D0009289

SHADOW DANCE

CHRISTINE FEEHAN

BERKLEY ROMANCE
New York

BERKLEY ROMANCE
Published by Berkley
An imprint of Penguin Random House LLC
penguinrandomhouse.com

ISBN: 9780593638712

First Edition: August 2023

Printed in the United States of America
1   3   5   7   9   10   8   6   4   2

For my sister Ruth. Love you so much.
This one's for you.

FOR MY READERS

Be sure to go to christinefeehan.com/members/ to sign up for my PRIVATE book announcement list and download the FREE ebook of *Dark Desserts*. Join my community and get firsthand news, enter the book discussions, ask your questions and chat with me. Please feel free to email me at Christine@christine feehan.com. I would love to hear from you.

ACKNOWLEDGMENTS

Thank you to Diane Trudeau. I would never have been able to get this book written under such circumstances without you. Skyler Cline for the hours of research with me. Shylah Sparks-Diehl for late-night encouragement. Denise for handling all the details of every aspect of my life that was so crazy. Brian for always answering the call and figuring out the math when it was making my head spin! I really must thank Lucia De Zuani for taking the time to explain the difference to me in her language between what one would call someone who does classical ballet and how one would refer to a ballerina. I learned so much from you! That made a difference in what Geno would call Amaranthe when he used an affectionate name for her. I appreciate all of you so much.

CHAPTER ONE

Geno Ferraro leaned one hip against the wall as he looked through the two-way mirror at the prisoner seated very uncomfortably in the metal chair in the middle of the interrogation room. The room was all about efficiency. Drains, overhead sprays and hooks, long counters laid out with power tools and instruments one could use to help the prisoner regain their memory very quickly if they'd mysteriously lost it. A shower. A toilet. A sink. Even a tub. Just about anything one needed for a successful interrogation if one was serious. He was *very* serious. Murder was a serious crime—doubly so if the victims were one's parents.

"Something's wrong, Stefano. I can feel it," he said, never once taking his gaze from the prisoner. "I don't want her to see you or my brothers. No one else. Fiero and Donte Latini, my main personal protectors, picked her up and brought her here. It couldn't be helped that she saw their faces, but I don't want her to see anyone else until I know what's going on. I sent for you because I need someone I can trust implicitly to help me figure this out."

Geno had been head of the Ferraro family in New York for years. The Ferraro territory was a crime-free, safe place for those who lived and worked in the neighborhood. *His* neighborhood. He knew every shop owner. Every resident. This was his community, and he was responsible for it. He took that responsibility very seriously. Ferraro territory started right on the edge of Little Italy and ran out all the way west through Tribeca to the Hudson River.

"I don't just know every one of the businesses and those living in my territory, Stefano, I know most of those in Little Italy. They know me and my brothers and our *famiglia*. They know they can count on us if there's need. Mama was raised with her second cousins, Viola and Noemi. Both married and became nurses. When they retired, they went to work in their husbands' shops. Viola's husband, Marcelle, had a hat store. Noemi's husband, Caio, had a very high-end watch shop."

Stefano Ferraro regarded the prisoner with shrewd assessing eyes. He ran the Ferraro territory in Chicago and had interrogated many prisoners under tough circumstances. He turned that piercing gaze from the prisoner to his cousin.

"There have always been petty crimes, thefts, tourists getting pockets picked, I was told, but our family was never asked to help," Geno continued. "Mama would visit her cousins and come home at times and tell us that the thefts were becoming more frequent, but no one thought to come to us. A few months ago, I could see concern on her face and strain on Papa's. He's always been distant, but he became even more so. I wondered why they didn't insist on investigating."

Geno pulled his gaze away from the prisoner to look at his cousin. Although they were somewhat close in age, he'd always looked up to Stefano.

"I rarely questioned my parents. Once they turned over the reins of the business to me, they no longer gave advice to me on any subject, including parenting. They made it clear they would only do their job and nothing more. My brothers, Salvatore and Lucca, don't remember them any other way, but I do. Not even concerning themselves with the escalating problems in Little Italy, with their friends and even *famiglia*'s livelihoods and safety, made no sense to me."

Geno shoved a hand through his hair. "Granted, in the beginning the crimes were petty. Stolen merchandise. Tourists being robbed with more frequency. But the thefts became more violent over a period of months."

"I take it your parents refused to turn the series of crimes over to investigators," Stefano ventured. His voice was low.

Geno sighed. "They wouldn't even discuss the subject, not even when many of the business owners began to look on the Ferraros with suspicion."

"Why would that be?" Stefano's expression didn't change.

"Many of the robberies occurred after hours. The safes were locked. There was no evidence of a break-in. No images were caught on surveillance tapes in the store or outside of it. Those who knew of our reputation began to worry that one of us was stealing and the others were protecting a family member."

"And yet your parents refused to order an investigation."

Geno nodded slowly.

"You could have ordered one."

"I could have, but I was gone more than I was home. We're short of riders, and I was continually taking rotations. I had hoped my parents would step up and see that there was a problem, especially as the robberies began to spill over into our territory. Not only didn't that happen, but when it did and I insisted we investigate, they threw roadblocks in the way of the investigation."

"That makes no sense."

"Nothing my parents have done has made sense since the night my mother woke me up and took me into their suite in the dead of night eighteen years ago. Their private surgeon, Dr. Mortan, was there along with Dr. Vargas, an anesthesiologist, Viola, Noemi and my parents' bodyguards. Blood was everywhere, and IVs were hooked up to my father with fluids and blood draining into him."

"You never really talked about that night, Geno."

"There was no explanation. His leg was amputated, but I don't know how he was injured. He never said. Neither would my mother. For one year, we weren't allowed into their suite. There was no contact with either of them. That night, my father gripped my shoulder with merciless fingers and stared at me with hard, pitiless eyes. I'll never forget the way his fingers dug into my shoulder or his eyes stared into me. He looked wild and not at all like my father. It was the first time in my life I was ever really afraid of him. He looked like a demon."

"He must have been in tremendous pain. You were thirteen. Your father was being prepped to have his leg amputated." As always, Stefano's voice was low and steady.

Geno nodded. "I know that now, but then it was terrifying. He said, 'You're a man now, Geno. You'll lead the family. You will guide the riders and protect the people in our territory. There can be no mistakes. None. All deaths will be on your shoulders. Yours alone. Do you understand? We look to you now.' Of course, I didn't understand. How could I? I was thirteen fucking years old. He wasn't making any sense. No one would answer any questions. His bodyguard grabbed me by my arm and hustled me out of the room. He threw me out and slammed the door shut. That was the last time I saw my father or mother for over a year. I was left to try to explain things to my two younger brothers when there was little or no explanation to give them."

Along with being head of his family, Geno had become leader of the shadow riders of New York, and it was an immense responsibility. A rider was able to slip through one shadow to the next finding portals to travel unseen anywhere he wanted to go. There was a terrible toll on the body. The rider trained from the age of two to be able to withstand the pull of the tunnels. They could tear him apart. More than once Geno had had to carry a dead rider from the shadows. The riders were required to always keep maps of cities in their heads because the shadows were so fast it was easy to get turned around, and again, once one was lost, there was no getting out. Shadow riding was extremely dangerous. Riders were tasked with the job of bringing justice to those who couldn't go through regular law enforcement.

"A series of trainers arrived from France," Geno continued. The Archambaults were considered the fastest shadow riders in the world. They policed all shadow riders and were the only riders who could investigate and assassinate a rider. "They trained me from morning until night on every aspect of riding and leadership. I was required to learn languages and interrogation. I was barely allowed to see my younger brothers and often heard the riders from France speaking in harsh voices to them. That was the only time I stopped what I was doing and intervened. I didn't care if I got in trouble with my trainers, and I would. They would be furious that I would dare to reprimand them for being so ugly with Salvatore and Lucca. I didn't have our father or mother to guide me, and my two brothers were so much younger. They were left alone and grieving for our parents. I didn't want strangers treating them so harshly. I understood they had to be trained to ride shadows and to pay attention to their other studies, but I wasn't going to allow anyone to be ugly to them. I just wasn't."

"That's why you called me," Stefano said. "And asked me all those questions about the way I balanced raising my siblings and training them to ride in the shadows."

"Yes. You had to raise your brothers and sister from a very early age, and you're the only person I've ever trusted, Stefano, with my brothers. I needed advice, so I called you. You'd been looking after your siblings since they were born."

The two men looked at one another, understanding and deep affection in their eyes for just one moment, and then movement inside the interrogation room drew their attention back to the present. The prisoner didn't turn her head, but lifted it slightly, just enough that she could shift her gaze around the room. They studied the prisoner through the glass.

It was extremely rare for a woman to be held in that room. In fact, Geno couldn't remember the last time it had ever happened. She had her head down, partially lying on her forearm where it was tied to an arm of the chair. She looked tiny, so slender she could have been a child.

"Who is she?" Stefano asked.

"Her name is Amaranthe Aubert. She arrived in the country five months ago from a region in the South of France. She dances and teaches ballet at the Ferraro Performing Arts Theatre Company. She is also working in Little Italy at their Performing Arts Center. From all accounts she's an excellent dancer."

"I take it your investigators have checked up on her in the short time they've had?"

Geno nodded. "She's danced all over the world. I've got a file on her, but nothing about her makes the slightest sense. At least there's no reason she should be sitting in a chair waiting to be taken apart by a man willing to be as brutal and as disconnected from emotion as I can be. I had even planned to ask Dario for help if need be."

"You changed your mind." Like Geno, Stefano hadn't taken his gaze from the prisoner.

"Something is very off here, Stefano. This is the third time she's done what she's doing. That stealthy scan of her surroundings. I don't go to the ballet. I've never had the time or the inclination to go until just now, just watching her, and that's a huge red flag given the circumstances."

Both watched as Amaranthe's dark eyes slowly moved around the room, taking in everything from the ceiling to the walls to the floor.

"I guarantee she knows the exact position of every single tool in that room. She'll be able to tell you the distance to every exit. She probably knows *our* escape routes," Geno said. "No ballet dancer would be sitting there that cool after being dragged into a basement by two bodyguards and tied to a chair with torture instruments surrounding her. She may be trying to look scared and intimidated, but she's not in the least afraid. Her brain is working on something."

Stefano considered the various possibilities, just as Geno knew he would. "You're keeping everyone away from her because you believe she's an assassin."

Geno's nod was slow in coming because he didn't want to believe it. She looked the least likely person in the world to be an assassin.

"The first murders were Viola and Marcelle. The hat shop was robbed, and both were stabbed repeatedly. Brutally. In fact, each had twelve stab wounds. It appeared personal to me, Stefano. Viola was seventy-two. Marcelle seventy-five. There was no need to kill them. Marcelle would have turned over the cash. The police were called. Naturally, our family was approached. For me that was a relief, although I would have insisted we investigate anyway. Viola and Marcelle were family."

The moment the murders had been reported to the police, he knew friends from Little Italy would end up in the parlor of his parents' home.

The way their family business worked was simple—yet not. Anyone could ask for a meeting with his parents. In their world—the Ferraros' world known as shadow riders—his parents were described as "greeters." They had a psychic gift, one that made them able to discern whether someone they spoke with was lying. Former shadow riders often took the job of greeters because every rider had to be able to discern a lie. Geno knew the gift was also aided by the casual conversation they had with the petitioner in the beginning of the interview establishing breathing patterns, heart rate and inflection in the voice.

No cell phones were allowed. No recording. Those asking for a visit were invited guests simply having tea or coffee and telling his parents what crime had occurred, what evidence they had and any suspicion they had of who might have done it.

The greeters listened but didn't participate in that part of the conversation, never taking part in discussions of crimes and never making any promises. That way, if a policeman slipped through their precautions, there was no chance of being trapped. If the greeters believed a crime had been committed and were willing to have the Ferraro family investigate, they never said so.

The greeters never indicated in any way that they were going to help. They simply inclined their heads, gathered whatever evidence had been brought to them and murmured their sympathies. They made polite conversation and then indicated the meeting was over, adding that someone from the family would check in with them occasionally to see if they needed anything.

At that point, all evidence was turned over to the investigators. The New York Ferraro family had two sets of investigators. Usually, one team investigated the petitioner and the other the suspect. Geno's cousins Lanz and Deangelo Rossi were exceptional investigators. There was very little they couldn't do on a keyboard. Team two was also made up of cousins, Beniamino and Davide Latini, and they were equally as skilled. Geno relied on them not only for their skills as investigators but for their accounting skills as well.

"In this case, there was very little evidence left behind. Anyone killing with a knife, particularly when stabbing that many times, usually will cut themselves and leave traces of their own blood behind, but they didn't. There wasn't so much as a hair. No fingerprints, no partial sole print of a shoe despite all the blood."

"A pro," Stefano said.

"A professional wouldn't stab someone that many times. He would kill quickly and cleanly. He'd get the job done and leave."

Geno took another long look at the woman slumped in the chair, looking fragile and defeated other than those eyes. Her eyes were dark brown, so dark they were nearly black. They didn't seem to miss much at all. Her lashes were thick and long, very feminine, adding to the dramatic sweep around her large eyes. Already, the lashes were falling, and she once again appeared to be that shaken prisoner, the epitome of a defenseless woman terrified of her captors.

"The second murder victims were Noemi and Caio. It was an exact match of the first one right down to the number of stab wounds and occurred thirty days after the first. Like clockwork, if you will excuse the pun, since it was a clock shop they robbed. No watches or clocks were taken, only the money in the safe. Although I'm not convinced there was money in the safe to take. The safe was open, but that doesn't mean Caio and Noemi had money in it," Geno said. "That was the conclusion the police came to, that it was a robbery."

"What makes you think it wasn't a robbery?"

"I think these are revenge killings, Stefano. And I'm beginning to believe another shadow rider family is involved."

Stefano sighed. "I was afraid you were going to say that."

"It's the only way they could get to my parents. *Both* of them." Geno indicated the woman slumped in the chair. "I came up with a trap to catch a thief. I believe whoever has been doing the petty crimes is helping the one doing the murders. The petty crimes are being committed to spread dissension and cast suspicion on our family. Unfortunately, I think I may have been outsmarted and brought the assassin right into my home, where she wanted to be all along. She was able to get to my parents, but she couldn't get to me."

Stefano studied the woman with his piercing eyes. Unlike Geno, he could step back from the situation and be completely unemotional. "I'm not in the least affected by the woman, whereas it is very clear to me that you are. Have you heard her speak?"

"Not yet. Nor have I seen her shadow."

"Yet you're convinced she's a shadow rider."

"I think she is, yes," Geno agreed. "And elite. Cool under fire. She'd have to be to stick her head in the lion's den. If she came here without backup, without a way to send her family members the coordinates to aid her, she has to believe she can kill me and escape."

"It's good you aren't underestimating her as most men would. It might be a better idea to have someone else interrogate her, Geno. If you're the target, it would be better not to give her access to you. We need the information she has. Dario can extract it without danger to himself."

Dario Bosco was one of the few nonriders in existence who knew of the shadow riders and lived. He was also a powerful crime lord holding a vast territory in Chicago for the Saldi family. The Saldi family was reputed to be the number one enemy of the Ferraro family. Emmanuelle Ferraro, youngest of the Chicago Ferraros and Stefano's sister, was wife to Valentino Saldi, who happened to be head of the Chicago Saldi family. Dario had been Valentino's enforcer for years and had the reputation for being vicious as well as able to get information from any prisoner.

Geno shook his head; his entire body rejected the idea. Every single cell in his body. He had such a visceral reaction to the idea of Dario interrogating Amaranthe that he knew he was in trouble. Had it been anyone other than Stefano with him, he wouldn't have said a word, but his uneasiness was the very reason he'd sent for his cousin. Stefano was the one person he trusted.

"I can't let Dario take her apart, Stefano. I haven't heard her voice. My shadow hasn't connected with hers. I don't even know if she's a shadow rider, but somehow there's a connection between us. I don't know what it is, but as much as I know she's a definite threat and she has information I need, there is a part of me that feels as if I need to protect her."

"You know it's too dangerous for you to be in there with her."

"I can't allow anyone else to take a chance. I do know without a doubt that she's lethal. She may look like a fragile little dancer, but I know in my gut she's anything but." Geno was certain he was right.

"Let's take this back to the house," Stefano said. He didn't wait for Geno's agreement, he simply stepped into a shadow and disappeared.

Geno watched the woman for a few more minutes, wondering if it would be better to simply kill her than take a chance on her killing anyone else he loved. Shadow riders executed criminals—men and women who had committed heinous crimes. Those criminals had somehow managed to escape justice and the riders had been called in as a last resort. He didn't know for absolute certain Amaranthe was guilty of any crime. He couldn't sentence her to death.

Swearing under his breath, he stepped into the nearest shadow and allowed the familiar wrenching pain to tear him apart, take his mind from the puzzle of the woman, to be replaced by a grid of the city as he made his way home.

Stefano waited for him in a chair in front of the fireplace in one of his three libraries. Geno preferred open spaces as a rule, but this library appeared small, mostly because of the tall walls of books surrounding him on every side. Geno liked real books. He had one wall that was enclosed and temperature-controlled so the vintage books were preserved carefully from the sun and no further damage could be done to them. He preferred to read them in the language they were originally written in and went to great lengths to acquire them.

"Tell me about the night your parents were murdered," Stefano said.

Geno poured two small glasses of scotch and handed

one to his cousin. "We'd taken an assignment in San Francisco. I was the primary rider. Salvatore and Lucca were the alibi with our cousins there."

Shadow riders rarely meted out justice in their own cities. They investigated and brought riders in from another city to do the actual assassination. If Stefano came in from Chicago to fulfill the assignment, he would do so with his brothers on a private jet. Several family members would come to party. One member would ride the shadows to the jet and board unseen. While the others partied in front of the paparazzi all night with the cousins in that city in front of cameras, the one in the shadows would dispense justice to the criminal. No one would ever know the Ferraros had anything to do with the death. They simply looked like they had too much money and too many toys.

"I appeared to stay home that night. Our parents always visited their friends and the priest in the evenings and took a walk around the neighborhood. Papa had a prosthetic leg, but at night he often used a wheelchair. He was doing so the night they were killed. They liked to go to the park after they visited the priest. That's where the assassin caught up with them."

"Even at their age and with your father in a wheelchair, he still had to be dangerous," Stefano pointed out. "Your mother was a rider as well, Geno. I don't care if this killer surprised them, how was he or she able to kill both? You had to have seen the reports. You know the sequence of events."

"Just as with the first two murders, Papa was killed first with a slash to the throat from behind. He was jabbed twice more, once to the jugular and once under his arm. That attack took seconds."

"In those seconds your mother had to have been alerted."

Geno nodded, swirling the scotch. "I've thought of this a hundred times. The killer rode a shadow right up behind my father's chair. That's the only explanation, or he would have known. My mother was facing my father."

"There was a second killer," Stefano concluded. "He or she came out of the shadows behind your mother."

"It had to have happened that way. The police had no idea my parents had the skills they did. If Mama was facing Papa and the killer emerged from the shadows to cut his throat . . ."

"He would have had to carry a knife through the shadows, Geno," Stefano said. "That would have been impossible. How would he have been able to do that? What composition would that have been?"

"It is possible. You know there are ways to make weapons out of natural materials. Our cousin Damian Ferraro has done it," Geno objected.

"He's a jeweler," Stefano said. "And yes, he does experiment for us. A good man."

"He can't be the only one able to come up with ideas like that. Your own brothers experiment."

Stefano took a drink of the scotch. "Suppose they managed to come up with a way to take a knife through the shadows and there are two of them. One emerges behind your mother. She's facing your father. How is it the police have no inkling there's a second killer?"

"Every stab wound was in the front and the pattern is exactly the same as on Viola and Noemi. It appeared as if the killer went straight from murdering Papa to stabbing Mama, and he stabbed her twelve times, just as he had stabbed Viola and Noemi. In fact, there was a transfer of Papa's blood to Mama."

"So the same knife was used on her." Stefano frowned. "If there were two people, what did the second killer do?"

"Inject my mother with a drug to prevent her from fending them off." That was the only conclusion Geno could come up with. "It had to be fast-acting and had to leave her system quickly for it not to show up when a tox screen was run. The ME didn't find an injection site, either."

It wasn't easy to calmly discuss the murder of his parents, but over the years, as head of his family and the shadow riders, Geno had learned to compartmentalize. He needed a cool head and to be able to think quickly. While he had initially disliked what he considered the overbearing and exacting Archambaults when they had arrived to take over his life at thirteen, they had trained him in every aspect of leadership.

They worked day and night with him on every type of self-defense and fighting technique they could teach him. They were never satisfied with his speed or reaction time. The Archambaults were the fastest in the world, and training with them brought his speed up, improving his reflexes and forcing his body into becoming a machine it would never have been without them. Not only his body, but his mind as well.

The Archambaults had rotated trainers and stayed throughout the years until he was of age, even after his parents opened the doors to their rooms. They never once consulted with his parents, only him. Every decision he made was his alone, but they asked him why he made each decision and discussed the consequences with him after.

They insisted on talking to him in various languages and corrected him on accents. He didn't have tutors the way his brothers did—the Archambaults tutored him while they worked out. He was forced to do several assignments at the same time to keep his mind working while his body did other things. They wanted certain muscle memory to be automatic, and eventually, even though in his teenage years Geno despised every single Archambault, he had to admit, they knew what they were doing. His brain worked at a high rate of speed even while he was in a fight for his life. He didn't have to plan his moves ahead of time, his body worked smoothly and efficiently. He still trained every day and left nothing to chance. He paid attention to instincts and every gut feeling. He might have an occasional drink of scotch, but it was rare.

Geno found, as he grew older, that he was grateful for

the men and women who had given up so much of their time to come and train him. In turn, he had trained his brothers and knew they were as safe as he could make them in the shadows. As suspicious as he had become when his parents had been murdered, he acted on his instincts as the Archambaults had taught him.

"You're worried these killers aren't just targeting your family," Stefano suddenly guessed, leaning forward. "That's why you held a private service for your parents and didn't even allow me to attend, isn't it?"

Geno nodded.

His parents were entitled to a show of respect from other riders. Normally, representatives from around the world would come to their funeral. But Geno and his brothers held a private closed service, sending out the word that they would hold a memorial service later.

"I couldn't take a chance with other riders. Certainly not with you or your *famiglia*. You are like my own. The same with our cousins in LA and San Francisco. I wouldn't risk you. I worry for Salvatore and Lucca all the time. Someone is behind this."

"The kills are not the signature kills of a trained rider," Stefano said.

Geno watched him closely. He always felt like he could learn from his cousin. Stefano was a shrewd man and very analytical. Not only was he a family man, but as head of the riders in Chicago, like Geno, he had carried responsibility from a very young age. He took that responsibility seriously and never stopped trying to do the best for his family. No one would ever have thought a Ferraro would have formed a partnership with a Saldi and yet Stefano had made it work. He changed with the times, but always kept his family safe. He played his hands close to his chest, not always consulting the council for the riders.

The Ferraro cousins were close. LA, San Francisco, Chicago, New York. They relied on one another because they were cut off from the other riders for the most part. Until Stefano had found his wife, Francesca, the others didn't believe they had a chance of finding a partner they could love and raise a family with. He had given them all hope. Now his siblings were married. His family had taken in Elie Archambault, and Elie was happily married as well.

"Why do you think they started here, with your family, if you believe their ultimate goal is to draw the other riders in and kill as many as possible?"

This was where he was on shaky ground, and Geno knew it. He didn't have much to go on, only the observations of a scared thirteen-year-old boy. But this was Stefano. Over their years together, they'd come to respect each other. If anyone would listen to him, it would be his cousin.

"I think these killings might have to do with whatever happened the night my father lost his leg. I know everyone was told he was in an automobile accident, but that wasn't true. He was wearing his rider clothes. So was my mother. I watched my parents all the time. I was very good at observation; in fact, it was one of the things my father always encouraged. They had been acting strange for a few weeks. They had meetings with other riders, but always denied anyone had come to see them. I heard the lies. I never saw the other riders, but knew they were there in the shadows. That night, other riders were in the room. Someone had carried my father into his room. My father was a big man. My mother couldn't have carried him."

"You didn't see anyone else?"

Geno took another sip of scotch. "No, but they were there. And I believe my father had gone into the shadows with a horrendous wound knowing he was risking losing his leg. He didn't want to be seen. To him, to keep the secret was worth losing his leg or even his life."

Going into a shadow tube with even a small wound was taking a terrible chance. The force the speed in the shadows generated could tear open any laceration and pump blood into the tube at a furious rate. If Geno was correct about his speculation, whatever secrets his parents shared with the hidden shadow riders had been worth his father's life—at least that is what they all believed.

"How would our enemy find out who was in the room that night other than your parents?" Stefano asked. "If you didn't know. You said the surgeon, an anesthesiologist, the two nurses, their bodyguards. Anyone else?"

"The riders hidden in the shadows I know were there. The priest. He was giving him the last rites as I was escorted out of the room."

"No one else."

"Viola and Noemi had no knowledge of shadow riding. They only knew we had several successful businesses and our *famiglia* made a great deal of money. Most of the family hasn't a clue about what we do, Stefano. My best guess would be the two of them told their friends about the hasty operation they attended at the home of a very wealthy man related to them, particularly after they had retired. Once they were working in their shops, they most likely got comfortable around their friends and began regaling them with amusing or exciting tales of their time as nurses. They wouldn't leave out going to the Ferraros' home for surgery."

Stefano let his breath out in a long sigh and then finished off the scotch. "If you're right about this, Geno, and you've rarely been wrong with your gut feeling, whoever is behind this has been planning their revenge for a number of years. They've had ears and eyes in our territories and in Little Italy. Who knows where else?"

"That's what I'm afraid of. I set a trap for a petty thief. I didn't expect to catch an assassin," Geno reiterated. "Now I have to figure out how to interrogate her without getting killed."

"You're absolutely set on doing this yourself." Stefano made it a statement.

"I refuse to put anyone else in jeopardy."

"I think there's more to it than that."

Geno shoved his hand through his hair. "Unfortunately,

you could be right. I'll know when I get in there. If I'm right about her and she's a shadow rider, I intend to compromise her shadow as fast as possible."

"Geno, that's dangerous to you," Stefano cautioned. "By compromising her shadow, you're jeopardizing your own."

"I'm aware of the risks."

Stefano studied his set features for a long time. "If you're determined, Geno, and I know how fucking stubborn you are, then you're going to do it my way. You called me here for a reason—that's to ensure your safety. That means you do what I say. Agreed?"

Geno hesitated. Stefano wouldn't have a qualm about taking out a gun and shooting their captive if she threatened Geno's life in anyway.

"You aren't going into that room unless it's my way," Stefano said, absolutely no compromise in his voice.

Geno knew he needed that assurance from Stefano. He just didn't know why.

CHAPTER TWO

The room smelled of urine and sweat. What it didn't smell of was terror, and it should have. The moment Geno entered, Amaranthe's head came up, her large dark eyes tracking him. She looked wary, like a wild animal caught in a trap and ready to fight her way out. She held herself still, not like frozen prey but more like a wary tigress waiting for an opportunity to tear him to pieces. Her hair was wild, coming undone from the multitude of pins so that it fell in waves and spiral curls around her little oval face, emphasizing her high cheekbones.

Geno snapped on the light that would cast her shadow on the wall behind her. At once the telling tubes reached out in every direction. His breath caught in his throat. He'd been right; he'd known she was a rider. The tubes were some of the strongest he'd ever seen. He moved to her left, staying several feet from her, making certain there was no way she could so much as reach him with spit. He wanted his shadow to connect with hers, but he had to wait for the others. He'd promised Stefano.

They studied one another openly. Her eyes by turns held sadness, anger, a fierce determination. They were beautiful, haunting, expressive. Absolutely captivating. She flexed her fingers, drawing his attention to her hands. She had small, delicate hands. Her feet looked tiny. She really did look like a ballet dancer.

The door opened and Dario Bosco sauntered in. A large man with wide shoulders and a ripped body, he wore a suit and no expression. He was easily one of the most dangerous men Geno had ever met. Dario positioned himself ten feet to the left of and just in front of the prisoner, well within striking distance of her with the set of throwing knives he had on display on the inside of his open jacket.

It was clear Amaranthe knew him, or at least of him, by his reputation. The color drained from her face, and for the first time, panic and fear warred with the calm in her eyes. Her gaze jumped back to Geno's face. He saw her swallow almost convulsively, but then her lashes swept down. When that thick black fringe came back up, there was steel there. Absolute, utter resolve.

Stefano Ferraro followed Dario into the room and positioned himself fifteen feet directly in front of Amaranthe. He took out a Glock and held it with deadly intent. There was no way to mistake the meaning in his hard features.

Valentino Saldi entered and crossed in front of the chair, barely sparing the prisoner a glance as he took up his position to the right of the chair the same distance as Dario from her.

The moment they were in position, Geno made his move, deliberately shifting spots. It only required taking a few steps forward so that his shadow connected with hers. The jolt of sexual awareness was savage and unexpected, so extreme it sent scorching heat rushing through his veins, flames blazed down his spine and jagged strikes of lightning forked straight to his cock. It was impossible to control that strong of a firestorm and he didn't try, allowing it to wash over and through him. His shadow tangled with hers fast, binding hers with knot after knot, eager to complete the connection between them.

"Stop. What are you doing?" Amaranthe's voice broke on a soft, low entreaty of total panic. "Damn you." The last was a hiss of warning.

Geno pressed a fist to his chest. The sound of her voice, those musical notes tuned specifically to him, broke open a place deep inside his chest that had been closed off. Something twisted at his heart, which had been made of stone. All along he had known this woman was meant for him. Almost from the moment he had laid eyes on the prisoner, he had been disturbed.

But she had betrayed all shadow riders. She had most likely murdered his parents or aided those who had done so. He had searched the world over for her. It wasn't as if he thought he was a bargain. Out of necessity, the Archambaults had shaped him into a ruthless, cold man. He'd had to become a machine at a very early age in order to carry the heavy weight of responsibility for so many lives. Still, he had lived with a strict moral code, and he expected that the woman destined to spend her life with him would do so as well.

He felt that first recognition of his true character, the one that came with the strength of connection through their shadows. She felt the full impact of who he was. What he was. Her gaze darted between Dario and him. Yeah. She got it. She had been afraid of the wrong man. She had counted on him being soft inside because of her connection to him. Like him, she had known the moment she felt him that they belonged, and she counted on him going easy on her.

Why she had come to his territory without doing research

on him, he didn't know. Any rider would have told her he was a man absolutely ruthless and as cold as ice when he needed to be.

"I see you understand me now," he said. "I'm going to ask you questions. It's important that you answer truthfully. Not only can I hear lies, but our shadows are connected. I have no sympathy for traitors. You have chosen to betray all shadow riders as well as the man who would have been your life partner."

Amaranthe frowned. Connected through their tangled shadows, he felt her shock. She was completely baffled by his declaration. "Traitor? You're calling *me* a traitor?" Her gaze slid around the room. "Two members of the Ferraro family are in an interrogation room with two major crime lords threatening a rider with torture, and you call me a traitor? That's rich."

Geno heard the sneer of contempt in her voice but read the underlying fear she couldn't hide from him in her body. He ignored both her contempt and the shiver that went through her. He added more ties to her shadow to make their connection stronger and buried his heart deeper in glaciers of ice in order to do what needed to be done.

"Did you kill or execute Viola or Marcelle Marino?"

"No." Her dark eyes flashed fire at him.

"Were you present when they were murdered? Or executed, if you prefer that term?"

"No, I was not."

"Do you know who killed them?"

"No, I do not."

Geno took his time searching every connection between them, looking for any sign of deceit. He couldn't find one, but still, there was a thread, something he was missing.

She's telling the truth, he communicated telepathically to Stefano. *But there's something.*

Instantly, Amaranthe's gaze jumped to Stefano as if she were aware the Ferraro cousins were speaking telepathically. Geno knew she couldn't possibly hear him.

"You knew of their deaths."

"Yes."

A one-word answer but no hesitation. She would know about the murders. She worked in Little Italy, and the murders were the number one topic of conversation. That question was more the setup for the next questions.

"Did you kill or execute Noemi or Caio Diliberto?" Geno asked.

"No, I did not." Her voice was stronger, ringing with the truth.

"Were you present when they were murdered? Or executed, if you prefer that term?"

"No, I was not."

"Do you know who killed them?"

"No, I do not."

Geno was certain she was telling the truth, yet at the same time, there was an uneasiness growing in him. Amaranthe might not be lying to him, but she was withholding a piece of the puzzle he would find crucial. He didn't shift his gaze to Stefano. There was no way for his cousin to do more than hear whether the prisoner was telling the truth or a lie. He wasn't connected to her in the way Geno was.

Geno stepped back into the stream of light to allow his shadow to further compromise Amaranthe's. The sexual jolt was far worse this time, rushing through him with the force of a freight train. It took her just as hard, driving the breath from her lungs, eliciting a muffled cry from her. She shook her head and even tried to move from the chair. When she did, the manacles fell from her wrists and dropped to the floor. Geno wasn't in the least surprised.

Ignoring the explosive chemistry raging between them, Geno was relentless. "Did you kill or execute Margo or Eugene Ferraro?" He kept his tone low. Compelling.

There was no accusation in his voice, but he didn't take his gaze from hers or pull his mind from hers. It would have been impossible for anyone observing him to know that the two people he named were his parents, but he was deeply embedded in her mind. She couldn't fail to feel the volcanic fury seething beneath the surface. He might cover it with a glacier of ice, dense and difficult for most to ever penetrate, but she was right there with him, and she could see into him, so he did not try to hide from her.

"I did not."

"Were you present when they were murdered? Or executed, if you prefer that term?"

"No, I was not."

"Do you know who killed them?"

"No, I do not."

He shifted gears smoothly. "Why are you in New York?"

She blinked. Her eyes widened. "I dance. I took a job with the dance company. Dancing is my passion."

She was telling the truth, yet not. It was a partial truth.

"I told you not to lie to me. The consequences of lying to me can be quite severe. Breaking bones in your feet would be the first retaliation that comes to mind. You are a shadow rider. Dancing might be a passion, but it would be a cover for you. You are here to assassinate someone. You came into my territory without first doing me the courtesy of consulting with me. That tells me you know far more about this situation than you are letting on. Again, why are you in New York?"

He kept his tone exactly the same, even when he made the threat to break the bones in her feet. He was matter-of-fact about the penalty for lying to him, and he made it clear he meant what he said.

She took her time answering, thinking carefully. His shadow continued to compromise hers, tangling them together until it was impossible to see where her shadow started and his left off. She shook her head, trying to dislodge him.

"I can't think straight. Why are you doing that? If something happens to me, don't you know what can happen to you?"

"What does it matter? You've ruined my future by betraying all shadow riders. Even if I survived whatever happens to you, what do I give to my future wife? A man who will never be in love with her. She'll always know that. Where's the honor in that?"

"Where's the honor in what you've done? The last thing I expected to find was the two of you." She nearly spat the accusation at him and then she shut down, pressing her lips tightly together, although her dark eyes sparked fury.

Her response was intriguing. Not only intriguing, but it was the first genuine reaction she'd given him.

"You just admitted you came to New York for something other than dancing. Why are you here?"

"I told you, I dance. If you check into my background, you'll see I dance all over the world. It's what I love."

"I did warn you." He stepped closer to her, making her very aware of his intention. Her bare feet were vulnerable and easily stomped on.

Geno knew he could never go through with it, not with her, and already he was beginning to have doubts. She might know something of what was going on, but she wasn't involved. There was far more to this than met the eye.

Amaranthe was already bent over. Her arms dropped toward her ankles. She didn't hesitate or stop, fingers manipulating the cuffs locking her feet to the floor, not even when Stefano cleared his throat to remind her he held a gun on her.

Before she could move toward the nearest shadow, Geno was on her, tackling her, knocking her from the chair, taking her to the floor. She was even tinier than he realized. He felt as if he had crushed every bone in her body. The moment she was under him, the defiance was gone. The fight was gone. She knew it was impossible to get away from him.

Geno felt the instant resolve in her. The movement in her jaw. Subtle. Her tongue sliding along the roof of her mouth, working to uncover a flat wafer hidden there. Alarm skittered through him.

He levered his body up and with both hands caught her jaw, his mouth coming down on hers, forcing her lips apart. One hand wrapped around her throat, making certain she couldn't swallow if she tried. His tongue sought the wafer. He was far larger than she was. If the poison, or whatever compound it was, was precisely made for her size, he had a better chance of survival than she did.

Geno clamped his tongue over the tablet, dug it away from the roof of her mouth and took it into his own. It was dissolving fast.

No. She fought him, trying to twist out of his grasp, turning her head. *Spit it out. You can't touch that. Spit it out, Geno. It's poison. Spit it out.*

He obeyed, turning his head to try to rid himself of the tablet, but most had absorbed into the tissues of his mouth.

Call in the Archambaults, Amaranthe. Don't trust anyone but Stefano and the Archambaults. Geno tried to warn her. He knew he wasn't going to make it. Hopefully, he had ensured that she would. She wasn't guilty of the crimes committed. Whatever she was doing in his territory, she hadn't been a party to the murders.

Amaranthe's heart rate accelerated to such a rate that the others in the room could hear it. Geno's did as well. Then abruptly her heart ceased beating. Geno swept his tongue through her mouth to try to clear the contents and spat several times to rid both of whatever compound she had tried to ingest. He rolled her onto her back and began doing CPR.

It's beginning to work on me as well, Stefano. Get the defibrillator. Call for a doc. I'm going to crash. Anyone breathing for us can't put their mouth on ours.

Stefano issued the commands and eased his cousin to the floor. "You ingested even more than she did." He started CPR on Amaranthe.

Call in the Archambaults, Stefano. You can't do this

alone. Someone is working to kill all of us or turn us against one another. She didn't do this.

"Shut the fuck up and breathe, Geno," Stefano snapped. "You die on me and I'm going to be so pissed I'll follow you to hell and bring you back."

Valentino caught up the defibrillator and hastily attached the electrodes and turned on the machine. "Get clear. Everyone needs to be clear." The machine began to analyze Amaranthe's condition.

The poison had to be absorbed through membranes. She tried to stop me. I'm not feeling so good, Stefano. I'm a lot bigger than she is. Hopefully, the tablet was designed for her size.

"Stay with me, Geno. Why would she try to stop you from absorbing the poison? Why wouldn't she want to kill you? You were about to torture her. Think, Geno. Keep your heart beating. Concentrate on the questions."

The machine told them Amaranthe had no heartbeat and began to count down to shock her heart. Geno nearly stopped breathing. Waiting. Nothing mattered to him but that machine and shocking life back into Amaranthe.

"Breathe, Geno. Don't you fucking die on me," Stefano snapped.

The machine shocked Amaranthe's heart. Once. Twice. The doctor rushed in with two of his aides. Her heart began to beat, but the rhythm wasn't steady.

"Poison," Valentino explained tersely.

"I'll need the compound."

Dario handed the aide two swabs. "Best we could do."

The aide took off running, presumably for a laboratory.

Geno's heart suddenly stopped beating. Immediately, Amaranthe's eyelashes fluttered. She turned her head toward him, then to Stefano. Clearly, she tried to form words.

"Tell me what kind of poison," Stefano demanded.

Valentino was doing chest compressions as Dario began hooking the defibrillator to Geno.

Stefano swore at her. "Tell me."

"He took most of it." She mouthed the words rather than voiced them, then tried again, murmuring. She sounded slurred. Disoriented. Her lashes fell. "Why? I tried to stop him. He isn't part of this, is he?"

"No. Fucking tell the doc what kind of poison," Stefano demanded. "Right now, Amaranthe."

She mumbled something again. Stefano leaned down in an effort to catch every word. Stefano related what she said to the doctor as she crashed again. Dario swore and began CPR.

The defibrillator shocked Geno's heart back into rhythm while the doctor's aide rushed to get the antidote for the poison. They'd texted the second aide in the laboratory, and he was already on his way.

Amaranthe Aubert stared up at the unfamiliar ceiling, trying to remember where she was and why she was there. Her chest hurt. In fact, her entire body hurt, but her chest felt as if a massive hammer had smashed her repeatedly. She scanned the room carefully, looking for cameras. There were no bars on the windows. She wasn't wearing clothes, but there was a robe hung beside the bed on a standing coatrack made of polished wood.

The room was beautiful with a hardwood floor and two wide windows overlooking the river. The bed was a queen and very comfortable. End tables with lamps sat on either side of the bed, and a reading chair was positioned across from the bed at an angle. The room was spacious and bright.

She sat up slowly, taking stock of her body and every sore muscle. She had no idea what day it was, but she was fairly certain she was inside the Ferraro home. The robe was close enough that if she stretched her fingertips, she could yank it to her. She hoped there wasn't a camera. She hadn't spotted one, but that didn't mean there wasn't one.

The robe fit as if it had been made exclusively for her.

Geno Ferraro was very wealthy. He could afford to have robes made for women he had inadvertently abused in his interrogation room. She forced her mind away from that particular fiasco, unwilling to face the consequences of what might have happened to him and the mess she'd made of everything. Finding a bathroom was paramount on her list of things to do.

The first door she opened took her straight to a private bath. It was immaculate and held her favorite brands. Someone had bathed her and washed and conditioned her hair while she was unconscious. The thought of being that vulnerable unsettled her. She'd been on her own a long time and never once had she ever been taken prisoner. She'd never failed in a mission, either. Or made such a huge mistake where an innocent man may have lost his honor and ultimately his life.

She covered her face. She would have to own up to her mistakes. There was no getting around it. And if Geno was alive, she would have to confess to him and apologize. She couldn't imagine facing him and telling him the truth. Why hadn't she seen the truth? She'd never made such an error before. The worst of it was, he'd been her contact—her backup. She just hadn't trusted him enough to talk to him. Pride. Ego. Fear. All those things. That shamed her.

She went back to her room and looked at the closet. If they had provided a robe and her favorite toiletries, perhaps there were clothes in the closet. Before she could explore further, a knock at the door had her scrambling back into bed.

The man opening the door was astonishingly handsome. He had dark eyes, chiseled features and very wide shoulders. He smiled at her. "My name is Elie Archambault. May I come in?"

Her heart sank. He certainly had the features of an Archambault. She nodded. Elie entered but didn't approach the bed. He took the chair across from her.

"Jean-Claude received an urgent call from Stefano Ferraro

on your behalf. He filed a report, which I have here for you to go over and add to. Before we get started, I need to inform you that I rarely act in the official capacity as an Archambault. I live in Chicago and work as a rider for the Chicago Ferraro family. Essentially, that would make Stefano my boss. I am, however, an Archambault, and I would never betray the code of my family. If you prefer someone else to give a ruling on this matter, I will inform Jean-Claude and he'll send someone immediately."

"I didn't ask Stefano to file a complaint on my behalf."

"Apparently, Geno Ferraro did."

"I'll have to take that up with Mr. Ferraro."

"I'm afraid that's impossible."

Her heart dropped. For a moment her lungs refused to work. "I don't understand. Are you saying Geno Ferraro won't talk to me, or he can't talk to me?"

"It's imperative we stay on track here, Ms. Aubert. These are serious charges being made against Geno Ferraro. Torture. Consorting with criminals. You did attempt suicide. You wouldn't have done so unless you felt there was no other way out for you."

"I have no complaint, Mr. Archambault. If I had one, I would have filed it myself." She was desperate to know Geno's condition.

"Please call me Elie. These charges must be dealt with. Jean-Claude is not going to be satisfied after reading this report that nothing was done."

"Elie, then. If anyone was at fault, it was me. And call me Amara."

"How were you at fault, Amara?"

"I was instructed to go to Geno Ferraro if I ran into any problem. I was told he was the one man I could trust. Instead, when I had the opportunity to speak with him, I didn't take it. I doubted him and in doing so put him in an untenable position. He believed me to be a traitor to the shadow riders and a party to those who murdered his parents. It certainly appeared that way. When I refused to answer his questions and he knew I was withholding information, he acted as if he might torture me. He didn't. At the last moment, I realized he didn't have any intention of following through with his threats. In fact, he saved my life by taking the poison himself."

She kept all emotion from her voice with tremendous effort. Was Geno alive? Surely, she would know if he were dead. Their shadows were so tangled together, she couldn't imagine that he could die without her knowledge. Still, she could barely breathe. She needed to see him—to just look at him and see for herself that he was alive and as arrogant as ever.

"That would be your sworn statement?"

"Do you think I want to admit to Jean-Claude that I screwed this up so badly? I wouldn't lie. I still have to face Stefano and Geno Ferraro and tell them the truth. I have no idea what Valentino Saldi or Dario Bosco were doing in the interrogation room, but I certainly couldn't talk about shadow riders in front of them."

"You are aware that Valentino Saldi is married to Emmanuelle Ferraro, Stefano's youngest sibling?"

Amaranthe shook her head. "I only familiarized myself with the New York branch before coming here."

"The Ferraro family is very close. New York, LA, San Francisco, Chicago. If you're talking to one, you're talking to all of them. If one needs help, they all come. Essentially, they are the Archambaults of the United States. They don't have too many other riders to help them out, so they rely on one another."

"You don't believe any of them would betray the others."

"No, I don't. And Geno would know. He was trained by the Archambaults exclusively from the time he was thirteen until he was twenty-one. At least two trainers were in residence with him until he was of age. Consequently, he became one of the fastest thinkers and riders we have. They shaped him into one of us. Geno has always had a gift when it comes to having a sense about people."

"He knew I wasn't telling him everything," she readily admitted. "He was extremely difficult for me to read. He came off very cold, as if he wore a mask. Just like an Archambault. That makes perfect sense."

She rubbed at her temples. A headache had been there from the moment she woke, just beginning to form at the back of her head, but now it had moved forward with a distinct roar. She felt a little sick and wanted to lie down. Elie was an Archambault. One didn't show weakness to an Archambault.

"Amara." Elie's voice was gentle. "The doctor said there were going to be aftereffects of the poison. Headaches. Nausea. Dizziness. He said to stay out of the shadows for at least a week. No dancing for at least that long. Certainly no traveling. Jean-Claude feels it's too dangerous for you to remain here in the States and would like you to return home as soon as the doctor gives you his permission to travel."

She shook her head and immediately subsided against the pillows. "Absolutely not. I have always completed my assignments, and I'll complete this one. I admit I screwed up, but I was making progress."

"Jean-Claude is head of the International Council of Riders as well as head of the Archambault family," Elie reminded gently. "He's responsible for your life."

"I'm well aware who he is." She crossed her arms over her chest, aware she looked stubborn, but she didn't know how best to appeal to him. Why was he living in the States and riding with the Chicago riders? "Do you have to put everything I tell you in your report?"

Silence stretched between them for so long she wanted to scream. She wasn't known for her patience, and yet Geno was important to her and so was her reputation. She pressed her lips together and forced herself to wait. Finally, Elie shook his head.

"It's at my discretion what to include. If you tell me something in confidence, I'll keep it that way."

"I saw Geno Ferraro on the street when he was talking to a group of men, and for the first time in my life I was intimidated. Keep in mind, I'm around riders quite often. I trained with Archambaults. I don't get intimidated. I'd never seen anyone like him before. Not to mention his size. When I was held prisoner and Dario Bosco came into the room, I'll admit I was scared. I'd heard about his ability to extract information through torture. I was certain Geno wouldn't do anything like that to me. But then my shadow connected with Geno's, and I could see inside him."

She shivered and wrapped her arms around herself. Her gaze collided with Elie's. "He was even more frightening than Dario to me. But our shadows just kept tangling, more and more. They were so drawn to one another. I didn't want it to stop any more than he did. I knew we were supposed to be together. I honestly couldn't think straight. I've always had a very clear mind and I can process information at an extremely rapid rate, but right then, around Geno Ferraro, my brain seemed to short-circuit."

She dropped her hands to the blanket and spread her fingers wide, shaking her head. "I would never want to admit such a thing to Jean-Claude. I doubt he would understand when I don't. I wouldn't want Geno to know, but I'm afraid he did. I think he took unfair advantage when he was interrogating me." She could feel color creeping up her neck to her face. Blushing. That didn't happen. Her headache was getting worse. This was a truly humiliating interview, and she hoped she would never have to face Elie Archambault again.

"Geno wasn't thinking so straight, either, Amara, or he would have known immediately something wasn't right, and he wouldn't have threatened to torture you."

Using the heel of her hand, she rubbed at her forehead in an effort to ease the throbbing ache. Elie was right. If Geno was as clear-thinking as an Archambault, he should have known she wasn't guilty, yet he had persisted in believing she had something to do with the murders despite her truthful answers. He had been just as affected by their joined shadows as she had been. That made her feel so much better.

Elie sat back in the chair. "Geno Ferraro compromised your shadow."

Amaranthe assessed his tone. There was a thoughtful note in his voice. Elie was definitely on her side. He had admitted to knowing the Ferraro family very well the moment he entered the room. He was considering how to handle the complaint to Jean-Claude.

"I believe it would prove very useful for you to stay right here with Geno Ferraro. The two of you should work to solve the mystery of who is trying to destroy the riders. Jean-Claude cannot possibly worry about your safety as long as you're under Geno's protection. I'm going to send him the report that you never made the complaint and feel that Geno acted within his rights. That there was a misunderstanding. You believe the two of you can resolve this case given time. But, Amara, you will have to reside here. Someone is targeting riders. We don't have a clue who is doing it. Margo and Eugene may have been older, but they were superb shadow riders. No one should have been able to kill them both. One, perhaps, but both? No."

"I understand. Geno may think differently." She hesitated, but she refused to lie to him. Lifting her chin, she met his eyes. "I don't think he wanted our shadows to tangle together. I believe he'll find a way to loosen the knots. He allowed it to better hear my answers."

"Perhaps." Elie stood. "If he only lightly wrapped his shadow around yours, he'll be able to get out of it. Otherwise, it will be difficult. At that point, you would be able to bring a very different complaint against him to Stefano

Ferraro. I think it would be wise of you to do so." There was a hint of laughter in his voice, although none on his face.

"I wouldn't do that. If he doesn't want me as a partner, I wouldn't force him."

"If he doesn't want you as a partner, he's an idiot. It was an honor to meet you, Amara. I'm certain we'll meet again very soon." He gave her a rider's salute and sauntered out, taking his papers with him.

Amaranthe turned over and buried her face in the cool pillows. At least he was going to recommend to Jean-Claude that she stay. Had she been forced to defy the council she would have, but it would have cost her position and she'd fought hard for it.

She desperately needed to go back to sleep. She didn't want to take anything for her headache, not on top of the silly drug she'd had embedded in the roof of her mouth. Only riders working alone in dire circumstances, those who might be subject to torture with no way to reach a shadow to save themselves, were given a tablet as a last resort. She had never expected to have to use one. Worse, she never expected to place another rider in jeopardy—especially an innocent one.

She covered her eyes and rocked back and forth. The light streaming in through the windows hurt. Everything hurt. Maybe she did need something after all. She wasn't nearly as tough as she thought she was.

There was a soft knock on the door. She didn't lift her head or answer.

"Ms. Aubert? I'm Dr. Veneto. I've been treating you. I imagine you aren't feeling the best right at the moment. Is there anything I can do for you?"

She was grateful he spoke softly. She indicated the windows, and he immediately pulled the drapes, darkening the room.

"I hurt everywhere, but the headache is the worst."

"I can give you something for that." She felt his fingers

on her wrist, taking her pulse, then a stethoscope listening to her heart.

She shook her head. "I just want to sleep."

"That would be best."

CHAPTER THREE

Amaranthe looked everywhere and at everyone in the room but Geno. He could feel how uncomfortable she was being the center of attention. Stefano and Elie sat across from her in the high-back leather chairs. He was seated directly facing her. For the moment, Val and Dario were in another part of the house, so she felt as if she could speak freely.

As usual, Stefano had his legs sprawled out in front of him and his fingers steepled together. Elie simply waited, as he already knew what to expect. Geno had set up the furniture so when Amaranthe sat in her chair and he sat in his, the light hit both perfectly so that if he shifted minutely, their shadows touched. It was a shit thing to do, but he didn't care.

He'd made so many mistakes with this woman. He'd spent time looking at the YouTube videos of her ballet performances, studying every move. She danced with passion. With exquisite sensual fire in every line of her body. Every character she portrayed was authentic, making her audience weep or applaud for her. It was no wonder she was sought after. Her reviews were phenomenal, and she deserved every accolade. He didn't know that much about ballet, but he knew body movement, and there was beauty and control in her lines.

He replayed every moment he had been locked in her mind in the interrogation room. He'd been so wrapped up in the fact that she'd been holding something back from him. Once their shadows had connected, he'd been shocked at the intensity of the physical chemistry between them. He hadn't been expecting that. The sexual pull had grown in power the more their shadows had tangled together, making it difficult to think clearly.

When he was alone in the evening before the morning meeting, he took his time replaying the things he saw in her mind, and he was able to study her character traits without the interference of his brutal sexual need of her. Despite her diminutive size and the beautiful, graceful dancer she was, she excelled at being a shadow rider. She was experienced, deadly, and very, very confident.

Amaranthe didn't seek out friendships—not in the dance world and not in the rider world. She moved from one city to another far too often. Her relationships with those around her were superficial at best. She hadn't sought out Geno Ferraro and didn't plan to, not unless she had no other choice.

"Who are you?" he asked her in the same voice he'd used in the interrogation room. Soft. Compelling. Insistent on answers.

"I'm Amaranthe Aubert, but friends call me Amara. Both my parents were from the Archambault line." She glanced at Geno and then shifted her gaze away quickly. "I have no family left, and the Archambaults took me in and trained me. I do love to dance and trained in ballet just as hard as I trained at riding from a very young age."

Elie frowned and leaned forward. "When you say *young*, how old were you?"

"I lost my parents, the last of my family, when I had just turned four. Jean-Claude took over my training."

Elie swore and leapt up, pacing across the room. He glared at Stefano. "I thought you told me Jean-Claude learned his lesson after he fucked up my life. He specifically trained her to investigate extremely dangerous riders. Her cover was her dancing. She had no family, so she was a perfect candidate for him. A fucking four-year-old."

For a moment, anger swirled beneath the surface, but Geno shoved it down. Amaranthe had no family. There was no question Jean-Claude had taken advantage. The Archambaults were ruthless. He knew because they had trained him to be ruthless. He never could have become the leader of his family and the New York riders if they hadn't given him the skills they had. Amaranthe would most likely be dead if she hadn't been given the elite training she'd been given—or Jean-Claude could have trained her to be a regular rider or one of his riders.

Stefano asked the question burning in Geno's mind. "I'm not certain I understand the difference between an Archambault assassin sent out and someone like Amaranthe."

Elie sat back in the chair. "The Archambault investigators use computers, just as our investigators do when complaints are made against a shadow rider or a member of the shadow-riding family. If that complaint is determined to be legitimate and the rider or member of the family needs justice served, a rider is dispatched, and the sentence is carried out."

"Amaranthe is not one of those riders." Stefano made it a statement.

Elie shook his head. "She is not. If a shadow rider is deemed extremely dangerous and the investigators can't find the truth through normal channels, an elite investigator is sent. They are rare. Only a couple. They go deep undercover. Sometimes weeks. Sometimes months. They conduct an investigation and send what they find and their conclusions to the Archambault investigators. An elite investigator not only is trained differently, but they are often born with a unique sense about them, a gift, that is highly developed to follow a trail others can't detect."

"I understand you're upset on my behalf, Elie," Amaranthe said. "But there's no need. I love what I do, and as a rule, I'm very good at it."

Geno didn't look at Elie or Amaranthe. He didn't expect the sudden smoldering sense of possessiveness rushing over him at the sweet tone she used when she spoke to Archambault. She even addressed him by his first name. He knew Elie. They were close friends. Elie was married and madly in love with his wife, Brielle. Still, even knowing that, it didn't stop the strange and very unfamiliar emotions welling up out of nowhere. Could he be jealous? Such a trait would be beneath him. The lack of control bothered him when he was a man always in control.

He shifted in his chair, so his large frame was caught in the light. Instantly, his shadow connected with Amaranthe's shadow, coiling around hers. This time he was prepared for the brutal sexual need surging through his body. He kept his cold mask in place, as if he weren't in the least affected, not even when she gave a shocked gasp and her gaze jumped to his. If she thought she was going to escape him because she was an Archambault, she had another think coming. He didn't give a damn what Jean-Claude or anyone else decreed, no one was taking her away from him—not even her.

"You don't understand the way the Archambaults work," Elie said, his tone soft, at once calmer and more controlled. "They see the potential in children, even toddlers. That's their gift. At least it's Jean-Claude's gift. If the child has no family, or the parents prefer not to have him or her around, all the better. You didn't have a chance at any other life, Amara. You should have had a childhood, not a life of duty. And don't tell me you had a childhood, because I know you didn't."

Geno was connected with Amaranthe, his mind touching

hers. He caught glimpses of her earlier life, small vignettes, a little girl forced to recite entire books in several languages while she punched and kicked a heavy bag. At night, alone in her bed, she would look at her feet—her toes were bleeding. His heart clenched hard in his chest. She didn't have anyone advocating for her. At least he stood for his brothers, and they had been older than she had been when the Archambaults had begun her training.

Amaranthe moved in her chair, doing her best to move her shadow out of the light. *If they ask me questions, I can't answer them properly.*

The intimacy of speaking telepathically added to the jagged white-hot lightning spiking between them. Every nerve ending was aware of her. Every cell in his body. Her breathless honesty was nearly as arousing as the way their shadows wrapped around each other so determinedly. He shifted back in his chair giving them both respite from the intense sexual tension.

Amaranthe took a deep breath and let it out slowly. She raised her dark gaze to his and sent him a tentative smile before turning her attention back to Elie and Stefano and their questions.

"The council sent you to New York without so much as informing Geno that you were investigating someone in his territory?" Stefano pursued.

For the first time she looked uncomfortable. Geno wished he hadn't pulled his shadow away from hers. He kept his gaze on her face. She had beautiful skin. Nearly flawless. There was one tiny scar along the right side of her chin, but one had to look very closely to see that little white line. Her lashes were very long and curved at the ends. She used them to veil her eyes when she didn't want them to know what she was thinking.

"I was to establish my cover. I applied for a job in the theater, both in Little Italy and at the Ferraro Performing Arts Theatre Company. The International Council of Riders has suspected for some time that there is a group—a faction—that is undermining shadow riders. They use young kids as their eyes and ears in the neighborhoods to commit petty crimes and to turn the people against the riders. Of course, the neighborhood knows nothing about the riders, only those in authority, such as Geno or Stefano. This group seems to be able to sow mistrust over time, and they do a fairly good job. After they manage to turn the people against those who have been protecting them, the murders start. The conclusion was the murders were done by a shadow rider—or a team of shadow riders."

"Was Geno a suspect? Was that why you didn't go to him and let him know you were in his territory?" Stefano asked.

"I wasn't to go to Geno unless there was trouble. He wasn't considered a suspect, and neither were his brothers, but everyone else in his organization was. Every rider who came through and worked under him was considered a suspect. I went to a lot of trouble establishing my cover as a dancer in both communities. It's a solid cover. If I were seen with Geno Ferraro, it would put me in his camp, something I can't afford as an investigator."

Stefano nodded. "Geno caught on to the neighborhood teens, younger men and women being used to spy, and he set a trap after his parents were murdered. How is it you were the one caught in the trap?"

"I teach ballet class to a group of children ranging in ages from very young to eighteen. During break I overheard one of the girls telling her friends she was afraid for her older brother. He'd stolen a wallet from a man at a restaurant on a dare. He was going to get a lot of money for the dare. The restaurant was owned by the Ferraro family, and everyone knew you didn't steal from them or the people who frequented any of their businesses. She was really frightened. She'd brought the wallet to the studio and put it in a locker. Her brother didn't know she took it. I think she planned to throw it in a dumpster. I thought I'd return it to the restaurant and simply say one of the children found it."

"But that isn't what happened," Geno said, speaking for the first time.

Her dark eyes met his. She shook her head. "I realized the minute I took it out of the locker that the wallet had a kind of a sophisticated tracking system in it. I ran the name of the gentleman the wallet supposedly belonged to. The identity was a good fake, but definitely a fake. Someone had constructed an entire background for this man and deliberately dangled the very fat wallet in front of a teenage boy. I wondered who would do that. I thought it would be a good idea to find out. Imagine my surprise when that man turned out to be Geno Ferraro. I was both shocked and horrified. He was the one man I counted on to be clear of this mess, and yet he was daring teenagers to steal for him."

Geno studied her averted face. Her dark hair partially fell across her high cheekbone on her left side. She had a beautiful face. "You didn't consider the possibility that there might be another reason that wallet led you to me?"

"I allowed your bodyguards to capture me and throw me in your interrogation room. They weren't very nice about it. There were a lot of threats. I recognized them and knew they worked for you, but until you walked in, I still didn't think you were involved. Not only did you walk in, but Stefano did, and with him, two major criminals. Valentino Saldi and Dario Bosco both have reputations and are known to be very dangerous men. I believed I had the upper hand until that moment. I knew I was in trouble and had to figure out how to get myself out of there."

"I should have paid more attention to my warning system," Geno said. "I knew something was off, but I continued to think it was off in the wrong direction. That made no sense. I knew you were mine, and I was pissed as hell that you weren't telling me everything."

Amaranthe frowned and shook her head, pushing at the thick mass of hair. "I'm not certain about knowing I'm yours, other than our shadows tangling together. But you had two criminals in the room. They weren't riders. I couldn't disclose shadow rider business to them even if I weren't aware they held two of the largest territories in Chicago."

"Valentino and Dario are family," Stefano said. "I know that seems impossible, but it's true. We make it work. We're careful of shadow rider business. They don't ask questions about our business, and we don't ask questions about theirs, although we've helped one another out upon occasion when the situation called for it."

"You aren't certain you're mine, Amara?" Geno asked softly. "There's still doubt in your mind?"

Soft color stormed her cheeks. She held her palm out toward him. "Don't even think about letting your shadow loose again, Geno. I'm still trying to figure out how to get back to my apartment and find Carlotta's brother without giving it away that I was the one who took the wallet out of the locker. I can't think about anything else, and you mess up my ability to think straight."

Before Geno could lay down the law to her, Elie did. "I think you've forgotten the council issued an order—you return to France, or you stay with Geno Ferraro, where they know you have a degree of protection. They want the two of you working together. If you don't follow their orders, Amara, you risk losing your job."

Geno raised an eyebrow at his errant woman. She might think she could run, but it wasn't going to happen.

"I don't see how they expect me to stay under the radar."

He wanted to smile at her snippy little tone, but he kept a straight face. "I contacted Damian Ferraro this morning. He happens to be another cousin of ours and a renowned jeweler. As a rule, it's very difficult to get on his schedule for a custom set of rings, particularly ones for a rider, but he was very accommodating. We'll announce our engagement. You're a dancer, not a rider. No one is going to question that I would be interested in a beautiful woman."

Her skin went pale as she shook her head. "No one in the

rider community would believe a Ferraro would ever consider marrying anyone who wasn't a shadow rider."

"Exactly," Geno said, his dark blue eyes drifting over her face.

Comprehension was fast. Her brain processed at a high rate of speed. She thought the way he did. A smile pulled at her full lower lip and lit her dark eyes until she looked as if she could stroke him with velvet.

"Exactly," she repeated.

"What does that mean?" Stefano asked. "What are you two planning?"

"My woman is a famous ballet dancer, a very big deal. I certainly would need to watch her perform. If there happen to be other shadow riders watching her performance, as well as two renowned heads of crime families from Chicago with their bodyguards, that would not be unusual," Geno said.

Amaranthe beamed at him, her entire face lighting up. Geno knew her reaction had nothing to do with the compliment of her dancing and everything to do with including her as a partner in catching the killers.

Elie and Stefano both shook their heads immediately. It was Stefano who lodged a protest. "You can't be considering using Amara as bait."

Amaranthe's dark eyes flashed with a dark flame. Geno filled her mind with warm amusement. *They persist in thinking you are like their women. Francesca, Stefano's woman, is soft and sweet and the center of the Ferraro famiglia. You will love her and want only to protect her. She is courageous and seeks to give Stefano a home and children. She nearly lost her life giving birth to Crispino, their son, and that was after losing at least two babies. She carried twins and only one, a little girl, Luciana, survived the birth. Again, Francesca nearly died. Stefano is very protective of her.*

How sad for them. Naturally, he would be protective.

Elie nearly lost Brielle when she was wounded and elected to save her bodyguards rather than go into a safe room. She's a shadow rider, but the shadows make her extremely ill. She is a superb investigator. In any case, neither man wants his woman to ride the shadows and work as an assassin.

Unlike you.

Unlike me.

Geno felt her genuine relief. She sent him another smile. Not only did he flood her with male pride in her but also a predatory possessiveness she couldn't mistake. He was not only a shadow rider—he was a hunter in the same way she was. He'd recognized that trait in her the moment his shadow had connected with hers. Whether the Archambaults had brought that trait out in them both or whether they simply had it embedded in their DNA, the result was the same—it was strong in them.

"Amaranthe explained what she was doing here and how she was trained," Geno said. "Elie, you reiterated what the Archambaults had taught her. I had the benefit of working with that family for several years, certainly not as many as she did. She may look delicate, but I can assure you, she knows what she's doing. I spent a great deal of time going over the report my investigators gave me on her background. Every place she danced. Those were the places she was undercover. I had them check and sure enough, a shadow rider died. She knows what she's doing."

"And you're willing to take the chance that you might lose her?" Stefano's hard features settled into a mask, his eyes twin sets of pure liquid steel.

"That's not fair," Amaranthe declared. "I'm a rider. Your sister is a rider and you send her out on rotations just as you do your brothers. I have different skill sets from most riders that make me even more suited to this kind of work. Why would you try to make Geno feel guilty for using every means possible to catch these murderers? They're not only going after his people, but other territories as well."

Stefano leaned toward her, his piercing gaze intense. "Because Geno had never had one good thing in his fucking life until you came along, and he deserves to be happy. You get murdered and he's going to go on a rampage the likes of which no one has ever seen before. I won't have the first chance of stopping him."

Amaranthe turned her gaze back to Geno. He felt the heat of her sliding into his mind filling him with her brightness. *Is that true?*

There was no point in denying it. *Yes. You can see what I'm like. Not the best of men.*

You're a shadow rider. A man of honor.

Not if someone took you from me. I would find those responsible. I would not turn my findings over to the riders from France.

A ghost of a smile touched her mind, but not her outside expression. *How very strange. I would be the same way if someone took you from me.*

You haven't decided you'll have me.

I know you're meant to be mine. I can walk away, but no one gets to take you away from me.

He raised an eyebrow and gave her his famous Ferraro stare, the one that scared the crap out of everyone. *You can try walking out on me, but that isn't going to happen. Not ever, babe.*

"Are you two having an argument?" Elie guessed.

Geno leveled the Ferraro shark's gaze at Elie. "We're just coming to an understanding. I'm being very polite and not adding more ties to our shadows since the two of you are in the room, but if she wants to keep up her nonsense, I'm going to ignore the fact that we aren't alone."

Technically that could be considered assault. You don't have my permission.

Call it anything you want, la mia danzatrice ombra. *And I have your permission. You could have leapt out of the chair the moment our shadows touched again, but you didn't. You could have protested to Elie or Stefano, but you didn't.*

She rolled her eyes at him, but again that ghost of a smile was in his mind. She liked him calling her his shadow dancer. "Is he always so arrogant and sure of himself?" she asked Stefano.

"Unfortunately, yes," Stefano said. "Clearly, neither one of you is going to listen to me. Have you thought this through, Geno? When she's backstage changing costumes, she's going to be vulnerable. Anytime she's performing and she's not with you, she'll be vulnerable."

"Not if Emmanuelle, Mariko or Nicoletta are in the shadows," Geno pointed out, naming the female shadow riders in Stefano's immediate family. "If Valentino is watching a performance, Emmanuelle will be here. He doesn't go anywhere without her. We both know that. She's head of his security whether he likes it or not. She most likely heads up Dario's security, and there's no way he likes that, but Emme isn't going to listen to either one of them. Mariko is fast in the shadows. I would trust her to watch over Amara while she's in her dressing room. If there's more than one assassin coming at her, the three women easily could handle them."

Amaranthe again smiled at his show of confidence in her and the unknown women.

"I believe we should announce the engagement immediately. Amara should move her things here, which would make it impossible for anyone to get to her, and we'll come up with a plan of action. Public visits we can control, such as going to the restaurant. It would be natural for me to introduce her to my cousins. She will need to go to her rehearsals and to teach her classes. Those are the places she will be her most vulnerable."

We'll have to come up with ways to ensure your safety, he added on their intimate path.

Amara nodded. "I had safety features built into my changing room at both studios where I teach and work."

"Those aren't going to be enough," Geno said. He sounded in charge. Implacable. She needed to know who he was.

An electrical current ran along his nerve endings. Sparks snapped and zapped, shocking his cells, coming far too close to certain parts of his anatomy.

She looked serene, but the woman had bit of a temper. Maybe more than a bit. He struggled to keep a straight face.

"You haven't tested my safety features. You haven't even looked at them."

"You're right, *la mia danzatrice ombra*, but I prefer to have every advantage when it comes to your safety. Stefano knows me very well when he says I wouldn't be much of a gentleman when I retaliated against anyone who managed to harm you."

"Is that what I said?" Stefano asked. "I meant to tell her you'd turn into a demon."

"Perhaps it would be best to keep that information private and not put Mr. Archambault on the spot when he has to make a report to the council," Amaranthe suggested.

Elie coughed into his fist. "I've been friends with Geno quite a long time now, Amara. I've sent my report to Jean-Claude and have no more to do with him or the council. My loyalties are strictly with the Ferraro family. I've lived here many years now and regard them as my family. Stefano's only telling you the truth."

"We'll work out the details together, Amara," Geno said, doing his best to find a gentler tone. He wasn't certain he had one. "You most likely have more ideas than we do. You've been at this longer than we have."

He wasn't going to concede when it came to her safety, but he recognized that she was extremely skilled, and that was who she saw herself as. She might look delicate and feminine. She danced with passion and sensuality, but the person she was inside was all warrior.

She studied tactics all the time. The intelligences she read were reports riders turned in to the Archambaults. She trained daily using programmed robotic opponents to ensure she continued to increase her speed. Her mind fascinated him. She solved puzzles at a fast rate of speed. Her predatory nature was hidden under her delicate beauty, but she was a hunter, every bit as lethal as he was.

Amaranthe sent him a small appreciative smile, clearly reading his opinion of her.

"When are your brothers returning home?" Stefano asked.

"In another week. They weren't happy I sent them away," Geno admitted.

"Have you already placed the announcement of your engagement in the society pages?"

"I sent it in early this morning," Geno admitted, a trace of amusement in his mind.

The smile faded from Amaranthe's face. "You did what? You didn't even consult with me first. We're just now discussing it."

"Do I look like the kind of man a beautiful woman with brains is going to say yes to when I ask her to marry me?" Geno raised an eyebrow. "Especially one who dances like an angel and kicks ass like the devil."

Elie burst out laughing. Stefano shook his head and regarded Amaranthe over the top of his steepled fingers. "Just remember the plan."

"He could have waited." She narrowed her eyes at Geno. "You could have discussed it with me first. That would have been the polite thing to do."

"I'm not considered polite, and you would have argued with me. In the end we would have been engaged anyway, so I just saved us a lot of time."

"We should go out a few times first and let people see us together. It's more believable that way."

Geno gave her his stone face. No one argued with his stone face. "You're staying here, where I know you'll be safe. We already established that rule, so it's a moot point about being seen together as if we were dating."

"Do you know what a partnership is? Partnership involves discussions."

"I'll have to look that up."

Her laughter was soft in his mind, stroking very unexpectedly like a caress along his nerve endings. She might have that hot little temper, but she had a sense of humor as well. He appreciated that trait in her. There was so much to her.

"So, your engagement will be announced. Did you call your brothers?" Stefano persisted.

"Yes. They wanted to come back immediately, but I told them to stick to the plan. I need another week."

Stefano nodded. "Tomorrow night we can take Amaranthe to the restaurant. Elie and I'll go with you. I'll have a few of my brothers come, but I don't want Francesca here until it's safe."

"Brielle has the instincts of a rider," Elie explained. "The moment anyone's in danger, she reacts like a rider, not an investigator. I've come too close to losing her, so I think I'll ask her to keep watch over Sasha, Giovanni's wife, and Francesca this time around. I don't like being away from her for very long, but she'll understand."

"Elie, you should sit this one out," Geno said. "I don't like that any of you are in danger."

"Actually," Amaranthe said, "all riders and their families are in danger. The target is your territory right now, Geno, but I guarantee, Stefano's is next if it hasn't already started. Or your cousins' in Los Angeles or San Francisco. It's happening in Europe as well. This is a vendetta, but the council isn't certain who's behind it. It's that subtle."

"If it came to their attention," Elie asked, "you had to have seen this before it started here in New York."

Geno felt her reluctance to impart information. As a special investigator, one working alone for the Archambaults and the International Council, she had to always keep her thoughts private. It was no wonder she was required to carry a fail-safe with her in the form of a poisonous wafer. She knew too many secrets the shadow riders as a community couldn't afford to have get out.

Geno struggled not to allow negative emotion for the International Council into his mind. He didn't like the fact that his woman was sent out with a poisonous pill to take if she should be captured in order to protect the institute. He didn't want to chance Amara believing he didn't think she could handle her job. She was alone when she worked, without any backup. In his opinion, that shouldn't be. He sided with Elie on the way Jean-Claude had arbitrarily decided her life for her.

"Amaranthe?" Elie persisted. "We need the facts if we're going to help put this together. Were your orders to keep everything from Geno or to share with him?"

She pressed her fingertips to the pressure points around her eyes. Geno felt the ache gathering in her head. She was still feeling the effects of the poison just as he was, but the antidote had worked. He was much larger, and his mass alone, even though he had taken the brunt of the poison, had allowed him to break it down quickly and recover faster than Amaranthe.

Amaranthe's gaze flicked to him. *You nearly died, Geno. You should never have taken that chance.*

You would *have died.* He couldn't help the censure in his voice.

She ignored him and turned her attention back to Elie and Stefano. "The International Council was contacted by the family of riders from Croatia. Like the Ferraro family here in New York, they are extremely small, only four riders for a large area. They noticed petty crimes, mostly among the young teens. In the beginning the crimes were outside their territory, but they were aware of them, then they began happening in their territory. Thefts. Robberies of shops. Tourists no longer safe. Mistrust spread where there had always been goodwill within their territory. The first murder was outside the territory, a priest. Then the greeters, the parents of the shadow riders, were murdered."

"A priest?" Geno echoed. An alarm went off. A young priest had been present the night his father's leg had been amputated. He had been giving his father the last rites when Geno had been forcibly removed from the room. "Father Brennen should be checked on. I should have thought to send protection. What the hell is wrong with me?"

"Who is Father Brennen?" Amaranthe asked.

"He gave my father the last rites when his leg was amputated all those years ago. My mother's cousins, Viola and Noemi, were the nurses attending the surgery." Geno hastily texted several of his men to get to the rectory to check on the priest and stay to ensure his safety. "It may have nothing whatsoever to do with what happened that night, but it seems too big of a coincidence that both women were murdered and so were my parents."

"I don't believe in coincidences," Elie said. "At least not that big."

CHAPTER FOUR

Geno studied Amaranthe's composed features for a long time before he allowed the pieces to click into place. "You had no way of knowing what happened when I was thirteen and my parents turned over leadership to me. As far as the Archambaults and Jean-Claude knew, my father was in a car accident. That was what everyone was told, including me. I suspected this attack on my parents stemmed from that night only because the murders tied together. But you didn't have that information. You weren't even born when my father handed leadership over to me. You couldn't possibly have known of that connection. How could you have chosen to come to New York?"

There was silence in the room. The sun shone through the wall of windows. The tiled floor and high ceiling with the wide-open spaces soothed him. He needed the minimalistic appearance his home offered. Simple artistic design. He was a big man and he needed space to move. Everywhere he looked the glass opened his home to the outside. At times—like now—he needed those views just to breathe.

It was a legitimate question. She had to have applied for her position in the ballet long before she came to New York to establish her cover. What had led her to New York? Geno hadn't informed the Archambaults of what had been taking place in his territory. They would be able to read about the murders, of course, but those came later.

Stefano and Elie exchanged long looks, both waiting for an explanation. Amaranthe remained silent, looking up at the high ceiling and then staring out over the water.

Geno broke the silence. "You were sent to Croatia to gather facts and come up with a conclusion. Would you share that conclusion?"

She sighed and pushed her fingers against her temples. Geno could feel the throbbing pain growing stronger in her head. She was very reluctant to talk about her report to the council, but he could tell she was going to capitulate. He willed the others to remain silent and allow her to set her own pace.

"I believed whoever these conspirators were, it wasn't a onetime thing. I felt it was a deliberate targeted attack. Yes, the riders were a small group and much more vulnerable than other families, but there was a reason other than that one that they were chosen."

Amaranthe frowned, and Geno could feel her reaching for an explanation, a way to try to get them to understand. "When I'm on the ground, on-scene investigating, I get strong impressions, and then I have to try to back those feelings up with facts to get the council to take what I say seriously. In this case, there seemed to me a ritual to the way the female rider was murdered. The precise stab wounds. The patient lead-up to the murders and the fact that two shadow riders— although older, they were still riders—could be murdered simultaneously was very alarming to me. This was meticulously planned and carried out. I believed that ultimately, they would have murdered the younger riders, but they didn't want to call any more attention to themselves."

She fell silent again, once more pressing her fingertips to the pressure points near her eyes. Geno wanted to call a halt to the inquisition. She needed to rest again. He indicated the water sitting on the end table beside her chair. She picked up the glass automatically and took a drink before continuing.

"The council didn't necessarily agree with my assessment—that the Croatia riders weren't chosen at random—that they were specific targets, and these people weren't going to stop. They also didn't believe the younger riders were under a threat. I still believe they are. I think if the success continues, the killers will become bolder."

Geno remained silent, shocked and astounded at how her mind worked. As far as he was concerned, Amaranthe Aubert was a total genius. She was not only beautiful and talented and an excellent elite rider, she had a mind to rival the best he knew in their business—Stefano.

She flashed him a look from under her long lashes, and he knew she was reading him. He didn't care in the least that she knew he thought she was the most amazing woman in the world. He admired her. Respected her. He hoped to hell the council did.

Elie asked the question. "Did the International Council take your report seriously?"

She sighed. "They didn't buy into the idea that the murders would happen again somewhere else or that the younger riders might be in danger."

"What is your percentage of being right when you hand in your reports?" Stefano asked.

"Until I made the mistake with Geno, and I suppose since I didn't send in a report, I'm still at one hundred percent. That's why Jean-Claude sent me here when I requested to come."

"You made the assessment that the next hit would be in New York?" Elie asked.

She nodded. "Yes. I had a strong feeling about New York. Small family of riders, a large territory to cover. Older family. There was something that pulled me in this direction. I told Jean-Claude I was certain—and I was. Every instinct I had said they were going to hit again, and it was going to be here."

"I wonder why the council disagrees with your findings when in the end, you prove to be right," Stefano mused. "That makes no sense."

"Sure it does," Elie contradicted. "They are in complete control. In the end, they reluctantly allow her to do as she wishes, but if something goes wrong, they can always say they knew she had blown it. They don't want her to get too big for her britches."

Amaranthe laughed. "You're terrible. No wonder you have such a reputation among all the riders. The legendary Elie Archambault, defying the Archambaults."

He flashed her an unrepentant grin. "I was a thorn in their side."

"I believe you still are." She matched his grin with one of her own, but that smile faded quickly, both on the outside and on the inside.

Geno felt a brief flash of another emotion, something very close to sorrow, and caught a look passed between the two Archambault cousins. They might be distant cousins, but they had an understanding of that lineage few others did.

Geno looked from one to the other, his mind racing. Elie had a temper, but he didn't show it to strangers, and Amaranthe was a stranger. Moreover, he had been asked by the council to see her in the capacity of an Archambault—something Elie rarely did. Why had he gotten so upset on her behalf?

Geno felt Stefano's gray eyes on him, and he looked directly at his cousin. Stefano was thinking along the same lines as he was. If the Archambault family, born with faster reflexes, was the only family allowed to bring justice to riders, if one of them went rogue, who investigated and ultimately was sent to carry out an execution order against an Archambault rider?

"You're one of the fastest Archambault riders they have, Elie," Geno said. He kept his tone mild. "The family trained you from the time you were a toddler, just as they did Amara. Were you asked to carry a special poison as well?"

Elie went very still. Stefano turned his head slowly to regard the man he had taken into his family.

Geno. There was a warning note in Amaranthe's voice. *You aren't being fair to him. That is the council's business. He has no choice but to keep information secret.*

Everyone has a choice, Amara. You could have died.

He wasn't here, she reminded. For the first time she stroked a little caress in his mind, attempting to soothe him.

"Yes," Elie admitted, his voice grim. "Yes, they wanted me to carry the same type of poisonous compound as Amaranthe. That was how I knew they were grooming her for a special type of service for them."

Stefano regarded him over the tips of his steepled fingers. "These people were extremely interested in Nicoletta, Taviano's wife, when it came out that she was related to the Archambault family, and her times in the shadows were incredible. Although she was already married to Taviano, they requested she be sent to France to train with them. Ultimately, were they looking to place her in a similar position as Amara?"

"I have no way of knowing for certain, Stefano," Elie answered. "They prefer unattached riders, but there are very few who meet their strict requirements for the job. Obviously, I did. If Nicoletta met their requirements, even as a married rider, they would want her."

"And so did Amaranthe," Geno supplied.

Elie's eyes met Amara's. His nod was barely perceptible.

"The council needs riders who will be able to bring justice to their own ranks," Geno said. "These special riders are trained for that. They must be faster than other riders and have that edge. And they can't be friends with the other riders."

"I'm uncomfortable with this conversation," Amaranthe said. "How is this pertinent to what we're doing here?"

Geno was silent for a moment, and then he glanced once more toward Stefano. "Because although my father was a Ferraro, his mother was an Archambault. He was incredibly fast in the shadows. It is entirely possible he was one of these riders trained to police others. I always wondered why the Archambaults trained me all those years and not Stefano or my cousin Severino, who heads up the LA family of riders. My reflexes are fast. At first, I believed it was because of the training I received from them, but I know I was born this way. Salvatore and Lucca were as well."

Stefano's gray eyes had gone almost liquid silver as he contemplated Amaranthe over his steepled fingers. "Let's get back on track. You had a strong feeling these men or women who murdered the riders in Croatia were going to strike again, and you convinced the council to send you to New York. How did you go about making certain your cover was established and there was no way to cast any suspicion on you?"

Amaranthe answered immediately. "I applied to both dancing theaters and was accepted. Fortunately, Geno, your mother was on the board for both, and she particularly liked my dancing."

He knew his mother loved the ballet. He loved books. She had introduced literature to him early as a way to make learning languages fun. Once he'd turned thirteen and his childhood had been taken completely from him, he had no time to enjoy the arts. He'd learned ballroom dancing because Ferraros were expected to be expert at all things. He'd learned to ski, snowboard, drive race cars, fly planes, but it was all part of his training. He couldn't be mediocre at anything. He had to be the best. He hadn't attended the ballet.

"I'm sure I will, too." Geno turned his attention to Stefano. "Does Francesca enjoy watching ballet?"

"The few times I've managed to take her to a performance, she has," Stefano said. "It's been several years since we were able to go with her high-risk pregnancies. We didn't go out much during those times. After this last birth, Francesca and I didn't feel like going out in public. Not too many outside the family knew we were expecting twins, so it did make it easier not to have to answer questions, but all the same . . ." He broke off, one hand shading his eyes for just a brief moment.

"I'm so sorry, Stefano," Amaranthe said, sincerity in her voice. "I can't imagine what you and your wife have had to go through. I appreciate more than ever the bond you and Francesca have with Geno that you would come to him when you and your wife prefer to be together right now. It says a lot about you both."

Geno knew how much Stefano and Francesca loved each other. Since she'd given birth, no one ever spoke of the difficulty or the fact that they'd had yet another loss. He'd been to their dinners, and they'd come to his home with their children, Crispino and Luciana. Francesca was always smiling and appeared happy, but Stefano hovered close, as did his brothers and their wives. Geno wanted to gather Francesca into his arms and hold her tight.

She's the heart of the Ferraro family, Danzatrice Ombra. She doesn't have a mean bone in her body. She looks after everyone. Geno didn't know how to explain Francesca to Amaranthe. *I can't wait for you to meet her. She changed Stefano's life completely. For that alone I'm grateful to her.*

"Thank you, Amara. I hope that you listen to my cousin when it comes to matters of your safety. He has a certain intuition, if you will. He doesn't always express himself before he acts, but you'll get to know him and hopefully will understand he is acting for your safety. I don't always explain myself to Francesca the way I should. I come off overbearing, and I know it hurts her when it's the last thing I ever want to do."

Geno knew Stefano was talking to him more than he was to Amaranthe. She smiled at his cousin. He wanted her to see what a good man, a good leader, Stefano really was. He always made the hard decisions, but he tempered his decisions with the love of his family and for the people in his territory.

"What do you think happened to your father that night, Geno?" Elie asked. "The night you were made head of your family? If you believe that was the key to these murders, then it is entirely possible whoever is behind this is after revenge. You must have heard a whisper."

Geno shook his head. "Not one single word. My parents remained in their suite for an entire year. Doctors and therapists came and went. They wouldn't allow us to see them. The Archambault trainers were allowed to go in after about three months, but not their children. Certainly not me."

"You honestly have no more idea today than you did when you were thirteen what happened?" Elie asked.

Geno's dark eyes were cold as ice as he shifted his gaze over Elie. "I knew they hadn't been in a car accident. Well, there had been a car wreck. They told a partial truth. I knew it was a partial truth. My parents were wearing their shadow rider clothing and they had come through the shadows. Other riders were there concealed in the shadows."

Amaranthe held up her hand. "Wait a minute, Geno. Your father was taken into the shadows after he was in that condition? With his leg already so torn? I thought he was driven back to your house. Are you certain?"

Geno found his fingers closing into fists just as they had that night. He had to fight to relax his hands. He wasn't thirteen and traumatized as he had been that night. He had gone down to their private parking garage. All their cars were accounted for. A day later, one of their cars, the Cadillac, was mysteriously towed to the garage, smashed, with blood on the driver's side. It had been just fine and in the garage when he saw it the night of his father's surgery. Geno recounted the story to them.

"They lied to me and to the other riders. I don't know who helped them cover up whatever really happened, but they did a thorough job of it." He glanced at Stefano and then away, ashamed that he had kept the truth from his cousin.

Stefano gave him an enigmatic smile. "We all cover up for our family members, Geno. If it was true, and your father was trained as one of these specialized riders, it's possible council members covered for him."

"They wouldn't have any business taking him through the shadows with a severe injury," Geno objected. "They'd know better. He would lose massive amounts of blood."

"They would expect him to suicide if he was caught by another rider," Elie pointed out. "They wouldn't want a trail leading home. They would take him through the shadows and, if he survived, come up with an explanation for his injuries."

"That doesn't explain the Croatia riders," Stefano pointed out. "Unless their parents had a tie to the Archambaults. This many years later it would be difficult to find it, especially if the council refused to answer any questions."

"It isn't even the same individuals on the council," Elie pointed out.

"I'm not eager to share my family history with the council at this moment," Geno said. "Nor do I want them to dictate to Amaranthe based on what they conclude if we share partial information. I want her to stay with me and give our relationship a chance."

"I think you've just about compromised her shadow in every way you could, Geno," Stefano pointed out. "Even the Archambaults can't argue with that."

Geno couldn't help the feeling of satisfaction that swept over him. Amaranthe rubbed at her head again and he needed to shut this down so she could rest. "I think she needs to lie down in a dark room for a little while. We can meet for dinner in a couple of nights and pick up where we left off. That will give us time to think about what we do know and what we need to know. Stefano, that gives you a chance to go home and see Francesca, and Elie, you can be with Brielle. I know both of you dislike being away from your wives for too long."

Stefano rose immediately. "Forgive me, Amara. I should have noticed you were getting tired. I think Geno has devised an excellent plan."

Geno frowned. He had known Stefano his entire life, and for the first time, his cousin appeared uneasy and eager to leave. Geno had the impression he wanted to tell him something but was holding back.

Stefano? Do you know more about this situation and don't want to say anything in front of the others?

Stefano didn't look at him. Didn't even glance at him. He continued walking toward the elevator. *No. I'm not sure why you would think that.*

Geno's unease increased, his gut knotting in the way it did when things weren't right. What was he thinking? Stefano was the best man he knew. If he had any suspicions, he would want to check them out before he presented them to Geno.

He knew Amaranthe had caught his brief prickle of unease, and before she could say anything, Geno called after his cousin. "As always, Stefano, you came when I needed you. I appreciate you. Elie, thank you, from both of us. Tell Valentino and Dario I'll explain as much as possible to Amara and will formally introduce them in a couple of days."

He ignored the way Amaranthe went very still in his mind, as if he, once again, had come under suspicion just by mentioning Valentino Saldi and Dario Bosco. He couldn't really blame her. It wasn't as if those names weren't in the news—and not in good ways. He didn't point out to her that the members of the Ferraro family were assassins, but the law would treat them as murderers just as quickly. They might look like glamourous playboys flying around the world in private jets, drawing as much attention to themselves as possible to make headlines, but Geno had learned they weren't all that much different from Valentino and Dario.

'd like to see your home if I'm going to be staying here," Amaranthe told Geno after the others left them.

She was certain Geno had given them some silent signal, but she hadn't caught it. He wanted them gone because he knew she had a blazing headache. She wasn't used to anyone looking out for her, and that made her nearly as uncomfortable as sharing the information they passed back and forth with the two men.

She got that Stefano was his cousin and he was there to help Geno solve the murders—and prevent any others—but at the same time, for her entire life, it had been drilled into her that she was never to give out information. She was to suicide before revealing details on any mission. Every cell in her body rebelled against sharing with anyone other than Geno. She knew it was impossible to keep details from him. Their shadows were tied together. Already, he was in her mind and could pick up information without her verbalizing.

"The others had been staying downstairs. I own a triplex apartment with a full-time doorman and concierge. The apartment encompasses the eighth, ninth and tenth floors and has eleven thousand square feet of living space. The eighth floor has four guest bedrooms with en suite baths. There's a recreation room with a terrace overlooking the water."

Geno rattled off the bare facts like a tour guide, but he didn't offer to take her down to the eighth floor to show her the guest bedrooms or the recreation room with its terrace.

"Geno." Amaranthe kept her voice gentle. She didn't want to sound as if she thought he'd lost his mind. She tilted her head up to look at him. He was extremely tall in comparison to her. She could have found him intimidating for that alone, especially since he seemed to be all muscle.

"You do realize that a doorman and a concierge have no hope of keeping a shadow rider from entering your home anytime they want to come in. You do it all the time when you're tasked with bringing a criminal to justice."

"I do realize that, Danzatrice Ombra. My cousin Ricco, out of necessity, invented a very handy item that blocked any shadow from getting through it. It fits beneath the door and isn't easily removed. One can't tell it's there. It certainly makes our homes and bedrooms far safer."

Relief swept through her. At least he was safe. His bodyguards couldn't possibly protect him from a shadow rider. Hopefully, he was right, and this device could. "Ricco didn't feel as if he needed to share this invention with the council?"

"No. We rarely share our inventions with the council, particularly when, in Ricco's case, more than one council member was involved in harming him when he was young."

"That was a long time ago, Geno, and those members are no longer serving," she reminded, sharing with him that she was up on the history of the failings of the council.

"We're on the ninth floor now," Geno continued, ignoring the conversation regarding the council. "As you can see, the great room has a double-height ceiling, an ethanol fireplace and walls of windows overlooking the water. The home office is on this floor, as well as a gourmet kitchen, dining room, gallery and a library. Each floor has a terrace, and all floors are connected by that very cool swirling staircase, which, frankly, is a work of art and one of the reasons I had to have this apartment."

Amaranthe had to agree she'd never seen anything quite like the stairway connecting the three floors. Now that the others were gone and she took her time to really look around the apartment, she was shocked that it wasn't anything she would have expected to find Geno Ferraro living in. She didn't know what that would have been, but not this.

Everything was white. High ceilings and walls of white. Long rooms that flowed into open spaces. White tiles on the floor. Glass walls. Even the dramatic swirling staircase was white. There were black accents. Thin stripes of black were here and there on the walls or ceiling. The grand piano was black. The furniture was white and very comfortable, accented by a white-and-black bowl artfully placed, but for the most part, the décor was at a minimum.

"The tenth floor consists of the master bedroom suite, spa bath, sauna and dressing areas. It also has a library and guest room with private bath." Geno continued to sound mostly like a tour guide, not as if he had tremendous pride in his home.

Amaranthe found his method of delivery interesting since she was in his mind and knew he enjoyed his home. It was a sanctuary of sorts to him. It wasn't simply a place for him to come back to at night and sleep. He did find a semblance of peace in the wide-open spaces and his tremendous views.

"The room I stayed in the last couple of days," she guessed. "That must be the guest room off the library."

He nodded. "The doctor wanted us close together. The training room and surgery are on the tenth floor as well." He paused as he led the way to the staircase. "Why do you suppose whoever murdered the parents of riders in Croatia stopped with those murders without killing the rest of the riders? You do believe it's their intention to kill me, don't you? And my brothers."

She answered without hesitation. "I didn't at first. Not until I realized you weren't involved. I think they intend to go back and kill the riders. They didn't want to draw too much attention to themselves the first time. I think they were practicing to see if they could get away with it. If they drew the attention of the Archambaults by killing the younger riders, too, they would have a much more difficult time getting away with their master plan."

"There is an elevator if you're too tired to climb the stairs, Amara. Or I can carry you."

She had to smile at the image in his mind. He liked the idea of carrying her. She might like the idea a little too much as well, and that was just plain silly. "I think I can manage."

"You do think they'll eventually go back to Croatia and kill the riders if they can," Geno ventured, indicating for her to start up the stairs.

The spiraling staircase was wide and gave Amaranthe the impression of climbing her way to the stars. She had no idea why, other than the clear stairs or the white modern, very cool enclosed banister that swirled in a long spiral from the eighth floor to the tenth in one continuous four-foot-high rail appeared to go on forever.

"I have a very strong feeling, Geno, but that's all. New York has even fewer riders here than Croatia. These assassins take their time. They have patience. I think they're still here, so they aren't finished. That means they're going to at least try for a rider."

"And you believe that rider is me."

"You set yourself up deliberately by sending your brothers away and then you set a trap with that wallet." She paused on the stair above him and flashed a smile over her shoulder. "You had no way of knowing I'd intercept the wallet."

His hand swept over her hair, for one moment tangling his fingers in it. A little shiver of awareness crept down her spine.

"No, but I'm grateful you did. We'll be able to figure this out so much faster together."

Even the sound of his voice was appealing to her. It was becoming harder not to make a fool of herself by flinging herself at him. Not only was she physically attracted to him, but she especially liked that he treated her as if she had a brain.

She had never had a chance to share her life with anyone else. She always thought she would have a difficult time being with another person for a prolonged period of time.

She hadn't considered herself lonely. She was used to spending time alone, and it felt normal to her—until she was with Geno. Until her shadow and Geno's shadow had tangled together.

"Just how compromised are our shadows?" She paused at the very top of the stairs and once more turned to look at him.

Geno crowded close to her. "I wasn't about to let you get away from me. We'd both be in trouble if either of us tried to walk away."

Her breath caught in her throat. "You risked your ability to be a shadow rider? You were that certain? You risked *both* our abilities?"

He nodded, his eyes darkening as his gaze drifted over her face. "I knew you were the one for me almost from the moment I felt your presence. Once I was in your mind there was no turning back, so I made certain there was no mistake."

"You have a ruthless side."

There was no humor in his smile. He looked utterly dangerous. Heat rushed through her veins and a dark thrill crept down her spine.

"It matches yours," he pointed out. "We make a good pair."

She liked that he saw that in her. Not only saw that she could be merciless but appreciated it. She was no shrinking violet. She couldn't afford to be when she worked alone for months at a time undercover, oftentimes investigating an Archambault. They were men and women with extraordinary senses. One walked a fine line when observing them.

"I think we do," she agreed.

She turned back to step onto the wide-open floor that was the primary bedroom suite. She could see the bed facing the long wall of windows. It was on a raised platform providing the best view of the water. She skirted the four-foot divider between the suite and staircase and entered the suite. Like the rooms on the other floors, this one was also white tile with white columns, although there were built-in bookshelves on the far end of the room.

"If your grandmother had ties to the Archambault line, and Stefano is your first cousin, that means he also has the Archambault blood in him as well." She couldn't help wandering around the floor. The room was extraordinary, just like the rest of the floors. The architect who had designed the apartment was famous for his work and rightly so. There was a second grand piano, this one smaller than the one downstairs but no less impressive.

"Yes. All the cousins have a bit of the Archambault blood in them, thanks to our grandmother." Geno reached out and gently shackled her wrist. "You're going to fall down. I can feel that headache getting worse. You can ask me all kinds of questions, Amara, but at least lie on the bed. Our grandmother was a cousin several times removed. Still, she had the bloodline and passed it to us."

He tugged her gently toward the elevated bed. It was much larger up close than it looked from a distance. When she hesitated, he picked her up and placed her facedown in the middle of the king-sized bed, coming down beside her. With a single click of a remote, he lowered privacy screens to darken the room. She hadn't realized the light was contributing to the headache.

"Thanks, that's better already," she murmured, closing her eyes.

Geno's hands went to her shoulders. He had big hands with strong fingers, and he seemed to know exactly where to find knots that were only making the headache worse.

"You must have a headache, too, Geno." It suddenly occurred to her that he had taken on more of the poison than she had. Despite the antidote, there were aftereffects. Or maybe the antidote caused the aftereffects. "Why can't I feel your headache?"

"Don't you think feeling your own headache is enough? I don't want you feeling mine."

"You're sharing mine. It's only fair." She couldn't help

the little spurt of amusement. Geno was such a law onto himself. "You do know you're going to drive me crazy with your arbitrary decisions."

"They won't be arbitrary most of the time. We're going to be partners. You have an incredible gift, and I'd be insane not to recognize that you're worth your weight in gold."

She couldn't help the laughter that escaped. The sound was muffled against the duvet, but it was genuine. "I don't weigh very much, Geno."

He bent his head and nipped at her earlobe with strong teeth. The sting changed her undignified giggle to a yelp and then back to real laughter.

"The point, *la mia danzatrice ombra*, is I'm looking forward to your input in every discussion. I think you're going to drive me crazy, not the other way around. I have the feeling you're going to get your way in all things." His phone played a little melody, and he removed it from his pocket.

"Hmm. That would be a miracle." His fingers were working magic on her headache. "I'm getting sleepy."

"Then go to sleep. You're safe."

"I've never slept with anyone in the same room. Or in the same house, for that matter, not that I can remember."

He pressed a kiss to the nape of her neck. "It's time you started getting used to it. I'll be a perfect gentleman—at least for now. It seems the priest is on a retreat. He's out of the city. Donte Latini texted me. He's one of my bodyguards."

"I find it extraordinary that shadow riders have bodyguards." She was so sleepy she could barely keep her eyes open. "Where were your parents' bodyguards? Why didn't they see anything that night?"

"Technically, my parents were no longer shadow riders. They were greeters and didn't require bodyguards, so they didn't use them. We don't have a lot of resources, so we're careful to use them only where we have no other choice."

She would have rolled over and put her arms around him, hearing the pain, regret and even guilt in his mind. It wasn't in his voice, but he felt it. He thought he should have insisted his parents have bodyguards while he went without, regardless of the rules of the riders.

"Geno." The need to comfort him was paramount, but she didn't know how. She had no knowledge of such things, and it left her frustrated and feeling lacking as a partner. She was always confident. To feel as if she wasn't good enough disturbed her.

"Don't, Danzatrice Ombra. You're giving me exactly what I need just by staying in my bed. Settle for me. I need to hold you." He curled his body around hers, wrapping one arm around her waist and laying his head close. "Just sleep, woman."

She drifted for a few minutes, but then it came to her, what she'd wanted to tell him. "Geno. They don't kill like riders. They may use shadows, but they don't serve justice."

His lips moved against the nape of her neck. "No, baby, you're right. They don't kill clean. They're out for revenge, not justice."

"I don't think they're trained riders," she said. "Not in the accepted sense of the word." Her hunch. She hadn't put that in a report because it made no sense, but she was certain she was right, just like she was certain the killers were turning their attention to New York. And that they wanted to kill Geno Ferraro.

They can't have you, she whispered into his mind as she drifted off.

CHAPTER FIVE

Amaranthe felt as if she were waking up in a different world. She lived a very strict life, one of routine and duty. She worked out. Meditated. Practiced her ballet. Stretched. Worked out more. She rarely had downtime. She didn't have breakfast on a terrace overlooking the water watching the sun come up with a man who made her laugh at the outrageous stories he told her.

She'd never before had anyone come to her small apartment with cases filled with clothing she never could afford to look at, let alone purchase. Geno sat in a chair on the ninth floor with a faint smile on his face while she tried on so many outfits, she thought her head might explode. Right there, in the middle of the great room, a fitting room had been set up for her to change in so she could put on the dozens of types of clothing from casual to formal.

This material is the same as the material our rider clothing is made from. What company is this? Amaranthe was excited.

She was from France and preferred to do most of her

shopping there. It was difficult to find clothing suiting her diminutive size that made her feel like a woman and not a child. This was a gold mine find—not only beautiful clothing in the perfect size, but pieces she could safely disappear into a shadow with.

Another cousin of ours, Andrea Ferraro Prescott, owns the company Ferraro Designs. She began experimenting beyond suits when it became clear the women needed clothes for other occasions. Emmanuelle and Mariko both volunteered to help with taking Andrea's designs into the shadows, and they love them. I told Andrea you might be interested in helping her as well.

How could they possibly make this many dresses and pants in my size? We only announced our engagement yesterday.

She walked out of the makeshift dressing room toward him, smoothing her hand down the navy glitter tulle cocktail gown that was her favorite. It felt fun and flirty and reminded her of a few of her ballet costumes, so it felt familiar. The V neckline held by spaghetti straps wasn't indecently low for her in the front, but the scooped back was daringly low. The fitted bodice was wrapped with fine ruched surplice and emphasized her small rib cage and waist. The knee-length A-line tulle skirt was very flirty, with flourishes and gathers, and she couldn't help the extra sway she put into her step.

Geno didn't say anything at first; he just looked at her, his eyes darkening with a look that sent little electrical charges flickering down her spine. She was utterly aware of him as a man. That made her aware of herself as a woman—so unlike her. She wasn't a woman who flirted with men. But Geno . . . Everything was different with Geno. Geno made the world brighter.

He shook his head slowly. "You know I'm reading you right now, and it's the other way around. You make my world so much better. I didn't realize I even had a sense of humor until you came into it. You make me laugh. Everything around me feels filled with hope and a sense of peace. Even my house already feels like a home just because you're here. I like sharing my space with you and having someone I can talk to."

Amaranthe really did feel as if she'd woken up in the middle of a fairy tale. To cover the fluttery feeling she didn't know what to do with, she spun in a slow circle to show him the sparkling dress with the low back.

"What do you think of this one for tonight? You said to expect quite a bit of press to be waiting for us."

"I think it's perfect. I have a navy suit that will match it." He looked up at the woman helping her. "Andrea, do you have shoes designed to go with this dress yet?"

"I'm sorry, Geno, we've designed them on paper, but they're not made up yet. I did bring a variety of heels for her to choose from that would go with the dress, but they aren't made of special materials. The good news is, I'll be able to leave the shoe drawings with you and the two of you can go over them and choose which ones you prefer for us to make up for you. Mariko and Emmanuelle often do ask us to do that. That way, they get exclusive designer shoes to go with their original gown."

"Please don't apologize, Andrea. You managed to come through for us on extraordinarily short notice. I have no idea how you did this, but I won't forget it."

Amaranthe knew he wouldn't. He sounded and looked sincere, but more important, she felt that sincerity in his mind. He did appreciate that Andrea's company had managed to ensure Amaranthe had clothing she could wear out with him, not feel inferiorly dressed, and yet still be able to make it safely into the shadows.

Geno had money. Not a little money. Lots of money. There was no getting around that. He was comfortable in places she would never consider going unless she stayed in the shadows while tracking a rogue. She didn't have the clothes to be confident in his world and appreciated that he thought of that for her.

You know I can't afford all these dresses, but I love this one. I really want it, Geno. I've got enough to buy this one for tonight.

Babe, really? "We'll take everything she liked, Andrea."

Don't argue in front of her, Amara. Her business is just getting off the ground. Her crew stayed up all night altering the clothes for your size and you're going to need all of those. We're all trying to help her as much as she'll let us.

Amaranthe bunched the sparkly tulle skirt in her fingers, trying to feel in his mind if he meant what he said or was trying to spare her embarrassment at not being able to pay such an exorbitant amount of money for clothes. She decided she would have to look at it as acquiring costumes. When she left a dance company, she didn't keep her costumes. It didn't matter how beautiful they were, they belonged to the company. She might just have to negotiate to keep this dress; that was how much she loved it.

"Thank you, Andrea," Amaranthe said. "I love all the clothes, but this dress is my particular favorite. It makes me feel beautiful and confident."

"You do look beautiful in it," Andrea said.

"You *are* beautiful," Geno said. "It doesn't matter what you're wearing. You're simply beautiful, Amara, inside and out." His voice was gruff.

Geno still wore his stone mask, but it didn't matter because she saw beneath it to the heart of him. She would always be able to read him thanks to the way their shadows had tangled together. She doubted if it was safe to allow her shadow to get close to his again. The moment it happened, the two shadows connected like magnets. The more it happened, the harder it would be to separate them.

Although Amaranthe hadn't grown up in a normal household, she had been warned to protect her shadow. She'd been told if her shadow was compromised and she couldn't undo the weave, if one rider walked away from the other and both were riders, neither would be able to continue riding the shadows.

She was a shadow rider. That was her identity. Who she was. Her parents had begun her training at the age of two. Jean-Claude and the Archambaults had continued it from the time she was four. She knew no other life. She doubted she would survive if she couldn't be a rider. Surely, Geno felt the same way.

She changed in the fitting room, mulling the question over. Did he? He had been so quick to take the poison from her, risking his life. He had known the consequences of ingesting the poison, and he'd still done it. There had been a quiet sorrow in him, an acceptance of death, as if he welcomed it. That bothered her. Geno had a huge family. She had none. No one. People weren't meant to spend their entire lives alone.

Amaranthe had known there was a high probability that she would die young. Her profession was high risk. Investigating rogue riders without any backup drove the risks higher than ever. Most of the time when she was sent in, thankfully, it was a false alarm and the rider wasn't guilty, but she had brought more than one to justice. It hadn't been easy, and it had become automatic to protect her shadow. Because of that, she hadn't believed she would find someone she would want to spend her life with.

Lunch was on the terrace of the second floor overlooking the sparkling water. Sunglasses were a must, but the view was impressive. She sat across the small table from Geno, still feeling like the princess in a fairy tale.

Geno had a way of focusing completely on her. Even with his eyes hidden behind sunglasses, she could feel the intensity of his gaze burning through her.

"Tell me about your dancing. Why you love it so much. I've taken over my mother's position on the board, but I don't know that much about ballet yet. I've been reading up on it, the difference between classical ballet and ballet. I didn't even realize there was a difference. I thought all ballet was the same and the training was the same until I started reading about it. It's very clear I'm going to have to watch videos and then the real thing. You'll have to help me learn. I wouldn't want to turn down the wrong students for scholarships or hire an instructor who doesn't know what he or she is doing."

Amaranthe couldn't help admiring the fact that he took replacing his mother on the board of directors seriously. Many men or women in his position wouldn't bother.

"Of course, I'll help you in any way I can. I love to dance, and I really love teaching anyone who takes it seriously."

"Tell me about how you got started and why you love it so much."

There was no denying the real interest in his voice. That was another thing she hadn't had in her life. No one had ever shown such interest in her opinions or why she wanted to do the things she did. The council studied her reports, asked her questions, often disagreed with her findings, and sent her on her way.

"When I was little, a toddler, my mother would take me to the ballet with her. I would sit spellbound. I loved watching the performances. If I trained without complaint for shadow riding, she would always reward me with dance lessons." She flashed a quick self-demeaning smile at him. "I think back then it was the sparkly outfits."

"Judging by the dress you chose for tonight, it may still be," he teased.

His playful bantering was another first for her. She found herself laughing. "That's probably true. But you must know I was trained in classical ballet because you call me *la mia danzatrice ombra* rather than *la ballerina*."

"I studied your file, and I'll confess I watched every video I could find of you dancing. You have the most beautiful lines. You're mesmerizing when you're onstage—from another realm. I can't even explain it."

She felt herself blushing when she didn't blush. Geno seemed to bring that out in her. "Thank you. That's a tremendous compliment."

"It's the truth."

"I wanted to train in classical ballet because precise, flowing movements appeal to me. Tradition is important to me. I think more so than for most people because I don't have a family."

She looked out over the gleaming water. The way the sun shone down and made what appeared to be diamonds sparkle and roll on the surface fascinated her. Geno not only had three entire floors of a masterpiece designed by a brilliant architect, but this view from every terrace facing the river was breathtaking. The glass walls inside his home gave him the same views, so no matter if he was outside or inside he had the feeling of open space.

"I understand," Geno agreed. "I do have a big family. We're loud when we get together, and noisy, and we tease one another. Taviano and Francesca usually are the ones cooking, although we all pitch in to help. Crispino is always underfoot and repeating every bad word he hears to get his father in trouble. We have traditions we follow. I can't imagine our lives without them. So, yeah, I get that."

Amaranthe tried not to stare at him. She didn't want to be so caught up in her fantasy she couldn't distinguish it from reality, but it was becoming difficult not to believe she could be a part of his life. The way he looked at her and spoke in that soft, utterly interested tone was seductive to someone who had never had anyone of their own.

"What else made you choose classical ballet?"

He sounded fascinated. Completely drawn in. She ran her finger down her throat to stroke the sudden lump there. This was what it would be like to have someone care. It was dangerous. If she allowed herself to trust that there was a real bond between them, and their relationship could work, and she came to depend on it . . . She shut down the consequences of loss. Right now, in this moment, she was going to enjoy what she'd never had before.

"There are ethereal qualities in the ballet that I get lost in. I disappear into the movements and simply become them. That and the aesthetics appeal to the artist in me. When I'm dancing, the music flows through me and I'm not there. It's just movement and artistry and the character if I'm performing."

She could see by his slight frown that he didn't understand, and she wanted him to. "It's such a beautiful world, Geno."

"You escape there."

"I'm totally free. All of me. Every part of me. The training is rigorous for classical ballet, just as it is for shadow riding. That's such a part of who I am. It's demanding and you must be disciplined and push through pain and discomfort with your eye on the goal every moment. So when I dance and everything comes together, the training, the flowing movements, the ethereal beauty, I feel as if I'm experiencing complete freedom. My spirit, maybe, but even my body is leaping high and soaring across the stage in an effortless way."

Geno flashed her a heart-stopping smile. He was really going to have to stop doing that or she might just keel over and faint. She hadn't thought of him as handsome. He didn't look like anyone's idea of Prince Charming. The angles and planes in his face were carved too deep, too severe to give him the classic handsome look. Instead he appeared all man, almost hardened. Scary dangerous. The intensity in his eyes and that hint of cruelty around his mouth didn't help with his image.

Geno fit the image of a man with money. He lived the lifestyle. He carried himself confidently and easily commanded any room he entered, but while Stefano looked sophisticated, Geno looked as if he belonged more in Valentino Saldi's world than the Ferraro world. He had that dangerous of an edge to him.

"You have the talent to dance with any of the larger, renowned companies. Surely, you've been approached. I've read through my mother's notes, and she observed that in her opinion, your dancing compared with some of the best dancers in the world. She would never say something like that lightly."

Amaranthe had to turn completely away from him. She'd never received so many compliments in her life—all of which appeared to be genuine. She heard the sincerity in his voice. She was trained to hear lies. It was one of her gifts, and Jean-Claude and the other instructors training her had insisted she develop that trait, testing her daily.

Geno tended to be casual when he gifted her with a compliment. He didn't make a big deal of it; he stated whatever he said as a fact. That was so much better than flowery compliments she would have known weren't sincere. The things he said would stay with her forever. She wanted to hold them to her and take them out when she was alone to go over every word.

"Yes, I was honored more than once with a request to try out, but I'm a shadow rider first. I work for the International Council, and dancing is a cover. That means I have to take work with the smaller companies just as I did here in New York."

"That means you will never have the chance to dance on a big stage with the best of the best, Amara. You deserve to be with them."

"I've had the privilege of working with remarkable dancers. If I'd stayed with one company, I never would have met these wonderful dancers, all of whom taught me something I had yet to learn. I'm a shadow rider, Geno. I wouldn't give that up for any reason. I love to dance. I do, but I'm a shadow rider first. That's who I am. It's who I was born to be."

Geno swirled water in the crystal glass, still looking at her intently behind his smoky glasses. "You do realize you trained from the time you were two, first by your parents, and then not only your training but essentially your entire life was shaped by the council. You could change the course of your life if you wanted. Your career in dance would take off and the Ferraro family would back you."

That offer was sincere as well. She frowned, trying to puzzle out what else she heard, what underlying note was there. He wore his expressionless mask, and the dark gray glasses covered the look in his eyes so she couldn't read him. It didn't matter. She knew the truth, and she was going to be honest with him about the things that counted.

"I'm a shadow rider, Geno. The offer would be amazing, but I would never voluntarily give up riding."

She felt his instant satisfaction. More than satisfaction, almost as if he'd been holding his breath, determined to give her an opportunity to change her path if that was what she wanted.

She studied his face. He was so much younger than she had originally thought he would be. Younger than Stefano when she had thought the cousins were the same age. She knew most people thought that because they were the head of their families and Geno looked older than he was, but in fact, he was several years younger.

"What about you, Geno? Tell me what it was like for you. You were so young when you took over for your parents, weren't you?"

He poured more water into her glass and added shrimp salad to his plate. "I was a kid, a teenager, so angry. Really angry. I knew my parents were lying to us. And I knew the Archambaults knew more than they were letting on. Translate that into being a reckless pain in the ass to everyone. I was big and fast and already very strong for my age. Put that together with angry, and you had a disaster on your hands."

Amaranthe had always had an empathic side to her nature, and she felt his memories of that teenage boy surfacing, the anger that was still smoldering. She couldn't blame him—his childhood had been ripped from him.

"We'd been happy, all of us. My parents were strict, but they were loving, especially my mother, and then all of the sudden they cut themselves off from us. It was bad enough that they'd done that to me, but Salvatore and Lucca were younger, and Salvatore was sensitive and sweet. He was very close to Mama."

She didn't think they were that much younger, but a few years made a world of difference in the early years.

"They were lost and that made me even angrier. Fortunately, I have a fairly decent brain and it didn't take me long to figure out that my parents weren't going to relent. I was angry with the wrong people. I might not like how strict the Archambaults were, but I realized I needed their knowledge not only for my survival but for Salvatore and Lucca's as well. So I changed my attitude and learned everything I could from them. Once I made up my mind to train and learn everything I could, I challenged myself daily to become faster and stronger. I learned everything they could teach me and constantly demanded more."

"I can't imagine what that must have been like for you."

"I had a teenager's anger and arrogance to spur me on. No one was going to be faster or better. I already considered myself smarter."

He gave her a little grin, but she felt his underlying sadness.

"The one thing I wouldn't let them do was tell me how to parent. That was all Stefano. At first, I thought my parents were going to come out of that room and at least talk to the boys, but after a year with no word, I knew they weren't. When they did open the doors and they acted like robots, I went to Stefano to learn what I could from him."

Amaranthe studied his face. His mask was firmly in place. "You're still angry."

He sighed and nodded, a slow, deliberate nod that had her heart clenching for him. She wanted to cover his hand with hers. Do something, anything, to comfort him. She just didn't know how.

"I wish I weren't angry at them. I thought they'd give me advice. Something. Anything. But they didn't. At least they would talk to Salvatore and Lucca like they loved them. But they didn't do that, either. They turned into strangers. Salvatore kept trying with them. He would go to Mama every day, but he got nothing back. I remember the day he came out of their suite and he was different, all the joy in him gone."

Geno sank back in his chair and ran both hands through his hair. It was one of the first signs of agitation she'd seen him make. He was normally very self-assured.

"Stefano has always been the man willing to make the hard decisions. You can count on him, but he tempers that with compassion. He has a temper, but he's all about discipline and control. He puts his family, the riders and territory first. He embodies what a leader should be."

Amaranthe waited to hear him out before she protested. Geno clearly didn't feel he was up to his cousin's standards.

"I knew someday I would inherit the responsibilities from my father and mother, but I thought Salvatore or Lucca were better suited. Truthfully, if I wasn't built the way I am, I could have seen myself doing the kind of work you do. I think when the Archambaults were training me, a time or two Jean-Claude may have even discussed something like that with them."

"Why do you think that?"

"They looked at Salvatore and Lucca, asking a lot of questions about the two of them leading the Ferraro shadow riders here if I were gone. It was the way they asked. I didn't know anything about the kind of work you do, but I had the feeling they were considering separating us. I made it clear that wasn't going to happen."

"Why? You must have realized that was your only opportunity to get out."

His fingers toyed with the crystal glass. Sure. Steady. She realized when he came to a decision, he had studied the problem from every angle. His brain worked at a high rate of speed. He might seem to come to a conclusion fast, but his decisions weren't without thought.

"My brothers didn't need me to abandon them the way my parents did. I'm not like Stefano. I knew that going into it, and I sat Salvatore and Lucca down and told them so. I told them I'd be making mistakes, but that I'd do the best I could. That I'd keep them safe, and every decision I'd make was with their happiness and safety in mind. I wanted them to know we were a family, and I wanted their input. We would work things out together, but in the end, I'd have to make the tough choices. I promised them I wasn't going anywhere."

Amaranthe knew right then her heart was in jeopardy if she stayed around Geno too long. He might seem as tough as nails, but his heart wasn't. He might think he wasn't like Stefano Ferraro, but when it came to his family and what he would sacrifice for them, he was.

"That's why you're so close."

"We're close," he acknowledged. "They aren't very happy with me at the moment."

"Did they forgive your parents?"

"I don't know. They talked to them more than I did. I treated them as greeters, members of the team. I made certain they had everything they needed, but I didn't give them any personal information. Not ever. Not on me and not on my brothers. Whether Salvatore and Lucca did, I don't know. I didn't ask. I figured that was their private business."

He removed his dark glasses, and she felt the impact of his deep blue eyes staring straight into hers. "I am not a forgiving man, Amara. When someone hurts a member of my *famiglia*, I don't forgive. Salvatore and Lucca were boys. My parents took something beautiful from them, and if they felt remorse, I never saw it, so no, I didn't forgive them."

A shiver of trepidation crept down her spine. Geno Ferraro would make a bitter, relentless enemy.

"It's best that you never tell anyone else this, Geno."

"Who else would I tell?"

"Elie Archambault comes to mind. You should never have sent a report to the council. They're going to be looking at you now. You never want their attention on you."

"I didn't want their attention on you." He covered his eyes once more against the glare of the sun.

She sighed. It was just one more reason to fall for him, and she didn't need any more reasons. She was trying to find excuses not to get her heart involved. "I'm used to dealing with them, Geno. Your parents never returned to being parents?"

He shook his head. "It was as if, whatever happened the night they told me I was to take over, they considered themselves dead as both riders and our parents. They interacted, but distantly. They showed no interest in us. I honestly wondered if they were the same people. If others had come back pretending to be them."

"Is that possible? Someone dressing up as them? Wearing masks? There are amazing reproductions of faces now."

"I studied them very carefully, their movements. Their voices. It was them. Something happened to them. Whatever it was killed their love for us. They couldn't even see us. Only each other."

There was no bitterness in him. He had accepted his fate, Amaranthe could tell, at least for himself. She didn't think he felt that way for his brothers.

"Do you really believe the murders now are connected to what happened all those years ago? How long has it been?"

"Eighteen years. It's been eighteen years. And I have this strong gut feeling that they are. They would never speak of it, but I think they did something wrong. Committed a crime along with other riders."

"Why would you think it was a crime?" Although that would make sense. Her mind began to race with the possibilities.

"The other riders hid in the shadows to keep their identities secret. They brought a wounded rider through the shadows, risking more damage to him and even risking his life. They lied about what happened and even manufactured evidence to back up their lies. They stepped down from shadow riding and refused to tell the Archambaults the truth. What other conclusion is there?"

Amaranthe had to agree it was a logical one. "Eighteen years is a long time to wait for revenge."

"It is, but if the grievance was big enough, I would wait, Amara. I'm a patient man when I have to be. When it counts."

He was silent for a long moment, and she didn't make the mistake of speaking. She waited, listening to the wind and the sound of her heartbeat. She knew whatever he was about to tell her was going to be huge and would reveal so much of him.

"Stefano isn't like Valentino Saldi or Dario Bosco, Amaranthe. I am. I would never forget if someone committed a crime against my *famiglia*, and I would wait a lifetime to retaliate. Stefano would do so through proper channels; I wouldn't. I wouldn't target innocents as these people seem to be doing, but I would take down anyone who harmed a loved one under my protection."

It was interesting to her that he aligned himself with Saldi and Bosco when it was clear that Stefano was the Ferraro closer to the two men. She could see that now, that well of darkness in him and where it had come from.

"Again, Geno, something better left unsaid."

"You need to know these things about me."

"Where do Valentino Saldi and Dario Bosco fit? I'm not comfortable discussing shadow rider business in front of them."

Geno studied her for several long minutes. "You aren't going to comment on the fact that I just confessed something pretty vile about myself?"

"No. You let me into your mind, Geno. Maybe not all the way in, but I see glimpses of you. The real you. You're quite different than you think you are. I really would like to know about Saldi and Bosco and how they fit into your world. Clearly, they have a place because you, your cousin and even Elie were far too comfortable talking in front of them."

"We consider them family. Both sides are respectful of

a line we don't cross. Stefano was careful to word things in such a way that Val and Dario had to swear allegiance to the family."

"You know outsiders can't know about shadow riders, Geno. Even within families, few know about the shadow riders."

"Val and Dario were already aware of the riders just from watching over the years. Val had been interested in Emmanuelle, and his family and our family were considered enemies. He has his own gifts. He watched us closely and observed us disappearing into the shadows. He never said a word to anyone, not even his father."

"Why would he keep that information to himself?"

"He's intelligent enough to know what we are and what kind of true enemies we would make. But in a word, Emme. He's in love with Emmanuelle, and he would never do anything to hurt her. She was under his protection, and that protection extended to her family. That's the way he works."

"And Dario?"

"He's loyal to Val and Emme. Fiercely loyal to them. I think he's extended that loyalty to Stefano and Francesca, but he'll always put Val and Emme first."

"I don't know, Geno." She wasn't convinced.

"When it comes to shadows, the Saldis have their own myth that seems to have diluted and disappeared for the most part. Fathers told their sons the story. Most have forgotten it, but Val was told by his birth father and then by his adoptive father, Giuseppi Saldi. He thought it was just a story until he noticed Emme's shadow at a party and his shadow connected with hers. Emmanuelle was a kid still, a teenager. She had no idea anyone other than a shadow rider would have the ability to compromise her shadow. At the time Val wasn't aware of the full extent of the consequences. It's a long story, but the bottom line is Stefano and Val worked out a deal."

"And you trust them to keep that deal? You're comfortable with the arrangement?" Because she wasn't.

"Let's just say, I like and respect both men. Like Stefano I believe it's safer to keep them close and know what they're doing at all times. With Emmanuelle, who is absolutely loyal to the shadow riders and her family, Stefano was brilliant in ensuring Valentino and Dario both gave their word of honor to uphold the agreement between families. If they ever did anything to put the shadow riders in jeopardy, Emme would stand with us against them, and both men know that. She's lethal as hell."

"Our women could be compromised by other Saldis if this gets out. Your family should never have kept this to themselves. The International Council should have been informed."

"We informed them as soon as we had as many facts as we could gather that would protect our female riders. Unfortunately, even Emmanuelle didn't have many facts because Val and Dario didn't. They had tried to find the original mythology in a library in Sicily but were trying to shut down a human trafficking ring and fighting for their lives. That's how we came to be allies with them. Both Dario and Val were nearly killed in an ambush, and we threw in with them to shut down the ring. That's when we discovered that members of the Saldi family had the ability to bind a shadow rider."

There was more, Amaranthe was certain, so she remained quiet without protesting. She didn't know what to say, other than the council sent her out without warning her to be careful of her allowing her shadow to seen by others as much as possible. They should have. They should have sent a warning to every rider—male and female.

"The book they need to study the mythology is written in an ancient language, one I doubt Val or Dario would be able to find an interpreter for, even at a university, at least one they would trust. Val's good with languages, but not that good. He doesn't go back that far."

Amaranthe heard the satisfaction in his voice. Not just satisfaction, but animation. "But you do. You have a gift for languages." There was an extensive library on the same floor as the master bedroom. There was a second library on the middle floor, where the recreation rooms were. She knew Geno loved books.

Geno's white teeth flashed at her. Briefly, but it was a genuine smile. "I love the written word and always prefer to read any story or document in the original language it was first written in. Translations are often interpreted incorrectly, as anyone going to another country and listening to an interpreter can tell you."

"Are you searching for this book that has the Saldi myth in it?"

"We can't do that," Geno denied. "It would be a violation of trust. We're being patient. Stefano has dropped the word occasionally to Valentino that I have extensive knowledge in ancient languages, but he only does so in passing, when the subject comes up. He acts like I'm an old soul who likes dead poetry behind my mask of indifference. Occasionally he tells Dario to study the ancient languages with me so he can quote poetry no one else can understand."

"He's planting the seed to have you read the book for them."

Geno nodded. "We need them to do the asking. We can't volunteer. It needs to be their idea. Stefano hasn't mentioned my penchant for languages in a while and he won't."

"Very clever." Amaranthe found herself smiling. She still wasn't certain of Val and Dario being so close to the Ferraro family, but she did understand the concept of keeping enemies close. Keeping an eye on them seemed like a good idea to her.

She really liked Geno Ferraro. More than she ever thought she could like another human being. She wanted the fairy tale.

CHAPTER SIX

Amaranthe found it was one thing to feel like she was in a fairy tale when she was alone with Geno in the unbelievable apartment, but it was an altogether different proposition being driven in a luxurious car to their engagement party, knowing the paparazzi were swarming around the restaurant. They had already run into a gauntlet of reporters with cameras as they exited the condominium, bodyguards shielding them as they were rushed out of a private door straight into the car with tinted windows that would take them to the restaurant, where she knew to expect the bulk of the paparazzi.

In his home, Geno was a different man, warm and doting, his entire focus on her, telling her funny stories about his brothers and asking her questions about her beloved ballet. When Geno had asked her point-blank if she would give up shadow riding for ballet, she could honestly answer him with a resounding no. She would never consider such a thing. Now, as the town car moved steadily toward the restaurant, the lively conversations she'd had with that Geno

Ferraro faded away to be replaced by the stranger sitting beside her.

In his dark navy suit, his shoulders seemed wider and his chest even thicker. He appeared more sinister and very much like a crime lord. He looked so remote, his hard features an expressionless mask. He had his phone out and was clearly receiving updates on what was happening at the restaurant. Who was there. How many. The security. He seemed completely engrossed with the news from someone watching the frenzy unfolding. The head of his security also chimed in occasionally. She knew because Geno would occasionally talk to him, asking questions and giving orders.

He didn't look at her. He didn't talk to her. He seemed completely remote and removed from her. What had she been thinking this entire time? She didn't fit into his world. She didn't live in the fast lane. She observed it from the shadows, but she didn't *live* there. It was exactly what she'd been thinking all along—a fairy tale. Fantasies no one really believed.

She brushed her fingers down the glittery tulle skirt in the hopes that it would give her confidence as the town car pulled into the circular entrance to the Luna D'Argento restaurant. The building had originally been a very large warehouse before the Ferraro brothers had converted it to a restaurant.

Constructed of gray, black and white stone, it was so large it had multiple entrances for the convenience of allowing for family dining on one side. Separately, a very upscale restaurant boasted an entirely different chef and staff for romantic evenings out. The back room was for private events or the family, and that room was kept locked. That was where their engagement party was being held.

It was silly how nervous she was. If they'd ridden the shadows to the restaurant, she was certain she wouldn't have felt the millions of butterflies fluttering like mad in her stomach. Suddenly, Geno's hand enveloped hers, thumb rubbing back and forth over the engagement ring he'd put on her finger. She glanced up at him, her fake smile in place, trying to reassure herself more than him.

She could do this. She played roles all the time. This was the role of a lifetime. She looked down at the ring on her finger, the one he was rolling under his thumb. He hadn't asked her formally. She wasn't certain what that meant. Were they engaged to be married, or was this a sham for the benefit of drawing out the murderers of his parents? Maybe she needed to really look at this like an undercover role, not as if he was going to be a permanent part of her life. She had wanted a home and family . . . No, she had wanted Geno Ferraro. He had been her fairy tale. Her Prince Charming.

Geno unexpectedly tightened his fingers around hers and brought their joined hands to his mouth to kiss her knuckles. "Are you having doubts about us again, Amara?"

His voice was so unexpectedly gentle she found herself blinking back tears. Geno Ferraro was a man of complete mystery to her. One moment he was as hard as steel, and in the next, so caring it shocked her.

Amaranthe attempted a humorous reply. "I suppose it's because I've never even dated. I don't exactly know about relationships. Are we undercover, Geno? You need to let me know what we're doing here, so I can get things straight in my head."

He turned her hand over and pressed his lips against the ring Damian Ferraro had created exclusively for her. "You're wearing my ring on your finger."

"I'm well aware, but props are necessary for any role I play."

The door opened to allow them out of the car. Her heart sank. She knew she could face Stefano Ferraro again, and any of the other relatives that might be waiting to congratulate them, but there were cameras crowding around. Geno Ferraro's engagement was big news. She wasn't as certain how to play the part of his glamourous fiancée.

Geno shook his head, and the door was closed immediately. He leaned forward and knocked on the privacy window. At once it came down and their driver turned her head. "Alice, would you mind stepping out of the car and giving us complete privacy?"

"Of course, Mr. Ferraro." Alice immediately vacated the vehicle, leaving them alone.

"The ring isn't a prop to me, *la mia danzatrice ombra*."

Now she was so nervous her mouth was dry, and her chest hurt. She wanted to disappear into the shadows and never emerge.

"Everyone's waiting, Geno. We should do this another time." Her voice was shaky, not at all like her usual confident self.

"Amaranthe. They can wait forever. We can turn around and go home if you prefer. This isn't about them. It's about us."

There was that gentle voice again. This time he caught her chin and tilted her face up toward his. He waited until her eyes met his. The impact was both breathtaking and intense when he was wholly focused on her.

She swallowed the terror rising up to overwhelm her. She didn't know how to do personal. "This is about baiting a trap for those who are killing shadow riders."

The pad of his thumb swept over her lower lip, and he shook his head, still looking into her eyes. "This isn't about that for me. This is about us. You and me. Our engagement. I meant my proposal. I want you to marry me. I want *you*, Amara. I think we're good together. I believe we fit. I hope you want me just as much."

She did want him. She just didn't know what to do with him. She had nice clothes; she didn't have his kind of nice clothes until he had bought them for her. She didn't have his kind of jewelry until he had provided several pieces for her. She didn't want to be in a relationship where she couldn't be a full partner. What did she bring to the table for Geno?

She didn't run in his circles. Yes, she danced in the

ballet, but she moved around too much to ever play for a big company. She received amazing reviews, but was never going to have that career, not when she was a shadow rider first—and she meant what she told Geno: she would always be a shadow rider first.

She didn't realize she was shaking her head until he framed her face with his large hands, stilling the movement.

"Baby, please just listen to me," Geno continued. "Hear me out. I don't want this just to be a role for you to play. I want you to feel comfortable as my fiancée. You were born to be with me. I was born to be your man. I've always known things. This is the strongest intuitive reaction I've ever had. Just tell me what you need to make you know it, too."

Amaranthe had expected him to be far older. She'd thought Stefano would be older as well. Having to be responsible for the riders and the territories from such a young age had made them both seem older, but they weren't. Physical age didn't matter. Geno was an old soul. It was there in his eyes, and she felt it when he weighed his answers before he spoke. He didn't think the way a young person would. He wasn't selfish in his thinking.

"You didn't ask me to marry you, Geno. Not really. I couldn't tell if you really wanted to marry me for me or to ensure the shadow-riding line. Or just to play this role so we could catch these murderers."

"It wasn't to play a role, and if we never have children, Amara, I'll be fine with that. I want you for yourself."

He sounded truthful. His voice was quiet but determined. His gaze didn't waver from hers. He could mesmerize her with those dark blue eyes.

"Do you want children?"

"With you?" He nodded. "I'm all about family. My brothers, my cousins. Mostly, now, I'm all about you. If you don't want to meet with everyone here now, we'll wait until you're ready. Amaranthe, this is for us. Our beginning. It isn't just a sham to catch murderers. We'll do that as well, but our beginning doesn't have to be that."

It felt as if her heart somersaulted. She reached up to frame his jaw with her hand. Who knew a man as dangerous and lethal as Geno Ferraro could be so intuitive? So caring?

"I want children," she admitted. "I want you to ask me properly, and I want you to be very sure. I don't want to marry someone who won't love me. All my life I've been alone, Geno. I never thought I'd be with someone, but when I considered it, I knew it would have to be with someone who would love me for me. They had to see me, flaws and all. I don't want you to think I'm ever going to be someone who sits on the sidelines, because I won't be."

"I see who you are very clearly, Amaranthe," Geno said. "I'm looking right into your heart, and I see what I want. I hope you're doing the same. I don't think this car is the place to ask you to marry me properly, but if you want me to be on my knee, I'll do it when I find the right opportunity. You have my word."

The tension in her eased. Geno wasn't playing a role. He meant when he said. He'd reassured her dozens of times, it seemed. She was the one without the confidence. She found herself searching his dark eyes. Ferraro eyes. They were dark, but not brown. Not black. They were actually blue, but so dark blue they looked black at times. He was a beautiful man, and he took her breath away.

She was never going to fit into his world. Never. But she would fit with him when they were alone. And as a rider, there were few her equal. She took a deep breath. Let it out. On sheer bravado, she made the commitment.

"Okay, then. Let's do this."

"As long as you're sure."

She nodded, never looking away from his dark gaze. She did love his eyes. "I'm very sure. I'm not going to doubt us again."

His smile was slow in climbing to his eyes, but when it reached them, it lit up the deep blue until her stomach began to perform loops and somersaults.

"You're lethal to women, Geno."

"Just to you, I promise."

He cupped the back of her head gently and bent to brush his lips across hers, featherlight, before she could protest that she was wearing lipstick. As kisses went, it was fairly virtuous. It shouldn't have made her heart pound like a drum out of control, but it did. He didn't stop there. He shifted her, easily bringing her onto his lap, urging her to straddle his thighs.

Amaranthe knew better, but she couldn't help herself. He mesmerized her. Large hands at her waist, he lifted her, and she settled one knee on either side of his thighs. His lips moved on hers again and again. Barely there. Whispering. Never hurrying. So light. Coaxing her with tenderness as if he knew everything she said was bravado. She was still afraid to go into his world with him.

Geno had kissed her with fire, but not like this. Not with tenderness. Not so she could taste raw emotion. He was giving her a gift—showing her how he felt. Her lips trembled beneath his. This was a terrifying moment even as she reveled in it. His chest was hard as it rose and fell against the softness of her breasts. His tongue slid along the seam of her lips, and her heart contracted.

I want you for myself, Danzatrice Ombra. You're the only thing I've ever wanted for me. The only woman I've looked at and known I had to have, or it would be no one. If you turn me down, there will be no arranged marriage. No children with another rider. You are my partner, Amaranthe. I feel it with every breath I take. Feel it, too. Want me the way I want you.

He whispered poetic words like that into her mind, and she knew she would never be able to resist him. It didn't matter that he was so far out of her league, and she had no idea how to be with a man like him, she knew she couldn't walk away from him.

She saw his absolute resolve. He meant every word he

said. His life had been dictated to him, his every path, his every breath and step. He was done with giving every aspect of his life to everyone else. He would choose his wife. The woman he would marry. If he couldn't have the woman he loved, he would choose to be alone. She saw that determination in him. When Geno made up his mind, he was absolute steel.

I'm so afraid I'll embarrass you, Geno. I have no idea what to do or say around these people. I don't belong with them.

His mouth brushed across her lips again. Gently. Coaxing. So tender her stomach did a slow somersault and her sex clenched. She held herself very still, frozen in place, but the need for flight was paramount. Every inch of the front of her body was pressed tightly against him. His masculine scent enveloped her so that each time she inhaled, she took him deep into her lungs.

You don't need to belong with them, Amara. You belong with me. I'm the one who needs you, not them. I don't belong. Haven't you noticed? I'm not the same as the rest of them and I make them uneasy. I've never minded, but I don't want you to feel that way. I don't want you uneasy around me.

How could he think that? Did she make him think it was him? She slid her palms up his chest and linked her fingers behind his neck, her mouth moving under his in answer.

It isn't you I'm afraid of, Geno. I love being with you, and I'm comfortable with you. It's the others in your world.

His teeth teased at her lower lip, tugging very gently while his palm curled around the nape of her neck and his thumb swept along her cheek.

Give yourself to me, la mia danzatrice ombra. I swear, you'll always be safe with me. I'll make you happy.

There was no resisting him. She didn't even want to resist him. He was right.

I want you to know you will always come first. Always.

What difference did it make if she didn't fit in with his circle of friends? With his family? She fit with him.

The council will lose their minds. She felt compelled to warn him.

Let them. I'll lose my mind without you.

He kissed her gently again and pulled back to look at her.

"My brothers fit with what a Ferraro should be. I made certain of that and still it wasn't good enough. They both feel as if they need to settle down immediately and start producing children to further the line. Francesca is practically killing herself to give the riders what they need." He framed her face again. "Not you, Amaranthe. They took enough from you. Your childhood. Your existence. They don't get anything else you're not willing to give them. And you won't kill yourself to give them our babies. Hopefully, you'll help me persuade my brothers to slow down before they commit to arranged marriages."

There was acute pain stabbing at him and she doubted he even knew. She detested that Geno hurt the way he did. The pain wasn't even for himself. This was for his brothers. He felt he'd failed them. She pressed closer to him and daringly ran her tongue along his bottom lip, tracing the curve.

She felt very small and delicate in comparison to his size. She'd never felt that way before. She had very firm muscles, but beneath her skin there was a layer of softness she'd never been so aware of until she was up against the density of his muscle mass. As his head descended, her lashes fluttered, and she veiled her eyes. She parted her lips, and his tongue swept inside her mouth, hot with a hint of spice, making her heart stutter.

She knew she would always be addicted to his taste. To this fire that he created. This was a slow burn that was like molten lava moving through her veins, so thick with desire she could barely breathe. Barely think. Her body went hot with need for him. He set up a craving that was never going to go away.

Amaranthe was overwhelmed with emotion, swamped with it. With the taste of it. Emotion surrounded her, pressed into every cell and bundle of nerves she had. She hadn't known love other than those first four years of her life with her parents—but she felt it now. Tasted it in Geno's kisses. There was no way to deny it. She'd never had that feeling, and now that she had, now that it was stamped into her every cell, she couldn't live without it.

Geno might think he was a brute of a man, but he was a miracle. *Her* miracle. She hadn't known love could exist for her. She hadn't known she could taste it or feel it or become addicted to it. She hadn't known she could feel that particular emotion, but he must have found a way through his kisses, or his mind, or sharing her cells to teach her, because she knew the growing feeling for him had gone from affection to love, and that made no sense when she barely had spent any real time with him.

You know me. Heart to heart. Soul to soul.

Yes, that was *her* Geno. He wasn't just that brute of a man he thought himself. He was her secret poet—the man who read everything he could get his hands on in every language he knew. She melted into him. Wanted to be even closer. Wanted to be skin to skin. This man would be forever her secret.

He didn't stop kissing her over and over, and she knew his passion for her was the real thing. Straddling him the way she was, there was no denying his body demanded hers. She had feared he wouldn't want her as a woman. He was fiercely aroused. He wasn't kissing her with the fiery passion he had before, but this smoldering burn felt as if he was claiming her. Was cherishing her.

There was no denying the gentle way he held her. She hadn't expected him to be so tender or caring, and that had disarmed her as nothing else possibly could have. His thumb stroked her cheek. That was all. Brushed with exquisite gentleness. She had to swallow back the tears clogging her throat.

She hadn't thought she had anything to bring to Geno Ferraro, but now she knew she did. There were few riders in the world like her. He had no idea who or what his partner was. He thought to keep the world around him safe. Everyone in it. He never thought about himself. He was willing to lay down his life for those he loved. She didn't look the part and that was more than half her advantage. She would protect Geno with the same fierceness he gave everyone else. She would give him her loyalty because he deserved it. She knew she could make him happy.

He was the one who broke the kiss first, drawing in a ragged breath as he lifted his head and stared down at her with such complete focus that she found herself shivering.

"I think we're very late for our engagement party, Geno," she whispered.

"We could turn around and go home." He sounded hopeful.

She laughed. "You're terrible. I'm the one who should be saying that."

He picked up his phone, looked at his messages and then showed them to her. "We've been officially summoned by Stefano."

"You don't seem concerned."

"He hasn't threatened to escort us inside yet. When that happens, we might worry."

She was reading the string of messages Stefano had sent. "Wait. What does he mean you've compromised my reputation and we'd better marry fast?"

He flashed her a very unrepentant grin. "What do you think those reporters are going to be saying playboy Ferraro has been doing in this town car all this time right in front of the restaurant, tinted windows and all? Ferraro men do have a certain reputation. There will be wild speculation and others telling the story as gospel."

"That's what they all think we were in here doing?"

He nodded. "Yes, ma'am, that's exactly what they think."

"I have to go out there and face them knowing that?"

He grinned at her, leaned forward and brushed another kiss over her burning lips. "You do look as if you've been thoroughly kissed. Maybe more. I did do a good job of it."

Amaranthe couldn't help but laugh, even though she should have been outraged. He looked more relaxed than she'd ever seen him. She leaned back and fixed his tie and then smoothed his jacket before she slid off him to pull down the mirror and examine her face. She did appear as if she'd been thoroughly kissed—and then some.

"You look beautiful."

She reapplied lipstick carefully. "Thank you. I don't think there's much I can do for my hair. It's looking like I took a walk on the wild side." Her eyes met his in the mirror, and she burst into laughter again. "Is that what you were going for?"

"I was going for any way I could keep you. I made up my mind I wasn't losing you. We had a beautiful day, but you began retreating and I couldn't reach you."

"You retreated," she accused. "You became Geno Ferraro, the man behind the mask."

His palm cupped her cheek, his thumb sliding into her hair. "I have to be that man when I go out into the public. Just like you're my classical ballerina."

Her eyes widened as knowledge burst through her. That was his role. He had taken it on at thirteen. He had to make others believe he was tough enough, even the Archambaults. He'd faked it until he was that man. Now, that was the demeanor he presented to the world. He slipped easily into the role, just as she did when she went hunting.

The dancer was her role. She hunted right out in the open. She was so good in her role she thought in terms of being a dancer, and she never once wavered, just as Geno hadn't. They were experts at what they did. It made sense for him to wear that mask and keep it on in public. People viewed him with trepidation. They respected him. They listened to him, and when he gave an order, they obeyed without question. He hadn't retreated from her. He had assumed his mantle of authority, the role he'd played for years.

"That makes so much sense, Geno. I misunderstood. I was so nervous, already feeling as if I didn't belong, and I didn't want to let you down."

"You could never let me down, Amara."

She turned toward him, letting him see her eyes, needing him to know she meant what she said. "I realize that now. You've more than reassured me, Geno."

"If at any time when we're in a public setting you feel the need for assurance, reach for me. We can communicate telepathically. Or just come straight to me, Danzatrice Ombra. You're more important than anyone. I'll never mind you interrupting me. Sometimes the men can be patronizing and the women catty in the circles I travel."

The honesty in his voice was humbling. She didn't know why she had doubted him. It hadn't been him, more herself. Amaranthe knew it wouldn't be necessary, but she nodded to let him know she would go to him if she felt slighted by anyone in his circle of acquaintances or nervous about their relationship again.

"Are you ready for this? They'll be in a frenzy. We need to give them the photographs they want," he cautioned.

"I'm ready."

"Stay very close to me and always do exactly what Donte and Fiero tell you to do."

Donte and Fiero Latini were Geno's personal bodyguards and the head of his security. They had the responsibility of training the other bodyguards. They took their jobs very seriously, and the little she'd observed of them, she knew they were good at what they did.

"I will," she assured, watching him text the head of his security that they were ready.

At once the car door was opened. In spite of everything,

her heart began to accelerate. Geno slid from the car, his large body shielding hers as she exited. She smoothed the bright sparkly navy skirt so that it swished around her legs with each step she took onto the pavement. There seemed to be numerous cameras going off and people calling out to Geno. He wrapped his arm around her, sheltering her with his larger body, drawing her front tight against his side. He paused for a moment, turning to face toward the line of men and women shouting at them.

Smile for them, Amara. Look happy to be my fiancée.

I am happy. Deliberately, she tilted her head to look up at him, smiling adoringly at him because she was happy, and she did rather adore him, and she didn't mind showing it to the world.

Most of the questions were directed at Geno, and he fielded them easily. It was evident he was used to dealing with the paparazzi. She noticed his expressionless mask didn't change, but his protective demeanor was very much in evidence. She also could see he made the media somewhat uneasy. They made their demands, but if he didn't like their questions, they didn't repeat them. The demand to see the ring was one of the loudest.

Geno threaded his fingers through hers and held up their hands, the ring facing the cameras. As soon as the reporters got their shots, Fiero stepped close and indicated the restaurant. Geno immediately nodded and lifted a hand to the rows of men and women with cameras.

Keep your head down and stay in the middle between the bodyguards. I've got shooters on the roof, but I'm not taking chances with your life.

You make a much bigger target than I do.

Donte and Fiero swiftly moved them toward the restaurant, Fiero in front, Donte behind them. On either side of Geno and Amaranthe paced two other bodyguards, Leonardo and Bravo Ricci. All four bodyguards were very efficient in the way they carried out their jobs. Amaranthe could tell they had been at it for a long time and knew exactly what they were doing. They flowed together and were in step with Geno.

"There are two different restaurants inside. This entrance takes you to the family restaurant. We thought it was important parents could bring children with them after work, have a good meal at fair prices and relax," Geno explained as a doorman opened and held the heavy oak door for them to pass through.

The architect had utilized the archways of the stone warehouse to help define the various spaces. The tables in the family restaurant were covered in simple red-and-white checked tablecloths. The chairs were comfortable-looking with high backs and sporting black legs. Around the long brick bar were high-backed stools with matching black legs. The bar held sparkling drinks for children to choose. Along one wall were small booths with red leather seating for two to four people. Overhead, strings of lights gave the impression of fireflies dancing across the high ceiling.

The bodyguards kept them walking straight through the family restaurant so Amaranthe didn't have time to really look around the way she would have liked. She only noticed that the area was extremely spacious, smelled wonderful and seemed bright and cheerful. They went through another private door and down a hall and immediately entered the next restaurant, which she knew had earned a three-Michelin-star rating. The chef was that good.

The same stone floor was underfoot, but the entire look had been transformed and was breathtaking. The atmosphere was darker and much more romantic. Small, intimate round tables covered with white cloths accented by very plush black chairs were in arrangements of twos and fours set distances apart to provide plenty of privacy for each couple or party.

Overhead, a network of tree limbs that appeared to be very much alive dripped with purple and white flowers giving off a faint fragrance of honeysuckle. Throughout the tree branches, tiny lights lit up the darker room. Those lights and the two fireplaces at either end of the large room were the only source of light other than the candles on the tables.

The bodyguards kept them walking, so again, there was no time to take much in when Amaranthe would have preferred to slow down and really look around. They didn't stop until they were right at the hostess station, where there stood a tall, slender woman with a wealth of black curly hair worn pulled back and braided across the top of her head, almost like a crown, and then secured at the nape of her neck so the rest of her hair hung down in a beautiful curly mass Amaranthe envied just a little. She had dark brown eyes and high cheekbones and clear, gorgeous skin. She also looked very familiar.

"Everyone is already waiting, Mr. Ferraro," the hostess greeted. "And may I say congratulations on your engagement?"

"Thank you, Penelope. This is Amaranthe, my fiancée." Geno kept Amara very close, under his shoulder.

It was a strange feeling for Amaranthe to know she was protected. She was used to being on her own. Geno was such a big man, and she had the small, slender body of a ballet dancer. His arm practically hid her.

She smiled at the hostess, trying to get a feel for how things worked in the restaurant. She knew the Ferraro brothers owned it. Penelope was such a beautiful woman, it would have been easy to be intimidated by her because she was clearly familiar with Geno, but she was very respectful, and not in the least flirtatious.

Penelope beamed at her. "It's lovely to meet you. My little sister, Jordan, takes dance lessons from you, and I've watched you work with her. You were so amazing. No one has ever taken so much time with her or been so patient. I wanted to thank you for that. Dancing means so much to her. Because she has a hearing disability, some of her instructors have dismissed her as if she has no talent."

The smile faded from Amaranthe's face. "Jordan has an

extraordinary talent. What do you mean they dismissed her? Who dismissed her?" When Geno's warm amusement slid into her mind, she realized she had unconsciously poured authority into her voice.

My warrior for the underdog.

Jordan does have talent. That's why I spent so much time with her. I thought maybe I was too hard on her at first, but she responded immediately. She even asked to stay after class to use the studio to practice more. I stayed with her and gave her some extra pointers. It really upsets me that any instructor would discourage her. She can hear clearly out of one ear, but the other is somewhat diminished. She wears a hearing aid but needs a better one.

"Ms. Marchel told her if she couldn't hear music, she would never be able to perform onstage. I pointed out that she hears, but she said her hearing wasn't good enough."

Amaranthe wanted to step into the nearest shadow and go visit Ms. Marchel to tell her a thing or two. First, Jordan wasn't deaf. Second, even if she were fully deaf, she still could dance. There are methods for teaching hard-of-hearing and deaf students. Ms. Marchel had been hired to teach everyone, not just a select few.

"Jordan has the potential to have a career in dance if she's willing to work for it." *Ms. Marchel and I will be discussing the inclusion of all students in her teaching, or she won't be working for the company.*

She felt Geno smile, but when she looked up at his face, his stone mask was in place. "It seems that Amara will take care of the situation, Penelope. If there is any further trouble with your younger sister, let me or one of my brothers know. We'll take care of it if Ms. Marchel doesn't listen to Amara."

"She'll listen," Amaranthe assured. *I've been looking into the various types of hearing aids Jordan might need to help her out.*

"Thank you both so much. Jordan means the world to

me, and she honestly works so hard at her dance. She's always practicing."

Penelope turned up her high-wattage smile and led the way to the private back room reserved only for guests of the Ferraro family. The heavy oak door was tall, thick and very wide, resembling a thatched wine barrel on the outside, with dark planks across it. Penelope opened it and stood back to allow them entry.

CHAPTER SEVEN

The event room, like the other two restaurants, was very large and spacious, but it was also filled with more people than Amaranthe had considered would be there. She also hadn't thought that each rider would have bodyguards.

Geno. She breathed his name.

She knew Stefano was there. He'd been texting Geno steadily, threatening him, although she was fully aware he'd been teasing—at least she hoped he was. She recognized his bodyguards. They'd been at Geno's house. She knew they were called Emilio and Enzo, and they were never far from Stefano. Even if Stefano gave them his death stare, they ignored him, which she admired them for. Neither man was the least intimidated by him. Amaranthe was used to standing before the International Council, and still, if she told the truth, Stefano Ferraro intimidated her just a little.

She had been certain Elie would return, and he had come with two bodyguards but without his wife. She'd wanted to meet Brielle. She wished Francesca had come as well, but she understood why Stefano hadn't brought her. He considered it too dangerous when they all were sure the ones murdering riders would most likely be in the restaurant somewhere. They would never pass up the opportunity to get close to so many members of the Ferraro family gathered in one place.

Right here, Danzatrice Ombra. You aren't alone.

Amaranthe was already feeling uneasy, and she didn't think it had anything to do with such a large gathering. *Do you feel something sinister close?*

Yes. No hesitation. *We knew we would be walking into an ambush.*

A bomb? There are a lot of innocents in this building, she was compelled to point out. It didn't feel like a bomb to her.

More personal.

That's what I think, too. But they were taking chances with lives. They had no way of knowing.

We can't live our lives in a cave.

Geno was right about that. She looked around the room. Like the rest of the building, the event room had been designed with care to every detail. It might be her favorite of all the rooms. The table was long and already held fresh warm bread and wine in elegant glasses. She saw the table could easily accommodate at least twenty people. The ceiling was high, and a very beautiful chandelier hung over the center of the table casting light throughout the room.

Amaranthe had never seen a chandelier like it. "That's so beautiful and unique."

Geno smiled at her, clearly pleased she liked it. "I saw a similar one when I was visiting with a friend in Africa and took photographs for Salvatore and Lucca. They were just as impressed as I was. They flew out to talk with the artists, a couple there, and brought the designs for the room. I believe there is something like three thousand hand-rolled clay beads. Stoneware. There's a mixture of crystal beads as well. Salvatore can tell you exactly how many and how it was constructed."

"It's gorgeous."

She looked around the room again. The fireplace glowed softly, adding to the ambiance. The stone floor gleamed. Double doors led to a covered terrace where it was clear the family could eat outdoors if they chose.

Valentino Saldi and his wife, Emmanuelle, were seated beside Elie. Emmanuelle was a beautiful woman. She was curvy with dark hair and vivid blue eyes. She looked very much at ease in the room filled with males. Amaranthe knew her reputation as a shadow rider. She had often gone to Europe and filled in for riders in countries when there was a shortage of riders. She didn't shirk duty. Not ever. The way Valentino looked at her, Amaranthe believed Geno—that the crime lord had married her for love.

Stefano was seated beside a man she knew to be his brother, Ricco Ferraro. Ricco had trained as a young rider in Japan. He was incredibly fast in the shadows and he'd been the central figure involved in the huge scandal that had brought down three of the houses of riders in that country. He practiced the art of Shibari, was considered an adrenaline junkie and was the family race car driver.

Beside Ricco was Ricco's wife, Mariko. She was from the very famous line of Tanaka riders in Japan. Shockingly, she had blond hair and hazel eyes, taking after her American mother. She might look demure and shy, but she was fearless in the shadows, whether she took rotations on her own or was the perfect partner with her husband.

Dario Bosco sat across from Valentino. It was no surprise that Dario was there. She knew that if Valentino was present, Dario would be. Dario had his own territory to rule over, but it didn't matter, he considered his first job to be head of Valentino's security, and he refused to relinquish that position. Amaranthe had to concede there was something noble in taking that position. After all, Dario's position was considered equal to Valentino's by everyone. Clearly, that didn't matter to Dario. Their bodyguards sat at the same tables or stood along the walls with the Ferraro bodyguards.

Beside Dario was the youngest Ferraro male, Taviano. He looked like a replica of his older brother Stefano, right down to the piercing eyes. Like Stefano, he appeared very sophisticated. Younger. Fewer scars, although she could see he had intimidation down.

Seated beside Taviano was his wife, Nicoletta. Nicoletta was a woman Amaranthe very much wanted to meet. There had been whispers about her. The Archambault family, in particular Jean-Claude, was excited about her. The council was excited about her. They wanted her in France to work with and had done their best to try to persuade Stefano to send her to them. She had no formal training in the shadows when the Ferraros began working with her, yet her times were unbelievable.

Don't you think it's significant that Nicoletta, you, me and Elie are here in this room? All of us could have been, or are, a part of the program the council has in place to police the Archambault riders. Are your cousins as fast as you? What about your brothers?

Everyone had looked up the moment they entered the room. A hushed silence had fallen. Ordinarily that would have bothered her, but she was trying to figure the significance of what had just occurred to her. There were several riders in the room who were blindingly fast in the shadows. After them, there were those that might be even faster. What did that mean? Because it couldn't be a coincidence that there were so many Archambaults migrating to the Ferraro family. Jean-Claude knew it and wanted to put a stop to it. Or did he? He knew the connection to his family through their grandmother. It might be a couple of times removed, but she was still an Archambault.

Geno knew immediately what she was thinking. His gaze followed hers to the two men lounging against the wall with the bodyguards. Salvatore and Lucca Ferraro.

Geno's brothers were very much like him—only he was right in saying they fit the Ferraro image of sophistication. They were tall and handsome and very fit-looking. She expected Geno to be upset that they had come against his express orders, but instead, there was instant softness, affection in his mind, although, looking up at him, there was no change in his expression. Along with that affection and yes, real love, there was alarm. Geno had become very alert to any possible danger. He scanned the room again, this time much more meticulously. She found herself doing the same.

"I see the two of you have no idea what staying put means," Geno greeted his brothers.

Both Lucca and Salvatore separated themselves from the bodyguards and sauntered across the room, their boots never making the slightest whisper of sound on the gray-and-black stonework. Their gazes moved over Amaranthe, taking in every detail of her appearance. They were every bit as sharp as Geno, she decided.

"Little sister," Salvatore greeted. He had a mesmerizing quality to his voice. "You must not be quite sane to let Geno put a ring on your finger and trap your shadow."

Amaranthe bared her teeth at him. "He's the one with the bad judgment. Ask anyone who knows me."

Lucca laughed. "You're like a fierce little terrier about to launch an attack on a tiger."

"That's what I prefer all my enemies to think."

"You're a dancer in the ballet," Salvatore pointed out. "I suppose you could attack with your ballet slipper."

"I suppose I could continue allowing you to make a fool of yourself," Geno said, his eyes darkening to black obsidian.

"We're just teasing the little ballerina," Lucca pointed out.

"Go sit down before I teach you some manners. You're sadly lacking," Geno instructed.

"We are just teasing her," Lucca repeated. "Welcome to

the *famiglia*. We're happy Geno found you." He stepped closer, and Geno intercepted him.

"What do you think you're doing?"

"I was going to hug her. I think that's tradition in families, Geno."

"I don't think it is in our family, Lucca. Especially when you were supposed to be lying low."

Lucca's eyes went flat and cold. "You set yourself up, Geno. And it looks as if you're setting up your fiancée as well. That's unacceptable. If she's your choice and is going to be our sister, we have every right to guard your backs. You don't get to take that away from us." There was a distinct edge to his voice.

Amaranthe thought he sounded very much like his older brother. Not only sounded like him, but when he turned abruptly and stalked to the main table, he looked every inch like Geno Ferraro. Amaranthe liked him a lot.

Geno narrowed his eyes at Salvatore. "I suppose you have something to say."

"Nope, I think Lucca covered it. In case you aren't paying attention, big brother, feel the air. You've succeeded in drawing out the enemy." He winked at Amaranthe and followed Lucca to the table.

So Geno wasn't the only Ferraro who had a sixth sense when it came to feeling danger.

Geno swore under his breath. "Things just got complicated."

"Maybe not. Maybe they got easier," she soothed him. "You won't have to worry about them so much. You were, you know. I could feel it." She looked up at him.

He stopped halfway to the table, his dark eyes moving over her face. "*Danzatrice Ombra*, I'm not certain you knowing what I'm feeling is always going to be a good thing."

She laughed. "I think it's a very good thing." She tugged on his hand. "I don't think your brothers believe we're really engaged. They seem to think you wouldn't tie yourself to a ballerina. I'm going to enjoy this dinner immensely, and I think you are, too. You just need to find your sense of humor."

Geno once more looked from her to his brothers and then sighed. "I don't think I have a sense of humor where the two of them are concerned." Placing his hand on the small of her back, he walked her to the table, where the others waited. "This is Amaranthe, my fiancée."

He proceeded to go around the table introducing her to everyone. Fortunately, she was very good at retaining names, and she knew who they were from prior research.

"I took pity on you, Amara," Stefano said. "I made most of the family stay home so you don't have to put up with too many all at once."

"You only have my annoying brothers and Dario to drive you insane," Geno pointed out.

"You can't put Salvatore and Lucca in the same category as Dario," Emmanuelle objected. "That's just wrong, Geno." She dipped a breadstick into salted olive oil. "They aren't *anything* like Dario. Geno, on the other hand, might be, Amara."

"What is Dario like?" Amaranthe asked, looking at the man who sat at next to Emmanuelle, seemingly unfazed by her assessment of him. Amaranthe could hear the affection in Stefano's sister's voice. If she could hear it, everyone else at the table could as well—even Dario.

"He's an arrogant, bossy ass and thinks he can tell me what to do," Emmanuelle said. "I'm head of security, but he thinks he is. I tell him what to do, but does he do it? No, he does not. Half the world wants him dead."

Dario raised an eyebrow. "Don't insult me, Emme. Only half? That isn't the truth. It's far more than that."

She rolled her eyes. "See what I mean about being arrogant? Don't flatter yourself. Darn it, Elie, you ate all the olives again. That second tray was supposed to be *our* tray."

"You were busy making eyes at Val. If you paid attention to the food and not to a husband you see every single day, you might manage to get your share of the olives." Elie was unrepentant.

Amaranthe listened to the banter swirling around the table as the Ferraro family gave one another a hard time while they ate fresh-from-the-oven bread and various cheeses with truffle honey, jams and spiced hazelnuts. Grilled flatbread with sun-dried tomato pesto, royal trumpet mushrooms, black olives and house-made cheeses. There were pan-seared scallops. Far too many appetizers for Amaranthe to consider ordering a main course.

Mostly, she kept her eye on Salvatore and Lucca. She was certain if Jean-Claude had given up on using Geno for his plans—and he had—then he'd focus on Geno's brothers. Geno was fast enough—but he hadn't been trained in the art of fitting in the way the rest of the Ferraros did. Jean-Claude couldn't control Geno. He couldn't mold him into the man he wanted him to be. Lucca and Salvatore were younger and more susceptible. They carried the Archambault genes. They'd be lightning fast in the shadows.

What is it?

I'm just wondering about your brothers. Which one has spent more time in Europe? You said you were worried about them. Why?

Salvatore trained in Europe and with various families for the experience. He goes there to help out or vacation. He recently told me he wants an arranged marriage. He's young for that. It worries me that he's so unhappy.

She couldn't help but rub at Geno's lower lip with her finger. "Stop frowning." *You do that a lot when you look at your brothers.*

I might have to kill Jean-Claude. Why would he deliberately target one of my brothers?

Amaranthe looked up at Geno, not that it did any good. His mask was firmly back in place. His anger was hot and raw, swirling beneath a dense block of ice in his gut. If she weren't so connected to him, she wouldn't know just how upset he was. It wasn't an idle threat he was making against one of the council members.

You aren't thinking straight, Geno. Put this in perspective.

What perspective? The man is all about power. He thinks he's losing his position because too many Archambaults are migrating to the Ferraro family. He doesn't want our family to become more powerful than his, so he's striking back. That's easy enough to understand. We don't want the power. We don't want to police other riders. He can have the job and all the power he needs.

Amaranthe felt eyes on them and glanced up to see Stefano watching speculatively. He knew they were communicating and guessed it wasn't a pleasant conversation, but he didn't draw attention to them. In fact, when Ricco started to direct a question her way, Stefano interrupted him with a query.

You're wrong about Jean-Claude's motivation, Geno. Amaranthe took advantage of Stefano's help. She knew the reprieve wouldn't last long. Soon, they would be engaged in conversation, and she wouldn't be able to get Geno to see the truth. He was too protective of his brothers. He was friends with Elie, and it was clear Elie Archambault and Jean-Claude had a past that wasn't good.

Jean-Claude and the Archambaults are responsible for policing the riders. Someone has to do it. No wants to do it, or likes it, but it's a necessary job, just as the council must have one or two riders capable of policing the Archambaults. Jean-Claude's problem has nothing to do with power and everything to do with genetics. If he can't find any riders to do that job, what happens then? You can ask Stefano that question. I'll bet he's already thought of it because he's talked with Jean-Claude on many occasions.

How do you know that?

I've been there when Jean-Claude was on the phone

with him. Your cousin is very well respected. I believe, but don't know, Jean-Claude consults with him.

He's brutally hard on the riders he trains.

Geno, think about it. If he's sending riders out to go up against other shadow riders who are fast and experienced, to give them the best chance, they have to be stronger and faster. When I find a dancer with excellent potential and they want a career, I admit, I work them harder than anyone else. Dancing is a grueling career. It's physically hard on the body and takes a tremendous amount of discipline. If they don't have what it takes, they need to know. Jean-Claude needs to know when he trains his riders that they can survive.

Geno may be the most protective man in the world, but he was highly intelligent and he could understand exactly the problem Jean-Claude was running into. Like every family, there were few female riders having children. The future looked grim for all the rider families.

Geno swept his arm around her. "I didn't think about that."

"Perhaps you should amend your bloodthirsty ways just a little bit."

Geno gave her his fierce, blackest scowl, which could stop anyone in their tracks.

Amaranthe's laughter escaped. She couldn't help it. "You're trying to look intimidating, but everyone here knows you, and I don't think it's working."

The moment she began laughing, all conversation ceased and she was the center of attention. Apparently, no one laughed when Geno gave them his death stare. She pressed her lips together to try to contain her laughter.

Glancing up at him, she fluttered her eyelashes. "I'm sorry, am I being disrespectful? Should I apologize?" She whispered it just loud enough that the others could hear.

"Knock it off, you little hellion. At least pretend to behave. Do you see how much trouble I have with my brothers? You start in and I lose all credibility. Don't make me laugh."

"She made you smile," Lucca said.

"I didn't smile," Geno denied, glaring at his brother.

"You did." Salvatore backed up Lucca. He looked around the table. "You all saw that. She made him smile."

"He's right, Geno," Emmanuelle said. She grinned at her cousin. "I thought maybe your engagement was for show, but now I think I was wrong. Not only did you smile, but when you look at her . . ."

Geno glared at her. "Don't say it."

"What?" Emmanuelle challenged. "That you look like you're crazy about her?"

"Here it comes, Geno," Dario said. "Emme is a nuisance that won't go away. Once she has you in her sights, she's like one of those vicious little terriers that grab at your ankle and won't let go."

Emme snapped her teeth at Dario and laughed. "Admit it, Dario, you're terrified of me."

The door opened, and four servers came in to take their orders, two men and two women. They split up, coming to either side of the table and working their way very efficiently down from either end. The room immediately went quiet as all of them studied menus and gave their orders.

Amaranthe realized they watched the servers just as carefully as she did. The feeling of malice had grown over the last hour. It didn't increase when the servers entered, but that didn't mean she wasn't going to be alert. Although the room was filled with targets, the main ones were Geno, Stefano, Salvatore and Lucca. Four primary targets. If she was guessing, either Geno or Stefano would be an assassin's dream goal.

Are you familiar with these servers, Geno? None of them are new, are they? In her opinion, it would be ludicrous to allow an unfamiliar person into the room with so many targets available to them.

They've all worked in the restaurant for at least eighteen months.

That didn't alleviate her worry. The troubles in Little Italy had started months earlier.

The Ferraro family acted perfectly normal, interacting with the servers as if they really were at an engagement party and ordering food and drink, not in the least worried their lives might be at risk. She did the same, easily playing the role. She was the ballerina everyone saw, looking delicate and fragile beside Geno. Each time he spoke to her, she would gaze up at him adoringly. That wasn't difficult to do.

Once the servers left the room, she contemplated the way the beautiful chandelier and the flames from the fireplace cast shadows throughout the room. Every rider had to know exactly where the shadows were. If any of the servers could ride the shadows, they now knew where those shadows were. There were several close to Stefano's chair.

Did your cousin seat himself there deliberately? That's the most dangerous spot in the room.

I'm well aware.

Geno's tone was clipped. He didn't like Stefano's choice of seating arrangements any more than she did.

"How did you two meet?" Ricco asked.

Geno sighed. "That's a tough one to answer, Ricco. I'd like to tell you I was interested in ballet and saw her dance. I did take over for my mother on the board of directors and certainly read all about her. We can leave it at that."

Emmanuelle's eyebrows shot up. She exchanged looks with Salvatore and Lucca. "Oh, no you don't, Geno. That's not going to work for any of us. That sounds like there's a *lot* more to the story. Amaranthe? Are you going to tell us?"

Geno leaned back in his chair and slipped his arm around Amara's shoulders. "Let's just say we met under bizarre circumstances and there was a very big misunderstanding. Little did I know there is a will of iron in this little package right here."

There was no denying the admiration, respect and even pride in Geno's voice when he spoke of her, and Amaranthe couldn't help the little glow. No one complimented her, and he did it so casually. It was just his tone, but it was enough to make her feel special to him. She didn't even mind that he referred to her as a "little package."

"Not good enough," Lucca said. "Go on."

Geno heaved an exaggerated sigh and shot a glance at Valentino and Dario.

Emmanuelle snapped her head up and looked at her husband. "Oh my God! You were there, Val. Dario? *Both* of you and you didn't say a word? You two are total sneaks. We are so going to have a talk about this." She pinned Stefano with a glare. "That means you were there as well. It was when we were all in New York and you said I could go shopping, no worries, you had Val's security covered."

"This is really getting interesting," Salvatore said.

"I agree," Ricco concurred. "Now you have to tell us. Val, Dario, Stefano and Geno add up to an interrogation. That would be a very big misunderstanding."

Nicoletta gasped and turned toward Geno. "You didn't."

Geno nodded. "I set a trap to bring those committing the murders to me. Or at least the ones helping them. It was fairly simplistic—a wallet stolen from a man standing right out front of this restaurant. We were just beginning to track it and the wallet started coming right for us. My men bagged my wild woman and took her to the interrogation room. Right from the beginning I felt something was off. Dario, Val and Stefano came at my call. I just had a bad feeling, but I didn't know what it was."

Lucca and Ricco exchanged a long look of sudden comprehension. "You knew she was the one, didn't you, Geno?" Ricco said.

"Not right away. I just knew something wasn't right with her being in that room. My mind kept trying to put her there, but it was at war at the same time, trying to make sense of what it was saying to me."

"How did you get the wallet, Amaranthe?" Mariko asked.

"One of the little girls I teach has an older brother and

he had stolen it. She heard him talking to his friends and recognized he was in trouble and very uneasy over the wallet. She brought it to class with her and put into the locker. She was going to talk to me about it after class, at least she told her friends she was going to. I took it out of the locker and was determined to return it to the owner with hopefully everything still in it. If her brother removed anything I could find out and get him to return it."

"But instead, Geno's bodyguards took you prisoner and locked you in the interrogation room," Ricco said. "That must have really frightened you."

"She didn't look very frightened to me," Valentino said. "In fact, she looked like she might take our heads off if we made one wrong move."

"She's all of five foot nothing," Salvatore objected. "I'm sure the four of you could handle her."

"Don't bet on it," Dario muttered. He reached for the olive tray at the same time Elie and Emmanuelle did.

Emmanuelle batted at his hand all the while glaring at him. "You don't even like olives. You're only taking them because you don't want me to have them."

"I've developed a taste for them. In any case I'm helping you keep your amazing figure, the one you're always complaining about."

"You don't need to be looking at my wife," Val said.

Dario made a disparaging noise. "That's just wrong, Val. And rather disgusting. Emme's . . . Emme."

"Let's get back on track," Emmanuelle suggested. "As much as I don't want to share my olives with anyone, I will, just to hear how Geno made a total ass of himself."

"We both did." Amaranthe shared the blame. "It wasn't just Geno. But we straightened it out and everything turned out the way it was supposed to be." She looked up at him because she couldn't help herself.

Geno smiled down at her and took her hand, threading his fingers through hers. "We did straighten it out."

"That's the sickening version," Dario agreed. "You Ferraros are a mess when it comes to your women. I'm including you, Val and Elie. You were around them too much and their pussy ways rubbed off on you. Your women run you and there's no hope for any of you."

"Is that true, Val?" Emmanuelle asked, fluttering her eyelashes at her husband.

"Absolutely, princess." He kissed her hand. "It's the absolute truth."

"I'll go along with that," Ricco said. "Mariko asks and it's hers. Not that she ever asks for anything."

"But I do, Ricco," Mariko protested. "Sometimes I ask you to tie me. It's so beautiful." There was a deliberate sultry note in her voice Amaranthe was certain she put in to tease Dario.

Nicoletta exchanged a grin with Taviano and then both looked at Amaranthe to include her in their amusement.

Dario just shrugged his shoulders. "Your brother used to be tough, Salvatore, but not so much now."

"Don't bet on it, Dario," Geno said, no expression in his voice.

Dario didn't look in the least impressed. Amaranthe wasn't, either; there was too much amusement and affection in Geno's mind.

"You straightened things out between you," Nicoletta prompted. "But how did you know you were in love so quickly?"

Geno's fingers slipped into Amaranthe's dark hair. "She has more courage than a lion. And she makes me laugh. I knew almost the moment I saw her that she was the one." He tugged at her hair. "I believe it took her a great deal longer."

"Not necessarily," Amaranthe objected. "I knew. I just didn't think I fit into your world."

"Why is that?" Stefano asked.

"I understand completely," Nicoletta said. "I felt exactly the same way."

"That makes no sense," Valentino said. "You're both intelligent, beautiful women. Taviano is a nerd and Geno is a brute. Why either of you fell for the likes of them, I have no idea. But then, I've never understood why Emmanuelle fell for me."

"You don't?" Dario's eyebrows shot up. "You set a trap for her, you cunning bastard. That's how you managed to get her to fall for you. Geno had his woman kidnapped and taken to an interrogation room."

"Looks like we should be taking notes, Salvatore," Lucca said. "Setting traps, kidnapping. If that's the only way we're going to get a woman of our own, we've got to follow our elders' examples."

"You're very funny," Geno said, sarcasm dripping heavily from his voice. "You're too young to find a woman. You can wait a year or two until you're more mature."

Ricco laughed. "Mature? You don't think Salvatore or Lucca are mature enough to be married? Taviano, what do you say?"

"Don't drag me into this argument. Geno just wants to take the spotlight off his meeting with Amaranthe. Everyone at this table knows he made a fool of himself, and she had to forgive something big. She's covering for him and he's dodging the question."

They don't know if I'm a shadow rider or not, do they? For some reason, that amused Amaranthe. They suspected. How could Geno fall so hard so fast if she wasn't a rider? But it had been known to occur. Riders had found mates outside of riders and made their bond work. *I would have thought Stefano would have told the others.*

No. Stefano wouldn't tell them. He doesn't give away secrets. As far as he's concerned that's my business to disclose.

The heavy door swung open to allow the servers, wheeling trays of food, to enter the room. Once again, they split off, the same servers moving to serve from either side of the table, two starting at one end while the other two started at the opposite end.

Amaranthe had been caught up in the teasing and fun of the Ferraro family dynamics, but the moment the servers entered, her attention centered on the servers. They were extremely professional, handpicked to serve the high-end customers who rented out the costly event room. They moved with precision, attending to every need, never running into one another, and serving each person at the table quickly and efficiently. She had to admire them while at the same time every alarm she had was going off steadily.

The most likely targets in the room were Geno, Salvatore, Lucca and Stefano. Her brain analyzed the danger to each of the four men. Why they would be the best target. What the repercussions would be if they were killed. Could an assassin kill them in a room filled with shadow riders and get away? If so, how? That would also determine who the best target would be.

The servers weren't wearing clothes that would allow them to disappear into the tunnel, so unless they planned to strip naked, they had already mapped out the room, the target and the shadows for the assassin. They had given the exact coordinates to the assassin. And they would cut off, even for a moment, the target from everyone else, so the assassin could make the kill and jump back into the shadows.

Not Lucca or Salvatore. The shadows were close, but not close enough. Their deaths would hurt Geno and the Ferraro family, but the impact wouldn't be so significant that the family would falter. Geno? She looked up at him. Maybe. Every intuition she had said no. It had to be Stefano. A shadow lay right behind him. Both a female server and a male server had come up on either side of him, one putting soup in front of him while another placed a salad down.

Amaranthe didn't wait. She launched herself, not caring she was giving everything away, her explosive speed and power, her ability to leap distances; nothing mattered but to get to the assassins in time.

Knees drawn to her chest, she cleared the table easily, throat punched the female server, knocking her back and away from Stefano, and shot her feet straight at the shadow rider as he emerged from the shadow behind Stefano, knife in hand. Both feet hit the rider with crushing force in the chest right over his heart, knocking him backward. Instantly, he was sucked into the shadow tube. Amaranthe kicked off her heels and followed him.

CHAPTER EIGHT

Salvatore made the leap nearly as fast as Amaranthe, catching the male server's arm as he tried to plunge a needle into Stefano's neck. Around Geno, the room erupted into chaos, but all he focused on was his woman disappearing into the shadows, feetfirst, after a man with a knife.

Ricco, Taviano and Emmanuelle rushed to cover their older brother with Elie, dragging him out of his chair and away from the two servers. Bodyguards surrounded the other servers, preventing them from leaving the room.

Geno, Lucca and Salvatore raced into the shadow to track Amaranthe and the assassin. Amaranthe left little behind in the way of a print, but the assassin was injured, and it was easy enough to track him. Where he went, Geno was certain, his shadow dancer followed. She was tenacious. She wasn't going to give up.

Geno, Nicoletta and I are coming in from the other side. Mariko was calm. *Tell Amaranthe to drive him this way. He won't even see us.*

Don't kill him if it's possible. We need to know who these people are and why they want our riders dead, Geno cautioned. *Amaranthe, you aren't injured, are you?*

The Ferraros would have the two servers to take to the interrogation room, and this time no one was going to ask nicely for information. They had attempted to kill Stefano. That was sacrilege. Better Geno. Better Valentino. That might have kept them alive, but nothing was going to save them from Dario. He let few people into his world. Stefano was one of them. He made a bitter, relentless enemy, and he knew more ways than most people to make a human being suffer. He would use every one of them to find out who wanted Stefano dead. Nothing, no one, was going to stop Dario, and Geno didn't particularly care. He felt the same way.

Danzatrice Ombra. Talk to me. Need to know you're safe. Nicoletta and Mariko are in the tubes, coming in from the south side. Herd the assassin their way.

He has a knife with a chemical that paralyzes on the blade, Amaranthe reported. *The knife is made of a different compound as well. I caught a glimpse of it before I kicked him back into the shadow.*

Geno didn't like the sound of that. Not because he worried about the knife, but because she acted as if she wasn't going to allow anyone else the possibility of getting injured.

Nicoletta and Mariko are seasoned riders, Amara. They can handle this assassin. Do you think he's an elite rider far better trained than our riders?

As was Amaranthe's way, she took her time turning the possibility over in her mind. *No. I don't think that. I think he's desperate. Desperate men or women can be very, very dangerous.*

Salvatore here, Amara.

His younger brother startled him. He had known Salvatore was a strong telepath and Geno had been looping his brothers into the conversation, but he didn't expect Salvatore to reach out on his own and loop Geno and Lucca in.

I'll cut him off from the east. Geno will tell Nicoletta and Mariko to make a little noise. He'll know you're behind him. He won't know how close. He'll run right into me.

That knife is worrisome, Amaranthe protested. *One slice into your skin no matter how shallow and you aren't going to move. He'll have you. That's how they're killing shadow riders. We need to find out who developed that compound.*

You know what I am. Same as you. I know what to look out for. Salvatore sounded—and felt—completely confident.

He could have it on his fingernails. On anything, she warned.

Geno didn't like the sound of that, but it was true. The male server had a needle concealed in his hand, but had the woman? What if this chemical had been on her fingernails? The Ferraros had chemists in their family. Many of the rider families did. They had no idea whose family was trying to wipe out the riders.

Salvatore. Amaranthe. We need this one alive. Drive him toward me.

We need you and Stefano alive, Amaranthe countered. *No matter what, Geno, we'll solve this thing, but they aren't getting either of you. They put at least three of their people on killing Stefano. It could just as easily have been you.*

Amaranthe was a good match for him. Geno might be frustrated that she didn't back down and give him what he demanded, but he knew she was capable—not only capable, there in the shadows—she might just be superior. He didn't know if she was faster than he was and he didn't care. It only mattered to him that she stayed alive.

He knew he could easily have been chosen and trained by Jean-Claude to be one of his "police force." He should have realized one or both brothers would be trained in his place once it was determined his character was a deterrent. Lucca was more like him. He appeared easygoing, but he had a streak of mean in him, just as Geno did.

Geno had always considered Salvatore the best of his

family. He had genuine compassion for others. Geno and Lucca had compassion, but it was buried deep, and it took a lot to bring it to the surface. With Salvatore, it was there immediately. He saw the best in people first. Geno and Lucca saw the worst—they expected the worst, and with the people they dealt with—they were usually right. Geno despised that he hadn't foreseen that Jean-Claude would choose Salvatore in his place.

Salvatore was a natural choice. He would see the need for someone to police the Archambaults. He wouldn't like it, but he would do it out of duty. He would see the need the council had for someone to go after rogue riders, extremely dangerous ones. Again, Salvatore would view the task as necessary.

Now, Geno could understand why his youngest brother had insisted he wanted to have an arranged marriage and settle with a shadow rider to produce children. Geno wouldn't be shocked if Jean-Claude and the council had pushed Salvatore in that direction. That was one order he could—and would—counter. Salvatore could wait a few more years on the off chance he might meet a woman and fall in love.

Now that he had a direction the assassin had taken and Geno knew where the other riders were, he stepped off the main tube he was using to follow Amaranthe into a much smaller feeder tube. It was slick as hell and fast as lightning. Instantly, it felt as if his entire body was being ripped to pieces. The faster the shadow tube, the worse the effects on the body. This one shredded, turning the body inside out, tearing the eyes from the sockets and leaking brain matter into the tube.

Geno had been shadow riding from the time he was very young. He'd experienced the various hallucinations produced from riding the more dangerous types of tubes while feeling torn apart. He had experience with every kind of shadow. The fast, slick ones were always the worst. Those were the ones most riders avoided if possible. They were painful, and riders could easily become disoriented and lost. Some lost consciousness. Once that happened, death could occur quickly. Geno's vision and reflexes always remained steady in the faster, slicker tubes, even when the hallucinations became violent. He never lost sight of his surroundings or the maps in his head. He hadn't even as a child.

He stepped from one shadow to the next, determined to catch up with the assassin. He was certain the man was heading for an old wine cellar at the far end of the docks that gave access to a storm drain. From there, the man would have a clear path to anywhere in the city.

The man was injured. The blow from Amaranthe had jarred his heart. She had put her body weight behind the double kick. Not only her body weight, but she'd also leapt through the air with good speed, and that had doubled the force of the jolt when she'd kicked him.

Geno made no sound as he came out of the shadows, halting just in the opening of the tube. He got his first good look at the assassin. He didn't recognize the rider. He didn't know the family the man came from. He was tall, blond. Now he was facing Amaranthe, his blue eyes narrowed and focused on her. She appeared tiny, a slender ballerina in her sparkling navy tulle dress, looking anything but an elite rider.

The assassin gripped a knife in his left hand, the blade short. Geno had no idea of the material, but it didn't look like any knife he'd ever seen before, only that the blade was very sharp and looked lethal enough.

"Get on with it, bitch," the man snarled.

The accent startled Geno. Definitely Australian.

"Who are you?" Amaranthe asked. Calm. Voice low. Compelling. "I don't think we've ever met. If you plan on killing me, the least you can do is introduce yourself."

"You shouldn't have interfered."

No trained assassin engaged in conversation. They got the job done. Geno would have killed Amara without hesitation. This man wasn't a professional as much as he'd like to think he was. The plan in the dining room had obviously been worked out ahead of time, but it was amateur hour. Now the Ferraros had two prisoners to interrogate, and Geno would bet neither prisoner had poison capsules to use the way Amaranthe had. They would wish they did by the time Dario finished with them.

"I couldn't let you kill Stefano Ferraro." Amaranthe sounded innocent, sweet. Even puzzled. One of her gifts. Her voice continued to be compelling.

She looked smaller and more delicate and fragile than ever. The Australian rider took a step closer to her and she appeared not to notice. She tucked her hair behind her ear. Geno noticed she wasn't wearing her engagement ring. What had she done with it? She was barefoot. She'd somehow kicked off her shoes when she'd hit the assassin's chest, leaving the heels behind in the shadow tube as she entered. How many hours had she practiced that move?

"Stefano Ferraro is a traitor to all riders and deserves to die."

Amaranthe frowned. "Do you have proof? If you do, you need to take it to the Archambault riders in France immediately to have him investigated."

The Australian halted all forward swaying and remained still the moment she sounded alarmed, as if she were willing to believe him.

"They would do nothing. He's too powerful."

Amaranthe bit her lower lip and gave a small shake of her head. "Did you try? If not them, then certainly the International Council would listen. They would have to listen. They govern all riders, including the Archambaults."

There was a hint of doubt in her voice, masterfully played. Geno focused his attention on the Australian's posture. He was much more relaxed. He had even released enough tension in his arm that it dropped slightly and the tip of the knife was no longer pointed upward toward Amaranthe's heart. She needed to keep talking to him in the sweet, innocent way she had, luring him in.

Geno sensed his brother Salvatore in the shadows to the right of him. Lucca was behind him. Both were utterly still, and he willed them to stay that way. The Australian made three of Amaranthe. On one hand, her diminutive size was a major part of the reason the assassin had relaxed, believing he had the upper hand, giving Amaranthe the advantage, but on the other hand, Geno knew if the man actually got to her, sheer bulk would count.

"They won't listen," the Australian said decisively.

"Did you already go to them and were turned down? There must be someone who would listen," Amaranthe returned, frowning, and biting on her lip. "The Archambaults are sworn to be impartial. Why would they be afraid of the Ferraro family?"

"Are you afraid of the Ferraro family?"

"I am just meeting them for the first time really. I met Stefano briefly. We barely spoke. Mostly, I think he wanted to ensure I was good enough to become engaged to Geno. Geno is head of the New York family, but Stefano is head of all the Ferraro families. Everyone defers to him, which you obviously know, or you wouldn't have targeted him."

The Australian indicated the shadow behind her. "I'm going to give you a chance to walk away. You aren't a Ferraro, and you have no part of this. Get rid of his ring permanently and get as far from that family as possible. Go back to being what you're born to do—dancing."

"Why are you doing this?" she asked again. "Someone other than you should know the truth."

The Australian narrowed his eyes, studying her face. "Why would you want to be with someone like Geno Ferraro?" Suspicion colored his voice. "Money? Power?"

Geno saw the tension creeping back into the assassin's body. If he could see it, Amaranthe had to see it as well. If she did, she didn't show it. She looked exactly the same, innocent and very disturbed over the things the man had revealed to her.

"Family," she supplied. "I've never had a family, and

Geno has a very large extended family. I can feel the tremendous care he has for them. I can't help but want that for myself and my children."

The moment the word *children* left Amaranthe's mouth, Geno knew it was a trigger for the assassin. He'd always sensed trouble before it happened. Geno hadn't been passed over by Jean-Claude to be chosen for the work Amaranthe and Salvatore were doing because he wasn't fast enough. He'd received training from the Archambault riders from the time he was thirteen until he was twenty-one, and to this day he sought out the best training possible. He had been passed over because of his dominant personality.

He burst from the shadow with blurring speed as the Australian reversed the knife in his hand and threw it at Amaranthe. She was already in motion, moving toward him, ready to block his knife arm. Salvatore was also in action, coming in from the right side, determined to control the knife arm attacking Amaranthe.

The assassin sent the blade streaking toward Amaranthe as she leapt toward him. Geno was there first, inserting his body between the poison-coated blade and his fiancée, slapping at the blade to deflect it away from his chest. The Australian had aimed for Amaranthe's throat, so the blade hit Geno in his midsection, barely penetrating the three-piece suit he was wearing. He had turned slightly, giving him the full protection of the material so only the very tip managed to make it through to his skin.

Amaranthe skidded to a halt behind him and then ducked around him. Salvatore caught the assassin's arm and spun him around just as the man attempted to draw a second knife from inside his jacket. Mariko and Nicoletta emerged from the shadows, and Lucca steadied Geno's large frame as Amaranthe tore open his jacket and shirt to get at the wound.

"What were you thinking?" she hissed at him.

Geno could see the fire in her eyes. It didn't happen that often, only once in a while, but when it did, deep in that dark brown were red sparks as if a volcano threatened to erupt. He loved that moment. Reveled in it. Found himself lifting his hand toward her face to cup her cheek and frame that perfect oval. His arm felt heavy and wouldn't cooperate. It dropped to his side and his vision blurred.

"La mia danzatrice ombra." He murmured the endearment. Said it with his heart.

"No, Geno. Don't do this. Why did you do this?" She sounded alarmed. Her eyes had gone wide with shock. So beautiful to him, all that dark chocolate framed with long, black feathery lashes.

"You need to be in this world far more than I do." He told her the stark truth. A gray veil covered his vision, and he couldn't see her face clearly. He tried to blink, but his lashes wouldn't cooperate. His lungs suddenly ceased to draw air, and his heart stuttered and then stopped.

Amaranthe followed Geno to the floor as Lucca laid him down. She ripped open his shirt and slammed her fist down over his heart. "You aren't dying, Geno. Lucca, make that scratch bleed. He didn't get much of the poison. Nicoletta, take the other knife to the lab and have them get us an antidote now." She was all business, taking charge.

"Do we need the Australian alive more than we need another person to keep Geno going?" Salvatore asked.

"No, we have two prisoners," Lucca snapped. "Get it done and start CPR. Amara and Mariko will tire fast. Nicoletta, call in the riders. Every rider we have available to us. We'll need riders for transport. Have the doc ready in Geno's apartment. Stefano can organize the transportation."

"Not through the shadows with his wound. It would be dangerous. We don't know the effects of the poison," Amaranthe objected.

"How do we explain what happened, taking him through the restaurant?" Mariko asked.

Amaranthe raised her head. "I'm not going to explain. Stefano can do that. He's the diplomat. But I'm not taking chances with him. I don't give a damn what Stefano has to say, head of the family or not." She said it defiantly.

Salvatore was tiring, and Taviano took his place, keeping the rhythm going, forcing Geno's heart to work. Lucca gave him air while Amaranthe carefully opened the wound around the scratch and encouraged it to bleed in the hopes of clearing any poison.

"Stefano is going to do what's best for Geno," Salvatore assured. "*We'll* do what's best for Geno, just like you." He caught her arm when she bent close to the wound. "What are you doing? Don't you dare try to suck the poison out. We don't need two of you collapsing."

"I'm smelling around the edges. My sense of smell is very acute. I also thought I might visually pick up a trace in the blood." Her voice was tight.

Stefano slid from the shadow to kneel beside Geno, his palm sliding over his cousin's chest. "How much time?" He sounded grim.

"Four minutes down," Amaranthe answered.

"Heartbeat," Taviano announced, his voice relieved. "Weak, but it's there. Not a rhythm."

"We can't have him in the tubes too long, not with a wound and his heart dicey," Stefano said. "The closest exit is just a few yards from here by a slower shadow. Mariko, have Fiero and Donte bring the car to that location immediately and call ahead for the doc to be ready at Geno's private entrance. Make certain it's clear."

Amaranthe had been touching Geno's mind. He was drifting somewhere else, somewhere between she couldn't quite reach. He was cold. Ice-cold. There was no sun. No warmth. It was dark and he was without direction. She needed to find her way to him to guide him back. Without warning he suddenly closed himself off completely to her. She felt the impact on her heart—her soul—as if a huge piece of her had been torn away and carried off with him.

"We're losing him. We're losing him," Amaranthe said.

"I can feel him slipping away." She nearly crawled around Stefano in desperation to get at Geno's chest. Taviano began chest compressions immediately.

Don't, Geno. Don't leave me alone. She'd never known she was alone or lonely until she'd shared his mind. Until she'd entertained the idea of discussions and laughter. Of family. Of children. Of belonging somewhere. Of fitting with someone. Their relationship had been too fast, but it was also a lifetime. They'd shared so much of themselves with each other through their connection. She couldn't imagine losing him.

"Keep calling to him, Amara," Stefano said.

Geno. She heard Stefano calling out. He sounded harsh. A complete authority. *Reach out to us. To me. To Amaranthe. You can't leave her alone. The family needs you. She needs you. Reach for us. Fight.*

How close to the surface was the spirit of someone who died? Close enough to call them back when doing heart compressions? How much of the poisonous compound had gotten into Geno's bloodstream and been carried to his heart?

Nicoletta was nearly spit from a shadow and slid on her knees to land beside Stefano. "Doc says to inject this straight into his heart, Stefano. It may or may not work. It's the only syringe we have capable of traveling in the shadows, so make it count."

Stefano didn't hesitate. He took the syringe from her, removed the cap from the long needle with his teeth and plunged it straight into Geno's chest, directly over his heart.

Amaranthe bit down hard on her lip to keep from crying out. Stefano was the most decisive person she'd ever come across. Ruthless. Just like Geno. The two were cut from the same cloth. Determined—so determined she couldn't imagine Stefano losing his cousin. Stefano just wouldn't let Geno die. No one dared disobey the man.

Her heart pounded and her nails bit into her thigh as she stared down at Geno's gray face. His chest suddenly heaved, and his eyes flew open. Taviano caught Amaranthe and dragged her back away from Geno as he began to instinctively fight.

"Geno, settle. We're here with you." Stefano's voice was absolutely calm. "Don't move around. We don't know how this poison works. We're transporting you out of here fast, so lay back and let us carry you."

"Amara. *La mia danzatrice ombra*. Where is she?" He had to reach for his voice, and it sounded far away to all of them, especially Amaranthe.

"Right here, Geno." She knelt beside him again.

He held out his hand. "He didn't touch you with that blade?" His voice was very gravelly, but still faded, as if he were far away.

She put her hand in his immediately, but he didn't close his fingers around hers. She looked up at Stefano for reassurance.

"Get him to the car," Stefano ordered, circling Amaranthe's shoulders with one arm. "The doc's waiting for him. He's got the antidote, and he can bring Geno back as good as new," he assured.

The riders lifted Geno and stepped into the shadow tube that led straight to the street where the car was waiting. Stefano and Amaranthe followed. Amaranthe was dismayed to smell the coppery scent of blood and occasionally catch of glimpse of dark splashes of red as she sped through the tunnel.

On the ride back to Geno's apartment, she stayed silent, trying to puzzle out how Stefano fit in with Jean-Claude and the International Council. A member of the Ferraro family sat on the council. Still, she was certain, it was Stefano who was held in the highest of regard and consulted in secret. She knew only because she stayed in the background, one of the council's hunters. Was it possible that Stefano was a hunter?

She studied him carefully under veiled lashes. He had far too many duties. She had no idea how fast he was in the shadows, but he certainly had the brains for it. He was shrewd and calculating. He was able to connect telepathically with others, strongly enough that she worried he might be able to catch her thoughts if she wasn't cautious. But no, he couldn't stay in too many places for long enough to be an elite hunter. He didn't have six months or more to give to that kind of investigation. What did he do for the council? For Jean-Claude and the Archambaults?

"Stefano, when Geno is better, will you please talk to him and make him understand he can't keep doing this? This is the second time now."

Stefano arched an eyebrow at her. He knew perfectly well what she meant. He had that look, the one that could make her temper boil over. She had one. A hot one. She always kept it under control, but men looking superior tended to set it off. Stefano had that look down to perfection.

Amaranthe let her breath out slowly. The only person in the world Geno might listen to was Stefano. She needed to stay in his good graces. Rumor had it that his wife was the sweetest woman on the face of the earth and would never defy him. Maybe she really wasn't cut out to be Geno's wife. Her heart stuttered. Clenched hard. She'd made up her mind that they fit. She belonged with him. She knew she was so much better with him—and he was so much better with her.

She took another breath. Let it out. "He keeps putting his life in jeopardy, Stefano. He risks himself all the time." Her throat closed, making it nearly impossible to breathe. "He's so careless with his own life." Tears burned behind her eyes, something no elite rider would ever do in front of Stefano Ferraro.

She looked down at Geno's face. His eyes were closed again, those dark lashes standing out starkly against his skin. Even unconscious he looked tough. She leaned down to whisper in his ear. "You aren't invincible, Geno. You can die just like anyone else. You have to stop throwing your life away."

She couldn't look at Stefano even though she spoke to him. "I think a part of him wants to die. Or at least he doesn't care if he does." To her horror she couldn't keep the anguish out of her voice. Stefano had to hear it. She was making a first-class fool of herself.

"Amaranthe."

Stefano's voice was gentle. That only made the tears burn closer.

"Look at me, sweetheart."

That was a command. No one disobeyed Stefano. He might sound gentle and caring, but he was definitely making a demand. She swallowed hard and lifted her chin, steadied herself and then raised her lashes to meet those dark blue eyes.

"Geno would never leave this world willingly now that he's found you, but he will protect you with his life just as I would protect Francesca. That's who he is, Amara. Fundamentally. At the very core of his being. Nothing I say or do will ever stop him, nor would I want to. He'll protect his family as I protect mine. He'll always put you first. You would have died if that blade had sliced into you."

She couldn't deny the truth of that. Pressing her fingertips to her throbbing temples, she just shook her head. "I can't watch him do this to himself over and over."

"Yes, you can. You're strong. That's why you're his perfect partner. That's why he fell so fast and completely for you. He needs a strong woman. Someone who can and will stand up to him. Geno doesn't fuck around when it comes to his emotions, Amara. You're it for him. I'm not going to pretend I wasn't worried about him before. I knew he was reckless and didn't give a damn whether he lived or died. We were all watching him closely. He didn't feel he had much to live for. But the moment he met you, all that changed."

The car pulled up to the private entrance of the hotel. Amaranthe could see that several of Geno's cousins and bodyguards were blocking the area around the sidewalk and door, so the men had a clear path to carry Geno from the car to the private elevator. She slipped from the car, wishing she believed the things Stefano said were true. Since Geno had met her, he'd nearly died twice.

The doors to the elevator closed noiselessly, and the car took them swiftly up to the tenth floor, where the doctor waited for them. Amaranthe trailed after the men as they hurried with their burden to place him gently on the waiting bed. Two nurses immediately went to work, finding veins, placing IVs, taking blood pressure, quietly reporting results to the doctor, who was already bending over Geno to examine him.

Stefano nodded toward the door, and Geno's cousins reluctantly left the room. His brothers ignored the order or just didn't believe Stefano meant them. Amaranthe refused to believe it, either. She stayed stubbornly close. Stefano took her wrist, his fingers a firm shackle, gentle but unbreakable.

"Let's go sit over here, Amara." He indicated the chairs she had barely registered as they'd entered the room.

She went with him because he gave her no choice, and she didn't want to make a fuss while the doctor worked on Geno. Salvatore and Lucca remained close, standing up against the wall, but where they could see their brother and everything being done for him. She envied them.

Stefano waited until she was seated and had turned her attention to him before he spoke again. "I saw the expression on your face when I told you he isn't being careless with his life anymore. There is no death wish. He looked at the difference in body weight, yours versus his, and calculated the odds fast. He knew if you absorbed the poison and it was deadly, you would die. He had good odds of survival. In both cases, he had you and other shadow riders close, and he counted on all of us to keep him alive. The odds were in his favor. They weren't in yours."

She couldn't argue with his logic. It was the truth. She would have come to that same conclusion. "He's so casual and deliberate about it. I don't know how else to put it. He just steps in and takes control. He's strong and I don't have a chance of stopping him because I have no idea he's going to take the hit until he's already done it."

"Are you blaming yourself for this?" Stefano indicated his cousin.

"The Australian was mine to bring in. I triggered him. I thought I was being careful, but I lost him." She raised anguished eyes to him. Guilt washed over her, and she turned to look at Geno lying so still and gray under his beautiful olive skin. "Worse, I was certain he'd keep the knife in his hand—that he'd come at me with it. I was prepared to block his attack, but he threw it instead. Geno somehow realized he was going to throw it and he stepped between us."

"Amaranthe." Stefano said her name gently, trying to absolve her of guilt when it wasn't possible.

"Don't. He was my job. I'd studied the way the others were stabbed. In every case they'd been struck repeatedly by the same blade. He'd come to the engagement party to assassinate you. I misjudged that he would kill you the same way the others had all been murdered."

"You don't know that wasn't his intention," Stefano pointed out. "You weren't his intended target. I was. You aren't thinking clearly because you're emotional. You've never experienced extreme emotion, have you, Amara?"

She pressed her lips together and once more looked at Geno, willing him to respond to the doctor's care. Very slowly, she shook her head. "No. I lost my parents when I was barely four. After that, I was never really allowed to be attached to anyone. I threw myself into training and dance. I lived for those two things, not relationships."

"I imagine Jean-Claude ensured you had the best instructors he could find for you," Stefano said. "He said he's always been proud of you."

Amaranthe frowned. "He spoke of me to you?"

"Not until I sent him an inquiry to make certain Geno wasn't being played. Then he had quite a lot to say." He glanced across the room and indicated Salvatore. "He left out a few things he should have told me. He'll hear about it. The bottom line to take away from this is to not beat yourself up. You're in unfamiliar territory. Falling in love. Learning about relationships. Having a man that insists and will always insist on standing in front of you when it comes to danger."

"I'm a shadow rider, Stefano," she reminded. She lowered her voice to a whisper. "I'm an *elite*. He can't be stepping in to save me every time he thinks my life is threatened."

"You blew your chance at cover in front of the entire family when you saved my life, Amara. You were far too fast, you, Salvatore and Geno, all three of you, but you especially. No one even considered that you were a rider, and then you blew their socks off with that little performance. And your man is never going to be any different. It doesn't matter how good you are as a rider, you're his life. His center. His reason for existing. How do I know? Because Francesca is mine. If I lost her, I wouldn't have much of a reason to continue. Geno feels the same. You're it for him. He isn't going to change. If you want to share his life, you need to love every part of him. That's the biggest part of who he is."

Amaranthe already knew what Stefano was telling her. She was just so afraid of losing Geno to that side of him. She was a rider, and she would never be able to be anything but who she was. She couldn't accept being responsible for his death. They would have to find a way to compromise because she wasn't about to lose him over their personality traits.

CHAPTER NINE

Geno woke with a hell of a headache, his heart pounding and a bad taste in his mouth. It wasn't the first time he had woken like that and he was fairly certain it wouldn't be the last. He knew he was home in his own bed, but already his hand was searching for her.

"Danzatrice Ombra. Where are you? Why is it every time I open my eyes, you aren't where you're supposed to be?"

He sat up slowly. Every muscle in his body hurt, especially his chest. He rubbed his palm over it as he looked around. His gaze collided with Amaranthe's. Her dark gaze stared directly into his, holding everything he could possibly want to see, robbing him of his breath before she managed to hide the yearning in her eyes.

"I'm right here, doing exactly what the doctor told me to do. Why is it the moment I move, you wake up?" she asked him.

Her expression was soft, concerned. That face of hers,

the perfect oval, skin inviting his touch. Still, she was upset with him and despite that loving look, he knew he was in trouble with her. Each time he woke, there was that distance she put between them.

"When I can't feel you against me, the nightmares start," he admitted. "I'd like to think it's a side effect of the poison, but more likely, I just need you next to me." He patted the mattress beside him. "Come here, Amara."

She sighed. "I'm still trying to come to terms with your insistence on placing your life in jeopardy. Once I can manage that, I'll be able to be in bed with you without staring at the ceiling with my heart pounding and wanting to cry my eyes out."

"Amaranthe." He said her name as gently as possible because, although she tried to sound valiant, she sounded lost and alone. "Come here."

She shook her head. "I can't. You scared me."

"You would have died."

"You *did* die. I watched you die, Geno. Right in front of me, you died. One minute you were there and the next I was completely alone. I had no idea what that was going to feel like, without you in the world."

She shook her head again, looking so forlorn it tore at him, his heart feeling more battered by that look than by whatever they had done to revive him, and they'd been very enthusiastic about pounding on his chest—at least it felt that way.

"I'm sorry, Amara, it was the best choice when all the choices were bad." He kept his voice as gentle as possible when he had never explained himself or been a gentle man. For her, especially to get that desolate look off her face, he would do anything he could. Give her anything he could.

Her long lashes fluttered. "Your death isn't the best choice for me or your family. Not for your brothers, or cousins, or the people in your territory depending on you. You have to know that, Geno."

"You aren't looking at this the right way, baby," he

pointed out softly. "I can see you have your mind geared in the wrong direction."

She frowned. That little frown twisted at his heart. For a man like him, one who felt little emotion, he found he was suddenly drowning in feelings.

"I don't understand. What other way is there to look at what happened?"

"I should be your hero, Amara." He made it a statement. Firm. "Just pointing it out."

Her expression registered shock. "Hero?"

"Yeah, babe. Your hero. Haven't you ever watched Superman? Or Batman? Or any of the Marvel movies?"

Amaranthe looked more confused than ever. Very slowly she shook her head. "Comics? What in the world do comics have to do with you almost dying?"

His eyebrow shot up. "It's no wonder you can't see the real picture, Danzatrice Ombra." He kept his tone soft and compelling. Loving. Tender even. "You don't know what a real-life hero is, not even when he's sitting in front of you. We're going to watch all the superhero movies and then you'll see this in an entirely different light." He poured confidence into his voice.

"I will?" ·

"Yes."

"By watching movies?"

"Exactly. You need a true perspective."

"Through movies." She sounded faint, but for the first time, there was a hint of amusement in her mind.

She would need her sense of humor with him. It was one of the first things about her he'd been attracted to. She laughed easily. He didn't know how when her life had been bleak. "I feel you've missed out on some very important lessons you'll need in dealing with your future husband. We can easily remedy that though. I have all the movies. We'll spend the next couple of days watching them back-to-back until you realize how you should see me as your hero."

"How many movies are we talking here?"

"I have an entire library of Marvel, Batman, and Superman movies. Have no worries. I have *The Green Hornet* and *The Crow. The Punisher.* All the Iron Man movies."

"This is a side of you I didn't know existed, Geno. Is it possible these movies influenced your behavior? When did you start watching the movies?"

"I read the comics first, before I began watching the movies. I'm a reader first. So first comics and then graphic novels and then the movies. I collect them."

"How old were you?"

He shrugged, happy he'd managed to distract her from her obsession with his near-death experience. "I started reading comics very early and collecting around ten. Seriously collecting at twelve. I've been at it ever since."

"You read and then watch the movies as well?"

"For fun."

"Do you go to the movie theater?"

He frowned. "No. Why would I do that? I have a perfectly good system right here."

"Do you go to Comic-Con?"

He narrowed his eyes, studying her innocent expression. His woman. She could be a mystery. "How do you know about Comic-Con if you don't know anything about the movies or comics?" He deliberately poured suspicion into his voice.

"Everyone knows about Comic-Con."

"I'm beginning to think you're playing me. You have watched the movies. You most likely watched *Wonder Woman*. Or *Black Widow*. No, *Elektra*. That was the one you watched."

She raised an eyebrow. "One I watched? Because they had female leads? Geno, I think you could just be skating the edge of being a male chauvinist. Is that why you keep throwing yourself in front of me when you think I'm in danger?"

All humor faded away. She had to understand him because he was never going to be anything but who he was.

"First of all, Amaranthe, I didn't *think* you were in danger. You *were* in danger both times. You would have died. I need to hear you acknowledge that to me, so I know you understand you wouldn't have survived. You had no chance."

She pressed her lips together stubbornly and looked down at her hands.

"No, Amaranthe, we need to get past this. You had no chance. You need to acknowledge that you know it."

She lifted her chin at him, her dark eyes beginning to smolder. God help him, he loved that fire in her, her ability to stand up to him.

"I know it *now*. You know it now. There was no way you could possibly have known it then."

"That isn't true. You had a wafer on the roof of your mouth that was designed to kill you if you were captured. You *knew* it would kill you. As soon as I became aware of it and your intentions, I knew I had a better chance of surviving simply because I'm twice your size."

"That time, yes. I'll concede that, but you didn't know me, Geno. You shouldn't have taken such a risk."

"I knew you. I knew the moment I laid eyes on you, and don't tell me you didn't know, either. When our shadows touched and then began coiling together, it was confirmed. I don't give a damn if I was too wound up to listen to my gut at that moment or you were, we both knew we belonged together. I wasn't about to let you die. It made sense for me to take the poison, spit as much as possible out and hopefully my body could take on the effects without it killing me before the doctor could administer the antidote."

"*Hopefully*. That's not a guarantee, Geno."

"Stefano was there. I had family around me. I knew the odds were in my favor, Amara. You had no odds in yours. Stop being stubborn. I realize I frightened you, and I'm sorry, but you aren't thinking logically. You need to do that for me. Weighing the odds, if the roles were reversed, what would you have done? Be honest with me and with yourself, Danzatrice Ombra." He used his most compelling voice, but also his most loving, tender tone, one he hadn't known he possessed until Amaranthe was in his life.

She took a deep breath and shook her head twice as if to deny what she was thinking. Then she pressed her fingertips to her lips. He hated the little shudder that went through her body. She was extremely distressed, and she wouldn't come to him for comfort. He needed her to, but he knew if he asked—or demanded—she would refuse. Right now, she needed to work this out. What he'd done, standing in front of her, risking his life, was a major problem for her.

Geno understood. She was a shadow rider and used to handling all difficulties on her own. She didn't want him to think she was less than he was—and he didn't. But he would always protect her with his life just as he would his brothers. That was ingrained in him. If her life was in danger, he would never be able to stop himself. That was who he was.

"I have to concede, logically, you made the right decision, and I would have made the same one." She admitted it in a soft murmur, barely heard. "But how could you possibly know what the Australian was going to do or even if the poison on the knife had an antidote?"

"I've told you, I sometimes know things before they happen. I've learned to trust those instincts. I knew he was going to throw the knife, and I calculated the odds of your survival versus mine. We were surrounded by shadow riders. We had cars that could get us to the doctor and riders that could take the weapon to the lab to analyze the poison. My chances were better than good. You're just too small in comparison, Amara. Again, Danzatrice Ombra, with logic, think about it. If you knew what was going to happen, tell me what you would have done."

"You're always going to have a larger body mass than I have, Geno. Does that mean you're going to step between me and whatever danger is coming my way as if I can't handle it for the rest of our lives?"

"Yes." He didn't hesitate. "Absolutely I will." He'd always been able to control his heartrate. He had the feeling the reason he couldn't control the sudden acceleration didn't have anything to do with the aftereffects of the poison and everything to do with his fears for Amaranthe. He still tasted the residual of fear of losing her that he'd awakened with.

"I'm a rider, Geno. I want to continue to be a rider. Do you plan to hold my hand in the shadows?"

"If I went into the shadows with you, I might hold your hand. I might try other things as well," he added in an effort to coax a smile from her. "Most likely, you'll take rotations as a solo rider. We're stretched pretty thin. These were extraordinary circumstances. Until we know the immediate danger is over, I'll be staying close to you and trying to keep my brothers close as well. There was hatred in that room when they went after Stefano. And I felt it again when the assassin was talking to you about the Ferraro family and the riders. They'll come at us again and again until we find out who is behind this and end it."

Geno studied her face for a long time when she remained silent. Finally, he held out his hand to her again. "I need you to come over here to me. If you don't, I'm coming to you. You don't seem to understand, Amaranthe. I honestly didn't give a damn whether I lived or died. Nothing much mattered to me until I met you. Now, whether you like it or not, you're the center of my world. I can't lose you, and I'll do whatever it takes to protect you."

"Has it occurred to you that I feel exactly the same way?"

"Come here, baby. You're too far away from me." His heart was still beating too fast. His mind felt a little too chaotic.

She hesitated. "You always get your way if I'm too close to you. We need to work this out, Geno."

"We are working it out. Just not so far apart."

She moved a little closer to him, but she didn't take his

hand. She came around to the side of the bed and regarded him warily. "I'm close enough, Geno."

He had long arms and he took advantage immediately, reaching out, catching her wrist and exerting gentle pressure until she climbed onto the mattress.

"Are you always going to insist on your way?"

She looked beautiful crawling across the short distance to him. He did his best not to let his body react. He hurt like hell, and he told himself to have more discipline, but she was just too damn sensual without even realizing it, especially when she got that snippy little bite in her voice.

"Not always," he said, mostly because he'd told himself he'd be honest with her. "But probably most of the time because you're sweet and I'm not."

"I don't have to be sweet."

Geno swept her against him. Close. His pulse couldn't seem to settle until he felt her soft skin, warm and alive against his. She made him smile. "Yeah, you do. And once you manage to get past the emotion, which I'm thankful you have, you'll see the logic because you're a logical person."

She leaned her head against his side. "I don't like you very much right now."

"I know, baby, I'm sorry. I can be a first-class dick. Saving your life and all. I really think it would be beneficial to watch these movies so you could change your view of my behavior and regard me as your hero. I think that would go a long way to helping our relationship."

She glanced up at the clock on the wall. "Your brothers will be coming in any minute. They've checked on you every hour on the hour. I'll ask their opinion. I presume they've watched these movies. See if they think your behavior was heroic."

Geno kept his expressionless mask on the outside, but inside he was smirking. He knew Salvatore and Lucca would back him up. His woman was important to all of them. There were always stories handed down in families, and his was no different. Once the eldest son found his woman, the others weren't far behind. That had proven to be true in Stefano's family. Every one of his siblings had found the woman, or in Emmanuelle's case the man, they were in love with.

"I'm certain my brothers have watched the movies multiple times, Amara. You'll enjoy them."

She steadfastly refused to turn her face up to his, probably knowing he'd kiss her.

"Hell of an engagement party," he commented, his gaze on the stairs. She was right, his brothers were on the way up.

"I thought so. What do you suppose happened when we all disappeared from that room? Penelope and the other servers had to have noticed we were gone."

"We always have an explanation," Geno said. "Stefano is careful. You notice there is a back way out. The patio is an extension of the room. Valentino and Dario don't ride the shadows. Most of the bodyguards and Emmanuelle remained to give the explanation that we were bothered by the paparazzi, and we left out the back with the others."

"I suppose that happens enough that it's a reasonable explanation."

He nodded. "Much more plausible than 'we disappeared into the shadows.'"

Salvatore and Lucca entered in near silence, their eyes moving over Geno with a hint of anxiety. He gave them both a quick grin to reassure them.

"I feel like someone beat me up with a baseball bat. It wasn't one of you, was it? Maybe giving it a little too much enthusiasm?"

Neither of his brothers responded to his humor, telling him they'd felt the same fear Amaranthe had.

"You died, Geno," Salvatore said, his tone low, almost accusing. "Right in front of us."

"It was heroic," he pointed out hastily and narrowed his eyes at his brother.

Salvatore nodded, following his lead. "It *was* heroic, but it was still a terrible thing for all of us to witness."

"Especially Amaranthe," Lucca added.

"She *is* struggling," Geno confirmed. "I told her it was because she's never watched a Superman movie and doesn't understand what a hero is."

Salvatore and Lucca simultaneously gasped and stared at Amaranthe in horror.

"That can't be true, Amara," Lucca protested. "Everyone has watched those movies."

She shook her head. "Don't start, you two. I know Geno saved my life. I just don't know if I can watch him do something like that over and over. And he will." Her voice trembled, breaking Geno's heart.

"Do you plan to keep putting your life on the line?" Salvatore demanded, scowling at her. "Because Geno isn't the only hero in the family. I'd have to get in on that action. You are the only sister I have."

"Yeah. If you're going to insist on sticking your head on the chopping block," Lucca added, "I'm going to have to play the hero as well. I can't be outdone by my older brother."

"Don't encourage her." Geno used his gruffest voice on his brothers. If his voice held a little too much affection, he ignored it.

He loved his brothers and couldn't help being proud of them. He'd scared them. He hadn't realized they would be nearly as afraid as Amaranthe, seeing him go down, but he should have. Both struggled to maintain in front of his woman, wanting her to believe they had every faith Geno would survive under any circumstance.

Amaranthe sighed. "I think all you Ferraros are alike. You think you can cheat death."

"I'm compelled to point out, we wouldn't have to be heroes if you weren't throwing yourself under knives all the time," Geno said. He tunneled his fingers in her hair, unable to resist another minute. So much silk. Very gently he began to massage her scalp, hoping to soothe her.

Lucca and Salvatore dropped into the two chairs facing

the bed. "I asked Lanz and Deangelo to check into the riders in Australia, Geno," Lucca said.

Salvatore laughed. "I asked Beniamino and Davide the same. They compiled their notes and sent us both a report on the three families."

"Lanz and Deangelo Rossi are investigators," Geno told Amaranthe. "As are Beniamino and Davide Latini. They're extremely good."

"I did study your family before I came," Amaranthe admitted.

"You moved like lightning," Lucca said. "Until that moment when you saved Stefano, I wasn't certain you were a shadow rider. I suspected you were a rider because you were engaged to my brother, but you are a ballerina. You look more like a ballerina than a rider, and you're so small . . ." He broke off when she glared at him.

"Why would Geno be engaged to me?" she asked in her snippy voice, the one that Geno really loved. His body, despite the damage began to seriously react.

"I suspected you might be pretending to draw out the murderers," Lucca admitted, sounding, and looking sheepish.

"Because of my looks?" Now she sounded outraged.

"Not your looks. You're beautiful. Your size. I just didn't think you could be a rider," Lucca said. "You're making me sweat. You'd better think twice about this one, Geno. She might be pint-sized, but she's scary."

Geno flashed a grin at his brother. "She is, isn't she? She'll keep you boys in line. Salvatore, since I noticed you were just as fast, leaping across the table to save your cousin, I'm rescinding permission for you to fill out the papers for the arranged marriage. You can wait a couple more years and see if the Ferraro prophecy holds for this family the way it did for Stefano's clan."

"What the hell was that, Tore?" Lucca demanded. "You were nearly as fast as ballet babe."

"You are *not* going to call me 'ballet babe,'" Amaranthe objected.

Geno was extremely happy his brothers were taking the spotlight off him and Amaranthe's mind off the fact that he'd nearly died. Her body felt less tense, and she was once again allowing him to slip into her mind a little at a time. He was careful, going slow, inching his way, making certain to keep his touch light. She was still very fragile, but she was willing to allow his brothers to distract her, and that was half the battle.

Geno's eyebrow shot up. "'Ballet babe'?"

"Look at her. She's a teeny-tiny ballerina. And she is a babe, Geno. You don't want me calling her 'hot ballerina,'" Lucca persisted.

"I'd have to beat you into the ground for that one," Geno agreed.

"'Ballet babe' isn't any better," Amaranthe objected. "I might have to beat him into the ground."

Lucca, Salvatore and Geno smirked. Geno hastily rearranged his expression into his stone mask.

"Babe," Salvatore said. One word. Gentle. Soothing.

"What does that mean?" Amaranthe demanded, sitting up straight and pulling away from Geno to include him with the glare she gave to his brothers. "I'm supposed to know what you mean by that one word and your incredibly condescending tone?"

"It means you're fast as lightning," Lucca said. He held out his fist. "But beating one of us into the ground isn't in the works. Killing yes, beating no. We're going to have the advantage through sheer strength and size."

She smirked and fluttered her long lashes at them. "I don't think you're using your brains, *brothers*, dear. Neither one of you would dare lay a finger on me. If you even looked as if you would, Geno would eat you for breakfast."

Amaranthe made the declaration with such confidence, as if it was pure fact. It was evident that she had no doubt that Geno would defend her even against his brothers—and he would—without hesitation. Not that either one of them would ever physically assault her. Both would defend her with their lives. He was certain Amaranthe knew that as well.

Salvatore sighed. "I suppose you're right. But then you're so compassionate, as much as you like to act tough, you wouldn't let him go all big brother on us."

"Which is why we're one hundred percent in your corner, Amara," Lucca added. "One thousand percent. Geno is so damn bossy it isn't funny. We've talked it over, and now that you're here, we think you can tame the beast."

"Or at least distract him when he's at his worst," Salvatore added.

"Do you two think I can't hear you?" Geno asked. "I might be a little weak at the moment, but my eyes and ears are working just fine."

His droll tone earned him a little feminine giggle from Amaranthe. He reached for his brothers on their private telepathic path. *Thank you. She was so upset with me. I'm always going to be that man who steps in front of her, and she's struggling with the concept.*

She'll have three of us stepping in front of her, Salvatore pointed out. *You struck gold, Geno. She's beautiful. I couldn't believe the way she was when you went down. Not just the way she saved Stefano, but when you went down, there was no other purpose in her mind but keeping you alive. If I had any doubts about her, they were gone right then.*

She'll learn who we are, Lucca assured. *She's intelligent and quick.*

"Stop talking to each other without including me. I'm beginning to think you're conspiring against me." Amaranthe searched each of their faces carefully.

"Nothing gets past you," Geno said.

"Geno, you're in so much trouble." Lucca looked gleeful.

"We were just assuring Geno you were in love with him and weren't going anywhere," Salvatore told her. "I saw the look on your face when he went down. He worries that you can't live with a man like him. With the way he is. He can't change who he is. Fundamentally, at his core, he's a man who protects his family. He protects his woman, his family. Lucca. Me. And here's the thing, Amara. You're our sister. You're family to me. To Lucca. We're exactly like Geno. We'll be the same way. Stepping in if we think you're in danger."

Geno's breath caught in his lungs. He'd spent so much time trying to get Amaranthe to move away from the fact that he'd almost died, and now they'd circled right back to it. He should have known Salvatore would be direct and honest with her. His brothers might tease her, but they wouldn't lie to her.

Amaranthe made a little moue with her lips and then nodded slowly. "It's taken me most of the night to process the fact that Geno has nearly died twice now because he's insisted on taking poison in my place and that he won't stop."

"Wait. *Twice?*" Salvatore glared at his brother. "You sent us away to safety and brought these murdering fuckers straight down on you."

"I *tried* to send you away," Geno corrected. "Neither one of you stayed where you were told. I think we need to have a family meeting and reset the ground rules."

"Don't change the subject yet," Lucca said. "I'd like to hear what Amara has to say."

She smiled at him. "Thank you, Lucca. All I wanted to point out is, just as I have to get to know and accept all of you as you are with your personalities, you have to get to know me and accept my personality traits. That might take a little more time. You look the part of big, strong men with iron wills. I look more like what you were teasing me about—the delicate little ballerina. I assure you, I'm not."

Geno didn't like the little confident smirk in her mind or the mysterious smile that was all too feminine and told them nothing but that she was going to be trouble.

"What does that mean?" Salvatore asked. He shot Geno a quick glance, hoping for an interpretation. "What does she mean by that?"

Lucca answered. "I'm afraid she means we took her size and the fact that she was a dancer at face value. What you're telling us, little sister, is that you very well could throw yourself in front of one of us."

"Don't give her any ideas, Lucca," Salvatore said. "She's damn fast."

"She already has them," Geno said. "I'm counting on both of you to be faster. You'd better step up your training with me."

Lucca groaned and wiped his hand over his face. "You're just using her as an excuse to make us work out with you every day."

"You already work out with me every day. I'm talking about working out twice a day."

"Adding ballet in will help with balance as well as endurance," Amaranthe added with a straight face. "Football players and boxers often take ballet to help improve their balance and endurance."

Lucca looked horrified. "I'm drawing the line. You're not getting me into tights, Amara. I know where you're going with this. Geno might want to prance around for you, but that's not happening with me no matter how cute you are."

Amaranthe collapsed face-first on the bed, her laughter muffled by the duvet. Geno exchanged a grin with his brothers. The sound of her mirth was so musically pitched, filling the room and lifting them up, making them feel lighter.

She sat up facing them, pushing at the clouds of hair tumbling around her face. "The visual is killing me. If the three of you wore tights and pranced around my studio, I don't think I could ever unsee that particular sight. As it is, I have a vivid imagination, and you've planted that in my head. Please don't ever do it again."

"You deserve it for making the suggestion in the first place." Lucca had no sympathy. "You can talk my brother into anything."

"Hey," Geno objected. "That's not true."

"It's clear she'll be able to." Salvatore backed Lucca. "Look at those eyes. And her eyelashes. If she asks me for anything, I'm not going to look at her."

"The lot of you are crazy."

"We always envied our cousins having Emmanuelle. And our cousins in LA and San Francisco. Both families have girls. We didn't get a female in our family. Just us," Geno said.

Lucca nodded. "Then we have the prophecy. We always say it's a crock, but deep down we really believe it."

"The prophecy?" Amaranthe echoed.

"I told you about it," Geno reminded. "The eldest Ferraro rider finds his true love and then the other family members find theirs."

"Geno is a . . ." Lucca looked across at his brother and waved his hand. "Hard-ass," he settled on. "He isn't going to change. We didn't think any woman would see past the stone mask to his heart. He's also extremely intelligent and needs someone with a quick mind to keep up."

"In other words," Salvatore interpreted, "he gets bored with conversation, men or women, in five minutes, if he lasts that long. We didn't think we had a chance in hell of the prophecy being fulfilled."

"Who knew someone like you was in the world?" Lucca continued. "Not only are you intelligent, gorgeous, a rider, but you can stand up to him—at least I think you can. You have fire in you."

"She stands up to me," Geno confirmed. Even he could hear the laughter in his voice. The respect and pride. He knew his brothers already felt his growing love for the woman whose shadow had connected with his. He wasn't going to try to hide it for his pride. He wanted them to know how much she meant to him.

He must have said the right thing because Amaranthe looked up at him, her dark eyes meeting his. There was that look he'd never expected to see in any woman's eyes, the one that shook him. He was okay with being shaken. He'd take that if she kept looking at him that way.

CHAPTER TEN

Amaranthe watched in a kind of dazed shock the way the Ferraro family prepared breakfast. Taviano and Emmanuelle clearly were the designated chefs. That didn't mean the others didn't help. Valentino and Mariko very efficiently chopped vegetables. Nicoletta and Ricco were doing something with dough and appeared quite skilled. Dario and Elie made lattes and coffees. Salvatore, Lucca and Stefano added leaves, making the dining table much longer, and put out plates, silverware and napkins on the long sideboard. It was obvious they had all worked together before. No one seemed to get in anyone's way.

She felt a little useless even peeling the already-cooked potatoes along with Geno. For every potato she managed to peel, he had three done. All the while the family worked together, they talked, teased and laughed. She let the talk and laughter surround her like a cloak. She'd always dreamed of a having a large family, one that got along and looked out for one another, but she never believed she'd ever be part of one. It felt surreal to be standing in the kitchen helping to make a huge breakfast while the members of the Ferraro family and their chosen trusted friends worked together.

She felt Geno's gaze on her, and she lifted her lashes. At once, the intensity of his dark blue eyes sank in. When he focused on her, he did so completely, and it always set off a chain reaction in her body.

"You always have to be careful what you wish for, Danzatrice Ombra. You now have the crazy family."

Emmanuelle glanced up. "Not all of us are crazy, Amara, only a couple."

"More than a couple," Nicoletta murmured. "Tell the truth."

"If she knows the truth about your family, she'll run for the hills before he can marry her," Dario said, without looking up. "In fact, if you're smart, you'll knock her up so she can't go anywhere."

"Do you have to be so old-fashioned, Dario?" Emmanuelle asked. "Women raise children on their own all the time. They don't need men if the men are overbearing."

"Not in my world they don't, princess," Valentino said unexpectedly.

"Or mine." Dario stated it as fact.

"I'll agree with that," Stefano said.

"That's a dictatorship," Amaranthe objected. "Geno, do you agree with that?" She kept her tone very mild.

Lucca and Salvatore both looked up sharply. "Don't answer," Lucca advised. "That's trouble right there. Real trouble. Remember what we talked about last night? I suspect that little ballerina of yours has a very bad temper."

Amaranthe raised an eyebrow at him. "I know what you're doing, Lucca, and it isn't going to work. I'm not going to be distracted. Geno must have an opinion on this subject."

"You already know my opinion on the subject, Amaranthe. If we have children, we'll raise them together. You don't like something I do, you tell me, and I'll fix it. I believe in communication."

Emmanuelle stopped working and stared at him. "I didn't know you were aware there was such a word as *communication*, Geno."

His cousins laughed. Geno gave her his death stare. "I believe, Emme, there's only one way to communicate with you. Hopefully, Val is familiar with it."

"There's two ways," Valentino corrected. "I'm more than familiar with both out of absolute necessity."

"Hey!" Emmanuelle glared at her husband as the room once again erupted into laughter. "You're going to pay for that."

Valentino didn't look the least bit intimidated. He flashed his wife a very intimate grin and passed the cutting board with the vegetables to Taviano. "Looking forward to you trying, Emme."

Mariko giggled and glanced at Amaranthe. "It took me forever to get used to the way they tease each other."

"I think it will take me even longer to get used to the way they can cook," Amaranthe said. "I don't think I'm ever going to be that skilled. Not ever."

"Geno's a very good cook," Salvatore reassured immediately. "You don't ever have to be great at cooking. I'm not bad. Even Lucca's pretty good on a grill."

"What do you mean, *pretty* good?" Lucca demanded. He scowled at his brother. "I'm hell on wheels on the grill. Not even Taviano rivals me on the grill."

Laughter broke out again at the deliberate outrage in Lucca's voice.

My brothers are going to any length to ensure I don't lose you. They don't have much faith in my ability to keep you.

Amaranthe touched Geno's mind. He didn't really think his brothers believed he wasn't able to keep a woman interested, did he? *Any woman would want to be with you.*

For my money. I have a lot of money, Amaranthe. My name. Our family name comes with quite a bit of prestige.

Women want you, silly. But they don't get you because

you're taken now. Your brothers love you and want you to be happy. They have complete faith in your ability to keep me. They just want me to know they accept me into their family. It's nice. I love how they love and champion you.

She did. She thought it was wonderful the way his brothers loved him. She felt their love. They surrounded him with loyalty—with love—the same way he did them. She couldn't believe that from such a terrible tragedy, she'd found happiness. She just had to keep believing in herself, that she fit with Geno. It didn't matter that his world was so different from hers; here, in his home, with this side of his family, his brothers and Geno close, she could fit.

T he Ferraro family called it breakfast, but Amaranthe was certain it was brunch and then some. She'd never seen so much food or such a variety. They acted as if it was normal. Immediately, the talk turned to business—and she realized that was normal as well. They seemed to switch easily back and forth between teasing one another and sliding into talking about murder.

"What did your investigators find out, Geno?" Stefano asked.

"There are three families of riders in Australia. It's a big country for them to cover. The Taylor family is in Sydney. Five boys, two girls. Lucky family for having daughters. The structure is sound. They have a good reputation. Greeters are their retired parents. A few cousins to help carry the load," Geno answered.

Amaranthe happened to be watching the others around the table and she caught a strange look between Taviano and Nicoletta. She couldn't quite interpret the look, but Nicoletta dropped one hand under the table, as did Taviano. Amaranthe was certain they linked their hands together. Neither changed expressions, but they definitely shifted in their chairs minutely, so they were closer to each other. Anything out of the ordinary was always a red flag to her.

She glanced at Stefano. He was stone-faced, which didn't surprise her in the least, but his gaze had touched, for one brief moment, on his youngest brother and then slipped back to his cousin. She filed that away as significant. Whatever Taviano knew and was withholding, Stefano knew as well.

She didn't call attention to either one of them but wondered if Geno had caught the nearly indiscernible byplay. She couldn't imagine that he hadn't.

"The Ryan family of riders are in Western Australia, residing in Perth." Lucca took up the report as Geno ate Italian sausage. "Seven boys, no girls. Not a hint of a problem with the family. The parents retired from riding and are the greeters. A tremendous number of cousins, just as in our family, so plenty of investigators, bodyguards and other help with their territory. It's a big territory. They have a very good reputation among all the riders in other countries."

Amaranthe kept her gaze on Taviano, Nicoletta and Stefano without seeming to. She'd perfected the art over the years, thankful for her long lashes and diminutive size. Often she could appear to be looking down at her food, or somewhere else, because she was so much shorter than most people. In this case, she was between Geno and Salvatore, and if she pushed back into her chair, she nearly disappeared, giving her a natural observation site as she appeared to eat.

Taviano had all but ceased eating. He drank his coffee but continued to hold Nicoletta's hand, his gaze fixed on his cousins as they reported on what their investigators had uncovered in the little amount of time they'd had.

She swept her gaze around the table to see if any of the other Ferraros or Elie, Dario or Valentino had the same reaction as Stefano, Taviano and Nicoletta. They didn't. The others appeared to be eating and paying attention to Lucca while they did so. There were no strange looks being passed back and forth. She turned her attention back to Stefano's youngest brother as she carefully ate strawberries and French toast.

Salvatore was next. He indicated the map of Australia that they had put up on a large screen on the wall across from the view of the water. "The third family of riders, the Thomas family, resides in Darwin in the Northern Territory. The parents died in a small plane crash when the oldest boy had just turned sixteen. He took over as head of the family and riders. There are four boys and one girl in the family. An aunt and uncle serve as greeters. They also have an excellent reputation."

Geno waved his hand toward the map. "Australia is huge for three families to cover. They do a good job of helping one another, and riders come in from other countries to aid them when necessary."

Elie nodded. "The Archambaults help out when they can."

"The families have always helped to train young riders," Lucca added. "Our investigators couldn't find that any of them were out of the country when any of the murders took place. Not a single family member. Their planes were on the ground, and no cousin was in our country. Obviously, we'll need to investigate more thoroughly; there wasn't time to really check each family the way we needed to."

There was silence as those at the table got up to replenish their plates from the warmers. Amaranthe didn't understand how they could possibly put away that much food. Geno remained sitting beside her. He sat back in his chair, looking relaxed, but he didn't feel that way. Inside he was coiled like a snake about to strike. She dropped one hand below the table to place her palm on his thigh, showing solidarity. There was no doubt he'd caught the exchange of looks between Taviano and his wife. He was also aware Stefano was withholding information.

Be very careful, Geno, she cautioned. She couldn't help herself. Stefano was a force to be reckoned with. He was also a man Geno respected and loved. If there were a falling out, it would hurt. She didn't know why the head of the Ferraro family would hold back crucial information, but there had to be a reason.

His hand covered hers. He took a sip of coffee, his gaze moving around the table, touching each of his cousin's faces and then Elie's. Finally, he settled on Stefano. "No doubt you put your investigators on this as well. Considering that my parents were victims of these murderers, I think it's a good idea to pool all information and see what we have."

Amaranthe was proud of him. There was no threat in his voice. Geno sounded the way he always sounded. Still, Stefano flicked him a quick, very sharp look from his dark, piercing eyes. He knew. How, she didn't know, but he was aware of what Geno was asking.

Stefano didn't look at his youngest brother. He kept his gaze fixed on Geno. "Naturally, we did investigate. I'm certain Valentino and Dario had their own investigators on it as well. Elie's wife, Brielle, is amazing with a computer."

Elie nodded. "She came to the same conclusion your investigators did, Geno. We have the report for you. She and Bernado Macaluso were very thorough, and they included more on the families, but nothing that is going to change what you already know."

Geno nodded but didn't take his gaze from Stefano. "I have a gut feeling Stefano's investigators may be able to point us in a new direction."

Stefano didn't so much as blink. "I'm not certain why you think my people would come up with anything different on these families that your investigators couldn't come up with."

Amaranthe listened to the cadence of his voice. Stefano had chosen his words very carefully. He wasn't lying, but he was misleading. It wasn't the most intelligent thing to do when he knew his cousin so well. At once she felt the difference in Geno. That ruthless quality in him rose like the tide. Did Stefano really think he was going to deter Geno? He had to know him better than that.

The room slowly filled with tension—with a dark antagonism that pushed against the walls despite the room being so spacious. One by the one the others became aware of the storm building between the two powerful cousins. The banter stopped and everyone fell silent. All eyes turned to the two men.

Geno and Stefano continued to stare at each other, locked in silent combat, neither giving an inch.

Amaranthe flicked her gaze to Taviano and Nicoletta, the only other individuals at the table who seemed to have the same information Stefano had. Nicoletta had shifted her body to partially conceal her husband from most of those seated across from them. Amaranthe could see him perfectly. There were tiny beads of sweat on his forehead. His breathing was elevated. His heart was racing. Nicoletta spoke softly to him, whispering in his ear, her entire focus on him.

Geno, look at Taviano. Something's very wrong. Stefano would never betray you or your family. If you had to hold back information from Stefano, you would do it for only one reason—the protection of Salvatore or Lucca. He's protecting Taviano. He's not going to back down no matter how much he might want to.

Amaranthe tried to be the voice of reason. Geno was hurt. Stefano had been the one constant in his life, big brother, father, the one person who hadn't abandoned him. In that one moment, he felt all the emotions he had when his father and mother had closed their door and never once spoke to him as parents again. He'd been locked out of their hearts. In some ways, Geno would forever be that child believing he had done something wrong, that he wasn't good enough, that he was undeserving of love. Now Stefano had rejected him just as surely as his parents had.

No one else would see it that way, but Amaranthe was in his mind, and she saw that thirteen-year-old boy's entire world crumbling. He loved Stefano and had believed in him when he didn't believe in anyone else.

Geno pressed his hand tighter over hers, so that her palm dug into the muscle of his thigh. She knew he wasn't aware he was doing so. She poured reassurance into his mind. She poured herself into him, giving him more of her than she ever had. She detested that he felt so alone and abandoned—that he was hurt by his cousin.

She didn't want to remind him again that he would protect Lucca and Salvatore because she knew he thought of himself as more of a sibling than a cousin to Stefano. The knife was sharp, and it had sliced deep.

Geno dragged his gaze from Stefano and rested it thoughtfully, speculatively on Taviano. His brain worked at high speed, and he was coming to conclusions just as she was doing. Stefano stood abruptly, the chair scraping along the floor, drawing all eyes to him.

"Do you really want to do this with me?"

"Yeah, Stefano." Geno rose as well. "More than anything, I really want to do this with you."

Amaranthe realized he did. Geno was that hurt. Anger layered over the hurt to protect him. The fighter in him was eager to do battle, to feel the satisfaction of physical combat. That same eagerness was on Stefano despite the surface sophistication. He seemed to need the physical battle just as much as Geno did.

Shockingly, it was Nicoletta who took charge. "Stop it, both of you. Geno, the information you're looking for that the investigators didn't find is quite simple. There was a fourth family of riders in Australia some time ago. They no longer exist. I believe they covered Queensland. Their actual territory was along the coast near Cairns. The family name was Boutler. None of them are left."

Amaranthe studied Nicoletta's features. She was a beautiful young woman. There was defiance in her posture. Her chin was up, and she showed the same protective trait toward Taviano that Stefano was showing.

Taviano is showing every sign of PTSD, Geno. Don't ask him any questions. Direct your questions to Nicoletta. Be gentle.

Amaranthe willed Geno to listen to her. He just couldn't

make the rift worse between him and Stefano. Sometimes things were difficult to repair.

"Do you know when the family died out, Nicoletta?" Geno asked, ignoring Stefano.

"It was approximately eighteen years ago. I don't know much more. I'm sure your investigators can find out further details."

"Thank you," Geno said. "I appreciate you letting me know, especially since I'm trying to discover who murdered my parents, and clearly the lives of my brothers are at stake." He looked around the room. "If you'll excuse me." He kept possession of Amaranthe's hand, forcing her to stand as well. "Enjoy the food. I'm still very tired, and I need to lie down for a while." He turned and left the room, taking her with him, not so much as glancing at Stefano.

Amaranthe moved up under his shoulder as they stepped onto the elevator together. It surprised her that he didn't take the stairs, given that he needed physical activity. Instead of punching the floor above for his room he punched the ground floor.

"I need to get out of here."

She wrapped her arm around his waist. "It's sometimes easier to breathe outdoors, isn't it? We can walk in the park or along the lake."

"I should have grabbed your coat."

"I'll be warm enough." She wasn't dressed for the weather, but she didn't care. She'd snuggle closer to him.

"There are shops. We can buy you a coat."

She hid her smile against his ribs. He didn't think anything of spending money on a coat she didn't really need. She already had a perfectly good jacket. Still, she wanted him out of the house as quickly as possible. The confrontation with Stefano had been brief, but it had taken a toll. It was so unexpected and out of character for both men.

They kept their heads down as they emerged onto the street via the private entrance. She had no idea how Fiero and Donte Latini knew they were leaving the building, but they were already outside, lounging against the wall as if they were just checking out their phones when they were clearly waiting for Geno to emerge.

"Which one of my brothers texted you?" Geno demanded.

Fiero smirked. "Both."

"You should have," Donte pointed out, all business. "You have Amara with you. These little bastards are coming at our family hard. Now that they know you're going to get married, they'll be even more determined to kill you—or her."

Geno nodded his agreement. "I wasn't thinking, Donte. Sometimes I just need to be outside."

"Leonardo and Bravo are with us as well. We aren't taking any chances with your lives," Fiero said. "They're scouting in either direction."

"We're going to walk along the river," Geno said decisively. "We'll stop at Miranda's and purchase a coat for Amara." He turned in the direction of the river walkway leading to the smaller clusters of boutique shops.

Amaranthe loved the feel of the breeze on her face. The sun was out and kept the temperature from being too cold as they moved together in silence along the sidewalk. There were several little squares with shops. The high-rises boasted well-known famous names, but Geno bypassed those and went straight to one of the smaller boutiques sandwiched between a jewelry store and a wine shop. Both buildings were quaint and small, but beautifully appointed.

Leonardo was already in Miranda's Miracles, checking the store before they allowed Geno and Amaranthe to walk in. Amaranthe didn't understand how an enemy would guess ahead of time where they would go. Why would a bodyguard have to check a store out before they went inside? She could understand them checking the street before they left the store, but it hardly made sense for him to go inside first.

"I don't think I'm ever going to get used to this, Geno," she admitted, breaking the silence between them.

His hand tightened around hers. "You will."

Geno felt and sounded sad. She moved closer to him. "Families have fights, Geno. They argue. But they get over it."

He didn't respond. Stefano had gutted him. Maybe Stefano didn't realize what he'd done, but then Stefano was too intelligent not to know. He had to be hurting, too. She couldn't imagine how they were going to repair the damage, but she knew it had to be fixed. She just wasn't equipped to do it. She had no family and no knowledge of how they worked.

She looked up at Geno's set mask as they entered the little boutique. He had withdrawn from her the moment she brought up families fighting. It occurred to her that she was new. Their relationship was new. Both were counting on the intimacy of their telepathic communication to allow them to have a fast and deep bond. Sadly, Geno had a telepathic connection with Stefano, and he'd counted on that to know they were always solid and close. She had been the one questioning their relationship, now she feared Geno would, and she couldn't blame him.

Geno's hand tightened around hers as the clerk hurried to greet them. "Geno, how lovely to see you."

Geno nodded his head at the woman. She looked to be about fifty, but Amaranthe recognized her as a former model and knew she was much older than that by a good fifteen years. She had great skin and a genuine smile when her gaze rested on Amaranthe and their linked hands.

"My fiancée, Amaranthe. We need a warm coat for her."

"I'm Miranda." The owner of the boutique smiled at her. "At last. A woman courageous enough to take on Geno Ferraro. I'm so happy to meet you."

"Amara, I need to make a couple of phone calls. I'm going to step outside. Miranda will take you around. Get anything you need or want. We can have everything other than the coat sent to the house." He bent down to brush a kiss on top of her head. "And don't give me any trouble about who is paying again. I don't like those kinds of arguments."

Miranda laughed as he walked out, Fiero and Dante moving fast, exiting first, with Bravo behind him. "He's a force to be reckoned with. We're cousins a couple of times removed. I've known him since he was a boy. Even then, once he made up his mind, no one could dissuade him." The smile faded. "None of us understood when his parents abandoned the boys. They just opted out after Eugene's accident. Margo and Eugene retreated so far from all of us, no one could reach them. It was sad to watch those boys go from fun-loving, happy children to very sober youngsters in a matter of months. Everything fell on Geno."

Miranda glanced toward the door, her beautiful face showing genuine affection. "He stepped up immediately, taking responsibility for his younger brothers. He always takes responsibility for everyone. He's a really good man, Amaranthe."

"Yes, he is," Amaranthe agreed, following Miranda to the rack of coats.

The boutique might be small, but every item had been chosen with care. They were unique, bought from artists Miranda had discovered in her travels and wanted to support. Amaranthe caught glimpses of hand-painted silk scarves and several flowing dresses that were gorgeous and far too long for someone as short as she was.

The boutique smelled subtly of fresh citrus and vanilla. There was a soothing quality to the aroma that appealed to Amaranthe and helped to allow her nerves to settle. She hadn't realized she'd been coiled so tightly.

"Have you had any items go missing recently? Little things? I've heard from some of the other store owners there has been a spate of robberies lately. Small things, but valuable. You have such unique, beautiful treasures, I would think the thieves would want to target you, but you also have a state-of-the-art security system."

"My security system didn't prevent the thefts," Miranda acknowledged. "Two weeks ago, a young woman came in and looked around. She was clearly a tourist, not unusual. I could tell she had money from the way she was dressed, but I was very suspicious of her behavior. She paid attention, without seeming to, to the cameras in the store. Also, the lights. I thought that was strange. She wore a thin pair of gloves the entire time, but she kept touching this one little clutch I had. It was beautiful, and it was one of the items that disappeared overnight. I believe she got in that evening somehow after I closed the store."

Alarm radiated through Amaranthe. The boutique had been visited at night by a shadow rider—a woman. She was certain of it. "Did you do anything different that day?"

Miranda nodded. "Normally, I'm open until eight on Fridays, but I had an appointment. A dear friend had flown in from Paris. I closed at six."

Closing early had most likely saved her life. The riders had come to kill to her, just as they had Geno's other relatives and his parents, but Miranda had been safely having dinner with a friend.

"Have you seen that woman since?"

Miranda nodded. "Just recently. Every morning before I come to work, I have coffee in that little café across the street. I like to people watch. She came into the square with a man yesterday morning. He was older by a good fifteen or twenty years, although I didn't think he was her father. Not a lover, either. He seemed to be giving her orders. In any case, she was very attentive. She listened and kept nodding her head. Twice she looked toward my shop."

Amaranthe took the coat Miranda held out to her without seeing it. She raised her stricken gaze to Miranda's. She was being targeted for murder. There was no doubt in Amaranthe's mind, but why? What had Miranda done that would bring these murderers down on her? Simply because she was a distant relative of Geno's? Did they hate his family that much?

If these people were willing to murder Miranda simply because she was related to Geno, surely Stefano had to know they would be willing to kill his children and wife. The more she thought about it, the less sense it made that Stefano had held back the information Nicoletta had provided. He had a wife and children he loved. What difference did it make to acknowledge there had been another family in Australia that was no longer working in Queensland?

Geno, these murderers are targeting Miranda. I think they are going to come here tonight or possibly tomorrow night.

There was silence while Geno considered what she told him. *Details.*

She repeated everything Miranda had said to her while she pretended to look over the details of the beautiful jacket the former model had placed in her hands.

At once the door opened and Geno came striding in with his bodyguards. His energy filled the store. Not just his energy, but his presence. He was a big man, and he seemed to dominate the wholly feminine space. His dark eyes glittered with menace. He looked very intimidating.

Amaranthe held up the coat. "What do you think?"

"I think you should put it on for me. It looks as if it might be a little big for you, but it is beautiful."

For the first time she really looked at it. It was gorgeous. She wanted it to fit, but Geno was right. It did look like it might be too big.

"It's supposed to fit oversized," Miranda murmured. "You'll see. I think it will be perfect for you."

Geno took the jacket and held it for her so she could slip her arms in the sleeves. It felt amazing on her, as if she was wrapping herself in a cocoon of warmth.

If I have to step into a shadow, I'd have to shed the jacket. Just drop it and go. It would be such a shame to lose it. I already love it, Geno, and I haven't even looked in a mirror.

"Miranda's right, Danzatrice Ombra, you look beautiful. The jacket looks as if it were made for you. We'll take it."

Fiero, Donte or one of the others will retrieve for you. Anything you need to leave behind, they'll keep safe for you, Amara.

What are we going to do about Miranda?

Tell her the truth and then take her place each night until they come for her.

Relief swept through her and with it a kind of overwhelming emotion she was unfamiliar with. Geno might be devastated by what had taken place between Stefano and him, but he would never allow anything to keep him from protecting those around him.

"What time are you closing the store tonight, Miranda?" Geno asked as he walked up to the counter with Amaranthe.

She slipped out of the jacket to allow Miranda to remove the tags.

"It's Sunday, Geno. I close early, around five. It only takes me about half an hour to lock the store up, and I go home and put my feet up."

"Amaranthe and I will slip into the back room of the store tonight around four. You carry on as if we're not here. My brothers may be with us. They pay no attention to any orders I give them, so even if I tell them to stay away, the likelihood of them listening is nil."

Miranda laughed, but she sounded nervous. "Your brothers are so delightful. Lucca takes me to lunch at least once a month. Salvatore drops by for coffee in the mornings quite often. You raised them to be fine gentlemen, Geno. I always enjoy dinners with you the most."

Amaranthe was happy to know Geno took Miranda to dinner and his brothers didn't neglect her. She hadn't mentioned a husband or children. She didn't know if the woman was alone in the world, but she thought she might be. That would be sad.

"You think that woman will come back to my shop after hours to murder me, don't you?" Miranda's voice was steady, but the hand she pressed to her throat trembled.

"Yes," Geno answered without hesitation. "But she's going to find me here, not you. You're going to be protected because I'm not losing one more person I love."

Miranda's eyes flooded with tears, but she blinked them away. Her chin went up and she gripped the edge of the counter. "Have no worries, Geno, I can act with the best of them. If she's spying on me, there will be no indication you're in the backroom."

"Even if Lucca's making a fool of himself, you have to be strong and not laugh," Geno warned with a straight face.

Miranda pressed her lips together to keep from smiling. She nodded, her eyes dancing once again. Her belief in Geno was absolute.

CHAPTER ELEVEN

wish I were taller. I could be out front taking Miranda's place."

Geno turned around to look at his fiancée. Both his brothers did the same. The three Ferraro brothers took up most of the space in the small back room. Amaranthe appeared very small, almost fragile. No matter her size, she was a force to be reckoned with. She always would be. She was lightning fast and very observant.

"You don't need to be bait. You managed to find out Miranda was being targeted when none of us knew. You saved her life. In a couple of minutes, we'll have her retreat to the bathroom and stay there. It will look as if she came back here. The assassin, if she's coming tonight, will enter and set up to attack."

"I doubt she'll be alone," Amaranthe cautioned. "I don't think any of the others were alone when they killed. I know the police reports said they were, but I don't see how it was possible, certainly not with your parents being riders."

Geno thought it was interesting that she'd gone to an

analytical voice without even being aware of it. His woman fell back on her training the moment she was in any situation where she perceived danger.

"Miranda isn't a rider," Lucca pointed out. "They will expect she'll be easy to kill. She was a model. If this female assassin talked with her at any length or studied her, she should know Miranda is as sweet as they come. She wouldn't hurt a fly. When we were kids, we would walk all over her."

Geno scowled at his brother. "And I beat the shit out of you for disrespecting her."

Lucca grinned at him and rubbed the back of his neck. "Yeah, you did, and we deserved it. There was no one as nice as Miranda."

"I take it she isn't married," Amaranthe ventured.

Geno sighed. "She was. She's a widow. Her husband was a fashion designer. They were crazy in love. The thing about our family, and that seems to include cousins, distant or not, we have the capacity to love deeply but only once."

He was trying to tell her she was safe with him. She always would be. He wasn't going to cheat on her. He'd never take the chance of losing her for a moment with another woman. He'd never want another woman touching him.

"Her husband died in a car accident," Salvatore said. "She was in the car as well. In Italy, a drunk driver hit them head-on when they were returning home from the airport. He was killed outright. Miranda was in a coma for a week. Geno flew to Italy and stayed until she was well enough to be brought to New York. She lived with us until she felt strong enough to get out on her own again."

"How horrible for her." Amaranthe sounded so sad, Geno wanted to put his arms around her. She was too compassionate. He didn't understand how she could be an elite rider and yet feel the deep well of empathy she had for others. "They didn't have any children?"

Lucca answered her. "That is one of her biggest regrets. She was at the height of her modeling career. They wanted children, but decided to wait a few years. It was too late after the accident for her to have a family. She never remarried. She asked Geno to help her stay here in the States. She didn't want to go back to Italy."

Salvatore took over telling the story. "In the end, she decided she wanted her own business, a little boutique with items she discovered herself from little-known designers she met in her travels but had made a huge impression on her. She went to Lucca; he's good at proposals, and he helped her plan it all. Then she came to me, and I found this space and helped her design the interior. Then we went to Geno so she could lay it all out. She wanted it to be strictly business."

Geno heard the pride in Salvatore's voice. It was impossible to miss it. They felt strongly about Miranda. She wanted to succeed on her own. She might need Geno's help to start a business, but she was determined she would stand on her own two feet. She made that clear.

"Lucca and I knew Geno would never turn her down even if her business was going to be a disaster. He'd find a way to turn it around for her, but she had the proposal, which was solid, and a good place for a store, in a high-traffic area. It was the right location for high-end merchandise like Miranda envisioned. One-of-a-kind items from artists all over the world. Miranda really has an eye for beautiful clothing, jewelry and other things. Her boutique has been very successful almost from the opening."

"She works too hard," Geno groused.

Salvatore and Lucca agreed with him.

"Did you manage to get everyone to leave?" he asked Salvatore and Lucca. "I'm sorry I put that on you, but I didn't want to start a fight. I don't want to look at Stefano until I calm down."

There was a small silence. Geno faced his brothers. Both wore a stony expression. That wasn't good.

"Tell me."

"Everyone left with the exception of Stefano," Salvatore

admitted. "He refused. Nothing we said could persuade him. His bodyguards, Enzo and Emilio, remained behind as well. Stefano convinced his brothers to go when they wanted to stay and talk to you. Everyone was upset, especially Taviano. There was an argument between Taviano and Stefano in private. In the end, Taviano and Nicoletta left, but it was clear they didn't want to go."

"You should have made it clear to Stefano that he wasn't welcome," Geno said, an edge to his voice. He felt edgy. He had to go back home and face an argument with Stefano—or worse, a physical altercation. The worst of it was, there was a part of him that welcomed that physical battle with Stefano. That was how hurt he was. How angry. How far he'd retreated into himself.

"I made it clear we wanted him to leave, Geno," Salvatore said.

"Both of us did," Lucca added.

"If you made it so clear," Geno pointed out, his voice low, but with a distinct growl in it, "Stefano would be gone, and I wouldn't have to deal with him when I get home tonight."

There was a long silence. Neither one of his brothers argued or debated with him when normally they would have.

"I might be new to the family circle," Amaranthe ventured, "but if I get an opinion, I think there are a few things none of you have considered."

"You don't have a clue what's going on, Amara." Geno cut her off. He couldn't listen to her, the voice of reason. She was going to leave just like everyone else in his life. She might as well do it now, before it would rip his soul out. He needed Amaranthe to want to be with him, but he couldn't take it if he believed in her and she abandoned him the way his parents had and now Stefano. Geno's chest hurt. He hadn't had physical symptoms like this since his parents had abandoned him.

The temperature in the tiny little room should have been hot as hell, but it suddenly dropped dramatically, the air chilling. He'd had very little reason in his life to feel ashamed, but he was overwhelmed with the emotion. He wasn't a fucking coward, but he was acting like it, deliberately trying to drive Amaranthe away when she didn't deserve it. He was treating his brothers like shit as well when all they'd done was support him. They'd supported Amaranthe without really knowing much more about her than he'd chosen her as his woman.

"I'm sorry. Amaranthe, I'm very sorry. Of course you have a say. You're part of the family and probably the only one of us who is thinking with your brain. Salvatore and Lucca, I owe you both an apology as well. I know dealing with Stefano is impossible when he makes up his mind to do something. That's what makes him so good at being who he is. I had no right to talk to any of you that way."

Again, there was a short silence. It was Salvatore who finally broke it. "We were all thrown by what Stefano did, Geno. I don't understand it any more than you."

"It isn't an excuse to treat you like shit after you cleared the house for me. That can't have been easy. And acting like an ass to deliberately push Amara away is not only stupid but an act of cowardice." He pressed his fingertips to the corners of his eyes. "Please forgive me, Danzatrice Ombra, and tell us what you were you were going to say."

I really am sorry, baby. I don't know what's wrong with me. He forced himself to look at her. He wanted her to see he meant his apology, not only to her, but to his brothers.

Amaranthe. The way she looked at him turned him inside out. Her dark eyes softened, and her face wore the sweetest expression. *I know what's wrong, Geno. Your brothers are just as confused as you are.*

They aren't acting like assholes.

You're acting hurt.

I'm striking out at the three people I love most in the world. I should be striking out at Stefano.

Not necessarily.

He sighed, his gut clenching. He didn't want to hear what she had to say because he knew it was going to be something reasonable. He didn't want to be reasonable. He really did want to hit Stefano. It would feel good to take physical action.

"Tell us what you think, Amara, although if I'm honest, I'm not positive I can listen with an open mind. I don't want to forgive him. I don't want to understand him. I just want to avoid anything to do with Stefano right now." Avoiding him meant avoiding violence because Geno wasn't certain he could see Stefano and remain in control.

"I'll admit, I feel the same," Lucca said.

"I want to hear what you have to say," Salvatore said. "Stefano wasn't acting at all like himself. Completely out of character."

"Geno?" Amaranthe waited for confirmation.

He forced himself to nod.

"Clearly, there was an underlying issue with Taviano," Amaranthe pointed out. "Stefano didn't want it coming to light. Whatever it was, it triggered what looked to me like a PTSD episode in Taviano. Nicoletta tried to cover for him, but I could see the signs."

"I did as well," Salvatore admitted. "Geno? You see everything. I've never known you to miss a single detail. What did you see?"

Geno had seen the signs in Taviano. He didn't want to admit it. Something had been very wrong with Stefano's youngest brother. That would mean Stefano was protecting him. If Geno were honest with himself, if the circumstances were bad enough, he might stand in front of Salvatore and Lucca, but he would have handled things with Stefano differently. At least he told himself that.

He sighed. He had to be honest. His brothers were waiting. He'd always been honest with them, no matter the cost, even when they were young. He hadn't softened the blows their parents had given them. They deserved the truth now whether he was ready to deal with it or not.

"Amaranthe's right. I noticed Taviano was having a difficult time. Elevated heart rate, sweating, his woman protecting him. Stefano was drawing attention away from him."

"Protecting him as well," Salvatore concluded.

"Most likely," Geno acknowledged reluctantly.

"How old would Taviano have been eighteen years ago? That's around the same time your father had his leg amputated, and you took over the Ferraro territory here in New York, right, Geno?" Amaranthe asked.

Geno nodded slowly, his mind jumping back on track. "Taviano would have been around ten. I'm three years older than he is."

He could see that shocked Amaranthe. He knew he appeared much older. The weight of responsibility did that to a man. He'd never taken his duties lightly. The safety and training of his brothers had been his number one priority, then learning to be the best shadow rider and leader he could possibly be.

He was also built very differently from Taviano. Taviano looked much like Stefano. Sophisticated. Handsome. Geno was more the brute force type, the criminal type—no matter if he wore a suit, he was always under suspicion. He took care that Lucca and Salvatore appeared to be much more like Stefano, although they did have similar builds to Geno. Genetics were a bitch sometimes. Still, they had the Archambault speed, and they'd benefited from years of training from the Archambault instructors even though he'd interfered when he thought the mentors had been too harsh.

"Do you have any idea where Stefano was eighteen years ago?" Amaranthe asked.

"I'm not certain where *I* was eighteen years ago," Geno said. "I'll have to give it some thought." He glanced at his watch. "Miranda needs to get out of the front of the shop." He texted her to close the boutique and then head to the bathroom and lock herself in.

Fortunately, to go to the bathroom, she had to first use

the small hallway and walk toward the back room. Geno instructed her to take an armload of merchandise as if she were bringing it back to box up for shipping. Miranda obeyed immediately.

Geno found himself relaxing. He hadn't realized he was so tense. Miranda wasn't a close relative, but she was one they had great affection for. He didn't want to lose her. Whoever these people were, they knew Miranda meant something to the Ferraro family.

"This female assassin will have a weapon or weapons tipped with poison," he reminded.

"Did Dario interrogate the prisoners?" Amaranthe asked. "Because I didn't hear a thing if he did."

Salvatore and Lucca exchanged a look between them before consulting with Geno. *You know Dario, Geno*, Lucca said. *He interrogated them. They weren't riders. They were hired and didn't really know crap. A ton of money exchanged hands. Dario was satisfied they couldn't tell him anything more.*

Geno sighed. "They were interrogated, Amaranthe, but they weren't members of the family committing the murders. They were hired—bribed with quite a lot of money to help. Dario was satisfied they knew nothing else of value, not even names they could pass on."

"I should have said," Lucca corrected himself. "He did give the names of a few teens that had been recruited to work for them. Stealing. Causing mischief. Planting seeds of doubt about our family."

Amaranthe smiled at them. "You actually didn't tell me about Dario's interrogation and the information he got out of the prisoners. Geno did, which means you told him because you were worried I wouldn't like Dario's methods."

"No one likes Dario's methods, but sometimes they're necessary," Geno said. "You're very aware of what happens in interrogations, Amara."

"Sadly, I am," she whispered and turned toward the front.

A woman emerged from the shadows and stood for a moment looking around the shop. The riders knew she was orienting herself before she moved around the store. They watched as she stealthily made her way through the racks to the edge of the hallway, where she appeared to be listening for Miranda's return.

Deliberately, Geno crinkled a sheet of the tissue paper Miranda used to wrap the articles of clothing in for shipping. The moment the assassin heard the crumpling sound, she drew a short-bladed knife and stood to one side of the open hallway door.

Geno held up his hand to stop the others from moving. *Lucca, you stay with Miranda. In case this woman manages to slip by, I want you to guard Miranda and make certain she's safe. Amaranthe and Salvatore, choose a shadow and come up behind her. If possible, we'd like to take her alive. If we do, we'll finally have someone who will be able to provide answers for us.*

You're using yourself as the bait, Amaranthe said.

He could tell she wasn't happy with him. What did she think? He'd let her be the bait? Not likely. He didn't care how fast she was. He could control the woman's knife with sheer strength alone. He rustled the tissue paper again and took a light step on the floor, allowing the tile to creak under him.

Amaranthe moved into a shadow and disappeared. Salvatore stepped up, toe to toe. *She's the real deal, Geno. Amara is. You've got it all right in front of you. I don't care what Stefano did to us. We're still a family. You. Lucca. Me. And now Amaranthe. Don't you fuckin' blow it.*

Geno might expect Lucca to come at him with a lecture, but not Salvatore. He nodded. *My brain's working again.*

Good. Salvatore stepped into a shadow and was gone as fast as Amaranthe. Geno found himself smiling. He'd raised his brothers to be men. They didn't take shit off anyone, not even him. He was proud of them. He liked that they stood up for Amaranthe.

In position, Amaranthe told him.

He waited, creaking another tile.

In position, Salvatore assured him.

Miranda is covered, Lucca said.

Geno immediately glided down the hall toward the main showroom, remaining perfectly silent. There was no more deliberately stepping on tiles that creaked under his feet. He moved in silence, going right up to the open door. Hearing her sudden gasping inhale as he loomed over her, he reached to shackle her wrist before she could strike with the knife. Ruthlessly applying force to the pressure points so her fingers went dead and she dropped the blade, he spun her around easily, locking her to him.

Salvatore and Amaranthe checked her for weapons, stripping her of two more knives before declaring she was clean. She glared at them with hate-filled eyes but refused to speak.

Geno didn't ask her to speak. He didn't need her to say a word, not there. He wanted her back in the interrogation room, where they could ask her questions and get much-needed answers. He waved Amaranthe toward the shadow that would take them out of the shop, into the street. She stepped into it. Salvatore waited, stepping to one side as Geno shoved the assassin toward the shadow.

Stop, Geno, don't bring her out here. She has a partner. She's in communication with him and he's waiting.

Amaranthe's voice didn't portray distress, but Geno wasn't taking any chances. *Salvatore, go. She may need help. I'll take this one out another way.*

Geno turned the woman and shoved her toward the back room. As he did, Salvatore stepped into a shadow to take him outside the front of the store to join Amaranthe.

Amaranthe hissed her displeasure in Geno's mind. *Her partner stepped into a short tube with so many feeders it's hard to track him quickly. Watch out, Geno. I think he's coming for you.*

He wanted to tell her to stay back, but he knew she

wouldn't listen. *Salvatore, do you see him or evidence of his passing?* The only thing he could do was try to have his brother keep Amaranthe safe.

Geno forced the woman into the shadow that would take them out the back door onto the small round porch that led to the street behind the boutique. The moment they emerged onto the porch from the shadow portal, his prisoner locked to his front, Geno knew it was too late. He tried to yank the young woman back inside the tube for her safety, but an older man was waiting for them, and he stepped right into her and slammed a knife into her heart.

"To keep you from the horror the monsters would subject you to," he murmured and stepped into another shadow.

Geno's first instinct was to try to save her. He knew the effects of the poison, but he couldn't stop himself from lowering her to the ground. Her eyes were already closing, breath ceasing, heart stopping by the time he had her flat on her back on the porch.

Lucca. She's down. Dead. I'm going after her killer.

Who's dead? Lucca demanded, fear in his mind.

The assassin. The woman. Her partner killed her. Geno included Amaranthe and Salvatore in his communication. *I made it easy for him.* There was disgust in his voice.

He stepped into the same shadow, careful, every sense flaring out in an effort to uncover the male, to see if he had waited for Geno to follow him. He had to know Geno would. He would be thinking in terms of an ambush. He could move much faster because Geno would have to be cautious, always cognizant of the man lying in wait for him.

Geno knew it would only take one slice of that poisoned knife to kill him. The doctor had the antidote, but it would be difficult to find him in the labyrinth of the shadow tubes. Geno knew, because he'd had to find more than one body of a rider to return the remains to the family, and it hadn't been easy. They'd never find him in time if he were cut with a poisoned blade.

He followed the faint trail made by the male assassin,

noting this man was far more experienced than the assassin who had tried to kill Stefano. This one had all the marks of a skilled rider—one who had been using the shadows for a long time and was familiar with the different elements of each feeder tube. He had known the young woman he'd murdered, yet he hadn't hesitated. In fact, as Geno pulled up the memory to examine it closely, there had been no sign of reluctance or distaste for the task. It hadn't bothered the man to kill her.

As he moved through the shadow, Geno contemplated that idea. They knew each other, that was for certain. In the brief glimpse he had of the man, Geno might have pegged him for her distant relative, a cousin or uncle. Most likely an uncle. There was no love on his side. He couldn't tell on hers. He hadn't been looking at her face. He couldn't see her expression. He'd read her body language. She had expected a rescue. She'd thought the man was going to shove the knife into Geno, not into her. Why hadn't he? The chances of getting to Geno were slight, especially with the woman solidly in front of him. Geno would have allowed the woman to escape to fend off the man, and the assassin had to have known that.

Geno came up on several feeder tubes, forcing him to halt and check each one for evidence that the assassin had entered one of them. If the assassin had known Geno would have to release the woman once the knife came at him, why hadn't he attacked? Geno would have done that to ensure her freedom. Yes, it would put him at risk, but now there would be two of them to take Geno down. It would be much better odds. After all, Geno was the ultimate target, wasn't he?

The tracks were very faint in a fast feeder tube that looped to his right. Every instinct screamed at him that he was being led into a trap. He'd always trusted his gut. Had the girl been a deliberate sacrifice? Had the murderers known Miranda's shop was being watched by his family? Had Geno made a mistake? He didn't think so. It was coincidence that they'd discovered Miranda was under a death threat.

He studied the feeder tube and the three closest to it. He could see the faint signs the assassin had left behind that marked the one he'd supposedly entered. The other two close to it were pristine. A rider could dive into a tube and clear the entrance without leaving a sign of passing if he wanted, but the portal would catch him and throw him into the slick fast-moving shadow before he was able to stop himself. Those small feeder tubes were pure hell when it came to riding them.

Still, his gut screamed at him he was in trouble. So where was the trouble coming from? He was a patient man when it came to hunting. He could be still for hours if need be. He remained exactly in place waiting to see if his quarry was in the entrance of the small feeder tube and if he had a partner creeping up behind Geno. He didn't feel anyone behind him. He didn't make the mistake of twisting around to see. Movement in the tubes displaced air and would tip off any experienced rider that he wasn't alone.

Geno waited. The feeling of danger didn't fade. He remained absolutely still just inside the mouth of the larger shadow where he could watch all three of the feeder tubes. It took another ten minutes before he felt a faint shift in the air right at the front of the feeder on his left. A gray outline appeared briefly and then the older man emerged fully from the feeder, stepping practically right into Geno. He was armed with a knife in each hand, holding them low, blade up, so he could sink the edge into Geno's belly before he saw danger coming at him.

Geno caught both wrists in an unbreakable grip, directing the blades away from himself, his thumbs digging into the assassin's pressure points as he stepped in close, crowding the man, knee between the man's legs. The assassin shifted his weight, trying to step back into the feeder tube. At once, the speed and force of the tube threatened to rip the man from Geno's grip. Instantly, the assassin threw his weight backward into the feeder tube, deliberately trying to fall onto his back and take Geno with him, rolling his wrist to turn the poisonous blades upward toward Geno's arms.

Geno recognized he was in a perilous situation immediately, not necessarily from the assassin but from the power of the feeder tube.

Behind them, Amaranthe slid, no more than a small shadow slipping beneath the assassin so when he fell, the man crashed precisely on the much smaller body. She wrapped her legs around his chest, both hands gripping his head, anchoring herself. The tube ripped at the three bodies, hurtling them through the shadows toward the next fork.

Geno seized the assassin's wrists, refusing to release him, keeping the knives out away from the man's body, no longer worried for his own protection. He was terrified the man might be able to use the poisonous blades on Amaranthe. The assassin fought like a man possessed. The slick feeder tube ripped and pulled at their bodies, spinning and tearing as if trying to take their skin, hair and eyes from them.

Beneath the assassin, Amaranthe seemed abnormally still, and for a moment Geno feared she'd been knocked unconscious by the violence of the shadow tube and the collision of the assassin's body with hers. Her hands and feet didn't loosen for a minute. She stuck to the assassin as if glued to him, but she was utterly still and quiet, barely breathing.

Geno realized what she was doing. In the violent turbulence of the shadow tube and with Geno's larger, very muscular body presenting such a clear threat, she was waiting for the assassin's brain to dismiss her. Geno aided her instantly by tightening his grip on the man and turning his wrists slowly but surely so the edges of the blades faced toward the assassin's skin.

Adrenaline and fear for his life made the man shockingly strong. He resisted hard, concentrating on keeping his hands away from his body, his gaze locking with Geno's.

Hatred gathered in those dark brown eyes. Whatever the reason this man had for targeting the Ferraro family for murder—it was very personal. Geno could detect fear, but there was so much loathing, so much it swamped him. Without warning, the man suddenly gave the appearance of giving in, his strength evaporating for a moment, arms caving, allowing the blades dangerously close to his thighs.

Just that fast, he turned the knives toward Geno's inner arms and pressed upward. As if she instinctively knew his intentions, Amaranthe struck, wrenching as she'd been taught from the time she was a young child, breaking the assassin's neck before he could complete his intention.

Geno hung on to the dead man until they reached the end of the feeder tube. One of the knives was lost to them, but the fist had locked down on the other. Geno cursed silently. It would take some time to find that knife, and he would have to. He didn't dare take a chance that a rider might stumble across it and get cut.

He dragged the heavy body from Amaranthe, leaving it in the mouth of the shadow so it couldn't be seen while he examined it for any identification. Salvatore came up behind them, the second knife in his hand.

"Any idea who he is?" Salvatore asked.

Geno shook his head. "He knew the young woman he murdered though. Killed her without hesitation and it didn't seem to bother him at all. She was shocked. Frankly, so was I. I expected him to go for me." His voice sounded deeper, had a heavier rasp to it. He cleared his throat. He detested the fact that he'd held that young woman in front of him and allowed the murderer to plunge the knife into her. He felt partially responsible.

"Geno, you can't take that on," Amaranthe counselled.

"She was young, Danzatrice Ombra, about your age. She had her entire life ahead of her. I think that man was using her the way they use the teenagers, recruiting them with promises of big money. The way they bribed two of our longtime employees."

"I've asked our investigators to look into our other employees just to make certain no one else is on their payroll," Salvatore said.

"Good thinking, Salvatore," Geno acknowledged. "We need to get back to Miranda. We'll let someone find this body, but we have to take the knives with us. This location is far from Miranda's shop. If the police ever connect them, they won't be able to bring Miranda or us into it."

The light would change in another few minutes, altering where the shadow lay, exposing the body. They stepped into the main shadow tube and rode it back to Miranda's boutique.

There were police cars and tape surrounding the back of Miranda's store. A small crowd had gathered, but two uniformed officers kept people from pushing near the yellow tape. Two men in suits stood just off the steps leading to the back porch. Lucca, his arm around Miranda, his body sheltering hers from prying eyes, was talking to the two men in the suits.

The man in the gray suit is Detective Patrick Bowden. He's a good cop. Very thorough. Watch every word you say to him because he doesn't forget anything. His partner is Terence Laker. They're sharp. They're friendly enough toward our family and willing to give us the benefit of the doubt—in fact, I grew up with Patrick—but they investigate any evidence that appears to incriminate us. We're very careful in our territory.

Geno and Salvatore kept Amaranthe between them as they approached the officers, showed ID and were allowed through. Their bodyguards had timed bringing their car just up the block as if they'd ridden there.

"Mr. Ferraro," Detective Bowden greeted. "I expected you." He glanced at his partner and then at Amaranthe. He nodded to Salvatore. "Unfortunately, Ms. Crespi found a body right on her back porch as she was leaving her establishment. She called it in immediately. She's very shaken up."

Geno went directly to Miranda and pulled her into his

arms, one hand pressing her face into his chest, his body language protective. She was trembling. "You should be sitting down, Miranda. Have you already given your statement to the police?"

"Lucca told me to wait for you and Vinci. Why would I need Vinci?"

"It's just a precaution to have him close when giving your statement, Miranda," Geno assured. "I need you to sit down. Patrick, I'm going to have Lucca bring a couple of the chairs out here so Amaranthe and Miranda can sit while Miranda gives you her statement."

"I'll help him," Terence Laker volunteered, just as Geno knew he would. More than anything it was a stall tactic to wait for their lawyer. He wanted to make certain Miranda was safe from saying anything inadvertently.

CHAPTER TWELVE

The police kept them for a long time at Miranda's Miracles. Geno was physically exhausted as well as emotionally drained, so much so he considered checking into a hotel for the night. The last thing he wanted to do was face Stefano and have another altercation with him. Geno couldn't imagine how tired Amaranthe or his brothers were if he was so drained.

If Stefano were already in bed, he'd be on the eighth floor in one of the bedroom suites. If he were up, insisting on a confrontation, he would be waiting to do so on the ninth floor. Even Stefano wouldn't invade Geno's personal space. There was no way he would be in Geno's bedroom.

Geno needed to know for certain if Stefano was still there. He didn't want Lucca and Salvatore going to their own homes. He much preferred keeping his family together where he knew they were safer. At the same time, he didn't want them to have to deal with Stefano. That was his job whether he liked it or not. He was head of the family, and the responsibility was his.

He glanced at down at his fiancée as they stepped off the elevator onto the ninth floor. She did look tired, much more fragile than usual. He stopped, sweeping his arm around her.

"Why don't you go on up to the bedroom and let me take care of this? I'll get us something to eat and bring it up to you."

Amaranthe smiled up at him. It wasn't a fake smile. Somehow she managed to find a way to light his world even in what he considered grim times.

Perfume, Salvatore warned.

Geno had caught that subtle fragrance. He recognized that scent. Already the smile was fading from Amaranthe's lips, and she turned her head in the direction of the great room. She'd caught that faint scent as well.

Kitchen, Lucca added. *Fresh bread. Spaghetti. Pasta.*

Geno went straight to the great room and the woman waiting for them, more than a little shocked that she was there.

Francesca Ferraro was a beautiful woman. It wasn't just her outside looks that made that determination; she was also genuinely caring and kind inside. There was compassion in her dark eyes when she rose immediately and without hesitation moved straight across the room to Geno. There seemed to be no doubt in her mind she would be welcomed. She wrapped her arms around his neck and kissed both cheeks, but he could see distress and anxiety in her eyes.

"I'm so sorry this terrible thing has happened. You are so loved, Geno. You, Salvatore and Lucca. And after you nearly died, Geno." She smiled at Amaranthe but went to Salvatore and then Lucca, kissing both affectionately before turning to Geno's fiancée. "I'm Francesca, Stefano's wife."

Geno's affection for Francesca was like that of a sibling. He had the highest regard for her. "Francesca, my fiancée, Amara. The love of my life." He added the last to assure her the engagement was very real, and he wanted Amaranthe to be treated as family.

"The boys made me very aware she was family. I'm sorry I invaded without giving you notice, but to be honest, I didn't want to give my husband a heads-up. If you knew, it was possible word would leak out and you know what a stubborn ass he can be." She gave Geno a faint hint of a smile.

For the first time, Geno could see doubt in her eyes, as if she was afraid she might not be welcomed in his home.

"I'm glad you came, Francesca. Speaking of Stefano, where is he?" He figured with Francesca there, she would temper Stefano's belligerent attitude.

Francesca looked torn between laughter and tears. "He indulged himself, drinking up your best whiskey. I think he might owe you several bottles. In any case, it took Taviano, Emilio and Enzo to help me get him into bed. I certainly hope he stays there." She smiled at Amaranthe. "Emilio and Enzo are cousins and personal protectors. They can handle him, thank God. They've been doing so for years, long before I came along."

"Taviano returned?" Salvatore asked. "Stefano was adamant he had to leave." He didn't admit that Geno, Lucca and he had sent all the family away.

"He and Nicoletta came to me and explained what had happened. They also told me other things that only Stefano knew, things he found out recently by accident. The three of us talked it over, and we believe you should also have the information. It concerns Taviano, which is why Stefano acted as he did. I'm not making excuses for him, but I do ask that you hear Taviano out."

Geno exchanged a quick look with his brothers and Amaranthe. "Francesca, no one in the family would ever refuse a request you make. Are the children settled for the night?"

"I left the children with my in-laws, Vittorio and Grace, and Giovanni and Sasha. They'll be just fine. There are plenty of people to watch over them. I think Stefano needs me more than they do."

"I think all of us here need you," Geno confirmed. "Before we sit down to talk, do you mind if we change and eat first? We ran into trouble this evening. Someone tried to murder one of our relatives and then me. They were stopped, but it wasn't pleasant."

"Oh, Geno." Francesca looked so distressed that he wished he'd kept the news to himself. He knew Stefano did tell his wife anything she wanted to know, but she didn't ask many questions. "There have been too many attempts on your life. One of these days . . ." She trailed off.

"It won't happen, Francesca," Geno denied. "My brothers and Amara stick to me like glue. I'm beginning to feel like Crispino." He referred to her son.

Instantly, she laughed. "He's a wild thing like you are. I think it's time someone took you in hand." She flashed another smile at Amaranthe. "You're going to have your hands full, not only with Geno, but with these two as well." She gestured affectionately toward Lucca and Salvatore.

Amaranthe nodded. "I've found that out."

"Taviano and Nicoletta are in the kitchen. We've been making dinner in case you hadn't eaten. It should be ready anytime," Francesca added. "I'll meet you there."

Geno watched her go. "I can't believe she risked Stefano's wrath to come. He's going to lose his mind."

"Taviano and Nicoletta accompanied her. And she has her own bodyguards," Lucca pointed out. "Stefano may make a fuss, but he won't really get anywhere. He acts tough with her, but one look from her and he's a goner. Everyone knows it."

Geno took Amaranthe's hand as they started up the stairs to his room. "Don't think that's how it's going to be with us. I'm far tougher than Stefano."

Salvatore spoiled the moment by bursting out laughing. Lucca snorted his utter derision. "No one believes you, Geno," Lucca called after them.

Geno gave his brothers the finger behind his back. It was childish, but the only thing left to him when Amaranthe gave one of her feminine giggles that managed to turn him inside out. He *used* to be tough. He had no idea where that had gone so damned fast.

"Wear something comfortable, Amara." He forestalled her questions the minute they got to the tenth floor.

"She looks like a glamourous movie star."

"She would hate that you think that of her." Geno caught her chin in his palm and tipped her face up to his. "When Stefano met Francesca, she was homeless. She had no money and hadn't eaten in a couple of days. Her friend Joanna had sent her money, and she had gone to Chicago on a bus. She had holes in her shoes, and she had given her coat to a homeless woman on the street because it was freezing. She'd saved some of the money Joanna gave her and rented an apartment. No furniture, but she had a sleeping bag. Francesca may have money now, but she knows what it's like to go without."

"Really? I would never in a million years have guessed that about her."

Geno brushed kisses over her upturned lips. "Stop doubting yourself."

"I'm not." She hesitated. "Not exactly. I do fine most of the time. The Ferraro family is glamorous whether you like to think so or not. They live life in the fast lane. I'm an observer. I live in the shadows, at least I always have, so I'm most comfortable there. I don't want you to ever regret choosing me, Geno. Every one of your sisters-in-law seems to be an amazing, accomplished woman. That's not even mentioning Emmanuelle."

She looked up at him and smiled. The moment she did, his heart began beating overtime. She did that to him so easily.

"And you're not accomplished?"

Amaranthe laughed. The sound alone made him fall deeper in love with her just because she brightened his world and chased away every negative emotion. "Shadow riders are, by definition, in the shadows, Geno. The world can't judge me on my shadow-riding skills."

He found himself smiling back at her, tilting her face up to his, one thumb sweeping over the tempting curve of her bottom lip. "Not your shadow-riding skills, your dancing skills. You pay no attention, but I read every review I could find. I read my mother's notes as well as the other board members'. You're quite famous in your own right. You easily could dance with a prestigious company."

Faint color spread under her skin and her long lashes veiled her dark eyes just for a moment before she lifted her gaze to his again. When she did, his heart nearly stopped beating. She had a way of looking at him as if he were the only man in the world. He was used to people respecting him. Fearing him. Giving him whatever he wanted. But not looking at him as if the sun rose and set with him. She humbled him. He wasn't, by nature, a humble man.

He bent his head to hers slowly. He needed to be slow to take her in. That beautiful face, the features so delicate, a perfect oval, high cheekbones, her large, dark chocolate, very expressive eyes surrounded by thick long lashes. He wanted to absorb her, memorize her, imprint her on his very bones for the rest of his life. He inhaled her scent as her lashes fluttered and lowered over her eyes. Her lips parted slightly. Her breasts rose and fell as he pulled her closer—into him—against his chest. She felt so small, yet perfect, as if she'd been made for him.

"I handed you my heart, Amaranthe." He whispered the admission against the soft curve of her lower lip, barely aloud, barely discernible. "I'm trusting you with whatever I have in the way of a soul."

Her slender arms slid up his chest, fingers locking around the nape of his neck as she gave him her weight. "You're safe with me, Geno. You'll always be safe with me." Her lips brushed along his. Featherlight.

He tasted her unique flavor in his mouth. He drew the

scent of her into his lungs. Then his mouth settled on hers, and flames instantly leapt between them. Roared over them. Through them. Engulfed them. He had no idea how she did that. It wasn't like he hadn't kissed a lot of women, but no one had ever swept him up in pure fire before. Or spun him out of control.

He didn't want to stop, but if they didn't, there would be no stopping. He lifted his head reluctantly, pressing his forehead to hers for a moment just to breathe her in.

"We must go back downstairs and face whatever Francesca and Taviano have to say. I need a clear head when I listen to them."

Amaranthe nodded and slipped from his arms. "My jacket." Amaranthe picked it up from the end of the bed and hugged it to her as if it was a special treasure. "Fiero or Dante remembered. I dropped it on the ground when I dove for the shadow. You said one of them would save it for me, and they did. I forgot all about it until we were on the back porch and the police were questioning Miranda. I didn't see it and felt terrible that I'd lost it before I even had a chance to enjoy it."

She hung it in the closet and stood there for a moment staring at the clothes. "Where did all these come from?" She turned to face him. "Honestly, Geno, do you have a magic wand or something? These weren't here when we left this morning."

He couldn't help smiling at her even as he was stripping off his shirt. If she looked at him like that every time he got her something, he'd be buying her gifts every single day. "We can't be late. I don't want dinner to be cold. Andrea delivered the clothes I ordered for you to the house and the staff put them away."

"Staff?" Her voice sounded a little faint. "You have staff?"

"I don't clean this place on my own. A young widow, Felicia Benson, started a business in our territory to support her three children. Naturally I supported her by using her service to clean the first floor of my home. She did such a stellar job that when she was able to hire more help, I added the second floor and finally the master bedroom. She's been working here for years."

Amaranthe leaned against the doorjamb, her gaze instantly sharp and watchful. "Do you keep track of the help she hires? Anyone coming into your home? Did she clean your parents' home? What about the shops where the others were murdered?"

That was why he was so completely in love with her. She looked like an angel, kissed like sin and that mind of hers never stopped working.

"There's an alert anytime anyone applies for work at any of the businesses in our territories, particularly ones we use or frequent. Our investigators immediately go to work finding out everything they can about them."

She nodded, but still looked thoughtful as she gathered clothes and headed for the shower off the library. Geno would have preferred to have her shower with him, but they never would have made it to dinner. He made up his mind she was staying in his bed with him.

There were no tables set up for their bodyguards. The Ferraros had never been elitists, not when it came to private family. If they were up very late and expected their personal protectors to be as well, they fed them. Geno realized not even Enzo and Emilio were seated in the room, and Francesca treated them as members of the family. The only ones seated at the dining room table were Taviano, Francesca and Nicoletta. Whatever Taviano had to say was extremely confidential.

Amaranthe was dressed in dark purple leggings and a lavender sweater that fell to her knees. Her dark hair was still wet from her shower, but she'd braided it and wound the braid in a crown-like knot on her head. Geno found that fascinating. As a rule, her hair was a little wild and out of control, with the thick mass of curls in direct proportion to the humidity. This was more like her ballet hair or rider hair. Strictly under control. Straitlaced. He slid his palm down her arm until he could thread his fingers through hers. He led her around the table to the chairs directly opposite Taviano and the women. He wanted to be able to catch every expression on his cousin's face when he said whatever it was he had come to say.

Taviano rose at once and gave Amaranthe his charming smile. "I certainly hope this meal ends better than the last two have."

"If it doesn't, we're eloping. The hell with engagement parties," Geno groused.

Lucca and Salvatore had entered behind them, and both laughed, but Geno heard the underlying strain in their voices. They were just as leery as he was. The last two meals hadn't gone well, and they had no idea what to expect. All three of them felt as if they were hanging on to Amaranthe by their fingertips when everything around them was trying to drag her away from them.

"I've never been a fan of long engagements anyway," Lucca said. "Just get it done and over. Get the ring on her finger. Say the vows and you're golden. She can't get away."

"Lucca," Francesca protested. But she was laughing. Shaking her head, her eyes meeting Amaranthe's as if to ask, what could she do?

Amaranthe laughed and sat in the chair Geno pulled out for her. "I'm going to eat fast, Taviano. I didn't get to eat anything this morning, so I'm not making the same mistake this time. Everything smells delicious."

"Don't let her size fool you, Taviano," Salvatore said as Taviano once again sat back down between Nicoletta and Francesca.

Salvatore took the seat on the other side of Amaranthe. Lucca took the chair beside his brother. Both greeted Nicoletta and Francesca with air kisses, simultaneously reaching for the bowl of angel hair pasta.

Amaranthe laughed, the sound one that unraveled some of the knots from Geno's belly.

"Leave some of that for the rest of us," he ordered his brothers.

Francesca's laughter joined Amaranthe's. "Believe me, Geno, I know how those two brothers of yours can put away the food. There's plenty."

"Geno, I owe you an apology. I'm sorry about this morning," Taviano said. "I couldn't speak up when I needed to. I would have avoided a lot of unpleasantness had I been able to do so. This isn't Stefano's fault. The failing is mine."

Nicoletta shook her head. "No, it isn't, Taviano."

He smiled at his wife. "I should have been able to speak about it, but the subject caught me off guard and brought up bad memories I have a difficult time coping with. Once I start down that path, it's very hard to pull myself back. I let all of you down, especially Stefano. Nicoletta and I went to Francesca to ask for her help. She seems to know how best to deal with Stefano when he digs in his heels. He's determined to protect me as if I were still ten years old."

Geno didn't take his gaze from Taviano. His cousin didn't look at him but concentrated on Amaranthe as if he were only speaking to her.

"We called my parents Eloisa and Phillip. We always called them Eloisa and Phillip. I referred to Eloisa as my mama to outsiders, but never to her face unless I wanted to annoy her. She didn't raise us. She didn't come to our room in the middle of the night if we were hungry or scared, even when we were infants. Stefano did. Even when he was just a boy. It was always Stefano. Eloisa detested children, especially her own children. Phillip was worse. They had children because it was expected of them, but they wanted nothing to do with us."

That's so sad, Geno.

But true. Eloisa was the bitch from hell. She made Emme's life a living nightmare. She made all of their lives hell, but it seemed she spewed a lot of venom on Emme.

Taviano glanced at Nicoletta and then Francesca. "Stefano waited for his opportunity to train with the Archambaults in France. He'd been invited numerous times, but he didn't go. He didn't want to leave us alone with the parents."

"They were that bad?" Amaranthe asked, her voice soft. Compassionate.

"You can't imagine how bad," Taviano said. "Stefano oversaw our training because Eloisa was extremely harsh. Especially when it came to Emmanuelle. Riders came from France to work with Stefano, but it wasn't the same as twenty-four hours a day with the various instructors for months on end. We all wanted him to be able to go. We knew he'd sacrificed so much for us. At the same time, the idea of being without him was truly terrifying."

Taviano indicated the bowl of spaghetti sauce. He had already managed to place the angel hair pasta on his plate, and he didn't stint adding a generous serving of the meat and mushroom sauce over it. Nicoletta added two crispy pieces of sourdough garlic bread to his salad plate.

"At the time an Italian family had offered to host me for training. I was nine and certainly old enough to go, but Stefano didn't want me to be gone while he was in France and couldn't reach me. Eloisa insisted. If he went to France, she wanted me out of the house. In the end, he agreed I could go because he had our investigators thoroughly check the family out, and I think he contacted them and threatened them. He told Eloisa I was to come straight back after the month was up, and she agreed. She gave her word."

Geno noted that Nicoletta was once again sitting close to Taviano. She didn't appear as if she had moved at all, yet she had shifted in her chair just enough that she managed to draw his attention. She handed Taviano her plate and he ladled the spaghetti sauce over the pasta.

"Just so you know, Amara," Lucca put in, snagging the basket of fresh bread. "Eloisa never kept her word to her children. She was a stellar rider, but the worst parent on the face of the earth because she didn't give a damn. Not about them as her children. Certainly not about them as riders. That reflected on her."

Geno quickly assessed Taviano's body language. He was uncomfortable, but he was in control, not like earlier at breakfast. Still, he loved his cousin. "Taviano, if this is difficult and too personal for you to tell all of us, we could go somewhere private . . ." he offered.

Amaranthe immediately put down her fork and nodded her compliance. "I have no problems giving you privacy, Taviano."

"It's easier telling you, Amaranthe," Taviano said. "You didn't know Eloisa and I can just talk it through with you naturally. If I don't talk about this, I'm just like everyone else. Sweeping it under the carpet so to speak. Letting them make me feel ashamed. That it was my fault. Francesca and Nicoletta are right. Stefano is taking this on himself. He just found out because I hid it from him for years. I shouldn't have. I kept what happened in my past a secret because Eloisa and Phillip were determined to make me feel shame."

This is making me very uneasy, Salvatore said to Geno. *I trained with that same family in Italy. They were a good family. I'm younger than Taviano and went there after he did, but I had the same instructors, didn't I? They were strict, but not nearly as strict as the Archambaults.*

Yes, Geno replied. His mind wasn't going to strict or cruel. Taviano had all the signs of a PTSD episode earlier that morning. Having been trained by the strictest of the Archambaults wouldn't have caused him to have been thrown into post-traumatic stress disorder.

"I enjoyed my time in Italy with the family there, but when it was time for them to send me home, Eloisa had made arrangements for me to go for further instructions with Jaspar and Beau Boutler, the remaining two riders from a family in Queensland. The family in Italy protested. I overheard them telling Eloisa no one sent trainees to the Boutler family, but she wouldn't listen to them."

Slowly, and very carefully, Geno placed his fork and knife on his plate, bile suddenly rising. He had some expectations of what Taviano might be about to share. All along he had seen this coming, but with the knowledge suddenly blossoming in his brain, his mind wanted to reject the images crowding in. He couldn't imagine how Stefano felt if Geno was feeling guilty and angry. He had no idea how he stayed in his chair when he needed to leap up and pace to remove the adrenaline flooding every cell in his body.

Amaranthe laid one hand on his thigh very gently. *You have to breathe, to be calm so he can continue. Do it for him, Geno. The walls are beginning to expand, and the room temperature is rising.*

She was right. He knew she was. She was the voice of reason—his breath of fresh air. Deliberately he concentrated on her. He couldn't look at his two younger brothers. If this had happened to either one of them, he would have gone insane. No one would have been safe. He would have turned into the ultimate predator and to hell with the consequences.

How could he possibly blame Stefano for wanting to protect Taviano? He would move heaven and earth to protect Salvatore and Lucca. Little beads of sweat formed on his body, and he had to force himself to breathe and remain calm, to keep his expression blank just in case Taviano looked up at him. So far, his cousin kept his attention fixed solely on Amaranthe.

She was soothing. Peaceful. He felt that in her. Francesca gave off that same inner calm. Both women seemed to be able to share that calming trait with those in the room, surrounding them with such tranquility it helped to level out the emotions despite the things Taviano was revealing. Geno realized what an asset Francesca had been to Stefano and what Amaranthe would be for a man like him. What was he giving her of equal value in return? What did any man give his woman that was of equal value?

Geno. Just his name. Breathless. Loving. The way she

whispered it to him. As if he was her everything, the way she was to him.

"The two men, Jaspar and Beau, picked me up at the airport and drove me to their home in the middle of nowhere. I had no means of communicating with my family. Eloisa told me I had to be with them for three months. Stefano had no idea I was there. I was cut off from the world and terrified. The men were in their late forties, and the moment I saw them, every instinct I had for self-preservation kicked in. I wanted to turn around and get back on the plane."

"Taviano," Geno cautioned. "You don't have to continue if this is too difficult."

For the first time, Taviano met his gaze fully. "Men never want to admit they were molested, Geno. Sometimes, as in my case, their fathers don't want them in their family. The things those men did to me for those three months were horrendous. On top of that, I was terrified they were going to kill me. They certainly threatened me with death if I dared to tell anyone. I turned ten when I was with them. It was one of the worst days of my life."

There was a stunned silence. Salvatore and Lucca had put down their forks and just sat frozen at the table as if unable to process the things Taviano was telling them.

"When I was able to go home, the moment Eloisa came to get me, I did tell her." For the first time, Taviano's voice changed. A note of bitterness crept in. "She had no sympathy for me. If anything, she was appalled that I hadn't been able to stop them. She didn't touch me and in fact told me to stop crying. It was a very silent plane ride home. I wasn't to talk to Stefano if he called. She had to speak to Phillip before she made any decisions."

"My God," Lucca burst out. "I knew Eloisa was a cold, unfeeling, heartless bitch, but seriously?"

"Lucca, honey, that isn't helping," Francesca said gently.

"I'm hearing this for the first time," Lucca reminded, pressing his fingertips to his eyes. "I love my cousin. I want to go find these people and rip them to shreds. I can imagine how Stefano feels. Taviano. Man. I'm so sorry. Had I known, I would have done my best to be there for you."

Nicoletta's smile was gentle. "I love that he has all of you." She switched her attention to Amaranthe. "I didn't understand family until I allowed myself to believe in the Ferraro family. Like Taviano, I was a victim of rape. Stefano and Taviano saved my life and, really, my sanity. I didn't trust anyone, and I detested myself. They were very patient with me."

Her smile included Geno, Salvatore and Lucca. "It took a very long time before I was nice to anyone including Geno, maybe especially Geno, because he scared me, and he was here in New York. I associate New York with everything bad, but it was his family that persuaded Stefano and Taviano to come get me."

Geno knew Nicoletta was diverting attention from Lucca and Salvatore, giving them time to process the things Taviano had revealed. She was also reassuring Amaranthe that the Ferraro family may have had a fight, but they were well worth the time and trouble in the end. Women. They were extraordinary.

"Phillip was so disgusted with me that he didn't want me in his sight," Taviano continued. "He threatened to leave Eloisa, to divorce her, if she didn't send me away."

Geno was shocked. Truly shocked. He had never liked Phillip Ferraro. He certainly hadn't respected him, but it had never occurred to him that he would turn his back on his own son.

"Eloisa convinced him to stay if he didn't ever have to deal with me. She promised Stefano would never be told, there would be no counselling, and no one would ever know. Then she threatened to send me away where no one would ever find me if I said one word to anyone. Phillip never looked at me or spoke to me again. I stayed out of their way and could barely bring myself to speak to Stefano. He knew something was wrong, but he couldn't find out what. I wasn't going to risk getting totally banned from my own family."

Another silence ensued. Taviano ate his spaghetti calmly. Geno glanced at Francesca. She looked as if she might cry, but she managed to find her meal very interesting. His brothers took their cue from her and ate as well. For him, the usually delicious food tasted like cardboard. If Eloisa had been alive, he might have hunted her down and strangled her.

"What happened to the two men?" Amaranthe asked. "Surely your mother at least asked the Archambaults to investigate."

"I heard her tell Phillip she was going to, but he forbade her. He didn't want anyone to know that his son had allowed men to play with him and use him as a toy."

Geno felt rather than heard Amaranthe's swift intake of breath. She dropped her hand to his thigh and pressed her fingers deep into his muscle.

His parents really were the worst.

Yes. I despised them. Now I know I had very good reason, even more than I thought I had.

"A while ago we were having a family meeting regarding Nicoletta's abilities as a shadow rider. The LA cousins were present as was Eloisa," Taviano continued. "Something happened, and for the first time in years, I suffered a post-traumatic stress episode. It was very severe. Nicoletta cleared the room and took care of it. Everyone left, other than Stefano. That was when he found out. He was devastated and he wanted to kill Eloisa. Phillip was already dead, or I think he might have killed him. He blamed himself for going to France. He's been fairly raw ever since."

"I can understand," Geno said.

"He didn't share, not even with me," Francesca said. "He wouldn't. He feels only Taviano has the right to share."

Geno understood what she was trying to convey to him. "Naturally Stefano believes that only Taviano can give permission to share his personal story." He needed to breathe.

Go outside and breathe fresh air. Instead, he persisted in gathering information. "What happened to the Boutler brothers?"

"I believed that Eloisa killed them. A few months later, I overheard her telling Phillip they were found dead. He was angry and demanded to know if she went behind his back and had the Archambault family investigate, and she denied it. I took that to mean she killed them. I told Stefano she did. I thought that might make him less angry with her. I didn't want him to end up in jail, stripped of his rider status, or worse, have the Archambaults sentence him to death, all of which could happen if he took matters into his own hands."

"Do you think Eloisa really killed them?" Geno asked.

Taviano rubbed his forehead as if it would help him to remember. "I did when I was a kid, but then I wanted to think she would do something like that for me. Just one thing. Now, I'm not so certain. I don't remember her taking any trips abroad. The more I've thought about it, the more I doubt that she would have bothered."

"We know for certain Stefano didn't kill them because he didn't know anything about what happened to you until recently," Francesca pointed out.

"And it wasn't the Archambaults because no one informed them," Amaranthe murmured, her tone thoughtful.

"I don't see how what happened to Taviano eighteen years ago could be connected to the murders now," Nicoletta said. "That makes no sense at all."

CHAPTER THIRTEEN

Whoever is committing these murders hates the Ferraro family," Geno said. "That's without a doubt. That man tonight looked at me with concentrated venom in his eyes. I'd never seen anything like it. They wanted Stefano dead. They were determined to kill him. They made it clear they wanted to wipe out every member of our family, even the children. They want us gone from the face of the earth. Every last one of us."

There was another silence. Geno found himself watching Amaranthe as she twirled her spaghetti around her fork. She ate her food with enjoyment, although she was refined about it. He recalled trying to teach his brothers table manners, stressing how important they were. He didn't like the Archambaults' way of instructing his brothers, but he knew manners would be essential. All the little refinements that they would need to fit in and be able to maneuver with ease in whichever circles they traveled.

"Do you believe these murders are connected to those despicable Boutler brothers, Geno?" Francesca asked.

"If so," Nicoletta continued, "how?"

"Eighteen years ago, my mother woke me and took me to their suite." Geno told the others in detail everything he remembered about the night his father had turned over leadership to him. "There were several shadow riders in the suite, but they hid their identities from me. At the time, with my father's blood everywhere and both parents acting so strange, the priest and surgeon acting as if my father was going to die, I didn't give it much thought. I had time to go over the details later. I don't forget details. They stay in my mind."

Amaranthe turned her face up to his. *You're frowning, Geno.*

He wasn't. He made every effort to keep his expression a blank mask. "It took me a very long time to sort out that there were many riders in that room that night hiding in the shadows. The car they claimed was in an accident was perfectly fine. I saw it. Later, it was damaged. My parents didn't care that I knew they were lying to me. They withdrew not only from us"—he indicated his brothers—"but essentially from everyone they really knew and cared about."

Amaranthe rubbed her palm soothingly along his thigh with one hand while she continued to eat as if she weren't aware he was in any way agitated. He knew he didn't appear so on the outside. He'd cultivated that calm look even when he raged inside. The mere mention of his parents could make him rage.

"They changed radically, became cold and distant. They wanted nothing at all to do with us. They went from loving parents to strangers overnight. If I didn't know better, I'd think aliens took over their bodies." He glanced at Salvatore, for the first time looking uncomfortable. "As time went by, I accepted that they weren't coming back to us, but I resented the way they treated Lucca and Salvatore. Salvatore is the youngest, and he didn't give up the way I did. Lucca had backed off as well, but Salvatore would seek them out. They made it clear they didn't want him around."

He didn't try to hide the grim loathing he felt for his parents. It was there in his voice. He'd disassociated from them. They'd hurt his brothers. That cut deep and wasn't something he could repair no matter how hard he'd tried.

"I went to them and told them as head of the family if they ever spoke to Salvatore or Lucca in such a manner again, if they hurt them like that, I would banish them. I meant it, too. I let them see I meant it, that my feelings for them were gone. I just turned and walked out. I didn't want their explanations even if they were going to give them to me, although I knew they wouldn't."

He didn't look at his brothers. He couldn't. He dropped one hand under the table to thread his fingers through Amaranthe's. He'd just confessed one of his gravest sins. He'd turned on his own parents. Now they were dead. Murdered. He'd move heaven and earth to find their killers and get justice for them, but he wasn't certain he could ever forgive them.

Salvatore cleared his throat. "I knew you threatened them."

Geno's gaze jumped to his brother's face. "You did not."

Salvatore nodded slowly. "I did. Geno, I followed you everywhere. I was terrified of losing you. We both were. And you were so pissed that day. I shadowed you to their suite. You didn't even knock. You just walked right in, and you didn't close the door."

He lifted his head and grinned at his cousins. "Geno seriously pissed is a thing of beauty. Scary as hell but still beautiful, especially when he's standing up for you. I realized for the first time that I may have lost my parents, but I had Geno and Lucca. Geno was going to be there for me no matter what. He didn't care if he had to go up against an adult. He took on our instructors and he took on our parents. I think that was the first day I began to feel I might be safe again."

Geno's gut clenched hard. He thought Salvatore would be angry at him. Salvatore, as a boy, had been very sensitive.

He had wanted his parents to love him. He'd needed that even more than Lucca and Geno. Both Geno and Lucca had been very protective of him, especially when their parents had been unbelievably cruel in the things they'd said to turn him away from them. The way his parents had deserted his brothers had only made Geno even more determined to watch over them and to create loyalty that would never be broken among the three of them.

"I suppose you knew as well, Lucca." He made it a statement, keeping his voice low, pretending he might be annoyed, when really, he was overwhelmed with emotion.

I blame you, he told Amaranthe.

She rubbed her head against his arm like a little cat, satisfaction sliding into his mind.

"Naturally." Lucca sounded smug. "Salvatore and I had to stick together in those days to figure out what the hell was going on. Those Archambault trainers were mean. The parents were zombies, and you were scary as hell. You didn't tell us what was going on."

"Because I didn't know."

"Yeah, we weren't aware you were as clueless as we were until we heard you talking to the parents."

Do they always refer to your mother and father as "the parents"? Because that's an odd way to put it. Amaranthe indicated the grilled vegetables. "Please pass the vegetables. If I don't take some now, Lucca's going to eat them all."

Her voice was very soft and tranquil in the midst of the overwhelming emotion. Lucca and Salvatore might be trying to make everyone laugh, but the reality was, it was a painful time. Their parents had slammed the door hard on them, rejecting them, and not one of them knew why.

In the years that followed, there had been many opportunities for Margo and Eugene Ferraro to tell their sons, to interact with them, to do something, anything at all to show them the family mattered to them, but they never so much as inquired about injuries sustained.

Geno had held the three of them together and proved

over and over he could be relied on. Lucca and Salvatore developed an unswerving loyalty to their brother. Geno loved them fiercely, protectively. He had made it clear he was willing to lay down his life for them. His opinion of his parents was something altogether different.

He knew the others at the table, no matter how his brothers tried to cover for him, had heard the bitter, unrelenting animosity he held for his parents.

He glanced across the table at Stefano's wife before reaching for the basket of bread. "Francesca, did you make this bread? It's really very good."

"Nicoletta did."

Lucca and Salvatore immediately stared in shock at Taviano's wife. Lucca arched an eyebrow. "You bake, too? I'm beginning to feel I need to be actively hunting for a wife."

Francesca burst out laughing, dispelling some of the heaviest of the tension in the room. "*Hunting*, Lucca? Women aren't prey to be hunted."

"Essentially, Francesca, they are," he disputed, reaching for the grilled vegetables. "You never know when you're going to come across the right one. Look at Geno with the teeny-tiny ballerina there. She wasn't easy to bag."

"*Bag?* Geno *bagged* me?" Amaranthe gave Lucca her fiercest scowl. "And stop calling me teeny-tiny."

Lucca responded with a grin. "You do look cute when you try to look mean. Geno's going to have a difficult time taming you."

"*Taming* me. Lucca, you're in grave danger of getting your ass kicked." Amaranthe narrowed her eyes at him.

"She could do it, too," Salvatore warned. "You saw the way she moved. She saved Stefano's life. I was right behind her, but I never saw anyone move that fast."

"Saved his life?" Francesca echoed. "There was a vague reference to an attack on Stefano before. What exactly happened?" She lifted her long lashes and looked around the table.

There was a long silence. Her gaze locked on Geno. He

knew it was inevitable that she would look to him for answers. Just as Stefano was head of the Chicago family, he was head of the New York family.

"Francesca." He used his most gentle, cautionary tone. "These explanations generally come from Stefano."

She laid her knife and fork carefully on the edge of the plate. "I know all of you think I'm very fragile and need protection because Stefano is so protective of me, and he demands everyone else give me that same consideration. It isn't true. I'm extremely strong. Do you know the real reason I insisted on having children? I know what all of you thought, that I was being stubborn and wanted my way."

"Francesca." Taviano was the one to protest.

"It's true," she said. "But I consulted with more than one doctor. They told me there was no real reason why I couldn't carry. Stefano wants children. He wants a big family. I'm his wife. I know him so well. He can try to say it doesn't matter to him, but I know it does. I know that has always been one of his big dreams and not because he's a shadow rider. He needs childhood to be different for his children. It took me a little while to give up working outside the home and understand that his need of me being there was more important. Once I could see what Stefano really needed, I wanted to give him everything I could to make him happy. He gives me everything. His every thought is for me."

"You're his entire world, Francesca," Geno said. "He couldn't bear it if something happened to you. He would never trade your life for children. You could still have children using a surrogate. Didn't you discuss that with him?" He tried to be careful, to choose his words, knowing she had lost one child full-term. He didn't want her to think he was blaming her. Stefano had explained the circumstances when he'd asked just a day or so earlier, and the baby had died just before birth. Francesca had nothing to do with it, but she would never see it that way.

She inclined her head. "We did discuss using a surrogate. But *I* wanted to give him the gift of children, and the doctors assured me there was no reason I couldn't carry. It's important to me to be the one to give Stefano the things that make him happy. I also had this idea of eventually being a surrogate myself for Grace."

She ducked her head. "Intellectually, I know the loss of our little girl wasn't my fault, the doctor reiterated over and over that it wasn't, but I couldn't help but feel I failed Stefano again. I lost several babies. I know I can't provide his children for him and that guts me."

Once again, she lifted her lashes and to Geno's horror tears swam in her eyes. "Honey," he said softly. "You give Stefano everything he needs."

She shook her head. "I don't. I want to, Geno, but I can't. It's so hard to know that I can't. You can't imagine what it feels like to love someone the way I do Stefano and know I can't give him the thing he wants most."

Geno didn't want to give her platitudes, not when it was clear she hurt the way she did. And he needed to learn from her. He had Amaranthe in his life. He was used to dictating, to getting his way. Amaranthe might have a steel spine, but she was soft inside like Francesca.

"The point I'm making in my roundabout way is I love my husband. I'm asking what happened, and I expect you to answer me. I'm not weak, Geno. Before I was with Stefano, I lost my parents, my sister was murdered, and I was homeless. I survived even though a madman tried to destroy me. After being with Stefano, we lost several babies. The adjustments to his lifestyle have been difficult as well. But I'm here. Still standing. Still loving that man. Again, as your sister, someone you love and respect, I'm asking what happened to my husband, and I expect you to answer me."

Her eyes were steady on his. Geno did respect her. He admired her. There was no getting around it. He lifted his gaze to Taviano. His cousin looked sympathetic but didn't offer to tell Francesca about the near miss on Stefano's life. They were going to leave that to him.

"You do know Stefano already wants to beat the crap

out of me, Francesca," he said, sitting back in his chair, regarding her steadily.

"That's exactly why I flew here, Geno." Francesca gave him her wide-eyed, innocent, sweet, serene look. "To save the two of you from being idiots. Neither of you would win that fight."

Lucca made a sound that could have been laughter but was hastily choked off when Geno's cold gaze slid over him.

"Probably not," he conceded to Francesca. It was the truth. They would have both been beat all to hell, but there would have been satisfaction in the physical combat for both. They needed that outlet. Now, with more understanding of the situation, Geno might still feel rage, but the emotion wasn't directed at his cousin. He didn't blame Stefano for his reaction as much. The sense of betrayal wasn't quite so acute.

"I'll protect you from the snarling wolf. He gets his way in most things," Francesca admitted. "Because most of the time it doesn't matter to me. This does. I'll be making that very clear to him. He'll understand."

There wasn't a single person at the table that didn't believe her, including Geno. Francesca was that sweet person, the heart of the family, but when she decided on having her way, she apparently refused to back down.

Geno gave into the inevitable. He didn't sugarcoat the details. He told her exactly what happened at the engagement party. Francesca didn't interrupt him, but several times her gaze shifted to Amaranthe and then Salvatore. When it came to the part where Geno took the poisonous blade, her face paled and her eyes went wide, but she remained silent.

When he finished, the silence lasted for some time. Nicoletta and Taviano began to clear the table. Salvatore helped.

Francesca finally met Amaranthe's eyes. "Thank you. Sincerely. Thank you. Stefano is my entire world. I don't know what I'd do without him."

"Geno made it sound like I saved him by myself. I had plenty of help. Salvatore would have gotten to him, and Geno was right there. But I'm grateful I was able to keep the assassin from harming Stefano," Amaranthe assured.

"I didn't really have the full picture of what was happening," Francesca continued. "Stefano did tell me that there was a series of murders here in New York and some of the victims were related to you, Geno, and to all of us. I didn't know them, but I felt terrible for you. Then your parents were killed. Of course, Stefano came to help. But I didn't realize there was an immediate threat."

"None of this explains how something that took place eighteen years ago with our parents," Lucca said, "and what Taviano experienced eighteen years ago could have any bearing on these murders. Or why these people despise the Ferraro family. How could they possibly be connected?"

"If Eloisa did kill the Boutler brothers, why wait eighteen years to strike back?" Geno asked. "And why go after my family first and not Stefano's?"

"But they didn't go after your family first," Amaranthe said. "I first came across them when I was sent to Croatia to investigate rumors involving shadow riders there. The Maric family covered a large territory and things were going wrong. In the end, both parents were murdered. The parents hadn't been riders in years. Strangely, they had abdicated when their son was very young, forcing him to take over as head of his family and head of the shadow riders in Croatia, just like Geno had to do here in New York. I don't know the precise timing of when they stepped down, but they did step down to become greeters. They hadn't suffered injuries, and they were needed as riders, but they refused to continue."

Geno frowned down at her. "You told me that you'd investigated the riders in Croatia, but you didn't go into detail. I had no idea the parents had stepped down years ago, Amara. Could it have been eighteen years ago? This can't be a coincidence. You did say you felt those riders were in danger. You included that in your report to the council. Why did you think they were?"

"I felt they were being stalked right after their parents were murdered. I had a strong feeling the murderers planned to return at some point even though I knew the immediate threat had moved to New York."

"That sheds an entirely different light on things, doesn't it," Salvatore said, once again seating himself at the table. "I sent word to Lanz and Deangelo to check into when the Maric riders stepped down and left their son to take on their responsibilities."

"But it still doesn't make sense," Nicoletta protested. "Why now? Why New York and not Chicago? And, I'm sorry, but I would bet my last dollar that Eloisa wasn't the one that sought out justice for Taviano. She would have been too afraid of losing Phillip, which meant she would have no longer been able to be a shadow rider."

"She could have gone on her own and killed them," Taviano said.

"You know she didn't." Nicoletta's voice softened. "You said yourself you don't remember her taking any trips. Stefano would have gone after them, but not Eloisa. For your sake, I wish it had been her, but I don't think it was and neither do you. So these people have no reason to go after your family, Taviano, if the death of the Boutlers were the catalyst."

"I don't see how it could have been," Lucca protested. "Why wait eighteen years? And certainly our parents didn't know about what happened to Taviano. I doubt the Marics in Croatia knew about the attack on him. They didn't avenge him. How could this all be related?"

"Well, we don't know much more about the why," Francesca said. "But I'm with Geno. I don't believe this is coincidence. How could it be with so many similarities?"

Amaranthe twisted the crystal water glass back and forth in her hand. "I think it would be a very good idea to have the investigators research whether any other riders turned over their territories to their children eighteen years ago. Also, find out what happened to the other members of the Boutler family. Did they die out? Did they abandon Queensland as they grew up and simply moved away? Most families remain as shadow riders. Were they female and moved to be with their husbands? I think it would be a good idea to locate any remaining relatives and see where they are now and why they left."

Geno agreed. He texted his investigators immediately. "I'll ask Elie to put Brielle on it as well. She's fast and thorough."

"We'll get our investigators on it, too," Taviano said. He was texting.

"In any case, I'll be going to work the day after tomorrow, and I imagine we won't have to wait long for these people to make their attempt for me," Amaranthe said. "I also have rehearsals for the performance that's coming up very fast. That same evening. So they'll have plenty of time to figure out when and where they want to strike."

It took discipline for Geno to sit quietly and not dictate an implacable denial. He saw it in his brothers' eyes. Like him, they were not willing to risk her. Amaranthe appeared serene, but he knew damn well she was aware she'd just thrown a stick of dynamite into the middle of the table.

"Is that wise, Amara?" Francesca asked. "Aren't you setting yourself up so these horrid people can murder you?"

Amaranthe smiled at her. "We must go about our lives as if we aren't on to them. They know we are, but they don't know how much we know. It's like a game of chess."

"It isn't a game when your life is at stake, Danzatrice Ombra," Geno objected. "You're the one who told me that. We don't know who these people are or how many of them are out there."

The moment he objected, Geno felt Amaranthe withdraw from him. She shut down. There was no change in her outer expression. She didn't remove her hand from his thigh, but she wasn't in his mind. She simply sat at the table looking as sweet as ever, but he knew he'd just blown it—and he knew why.

He wanted her to accept him for who he was. He'd laid that out for her, but was he doing the same for her? She had his back right down the line, in front of everyone, making it known she stood with him, but had he done the same? He hadn't because he wanted to wrap her up in a cocoon and ensure she was safe. As far as he was concerned, he would be happy to keep her in a locked safe room until the crisis was over—but Francesca had made a very important point. He'd be a first-class idiot if he didn't pay attention.

Amaranthe was not Francesca. She wasn't Grace. She was an elite shadow rider. She went out on her own for months investigating other shadow riders, including Archambaults. He had to give her the respect she was due. He was thinking of his needs, not hers. Their relationship was going to be all about walking a fine-edged sword.

He slipped his arm around her shoulders. "Amaranthe is not only a superb shadow rider, she's one of the fastest I've ever seen. She knows what she's doing. As much as I want to put her in a safe house, that's not our dynamic. We're partners. We'll come up with a plan for her extra vigilance."

He leaned down and brushed the top of her head with his lips, forcing his heart to stay at a steady beat. "No doubt, she's one step ahead of me and has already come up with something brilliant. I'm still back at the protecting-my-woman-by-being-a-caveman stage."

"Right there with you, Geno," Lucca said, his tone filled with censure. "Caveman sounds good to me. For a teeny-tiny little thing, Amara, you are one giant package of trouble. You are going to be a pain in the ass."

Amaranthe smiled at Lucca, her entire face lighting up. "I'm so pleased you finally see the reality of the situation, my brother. Sisters are supposed to be a pain in the ass."

Lucca covered his face with his hands. "Do you have to

sound so damned happy about it? You sound just like Emmanuelle. She's the epitome of a pain in the ass."

"She's much quieter than Emme," Geno said.

Lucca pulled his hands down and glared at his brother. "Do you think that makes it any better? It doesn't. She just sits there looking all sweet and little and delicate. That's deceptive as hell. She's really like some copperhead, about to strike and you won't even see it coming until it's too late."

"Lucca," Francesca objected. "You just implied she's a snake."

"I didn't imply," Lucca denied. "I full-on accused her. The woman has venom."

Amaranthe laughed. "At least he's beginning to understand me, Francesca."

Thank you, Geno. I know that was very difficult for you.

That soft voice got to him, turned his heart over, told him he'd done the right thing.

You have no idea. She would never know what it cost him to stand with her in front of his family, knowing she was going to be a target for killers. The idea went against his nature. He would have to do everything in his power to make certain she was safe. She'd just have to live with that side of him.

Her palm slid along his thigh muscle in a soothing caress. "Lucca, I really hope the woman you find is going to be fierce. She'll need to be."

"Don't wish that on me."

Salvatore, I'm counting on you to help me protect her. Geno didn't look at his brother. He was certain Salvatore had received the same training as Amaranthe had and that he sometimes worked for the International Council. Maybe not often, but he did it. Geno had seen him move. He would count on him to protect Amaranthe.

As if she could read minds, Nicoletta volunteered. "Taviano and I aren't scheduled to work the next few days. I can go everywhere with you, Amara, and stay in the shadows. No one knows we're here."

"We've got a couple of our best scientists working on a remedy to make us immune to the poison, but they've just started," Geno said. "Those people took their time developing these weapons to get through the shadows. And the compound for the poison is complex."

"Emmanuelle and Giovanni excel in working with chemicals. Don't you remember Emme blowing things up all the time?" Taviano asked. "The moment she managed to get a tiny bit of that poison, she called Gee, and the two of them have been locked up together breaking it down. I'm betting on them."

"In the meantime, it's extraordinarily dangerous. I should know," Geno said. "I'm a big man, and it nearly killed me. Nicoletta and Amara are both small. The woman the assassin murdered on Miranda's back porch weighed more than either of them. Had he not stabbed in her in the heart, she would have died from the poison anyway. It's a very lethal toxin."

"Nevertheless, Geno," Nicoletta said, "Amaranthe is family. You're family. We stick together no matter what."

Taviano nodded. "That's why Stefano stayed when he sent the rest of us home. He knew he didn't handle things very well. What he'd learned about the past was still too raw. He stayed to make things right with you."

"I know," Geno agreed. "But risking Nicoletta when we have so few . . ."

"Don't start with the woman thing," Nicoletta interrupted. "All of us are needed on this. I'm not willing to lose you or Salvatore or Lucca, certainly not Amaranthe. Especially since she clearly can drive Lucca crazy. That's a bonus right there."

Lucca groaned. "You have to keep Nicoletta away from Emme, Taviano. Already, she's rubbing off on her."

Taviano burst out laughing. "That isn't going to happen, and you know it. Emme's too much fun."

"Valentino was supposed to tame her."

Amaranthe rolled her eyes. "You persist in thinking women need to be tamed. That's where you go wrong, Lucca. Has he always been so bullheaded, Geno?"

"He gets worse," Salvatore volunteered. "He has anti-quated ideas about women."

Amaranthe looked up at Geno. "I wonder where he got those ideas."

Another round of laughter, and Francesca pushed back as if she were going to excuse herself.

Geno shook his head slightly. "Don't go yet, Francesca. I'd like to revisit a couple of the things you brought up if you don't mind. I think it's important."

Beneath the table he wrapped his fingers around Amaranthe's wrist, sliding his thumb along the back of her hand in long caresses.

Francesca subsided immediately, her large eyes fixing on his. "What is it, Geno?"

"You know I'm not like Stefano. I'm not smooth or sophisticated when it comes to saying the right things, especially to a woman. I'm going to give this my best shot because there isn't another woman who has helped me more when it comes to learning about relationships."

He hesitated. "It's far more than that, Francesca. I'm going to make an ass out of myself, but some things need to be said. I love you. Feel like a damn fool saying it right out loud in front of everyone, but I don't love that many people."

Tears glittered in Francesca's eyes, and she gave Geno a watery smile.

He held up his hand before she could speak. "You need to let me try to get this out. Men think very differently from women. You obviously don't view yourself the way we see you. Or at least the way I see you or Stefano does. I know how he thinks and feels about you because, for one, he tells me, and we're both men. I can see it every time he looks at you."

Geno looked down at Amaranthe. "You give to all of us, Francesca. Just tonight, I would have made so many big mistakes in my relationship with Amara that would have hurt her. The last thing I ever want to do is hurt the woman I love. And it would cost us valuable time in our relationship when we need to be completely in sync to survive. You did that for me. Gave me guidance when I needed it most. You do it all the time."

Francesca shook her head to deny what he said.

"You do," Salvatore confirmed. Lucca echoed him.

Taviano and Nicoletta added their endorsement to their New York cousins.

"Why do you think I went to you, Francesca?" Taviano asked. "I trusted you to give me good advice, and you immediately came up with the right answer. We flew here together and told Geno everything. We're sorting it out, thanks to you."

"You're the heart of the family," Geno continued. "You think you don't have worth because you can't carry babies in your body for Stefano. I'm a man. I can tell you, Stefano has never even considered that you would think that way. He doesn't think that way. The thought would never enter his mind, and he would be horrified that it has ever entered yours. His entire world is Francesca Ferraro. Keeping you healthy, happy and safe is what he focuses on. Not having children, Francesca. You. He focuses on you. How do I know? Because I would never think about having children over Amaranthe. Not one time. You have to trust me on this."

"But . . ." Francesca started to protest.

Geno stopped her again by holding up his hand. "You're not really listening, honey, which isn't like you. You need to hear me because what I'm saying is the absolute truth. Just for one moment, don't have rebuttals in your head. Just listen to me. I'm telling you how men think. How Stefano thinks. Stefano wouldn't trade you for one child. Not one. He wouldn't consider it, and he'd never regret his choice."

He brought Amaranthe's hand from under the table and pressed her palm against his chest over his heart. "I never once, not for a single moment, believed I would find a woman who could accept me, let alone love me. I thought I'd either have to marry someone who would never care for me but would have my children, or I'd be alone for the rest of my life. I knew I would choose to be alone. Stefano felt the same way. He didn't believe a woman could ever love him. Then you came along, Francesca. You, with your compassionate heart and your kindness and your wisdom and patience. You were willing to take all of us on. We're all fucked up, but that doesn't seem to matter to you. No matter how bad it gets, you stand with us."

Francesca brushed at the tears on her face. "You aren't fucked up."

"Honey." He gave her the endearment softly. "I'm making a point here that you need to think about and then discuss with Stefano. He doesn't give a damn about anything but you. Tell him how you feel, why carrying his babies yourself was so important, because he clearly doesn't get that. I wouldn't. He'll think you're crazy, but he'll love you all the more for it. He'll also reassure you in ways I can't that it doesn't matter to him. The gift of you, of having you and you loving him, is more than enough. Just do this for me, Francesca. I swear I'm right about this. I hate that you're hurting, and you don't realize how important and loved you are."

Francesca stood and came round the table to circle his neck and lean into him. "I'll talk to him, Geno. Thank you. I love you so much." She kissed his cheek and then bent down to do the same to Amaranthe. "Good night, everyone."

CHAPTER FOURTEEN

Clouds trailed across the moon when Geno woke. He hadn't lowered the privacy screen yet. He was used to waking several times at night. He often walked outside on the balcony overlooking the river just to breathe in the air. Now when he took a deep breath, it was Amaranthe he breathed into his lungs. The scent of her. That subtle, unique fragrance he had to be close to smell.

He lay in bed, feeling her body next to him. That delicate feminine form. Women had soft, beautiful bodies shaped so differently from men. Amaranthe had braided her hair in a loose weave and the braid lay curled against the dark pillowcase spotlighted by the moon peeking out of the drifting clouds. Because she had thick hair, it was still a little damp from her shower earlier, before dinner. He loved the fact that her hair could be all curls and what she considered frizz when she didn't tame it. He didn't want her taming it. But then, when she was all prim and proper for her dancing, he had to admit he loved that look as well.

He had looked up every single video on YouTube he

could find of her performances. He'd been shocked at how many there were. When he first had woken from his poisoned state and the doctor hadn't allowed him to do much but lie in his bed, his body responding sluggishly to the commands of his brain, he had used that time to watch her dance. She had stolen his breath—then his heart.

When she moved across the stage in her costumes, completely consumed by whatever character she played, she seemed an ethereal creature from another dimension. Watching her perform, he couldn't imagine her as an assassin, stalking her prey through the shadows. She was too beautiful, far too delicate and alluring. One of the things that struck him is reviews repeatedly said her performances could bring tears to those watching her every time. She was exquisite in whatever role she was given.

Amaranthe lay on her side, so slight she took up little room in his bed, barely there, yet dominating the space. She wore a silk crop top with a pair of little boy shorts he was certain she didn't need. The clothes were more for her modesty than anything else. He found the way she was such a mixture of pure confidence—his fierce warrior and beautiful dancer—and introverted woman fascinating. But then, he found everything about her captivating.

He bent his head close to her bare skin to draw her into his lungs with every breath. His heart stuttered. Accelerated. Began to race. He needed to take time to commit every single inch of her to skin-to-skin contact, to imprint her on the pads of his fingers and know her on his lips. Already he could taste her in his mouth. She had set up an addiction with that first kiss. Who knew, when he had been with so many other women, that one taste of Amaranthe would wipe out every other woman who had come before? He couldn't remember a single one.

He craved her. Every inch of her. He wanted a slow burn, not a roaring fire. Eventually, that would come. How could it not when she sent flames rushing through his veins like a wildfire? His cock hardened into an unrelenting ache, reminding him he was alive and with the woman he not only loved but desired. This slow exploration was perfection.

Geno pushed the back of her silk crop top up to her shoulders to reveal her spine. He used the tips of his fingers, going very slowly, much like opening a gift, because that was what she was to him. She had such a beautiful, feminine line. He brushed the pads of his fingers very lightly, seductively, from her shoulder to the curve of her buttocks, following her spine, deliberately awakening every nerve ending he could.

She moved. Her eyelashes fluttered. Lifted. Her legs shifted restlessly. "Geno." There was an ache in the way she whispered his name.

"Lie still for me, *la mia danzatrice ombra*." His voice was unexpectedly gruff.

Her lashes drifted down when he brushed the bare skin of her back with his lips. Featherlight. He barely touched her, already shaking with need. Her body reacted with a shudder of pleasure.

He swore electricity sizzled through him—hot and bright, snapping and crackling, buzzing loud in his ears. The pulse of his heart thundered through his cock like a jackhammer, so his heavy erection jolted against his abdomen and leaked pearly drops. Flames licked along his veins, settling in as if they'd found a home.

He'd known rough his entire life. He'd grown up a dangerous, edgy, brutal man, but with Amaranthe, there was an unexpected side to him. An unexplored river of tenderness that flowed out of him when he was close to her. He felt gentle when he was with her. Protective. He had a need to slow down and savor every moment with her, to feel every merciless aching desire in his body.

With Amaranthe he was free to allow himself to be in a world of pure feeling, of emotion wrapped in desire and love. He let himself drift there with her, a part of the night and those clouds floating around that sliver of the moon, part of that slow, steady burn. He'd never known anything like it. Anything as good.

Geno followed the trail of her spine with his lips, sipping at her soft skin. Lapping with his tongue to get a little more of her taste. Nipping with his teeth, causing a sting and then removing that sting with a swirl of his tongue, intrigued by his body's reaction. The blood in his veins heated so the flames thickened to molten lava, a bright hot red mass spreading outward. Burning through him.

He'd never cared for another woman. He'd never spent time on a woman or wanted to take time with one. He used them the same way they used him. Amaranthe was different. Being with her was all about caring. He was feeling his way. Learning what she liked. What brought her body pleasure. The subtle signs, quick inhales, goose bumps, little shudders, restless shifting of her hips, soft moans escaping. Those signals fed his rising desire.

He turned on his side to better study the symmetry of Amaranthe's facial structure. A faint smile curved her lips.

"You're staring at me."

"Looking," he corrected. He slid the pad of his thumb over the soft curve of her bottom lip. "Maybe staring. It's hard not to. You're so beautiful."

"The things you said to Francesca were beautiful, Geno. She needed to hear them. I was astonished that she doesn't have confidence in herself."

Her long lashes lay like two thick crescents against her skin, the tips curving upward just slightly, intriguing him. But then everything about her intrigued him. He could watch her for hours and never get bored.

"Amara, you often will suddenly lose confidence in yourself for no apparent reason. I'm always astonished when that happens. If there's one woman on this earth who should have absolute confidence in herself, it's you."

Her lashes lifted, and he was suddenly staring down into her dark eyes. His heart instantly accelerated at what he saw there, and little flames began licking like hot tongues down his cock. He'd never thought to see love in a woman's eyes. He was certain it was there when Amaranthe looked up at him.

"Don't ever say you don't know how to talk to women, Geno," she murmured. "You do just fine."

"Do I?" he murmured, looking down at his own personal miracle. "I think you might be just a little sleepy and don't know what you're saying."

Geno caught her hip, flexed his fingers and then tugged, urging her to turn onto her back. He needed to kiss her. It wasn't a want anymore. It was an overwhelming need. He kept his gaze locked with hers. Let himself drown in the dark brown of her eyes and what he read there.

Amaranthe put a deterring hand on his chest. So small. There was just the beginning of trepidation. Of alarm. "Geno. Wait."

He slid the pad of his thumb over the curve of her bottom lip. "I need to kiss you, baby. Right now. If I don't, I might die. It could happen."

He was rewarded with that little flare of amusement he knew she'd give him, washing out the apprehension for that one moment. He didn't wait for a protest. She wanted him. That wasn't the problem. Desire was there in her eyes.

His head descended toward hers. Slowly. Very slowly. He kept his eyes open, watching her expression as he moved toward her. Her eyes were so large, lashes long and thick, tipped up at the ends. He'd noticed how long and feminine her lashes were right away and how they drew attention to the dark color of her eyes. She had large eyes, very expressive. Almost haunting. Up close he felt as if he could drown in the deep wells.

Geno read gathering desire. More. It was the more that mattered. The beginnings of love. Real love. His heart clenched hard in his chest. Not just beginning. She might not even know how much she had already invested in him, but Amaranthe was a woman who felt things deeply. She was loyal. She would be faithful. And she had already given herself to him. He read that in her dark eyes before she managed to veil them as her lashes came down.

He framed her cheek with one hand. Just the feel of her soft skin in his palm astounded him. Anticipation of her unique taste filled him. He suddenly craved her kisses. His heart pounded even harder than it had been—wild now for her. He maintained control. He was feeling his way with her, but he needed the feel of his mouth on hers. *Needed* that more than he needed his next breath.

He brushed her lips as gently as he possibly could. Deep inside, he felt like a feral predator, hungry beyond all reason. Lust rose sharply but was tempered by the overwhelming love he felt for her. His emotion allowed tenderness to coax her lips apart for him rather than just take. He wanted her to feel the way he would always cherish her. Would always protect her. Mostly, he wanted her to feel loved.

Her lips parted, his tongue swept inside and he was drowning. He hadn't known one could taste love, but it was there. He was lost in everything Amaranthe. The delicate nuances of her. The subtleties of her. He had never experienced euphoria kissing a woman, but Amaranthe managed to take him there.

"Too many clothes on, Danzatrice Ombra. I need to feel every inch of you." He murmured the half command, half entreaty against her lips and then bit down on the bottom curve, nipping lightly and tugging.

Once again, she put her palm on his chest as if to stop him. He lifted his head, his gaze drifting over her face to read her expression. "What are you afraid of, baby?"

"Letting you down." She whispered it like a confession.

He rubbed his lips over hers to erase her frown. "How could you possibly let me down?"

"You do realize I have zero experience, Geno."

She sounded so anxious he found himself more protective of her than ever. He caressed her cheek with the pad of his thumb.

"Zero experience?" he echoed. She kissed like a fucking

dream. He'd known she wasn't experienced in the kissing department. That hadn't mattered in the least. She could melt his heart. Melt his brain. Send flames rushing through his veins. Put absolute steel in his cock. She didn't need experience.

"I'm not going to measure up. You've had a lot of women. I've seen all the magazines." The admission came in a soft whisper. Her eyes avoided his.

Geno couldn't deny the hundreds of photographs deliberately published on social media. Seeking out the paparazzi was a good part of the cover for the shadow riders. Everywhere they went they were photographed, usually with a famous model, a movie star or a woman from their same social circle, so the speculation whether they were serious and would soon be taken from the market hit every tabloid and was widely circulated. They were adept at creating headlines and staying in the spotlight. That was what gave them airtight alibis when bodies dropped. They were rarely serious suspects, not even in the death on Miranda's back porch.

He brushed kisses over her eyes and then along her high cheekbones. "The pressure isn't on you, Amara. It's all on me. I need to make it good for you. Believe me, baby, it's going to be good for me. I have to make certain your body is ready for mine—go slow enough to prepare you. The first time isn't always wonderful for the woman, at least that's what I'm told. I wouldn't actually know. I've never been with an inexperienced woman. So if things don't work out perfectly for you, that's on me, not you."

Her long lashes lifted, and he found himself falling into those beautiful dark pools. "Geno, you can't believe that."

"I *know* that, but it's all right. We're going to have lots of time to get it right. Right now, I think the clothes need to go. Are you comfortable with that?"

He brushed his lips back and forth gently over hers. Coaxing her. Shamelessly tempting her. All the while the pads of his fingers caressed the bare skin of her stomach.

Blatantly seducing her. If anything, touching Amaranthe so intimately was only increasing his hunger for her. Her skin was exquisite. He could feel muscles running like steel beneath the satin.

Outside the wind picked up speed pushing the clouds across the sky a little faster, an ominous warning of the predicted storm. Geno liked storms. He especially liked to watch them from the glass wall as they came in over the river. Dark threads formed clouds spinning and rolling, blocking the silvery sliver of a moon. Occasionally, in the distance, he could hear the rumble of thunder. The sound matched the pounding of blood in his ears.

Geno pulled Amaranthe's top over her head and tossed it away from them. She didn't protest, but her body flushed a beautiful shade of rose, and her breathing turned ragged.

"My breasts are too small."

"Who told you that?" he demanded. He lowered his mouth to her chin and then nibbled his way to her throat. "Your breasts are perfect." As far as he was concerned, they were.

He kissed his way to the top of the slight curves, the heavy shadow on his jaw sliding over her tender skin leaving behind his mark on her. Very gently he lapped at her right breast and then stroked her nipple with his tongue. She circled his head with her arms, her breath hitching, her body sliding against his restlessly.

"Geno." She whispered his name, an ache in her voice.

He tugged very gently on her nipple with his teeth before drawing the small, very sensitive breast into the heat of his mouth. He gently pinched her left nipple and then kneaded and rubbed her breast while he suckled strongly, using his tongue to flick and play.

He felt her body's response, the flush of heat from breast to core, her skin growing hot until she seemed a living flame. An electrical charge zapped down his spine and over his body to hers.

"I'm getting rid of the panties, Amara," he warned her,

sliding his hand down her flat belly. Taking his time. Savoring the feel of the muscles under her satin skin and the way she made a slight strangled sound in the back of her throat. Her eyes went wide in a kind of shocked daze.

He waited a heartbeat. Two. He didn't want her to panic. "Tell me what you're feeling, Danzatrice Ombra," he coaxed while he drew the little boy shorts down her dancer's legs one-handed.

"Hot. Like I have a terrible fever, burning from the inside out," she answered instantly. Honestly. "I've never felt like this before, and it's magical but frightening because I feel out of control. I've never been out of control."

He kissed her again, not only because he wanted the taste of her in his mouth, but to erase the wild panic welling up in her eyes. He wanted only pleasure there. Desire.

Lifting his head, he kissed and nibbled his way to her belly button. "You aren't supposed to be in control, Amara."

"I feel like you're taking me over," she whispered.

He liked that. He claimed her with his mouth and hands. Gently. Tenderly. Not forcefully when there was a part of him that felt like a caveman wanting to make her his own cavewoman.

"If I am, Danzatrice Ombra, that's only fair. You took me over almost from the moment we touched minds. You're wound so tight inside me, I know you're there to stay, and I'm good with it. I want to belong to you."

Once more he kissed his way to her breasts, noting how sensitive she was. He licked at her nipples, flicked with his fingers, tugged and rolled before drawing one breast into the heat of his mouth. Instantly, she cradled his head to her while he suckled first one small mound and then the other, seducing her with his mouth, teeth and tongue.

Amaranthe reacted with a breathy little moan when his tongue flicked and his teeth tugged. He moved lower, tracing her small rib cage and then her stomach, familiarizing himself with the shape of her body. He nuzzled the indentation along her hips and then moved back to her intriguing little belly button, swirling his tongue there.

"You should wear a chain of diamonds around your hips and dance for me," he murmured against her bare skin. "I'll have to get you one."

One hand slid between her legs to feel her damp heat. Her legs shifted. Moved restlessly.

"You've got my body coiling tighter and tighter like a spring," she hissed. "I swear, I'm going to burst into flames."

He lifted his head just enough to meet her eyes so he could smile at her. "That's the idea, my beautiful dancer. We're going to burn together. Would you dance for me in a chain of diamonds?"

Very gently he parted her legs, listening to the little hitch in her breathing. He loved that rush of sound—like music to accompany the gathering storm outside their bedroom wall.

He waited for her answer, breathing a steady stream of warm air against her damp entrance, manfully ignoring his need to devour her. She was so tempting, laid out for him like a feast. The rain began to fall, the wind pushing the drops hard against the thick wall of glass, so that it sounded like musical instruments playing along with her little moans.

"Baby, are you going to answer me?"

She swallowed down another gasp, her fists in his hair. "Diamonds seem a little excessive, but anytime you want me to dance for you, I will."

He liked her answer, even though she sounded shy.

"Diamonds around your hips when you dance wouldn't be excessive," he assured. "They'd look beautiful and catch the firelight if we had the fire going. Ballet slippers and diamonds. Nothing else."

He nuzzled the dark curls of her mound. Wild, the way he knew she'd be in bed. She gasped as her legs jerked. He caught her thighs firmly in his hands. He had large hands and could wrap his fingers around the upper part of her legs.

"Geno, I can't breathe."

"Yes, you can. This is something you're going to love. A gift. I've been fantasizing for a while now, growing hungry. Craving the taste of you. I could devour you, eat you for breakfast every morning before we get up."

Spicy honey glistened at her entrance in invitation, telling him she liked the idea. He ran his tongue up the inside of her left thigh, interspersing lapping with nipping and kissing until he was so close to the temptation of her slick honeyed spice. He couldn't stop himself from tasting her. She cried out when he swept his tongue across her entrance to collect that addicting concoction. Before he could get caught up in devouring her, he switched his attention to her right inner thigh. Building anticipation was half the seduction.

Geno wanted Amaranthe's first time to be as pleasurable as it could possibly be. That meant preparing her body for him. Getting her mind in the right place. This time was for her—not him. No matter how much he wanted her, he had to go slow enough that her body could accept his.

The storm outside seemed to have found its way inside his skull. Thunder crashed in his ears and roared through his veins. The veins of lightning forking in the clouds found their way into his body, sending jolts streaking through him straight to his cock. He did his best to ignore the brutal need hammering at him the way the storm pounded at the glass walls.

He settled his broad shoulders between her legs. She was a dancer and had an amazing ability to stretch. He took advantage. His shoulders were very wide, and he was grateful for the room. He intended to take his time and enjoy every second.

Amaranthe tried not to hold her breath as she stared at the lines carved deep into Geno's face. He looked the epitome of carnal lust, of forbidden sensual temptation, of genuine love. When he spoke, he always had that raspy growl to his voice, but now, when he was on the very edge of control, he sounded even more wild. Almost feral. The sound gave her goose bumps. Sent a thrill down her spine.

When he wrapped his hands around her thighs and spread her legs apart to wedge the width of his shoulders there, her heart nearly beat out of her chest. Her pulse raced out of control when his tongue ran up her thigh. Her hips jerked of their own volition, and he tightened his hold, clamping his fingers around her thighs to hold her in place.

His tongue swiped through her folds in a gentle foray, and she lost her ability to draw air into her lungs. Nothing had prepared her for the absolute dazzling pleasure. Bliss rolled over her in a wave and joined that knot coiling tighter and growing larger, threatening to overtake her.

"Geno," she whispered his name in awe when she could find air.

"You taste good, *la mia danzatrice ombra*, so damn good. Nothing will ever taste as good as you. Nothing."

He didn't move his mouth from her slick entrance, so she felt every breath, every syllable as he spoke. He began to lap at her the way a starved feral cat would devour cream. At first licking over and over and then becoming aggressive. Greedy.

Sensations poured into Amaranthe's body. Her brain melted into pure feeling, unable to think, to process. There was no getting ahead of the fire racing through her bloodstream or her raw, oversensitive nerve endings that seemed to be detonating every single cell in her body in a fiery explosion.

Geno didn't stop, as the tension in her deepest core coiled tighter and tighter. The pounding between her legs grew into a terrible demand there was no way to ignore. The fire grew too hot, and she had no idea what to expect. She felt as if she were on the edge of a giant cliff and any moment she might tumble off.

I'm going up in flames. You have to stop. She wasn't

pushing him away like she should be. She was holding him to her, terrified he would stop, terrified he wouldn't.

His tongue plunged deep, stroked and flicked, scooped and collected more and more of the honeyed spice he seemed so addicted to. His tongue stroked and circled her sensitive, inflamed clit and she found herself crying his name softly, imploring. Pleading. For what, she didn't know.

Lightning lit up the night sky. Inside, white-hot flashes of jagged lightning arced through her body, striking in every direction, hitting every nerve ending, sending hot pleasure bursting through her. The room faded away. The bed was gone. There was only Geno and his wicked mouth. His tongue and his teeth. The fire he created. She couldn't breathe. She wasn't going to survive if he took her any higher.

Let go, Amaranthe. Trust me to catch you.

He was really saying, *Be with me. Give yourself to me. Stay with me. Know in your heart I'm the one.*

Geno was her one. Her only. She was that certain of him. But that tension gathering inside her was overwhelming. Coiling tighter and tighter until she could only hold on, fear streaking through her along with that bright, hot pleasure that was spiraling out of control while she desperately tried to hang on, thinking she might go insane if he kept going.

It's too much. Really, it's too much. The fiery need had grown into a wanton lust. She barely recognized herself. She couldn't think. Her mind was in complete chaos. There was no release she desperately needed, only the relentless climb as Geno drove her higher and higher with the way he devoured her so greedily.

Baby, give yourself to me.

He knelt between her thighs, pulling her body to his, wrapping her legs around his hips. For the first time, Amaranthe's gaze landed on his cock. Geno was muscular. Big. More than big. His cock was no exception. He was built the way she imagined the Greeks had defined their gods to be.

Tall and wide. Even kneeling between her legs, he was massive in comparison to her. Why hadn't she noticed?

She began to shake her head, intimidated and frustrated. She needed him desperately. *Desperately*, but there was no way he was going to fit.

"Geno," she whispered aloud, tears burning behind her eyes, because she wanted him that much. She loathed her size in that moment when it had always been an asset in everything she'd ever done.

He reached down with one hand and blanketed her body, his mouth crashing down on hers, claiming hers. Just that fast, every protest melted. Sanity was gone. The flames were back, licking over her skin and rushing through her veins. He kissed his way down her throat to her breasts, that stubble on his jaw scraping along her sensitive curves just before his large hands cupped, kneaded and squeezed until she couldn't stop moaning and begging him.

She didn't even understand fully what she was begging for, only that he had to do something fast. She arched into his hands, and he tugged and pinched her nipples. Lightning streaked straight to her clit. She muffled her cries against his chest as she felt something very large, very hot and hard lodge in her entrance and begin to push steadily, relentlessly into her.

He moved back, taking her open thighs with him, wrapping them around his hips, looking down to where they were joined. One hand circled the girth of his cock. She was so slick. So wet. She could see just how wet with her curls clinging to her.

"You're so beautiful, Amaranthe," he whispered. "Look at you taking me. Look how incredible you are. I've never seen anything so sexy."

There was awe in his voice. She could barely take her eyes from his. Geno was looking down at the joining of the two of them with such awe, but more than that. Disbelief. He suddenly lifted his gaze to hers and there was stark love there. Raw. Visceral. Primal. So much so she barely comprehended the steady pressure, the burning and stinging as he pushed forward, easing into her.

"You're so perfect, Amaranthe." Geno was back to staring at their joined bodies. "You're so tight I can feel your heart beating around my cockhead. Squeezing. Fucking paradise." He sent her a quick grin and went back to looking at the two of them.

He seduced her with that smile. That look. She was lost there in his eyes, trapped in his joy, in the feral, primal love he had no trouble showing her. He continued to push steadily into her, her tunnel straining as he hit her thin barrier. She was soaked, welcoming him, but it didn't seem to matter. It stung. Burned. She was afraid he was going to split her open.

Amaranthe knew it wasn't going to work. "Geno," she whispered. "You're not going to fit. You're just too big." Despite trying to remain relaxed, she stiffened, her thighs tensing around his hips, instinctively fighting his invasion. Self-preservation was just too strong, no matter how much she wanted him. No matter how much she wanted to please him.

Even as she protested, her body was still trying to find a way to accept him. She didn't push him away, but instead, tried to impale herself on that long, thick pole.

"You were made for me. You're slick, baby." His hand slid up her belly to the curve of her breast to her nipple. "So slick. You're just afraid because it's all so new." He waited another heartbeat. "If you want to stop, Amaranthe, we'll stop."

She could tell it would practically kill him to stop. It cost him just to ask her. Did she want to stop? She was terrified to continue. On the other hand, as much as it burned and stung, there was another sensation creeping in that overshadowed the discomfort at times. It was just hovering out of reach. And then there was that look on his face.

She shook her head. "Don't stop. Not yet."

"Babe, I might not be able to stop later. I'll try but . . ."

He broke off. Sweat beaded on his forehead. His fingers moved over her breast and flicked her nipple and tugged gently. Fire raced from her breast to her sex. She couldn't help her reaction to his touch. She had such a weakness for him. He had that sensual mask again; the alluring one she couldn't resist.

"Don't stop."

Geno pinched her nipple hard, and lightning streaked straight to her clit. At the same time, he surged forward, driving his cock through the thin barrier and deeper. Deeper still.

"Geno." She tried warning him. He was so hot. Splitting her. She took a deep breath, willing him to fit. Willing her body to take him inside all the way. It hurt. But at the same time . . . she didn't want to stop.

"That's right, Danzatrice Ombra. You've got this." His voice was an even deeper, sexier rasp. He sank another inch, his length fiery hot. Spreading her open.

Amaranthe felt too full. Stuffed. She could feel the large vein running along his cock. His heart beating through the wide girth. She shook her head as he eased in another inch. His fingers dug into her thighs, holding her firmly in place. He suddenly surged forward, driving himself forward like a spear all the way through her tight folds until she had every inch of him in her.

She caught at his forearms, digging in her fingernails, a small moan escaping as the burning and stinging increased.

Geno stayed still, their bodies locked together, his forehead pressed against hers. His breathing was as labored as hers. She felt the pulsing of his cock in the tight silken tunnel as her sheath attempted to strangle the massive invader.

He swore over and over under his breath. "Nothing has ever felt this good, Amara. Nothing. I'm waiting for your body to catch up. God, baby, you need to catch up."

She felt her body begin to relax and she took several long deep breaths. He pulled back his hips, withdrawing from her. Without warning, he sank deep again, driving straight through her folds without hesitation.

She didn't know if she liked the sensation or not. It was painful, yet it wasn't all painful. He filled her completely. She tightened her legs around his hips and caught his rhythm, her body naturally following his lead. She couldn't find her voice, only moan.

His movements became faster. Harder. Each time his cock pumped in and out of her, streaks of fire encompassed her entire body, drowning her in the sensations of both immeasurable pleasures mixed with sharp stinging and burning. Half of her pleasure was just the way he was looking at her, as if she were everything to him. His entire world. As if his cock fitting into her body was a miracle he hadn't expected, and now that it had, he never wanted it out.

He began to shake his head from side to side. "Too soon. You're so perfect, babe. I can't hold out. I've never felt like this."

If it were possible, his cock was getting bigger, pushing at the already tender walls of her sheath. Then he thrust hard. Fast. Jerking out a jolting rhythm as hot ropes of seed coated the spasming walls of her tight tunnel. He collapsed over her, fighting for breath, his cock still jerking, his mouth finding her neck.

She lay still, trapped beneath him, unwilling to attempt to process what just happened, whether she liked it or she didn't. She wasn't certain. She gave a little gasp and turned her face to the side in an effort to breathe.

"Geno."

He lifted himself up on his elbows. "Sorry, Amara." A slow smile lit his eyes, turning them a dark shade of blue. "Next time, I'll get your body there, I promise."

She wasn't going to think about next time, not when there was a persistent burning throbbing between her legs. She flung one arm over her eyes. "I'm never going to be able to walk again."

Geno removed her arm to look down at her, his frown

very much in evidence. "Did I hurt you? I tried to be gentle. I was careful knowing it was your first time."

Amaranthe tried not to show alarm. "Careful. That wasn't—um—enthusiastic?"

He swore under his breath. "I'm going to get you in the Jacuzzi. Maybe that will help with the soreness. I can call the doc if you think we need him."

She pressed her fingertips over her lips to hide her smile. "We definitely don't need the doctor. It was my first time, Geno, and you're big. I'm bound to be a little sore. I think the Jacuzzi will help a lot. In case you're wondering, I liked it and hope to repeat the experience." She would die of embarrassment if he called the doctor.

Geno smiled at her as he slid off the bed. She tried not to look at the mixture of blood and other evidence of their joining on his cock.

"You liked it?" he repeated. "I think I'm going to have to put a lot more effort into our next time."

"Your effort was just fine. More effort and I really wouldn't be able to walk."

He brushed a kiss on top of her head. "Babe, you didn't have an orgasm. That's a matter of pride with me."

"Women don't normally have them the first time, especially when their partner is massive enough that part of the time there's a bit of a burning sensation. I couldn't decide if it hurt or if it was beautiful. I'm not into pain. If I were, we would have been golden."

He groaned and put a hand over his heart. "That's it, woman. I'm getting you into the Jacuzzi and then we're repeating the experience, so I can do a much better job. We'll keep going until I get it right. You've wounded my pride."

Amaranthe found herself laughing. "Your pride is just fine." She didn't think repeating the experience right away was the best idea in the world. She might really be scarred for life.

"Seriously, Amara, we'll do much better the second time around."

"I know we will. I'm going to soak in the Jacuzzi, and I'll feel fine." She hoped so. She didn't want to be afraid of having sex with him. It had been good—sort of. It was just that he was intimidating. Her body was bound to get used to his. Right?

CHAPTER FIFTEEN

From the first moment Amaranthe entered the dance studio, she felt the subtle difference in atmosphere. It wasn't as though she could put her finger on exactly what was wrong, but a note of discord had been introduced into the normally tranquil and composed dance world. This particular class was made up of various ages, from extremely young, just starting out, to teenagers who had been taking ballet for several years.

Ms. Lyna Marchel, one of the dance instructors, helped to teach the class. She was very exacting, but quite good at her craft. Unfortunately, Amaranthe had noticed she tended to play favorites. The more money a client's family had, the more she catered to that child, whether they had talent or worked hard or not. She was in a foul mood, already haranguing the students and telling them to hurry to change, that she didn't have all day to wait for them.

Nicoletta, do you feel the animosity? Can you tell where it's coming from?

The higher the level of enmity building in the large studio, the calmer and more tranquil vibrations Amaranthe ensured she gave off. She had little pods in various corners of the room with soothing aromatherapy scents she activated to help counter the gathering hostility.

I definitely feel it, Nicoletta confirmed. *I searched the shadows to see if someone else was here, but we're the only riders in the studio or dressing area.*

Amaranthe reached out to Geno, but she looped in his brothers and Nicoletta. He was close, patrolling with his brothers on the street and around the studio to ensure no other riders were attempting to get close to Amaranthe.

Geno, this is the exact way the other businesses began to have problems. It started with teenagers doing little things. There are two girls here, Jenny Porthman and Reba Salsberry, regular students, who I suspect are introducing gossip and negative energy into the studio. When I'm close to them, I can feel the hostility pouring off them in waves. There is one other girl as well, I'm not as certain of. She's very good friends with them. Her name is Priscilla Clake.

Priscilla was the oldest at seventeen. Reba, the youngest at fifteen. Although Jenny was sixteen, she was clearly the leader of the trio.

Have you always gotten along with them? Geno asked.

Amaranthe had. She liked the girls, and they'd always seemed to like her. She couldn't imagine what had changed. How did the murderers manage to control the teens like they did? What were they doing to get them to agree to turn on their neighbors and friends? If she could figure that out, she might be able to stop them from using the teenagers. She put the question to the others.

Money, Lucca guessed. *They're paying them lots of money.*

They must be blackmailing them, it can't just be paying them, she speculated. *Some of them might be willing to turn on family and friends for money, but not so many. Especially when people start getting hurt or killed.*

How do you think they are blackmailing them? Nicoletta asked.

Amaranthe moved around the studio, watching as each girl came out of the dressing room and began to warm up on the mats. Lyna Marchel pursed her lips and glared at the older girls, who talked in low tones as they went through their basic stretches, but she didn't reprimand them.

Ten-year-old Carlotta hurried out of the back room and barreled straight into her best friend, Selena, another ten-year-old. Selena fell backward, landing hard on her bottom, ripping her bright orange-and-pink leotard. She immediately burst into tears.

"You did that on purpose because you wanted my leotard," Selena accused, sobbing hysterically. She rubbed at her eyes with her fists. "Look what you did. You ruined it."

"I didn't do it on purpose," Carlotta denied. "I wouldn't do that."

"You horrid child." Lyna, her face twisted into a mask of hatred, stormed over to Carlotta, towering over her in a threatening manner. "What a terrible thing to do out of spite and jealousy."

"I didn't. I didn't." Carlotta began to really cry.

"Your parents are going to pay for her beautiful leotard. Go right now into the changing room and wash your face. You have no reason to be blubbering like a baby."

"Lyna," Amaranthe said softly, "I'm sure it was an accident. Carlotta, go wash your face while I take care of Selena."

"I can help Carlotta," Jenny volunteered.

Lyna drew her breath in with a soft hiss. "Did you just reprimand me in front of the students?" she demanded, scowling down at Amaranthe. She deliberately stepped right into Amara's personal space.

Amaranthe smiled at the other instructor without giving ground. "Of course not. Let's try to settle these girls down. I really could use your calming influence."

Lyna's scowl grew even darker. "Don't pretend you're

my friend. You came here and took over my job, and now you're deliberately undermining me in front of the students." She narrowed her eyes at Amaranthe. "You're not going to get away with it. I'm gathering complaints and signatures to have you removed." She looked past Amaranthe to the group of teens watching them and nodded her head as if they were all behind her.

Amaranthe followed her gaze to see Reba and Priscilla holding hands. Neither looked triumphant. Both appeared distraught. Selena continued to wail loudly, touching the small rip in her leotard.

I don't think this girl Jenny is trying to console Carlotta. She's whispering to her, but I can't hear what she's saying because the water is running. The more she talks to Carlotta, the more the poor little girl is crying. There's something about Jenny's body posture that's off, Amara, Nicoletta declared.

I'm coming in to help you keep an eye on them, Taviano said. *Everyone's dressed now, right? I don't like the way any of this is playing out, especially the way the other dance instructor is acting. Could she be programmed to attack Amara? We're thinking in terms of a shadow rider attacking one of us, but she could just as easily whip out a poisoned knife and cut her. Or one of the teens could.*

Amaranthe hadn't considered that idea. The way Geno swore, he hadn't thought of it, either.

I don't like this, Amara. I thought we had the studio as safe as possible for you, but this is a game changer. They could have programed Marchel or one of the teens to try to kill you.

Amaranthe didn't want Geno to insist she send her students home. That would be a win for the murderers.

This is how it always starts with the businesses, Geno. People are accused of stealing. Everyone becomes suspicious of one another. Businesses begin to lose money because customers no longer trust them. Employees turn on one another. We're seeing it happen firsthand, and we have to figure out how they're doing it.

Ignoring Lyna, she went around her to crouch on the floor beside Selena to examine the small rip in the leotard. "We can fix that right up. I have a sewing kit. Come with me. There's no need for all those tears."

I think the way they get the teens to cooperate other than with money is using the sextortion scheme that's so alive and well today, Amaranthe explained. *It's extremely popular, and so many kids fall for it. They go online to sites where they know their parents can't track them, and they meet other "kids." They think they're connecting with someone who understands them. These are adults who know what to look for in vulnerable teenagers, or sometimes the children are even younger, elementary school age.*

She led Selena over to the entrance, where the sewing kit was kept in a drawer in a small desk.

Once the "friend" knows all the right buttons to push, all the right subjects to talk about and emotional issues to cover, the child is comfortable and opens up to them. The child feels as if they have a true connection for the first time.

Most of the other students were in the studio warming up. Lyna organized them by age. Seven and under, eight to twelve, and thirteen and up were the three age groups. The classes provided to new students and private lessons were given at different times. This was a special class for extra practice more than anything else, and Amaranthe enjoyed working with all the students. They were dedicated to learning their craft.

Once their target is comfortable with them, they begin to pressure them for photographs or videos. Usually, the child won't comply at first, but photos are sent to them. Naturally, they aren't of the real person talking to them. That person is an adult, not a teenager. The adult keeps working them, insisting on the photographs and videos until the teen caves. Once that happens, the child is trapped.

Nicoletta made a small sound of protest. *They would feel so hopeless.*

Yes, Amaranthe agreed. *Most of them won't tell their parents or any other adult. Many end up suiciding; they're so distraught when they're threatened with extortion. In this case, these people seem to be forcing the teens to steal from local businesses as well as spread gossip.*

Geno had been observing Lyna Marchel from the shadows. *I can't imagine that she would send naked pictures to anyone.*

No, she's always held a grudge against me, although she was never rude to me. We got along. She didn't want me hired, Amaranthe confirmed. *I don't think it was difficult to recruit her.*

She has no idea you're engaged to me, does she? Geno asked.

It doesn't seem so. Amaranthe led Selena over to the group of eight- to twelve-year-old girls. Carlotta was back, and Amara kept a sharp eye on her. She was having a very difficult time. Normally, the ten-year-old was very good, but now she couldn't transition from one position into the next, not even with the aid of the bar. Her eyes were red and swollen from crying so much, and no amount of cold water was going to alleviate the symptoms.

Lyna Marchel didn't help, scowling at the child and stomping over to put the little girl's feet or hands into the correct position. Twice she snapped at Carlotta, telling her to pay attention. That brought a fresh flood of tears to Carlotta, and Lyna rolled her eyes in disgust.

"Do you need to go home, Carlotta?" she demanded. "Stop this nonsense right now."

Jenny snickered. The moment she did, two of Carlotta's closest friends, Selena and a young girl of nine named Debbie Atwater, laughed. Amaranthe instantly stopped the music playing in the studio.

"That will be enough of that. Jenny, you can call your parents to come and get you. I won't have you bullying other students in this class. You're far too old to pick on younger students. Ms. Marchel, you and I can discuss how best to help the students when they're having difficulties after this class. I want all of you to sit on the mat in your groups and start stretching."

Jenny tossed her head, sending her hair flying. "I can't possibly call my parents. They won't like it. They pay good money for me to take this class." She looked to Lyna Marchel for confirmation. "It isn't happening."

"I'm afraid it is, Jenny. If you don't call them yourself, I'll be forced to call them and have you removed from the program altogether."

"You don't have that kind of authority," Lyna snapped, raising her chin in a challenge to Amaranthe. "No worries, Jenny. She's just trying to act as though she owns the studio. Once the board hears what she's doing, they'll fire her. You don't have to call your parents."

Amaranthe shrugged. "Keep stretching, girls," she said to the others.

The door to the studio opened, and first, Fiero came inside. Then Geno's wide shoulders filled the frame. She glanced up and sent him a brief smile. Behind him, Salvatore and Lucca shadowed him. All three were dressed in three-piece suits. Behind them, Donte followed. The two bodyguards broke off and stood against the wall.

The girls gaped at the men, the teenagers whispering, giggling and covering their mouths.

Geno went straight to Amaranthe. "Danzatrice Ombra, Stefano would like to have lunch with us. Will you be able to have the time off?" He lifted her hand with the ring on her finger to his mouth and kissed it before turning to Lyna Marchel. "Good morning, Ms. Marchel. I trust all is well this morning?" He looked around the studio. "Girls."

The giggles grew louder.

"Sadly, Geno, we're in the middle of an incident," Amaranthe said. "I was just about to call the parents of one of the students. She's no longer welcome here. She was bullying a younger student, and when I told her to call her parents to take her home, she refused. That is grounds for her dismissal. Unfortunately, Ms. Marchel backed her and is insisting Jenny can stay and that the board will dismiss me."

The air in the room seemed to be difficult to breathe. Tension built. Geno turned slowly to face Lyna Marchel. "You didn't back the headmistress of the studio? In fact, you incited a student to go against her instructions?"

For a moment, Lyna's lips trembled, but then she firmed them. "She overstepped her authority. She can't throw out one of our highest-paying clients without board approval."

"Actually, Ms. Marchel, that isn't so. Had you read any of the many regulations the board sent you when we were trying to get you to take the job of head instructor for the studio, you would have known that."

Lyna gave a little sniff of disdain. "What I do know is the board made a huge mistake choosing this woman as the head instructor. She may be brilliant at dance, but she has no business sense. You don't cater to the poor students and simply dismiss the wealthy because they have a sense of entitlement. You learn to work with them."

"You don't believe in treating all students the same?" Geno asked, his voice pitched very low. That should have been a warning.

"No, of course not. They aren't the same. She's far too young to understand what it takes to run a successful dance studio and theater. Girls like Jordan"—she poured contempt into her voice—"may have some talent, but she's handicapped and has no money. What's the use of giving time and energy to her? Someone like Jenny, who is difficult and entitled, has talent and money and will go a long way given the right instructor. She would bring prestige to our school."

Geno shook his head. "That isn't what our mission statement is, Ms. Marchel."

"Mission statements sound good for publicity and fundraising, Mr. Ferraro," Lyna said defiantly.

"It's too bad that you feel that way, Ms. Marchel, after all the years you have worked for us. We've valued your time with us, so much so that we encouraged you to take the position as head instructor, but you adamantly refused. You've left me with no choice but to terminate your position."

Lyna gasped. "You can't do that."

"I assure you I can."

"Only the board can do that."

Geno smiled at her—a predator's smile. "You seem to forget we own the school. My brothers and I not only own the studio and theater, but we make up the majority of the board as well at the moment. You don't read the fine print of the contracts you sign, Ms. Marchel, but you're more than welcome to take the contract to a lawyer and they'll do it for you. Please pack your belongings and vacate the premises immediately."

He turned his back on her, clearly dismissing her. "Have you called the student's parents? She can leave as soon as her parents get here."

Jenny shook her head and crossed her arms over her chest. "I didn't do anything. She's lying."

"You would like me to believe my fiancée is lying to me?"

Jenny paled. "Your fiancée?" she whispered.

Behind him, Lyna gasped. "What? No wonder she's so sure of herself. I suppose I should have slept with you, and I could have gotten my way," she declared in a sneering voice. "Girls, let that be a lesson to you. Sleep your way to the top."

Jenny giggled.

Geno let his breath out in a long slow hiss of displeasure. "I would have let you leave with full pension, insurance for life, retirement, everything, but not now. You'll find yourself with nothing when I'm finished with you. Get out before I have my men throw you out."

His voice was pitched low, but so scary, Lyna turned and

rushed out of the studio. Amaranthe laid her hand very gently on his forearm. She could feel the anger coiled hot and bright in him. Not only in him but in his brothers as well. Strangely, she felt that same anger emanating from his personal protectors on her behalf. They hadn't liked the accusations Lyna Marchel had raised against her in front of her students any more than Geno had.

Don't alarm the students or give Jenny any more fuel for gossip, she cautioned. *These people want to alienate your family from all the businesses in your territory. This is exactly the kind of thing they can use.*

We can turn the tables on them, he countered.

Amaranthe ignored Jenny and once again turned on the music so the girls would have something to begin their stretches to.

"Let's get to work, girls. Get back into your groups and begin stretching. Drama's over. We still have time to work on our basic positions," she announced.

How do we do that?

The girls quickly hurried to their mats. She took the youngest group to the bar.

Someone will contact Jenny. She seems to want to engage with them rather than fear them, Geno said.

It was true, Amaranthe had to admit. *She feels powerful. In her family, she feels out of control. Those using her haven't sprung it on her yet that she won't get her photographs back. She likes being a bully and having others afraid of her. A part of her believes she can bring the great Ferraro family down.*

Nicoletta weighed in. *I understand her way of thinking, unfortunately. When you've felt small, without any control, and you suddenly have power, you might be willing to do anything to keep it.*

She has choices, Lucca said. *She knows she's hurting people. She doesn't have the kind of life you did, Nicoletta. She's an entitled brat.*

How can you know that? Nicoletta asked. *Just because*

she comes from a wealthy family doesn't mean she isn't abused either physically or emotionally.

Amaranthe had to agree with Nicoletta. She'd investigated more than one family considered to be beyond reproach and found very dark hidden secrets.

Jenny's family is very entrenched in the social circles, Salvatore informed them. *They hold quite a few fundraisers. They sat on the boards of many charities with our parents.*

I'm aware, Geno acknowledged. *I'm also aware, one misstep and they can fall out of favor. They're aware as well. Their daughter hasn't learned that lesson. She doesn't appreciate the privileges she has from being their daughter. All the money spent on every interest she has. The education she receives. The clothes she wears. The vacations she takes. She acts out because she thinks she's restricted at home when they say no to her. I've heard her mother talk at the board meeting to some of the other mothers asking what to do.*

When Jenny began acting out and her mother asked for help, we had the investigators check their family out to ensure Jenny wasn't being hurt in any way, Salvatore explained. *She wasn't, Nicoletta. She craved attention all the time, and if her parents told her no, she threw tantrums. Big ones. She would lie about her parents to anyone who would listen to her. Unfortunately, they bought her way out of trouble instead of allowing her to suffer the consequences. That just reinforced that she could do whatever she wanted.*

Amaranthe helped the youngest girls go through their positions while the other two groups stretched on the mat. She ignored Jenny who took turns glaring at her defiantly and trying to flirt with the Ferraro brothers and their personal protectors.

The youngest hopeful ballerinas were very cute and clumsy, making the others smile as they did their best to get their feet and hands into the right positions when Amara called them out. The familiar music, the scent of the essential oils, the act of stretching accompanied by the sight of the little girls attempting to do their best at going through each of the classical ballet positions, helped to drive away much of the ugly atmosphere in the studio. Without Lyna Marchel to fuel Jenny's gossip and bullying, it was much more difficult for the teen to spread her ugly attitude to the other girls.

That girl is looking to stir up trouble, Lucca announced, watching Jenny.

I called her mother. She's on her way. We'll see what happens when she shows up, Amaranthe said.

Amaranthe led the little girls back to their mats and called the next age group up. Carlotta and Selena were in the group. Jenny kept trying to get Selena's attention, but Amaranthe inserted her body between the teen and her intended target to prevent Selena from seeing Jenny giving her signals. It was clear she wanted Selena to ridicule Carlotta in some way. Carlotta was quite good already, one of the best in her age group. It was clear she practiced, stretched and worked on her core. Her two friends Selena and Debbie weren't quite as good, but they had the potential to be if they worked the way Carlotta did. Carlotta had single-minded purpose, even at ten. She had the dream of being a ballerina and was determined to succeed.

Carlotta was very sensitive and emotional. She also was on scholarship. Her family had very little money, a fact that Jenny knew and frequently told the other children. She made fun of Jordan for the same reason. Jordan was targeted because she was hearing impaired and had little money. As a rule, Jenny had kept her bullying to a minimum, but as she was Ms. Marchel's favorite student, more and more she had begun to act a little bolder.

At first, Jenny had tried to curry favor with Amaranthe, but Amara didn't play favorites in class. She was a strict but fair instructor. She took dance seriously, just as she took riding shadows seriously. The only dancers who could play around in class were the little ones. She wanted them to have fun and learn to love ballet.

Geno and his brothers leaned against the bank of windows, arms folded, seemingly watching the girls go through the classic ballet positions. They were really studying the position of the shadows in the studio. Amaranthe was just as careful as they were to avoid being close to a shadow just in case one of the assassins burst out of an opening to attack with a poison blade.

Jenny's up to something again, Nicoletta warned. *She's whispering to the girl next to her.*

That's Priscilla. Priscilla Clake was older than Jenny by a year but an introvert. She rarely talked. She kept shaking her head, refusing to look at the younger teen. Abruptly, she laid her head flat on her legs in a long stretch, attempting to ignore Jenny altogether.

Jenny muttered something under her breath. It appeared as if she didn't like that the atmosphere in the studio had calmed, and no one was paying the slightest bit of attention to her. She used her foot to shove at Reba. Reba was on the mat beside Jordan. Jordan stretched, her head turned toward the girls working, a smile on her face. Jenny indicated for Reba to kick Jordan. Reba frowned and shook her head. She tried to look away from Jenny, but Jenny shoved her foot at Reba again and indicated Jordan.

Amaranthe sighed, stood up and walked over to the group of teenagers. "Jenny, you really are the most immature, childish girl I've ever had in one of my classes, and I've taught all over Europe in the most prestigious schools. You wouldn't have lasted five minutes. You have no discipline at all."

Deliberately, Amaranthe was as cutting as possible, setting herself up for the girl's retaliation. The hope was that Jenny would run straight to her handlers and demand justice for the humiliation in front of her friends.

Her face bright red, Jenny leapt up, taller than Amaranthe, her fist shooting out toward her face. Amara blocked the punch.

"I do believe that is considered assault, Jenny," she said. "And in front of witnesses, too."

The other girls gasped. Three of the younger girls began to cry.

"You'll have to press charges, Amara," Geno said, on his feet. "She can't keep getting away with her bullying tactics."

The door to the studio opened and London Porthman hurried in. She stopped abruptly when she caught sight of Geno, Salvatore and Lucca. Immediately, she broke into a huge smile. She was a woman of about forty with blond hair and blue eyes. She had a very trim figure and was tall like her daughter. She wore slim wool trousers and a blue silk blouse with a dark brown topper over it. She looked extremely chic.

"How lovely to run into the three of you," she said. "I can't remember the last time that happened." Her gaze swept past them to take in her daughter, who stood with both fists clenched, her face red and a scowl twisting what could have been a pretty face into something nearly ugly.

London looked around the room at the crying children. "What's going on, Geno?"

"Your daughter just tried to assault the instructor. Fortunately, she was able to block the punch before she was struck in the face. As you can see, Jenny being physically violent toward Amaranthe upset the younger children. I've advised Amara to press charges. It won't hurt Jenny to spend the night in a facility. As it is, she's banned from this school, and I'm going to see to it that she won't stand a snowball's chance in hell of getting in any other school I oversee or have any influence with."

Jenny paled. "He can't do that. She's sleeping with him, Mom. That's why he's taking her side. They're making this entire thing up. Reba and Priscilla will tell you the truth. He's only saying that because she's sleeping with him. She even made him get rid of Ms. Marchel."

London turned to Geno with a shocked look on her face.

Ignoring her, Geno centered his attention on Jenny. "Why would you give your mother partial information? Are you hoping she says something to anger me? Or upset Amaranthe? Do you have any concept of the difference in our social status? If your mother were to lose her social status, you would no longer be welcome at any of those events you love to go to. None of the privileges you have right now would be yours any longer. You're dependent on your parents' status. They own certain companies. Do you know what I can do to those companies, Jenny? Do you have any idea what would happen if they angered me because they insulted my fiancée the way you have?"

"Your fiancée?" London whispered.

The girls in the studio murmured to one another in a wave of approval.

Geno took Amaranthe's hand and turned her wrist over to bring up her fingers, showing off the ring. She understood that he wasn't just warning Jenny he would retaliate against the teen, but that he would take down the entire family if anything else were done to his fiancée. She was beginning to understand just how ruthless the Ferraro family could be under the right circumstances—when they were protecting the ones they loved.

The idea that Geno Ferraro could love her astonished her. Her gaze jumped to Salvatore and then Lucca. They were there to defend her as well. Even though she found Geno's voice and demeanor chilling, she still felt wrapped up in a warmth she'd never known before.

"Jenny knows Amaranthe is my fiancée, London. She knew when she defied her, refusing to stop bullying the other girls. She knew it when she refused to call you after having been given a direct order. She knew it when she tried to punch Amara. And she knew it when she tried to get you to say something derogatory to her," Geno accused, never once raising his voice.

"Jenny." London barely breathed her daughter's name. "How could you?"

"Mom, just pay him off. Pay whatever they want. I *have* to dance. I don't care who she is or if they're sleeping together. Just pay them whatever they want." Jenny's eyes filled with tears, and her voice hit a whiny pitch.

Amaranthe could see the teenager was very used to manipulating her mother. London hesitated and looked imploringly, first at Geno, who gave her his expressionless mask, and then to Amara.

"I'm sorry," Amaranthe said as gently as possible. "She can't come back. She went way over the line."

"I wouldn't allow her back even if Amara insisted on giving her another chance. First, she isn't sincere. Those are crocodile tears," Geno said. "And second, she tried to physically assault my fiancée. That's unforgivable. Take her home, London, before I insist Amaranthe press charges against her."

"No." Jenny spat the word out. "No! Mom, *pay* them."

"Money isn't going to work," Geno said. "Please take her home, London."

"You're going to be sorry. You think you're so high and mighty, but you'll see," Jenny threatened. "You aren't the only one with friends."

Lucca threw his hands in the air as if he couldn't take one more moment of the teenage tantrum and slipped out the door of the studio. Fiero went with him, straight to the car parked at the curb, opened the door, his body blocking the view of the Ferraro brother for just a moment. Then Fiero closed the back passenger door and leaned against the vehicle his hands loosely at his sides, looking deceptively casual. It was impossible to see inside the dark tinted windows where Lucca had supposedly entered the back seat.

They'll contact her online, Salvatore warned Lucca.

You'll have to stay very close. She isn't going to wait. She'll text them the moment she gets her phone back.

They won't text her openly. They'll have a meeting place that can be permanently erased, Amaranthe said. *She'll need privacy.*

I'm on her, Lucca said. *The little brat won't see me. I'll get the information for Lanz and Deangelo. They'll be able to track whoever is behind this.* There was absolute confidence in his voice.

Watch yourself, Geno cautioned.

"London, I'd take your daughter's phone and devices away from her and actually punish her this time. She should have consequences," he added aloud.

"Fuck you," Jenny snarled, following her mother out of the studio.

London hastily shut the door before her daughter could say anything else. Amaranthe watched the two walk up to a sleek little Porsche, Jenny screaming at her mother the entire time.

She turned back to the other students and held up the hand with her engagement ring, a smile on her face, determined to get them all laughing again. The girls could be romantic, and they all thought the Ferraros were the epitome of Prince Charming. It wasn't difficult to get them to admire the ring and then show off their talents for Geno and Salvatore.

CHAPTER SIXTEEN

Stefano stared in silence at the water glittering like diamonds for a long time. The sun was setting, turning the surface a mixture of orange and red. The sky had even more colors, with various shades of reds and pinks in addition to the orange. It was rare to see those colors in the sky, even over the river. Although the sky looked clear, Geno wondered if another storm was moving in.

"It's too late to give you advice, Geno. But if I could, I'd tell you not to fall head over heels in love with that woman. Look at me. Look what Francesca's done to me." He sounded mournful.

Geno just managed to keep from laughing. "Francesca is the best thing that ever happened to you, Stefano, and you know it." He kept his tone very mild. He had no idea what kind of mood his cousin was in, and he wasn't taking any chances.

Stefano spun around to face him. "*Exactly*. Should she be here? She's surrounded by danger. Does she know it? Yes. Does she care? No. I told her she had to leave. She looked me right in the eye and told me she wasn't leaving. She said, and I quote, 'Stefano, I don't ask you for much and you're going to give this to me. I'm staying with you to see Geno and Amaranthe through this. All of you need me and I need to be here. So you're giving this to me. The subject is closed.' What the fuck do I do with that, Geno?"

Geno sighed. "I guess you give her what she's asking."

"She wasn't asking. She made that clear. She got on a plane while I was drunk out of my fucking mind. I had her fully protected where I knew she was safe and none of these crazy bastards could get to her or the children. Did she stay put? No. She commandeered the Ferraro plane and came here. She's never done anything like this in her life. No one dared say no to her, either. They just did whatever she told them."

"I would have," Geno conceded.

Stefano pushed his hand through his hair with another sigh. "My Francesca. Such a sweet little angel. Do you know what she told me, Geno?"

Stefano paced across the room, his movements as always fluid and graceful. He was a man who looked good in his suit.

"Francesca told me she wanted to be the one to give me the gift of a child. She doesn't seem to understand that *she's* the gift. She cried. I fucking hate when she cries. It tears me up inside." He fell silent again and then turned to face Geno.

"I apologize for the way I handled this thing with Taviano. There were so many other ways I could have done it. I could see the moment Australia came up and the name of the Boutler family in Queensland was mentioned, it threatened to throw him into another post-traumatic episode."

Geno tried to interrupt him. "Stefano . . ."

Stefano shook his head. "Let me. I need to talk to you about this. I should have. Not there in front of everyone, but I could have indicated to you that I had things to say privately. I felt so guilty when I first learned what happened to

Taviano. I felt such rage at the parents. I'd never felt like that before. I have a temper, but I honestly felt if my mother were standing in front of me, I was capable of strangling her. She allowed a ten-year-old child to suffer without counselling, to be separated from all of us and to believe he was in some way responsible for what happened to him. I truly hated her, Geno."

Geno could understand. Geno loved his cousins and he felt anger toward Eloisa and Phillip that they were so selfish that they wouldn't care for their children.

"All I could see was my baby brother suffering all over again," Stefano admitted. "I couldn't protect him all those years ago, so like a fool, I made matters worse. None of the family knew anything, but with the way I acted, and with your reaction, they're all questioning my behavior. Now with Francesca using our private jet when she's never done such a thing, believe me, those questions are really multiplying."

"Stefano, I would have done the same had it been one of my brothers. I observed Taviano, but I wasn't comprehending what I was really seeing. It was Amaranthe who pointed it out. I was so angry when I thought you were shutting me out that I didn't want to hear her."

Stefano sighed. "Our women. We think they're the emotional ones. They see us so clearly. Taviano went to Francesca and asked her what to do. She told me I could have handled the situation so much better. She even told me several ways I could have. At the same time, she was sympathetic and sweet as only Francesca can be."

Geno understood exactly what Stefano was saying. Francesca could reprimand and yet still be compassionate. It never felt as if she were putting you down.

"Francesca is one in a million, Stefano. I believe Amaranthe is as well." He paused for a moment, listening to the laughter coming from the kitchen. Their family. It was amazing how when they were altogether, he felt so much more relaxed.

Stefano nodded. "I want that for you. After all you've been through, I want her to love you the way Francesca loves me."

"I believe she's getting there. I see it when she looks at me. She's never had a family and we intimidate her just a little bit. She wants us though. She definitely accepts Salvatore and Lucca."

"That woman is lightning fast. I've never seen anything quite like it," Stefano admitted. "I've known there were elite riders. There had to be. Elie and I even discussed it, but to see her in action was shocking. I've had conversations with Jean-Claude that I know pertained to cases he was worried about. Later, I wondered if he sent an elite rider to investigate."

"He wanted to have me trained, but I didn't fit the mold," Geno admitted. "So unbeknownst to me, he had Salvatore trained. Lucca is too much like me. We don't conform."

"He clearly wanted to train Nicoletta," Stefano said. "I can understand when there is such a need. At the same time, it's sad enough the way we must train our children. When Emmanuelle fell in love with Valentino, I had to take a good hard look at what a shadow rider is and face up to what we really are. Our family wanted to condemn him, not only for what he does, but for claiming Emme. I tied Francesca to me as fast as I could. My brothers did the same as soon as they were certain the woman was the right one. How could we condemn Valentino for doing exactly what we did?"

Lucca stuck his head in the open archway. "Come eat, you two. You know Taviano and Salvatore. They won't leave you anything if you're late. Not even Francesca is going to save you, and she'll try. Don't put her in that position."

Stefano and Geno followed Lucca back to the large dining table, where the food was in silver warmers along the opposite wall. Stefano stopped to circle Francesca's waist and drop a kiss on the top of her head.

"You'll be happy to know Geno and I have made our peace, *bella*."

Francesca tipped her head back, her dark eyes shining at him. "Well, of course you have. I never had any doubts." She sent Geno a dazzling smile.

"It was a long day for Amaranthe," Geno said as he came up beside his fiancée to serve the lasagna onto her plate. "The studio felt as if it were under siege. All the little girls were crying or angry. Ms. Marchel turned into the biggest bitch of all time. She never wanted the job Amara eventually was given but acted jealous because Amaranthe was head instructor. She was offered the job several times but turned it down. She knew it was the head instructor position."

"Amaranthe dances better than she could ever have hoped to dance," Salvatore said, seating himself at the table. "She's beautiful, and every prestigious dance company would love to have her as their principal dancer. Ms. Marchel was never going to be anything but a mediocre dancer."

"That isn't very kind, Salvatore," Amaranthe said as she carried her plate to the table.

"I'm not being rude, I'm stating a fact. I also think she has the hots for Geno."

Geno snapped his head around to glare at his younger brother. "She doesn't."

"Yeah, she does," Lucca confirmed. "There's nothing like a woman scorned. You never so much as looked at her, which was probably fine. She most likely has all kinds of fantasies about you. Hot ones."

Geno threw hot sourdough bread at his head. Lucca picked it one-handed out of the air with a grin.

"She didn't. Amaranthe, that hideous woman never even looked at me," Geno assured.

"I suppose I'll have to get used to you being a sex symbol to all these women," Amaranthe said with a pathetic sigh. She looked at Nicoletta and then Francesca. "It really is a challenge putting up with these Ferraro men and their flirtatious ways, isn't it?"

Geno nearly choked on the water he was drinking. A roar of laughter went around the table. Lucca nearly fell off his chair.

"I'll give you that Stefano could be considered a sex symbol, but Geno?" Lucca asked when he could finally speak.

"Have you ever actually looked at the magazines all of you are in?" Nicoletta inquired very softly, pinning Lucca with her large dark eyes. "Believe me, all of us have looked at them, with your ten thousand women hanging off your arms."

Geno groaned. "Don't, honey. I'm still trying to convince Amaranthe I'm not the kind of man women want to take home to mother. Well, except her. She wants to take me home."

"I do?" Amaranthe's eyebrow shot up.

"Yes." Geno was very firm. "You do."

His phone buzzed. The downstairs desk informed him that Detectives Patrick Bowden and Terence Laker were there to see Geno, Salvatore, Lucca and Amaranthe. Geno sighed and gave the okay to have the two policemen come up to his home.

"For them to want to see the four of us, this has to have something to do with what went on in the studio this afternoon."

"Put your lawyer on standby," Stefano suggested.

Geno texted Raffaele Rossi to let him know the detectives were on their way up and he wanted him on standby.

Raffaele texted back he would be dropping by.

Francesca got up and added plates and silverware to the sideboard. "Perhaps we should invite the detectives to dinner."

"Only you would think of that," Stefano said.

She smiled at him. "It never hurts to be polite. It will make it much more difficult for them to be nasty to us."

Geno liked her thinking. That was the thing about Francesca—he always managed to learn something from her. She was right. Inviting the detectives to sit down and eat with them, even if they refused, would make it much harder for the two men to say or do anything that would be impolite, especially with the women in the room.

"How is it this detective became your friend, Geno?" Taviano asked. "He couldn't have grown up in your circle and you didn't attend local schools. None of us were allowed. We were all on accelerated programs. Where did you meet him?"

Geno glanced at his brothers. Lucca grinned at him. Salvatore raised an eyebrow. Geno leaned back in his chair and slipped his arm around Amaranthe's slender shoulders. He found himself being very aware of the difference in their sizes since he'd made love to her. It hadn't been a thing before. Now it was.

"Geno?" Francesca prompted.

"His mother, Mauve Bowden, was a piano teacher," Geno admitted with obvious reluctance. "She came to our home and brought Patrick with her. He was my age. His mother was nice. I really liked her."

"We all did," Salvatore added. "Patrick was like her. She was like Francesca. She always saw the best in people."

Lucca nodded. "And she brought out the best in people."

"In some ways, Patrick inherited that trait from her," Geno continued, grateful the topic was off piano playing and back onto the detective. "He was always kind. He has good instincts as a detective. I've often wondered if he has a strong psychic ability, because he gets on the right track fast even when there's very little to go on. I've followed his career."

"Becoming a police officer seems a strange career choice for a man with his character traits," Stefano ventured.

"The Bowden home was broken into, and Mauve was violated and murdered."

Geno's voice went completely expressionless. He couldn't

help it. He'd lost his parents by that time. They'd shut themselves behind doors, and those doors may as well have been
a brick wall. Mauve and Patrick had continued to be in his
life until then. The blow of losing her had been visceral.
He'd been eighteen.

Mauve might not have known what was going on in his
household, but she was shrewd enough to make a good
guess, and she treated not only Geno but also his younger
brothers with extra kindness. With extra care. She showed
them love without making them think she felt sorry for them.

The loss of Mauve had gutted him, and Patrick had seen
his reaction before Geno had been able to mask it. That was
probably what had bound them together after her death.
Patrick had needed money, and Geno hired him to continue
his piano lessons. Eventually, Geno found out through their
conversations that Patrick wanted to go to the police academy. His mother's killer had been found but wasn't con-
victed. He was certain the man was guilty, but the evidence
had been compromised.

Geno had provided the money for Patrick to go to the
academy through a scholarship. He had no idea whether or
not Patrick was aware the money came from him, but Geno
never said a word about it to the man, nor would he. There
were many such scholarships for those residing in the Ferraro territory. His family looked after the people they considered their own and tried to give them every chance to
succeed in education and business.

After Patrick became a policeman, they saw little of
each other. Over the years, their paths went in two different
directions, but when they did see one another, they remained
friendly. Geno respected Patrick and kept track of him. Patrick had been brilliant at police work. He was diplomatic
with people and had a good reputation. Geno had expected
nothing less of him.

Once Mauve's killer had been released, Geno had both
teams of investigators thoroughly look into the crime and
the mountain of evidence that had been unable to be used

in the trial. He had them investigate the suspect to determine whether they believed he had been the one to rape and kill Mauve. There was more than enough forensic evidence on Mauve's body and in her house to convict the man. His DNA was everywhere, but it had been contaminated and was unable to be used in court.

Geno took a deep breath, his fingers dropping to the nape of Amaranthe's neck to massage any tension there. The tension was really in his neck and shoulders. "That was the most difficult moment for me as the leader of my family and the shadow riders. I wanted to be the one to bring justice to Mauve's killer," he admitted to his family. "It was so hard to make the decision to follow protocol and turn the evidence over to Stefano and allow the Chicago riders to handle it while we looked like dumbass playboys partying it up with our cousins, showing them a good time in the clubs."

"He's dead," Stefano reminded. "Justice was served. Not revenge. Justice."

Geno inclined his head. "I'm not always as evolved as you, Stefano, no matter how hard I try."

The elevator opened, and the app on Geno's and his brothers' phones announced the visitors. Salvatore immediately got up to escort their visitors through the great room to the open kitchen and dining area.

The two detectives looked startled to see the amount of people seated around the table. Geno rose immediately, offering his hand to Patrick first.

"We were just sitting down to dinner. A few of my cousins are here celebrating my engagement to Amaranthe. You met her the other day, Patrick. This is Detective Patrick Bowden, everyone." He switched his gaze to Bowden's partner. "And his partner, Detective Terence Laker. You're welcome to join us. Francesca and Taviano are excellent cooks. There's plenty of food and plenty of room at the table." He waved toward the sideboard, where delicious smells were emanating from the warmers.

"I'm sorry to come at a bad time, Geno," Patrick said.

Geno noted he sounded apologetic. Their phones played again, and Raffaele Rossi strode in. He wore a dark blue suit. His dark hair curled in every direction. He looked more like a model and less like a lawyer than anyone Geno could imagine. He was a shark in a courtroom.

Grinning, he winked at them. "Sorry I'm late, everyone. Met a girl on an elevator." He stopped abruptly as though just seeing the detectives. "I see we have company. Is this an official visit, gentlemen?"

"We have some questions for Geno, Salvatore, Lucca and Amaranthe," Patrick said.

Geno gut clenched at the inclusion of Amaranthe. He glanced at Stefano and then his brothers.

Amara, don't answer a single question without Raffaele's consent or input. Something is going on here other than a follow-up to the death of the woman at Miranda's.

Amaranthe didn't make the mistake of looking at him. She smiled at Nicoletta and indicated the bowl of fresh-baked sourdough bread. Nicoletta passed it to her immediately.

Raffaele glanced at his watch. "This late? Must be important." He went from handsome, cocky young man to serious lawyer in the blink of an eye. "Is it so important they should stop eating with their cousins, or can you ask your questions while they eat hot food?"

That put the detectives on the spot. Patrick and Terence had come up to Geno, clearly hoping to appear casual with their questions. If they insisted on a separate room, taking the couple from their hot meal, it would look more like an interrogation.

Terence waved Geno and Raffaele toward the table.

Geno pulled his chair closer to Amaranthe. "Our engagement party is once again interrupted, Danzatrice Ombra. I'm not certain what else we can tell you, if anything, about the woman at Miranda's, Patrick. Or who might have wanted to kill her. She was a complete stranger."

"That investigation is ongoing, Geno," Patrick said. "This has to do with another matter altogether. Apparently, there was some incident that happened in a dance studio you own. All of you were present."

Geno's brows drew together. "Incident?"

Raffaele waved him to silence. "You'll have to be more specific, Detective. I'm sure many incidents happen in a dance studio. Did someone file a complaint against one of my clients? What are we talking about here?" Although he was helping himself to food from the warmers, he sounded very serious.

"Was there a problem with a teenage girl named Jennifer Porthman?" Terence asked.

Lucca sighed. "She was very disruptive and made the younger girls cry. We were there to talk to Amara for a minute. The way she kept interrupting class and disrespecting the instructors was too much for me. I went outside and waited in the car so I didn't have to watch her pathetic little show."

"Lucca," Raffaele cautioned.

Lucca put his hands in the air. "That's my statement. He wanted one, I gave it to him."

"Jenny believes her parents can pay her way out of any trouble she gets into," Salvatore concurred. "She was asked to call home, and she escalated her behavior rather than comply, believing the studio would accept money rather than have her leave."

"Where were you when this happened, and what did you do?" Patrick persisted.

"Before I allow him to answer," Raffaele said, waving a forkful of lasagna so the aroma permeated the air, "has this girl or her family brought charges or a complaint against any of my clients?"

"No," Terence said, his gaze on the fork. "We would like these statements."

"I was leaning against the bank of windows at the street entrance. Lucca had been next to me before he left. Neither one of us went farther into the studio because they were conducting classes, and there were a lot of little girls in there. I didn't *do* anything. It wasn't my place to do anything. Technically, I own the business with Lucca and Geno. So yes, I concurred with the decision to have the girl permanently removed from the class when she refused to cooperate, but I didn't do anything other than observe her bullying, swearing and trying to take a punch at Amara."

The moment he admitted the teenager had taken a punch at Amaranthe, Salvatore was stricken with guilt. *I'm sorry, Geno. Amara. I shouldn't have said that to them.*

They already have that information, or they wouldn't be here to confirm it. We had to admit it to them, or they'd believe we're trying to hide it, Geno said. *But, Amara, you don't say one word without Raffaele's consent until we know what this is about. Who knows what that hideous little girl has done now.*

"Ms. Aubert, would you tell me what happened?" Terence asked. He wandered over to the sideboard and lifted the lid on the lasagna, inhaling the aroma.

"Amaranthe, don't answer his question," Raffaele interrupted. "We've been more than cooperative. Put the lid back down, Detective. Why exactly are you here? I'm not allowing my clients to answer any further questions until you let us know what is going on."

"It's odd that neither Lucca nor Salvatore mentioned Ms. Marchel as being part of the problem," Patrick observed.

Geno sighed. "Seriously, Patrick? Detective Laker asked if there had been a problem with a teenage girl named Jennifer Porthman, not if Ms. Marchel was involved. Had that question been asked, it would have been answered."

"Did Ms. Marchel file a complaint against any of my clients?" Raffaele asked.

"No," Terence assured them.

"Spit it out or we're done," Raffaele snapped. "We'll make an appointment to meet with you at the station if you want any other questions answered."

"Geno." Patrick ignored Raffaele. "Who the hell has it in for you? Who wants you implicated in murder? Every time I turn around, someone you know is either robbed or murdered and your name comes up."

"Patrick," Terence cautioned.

"For God's sake, Terence. We checked his alibi every time. We know where he was tonight. We saw him."

"He's a billionaire. He can pay for whatever he wants."

Good cop, bad cop routine in your own dining room? Stefano asked.

"I've known Geno a long time, Terence, and in any case, I can tell you, someone's out to get him, not the other way around." Patrick looked stricken. For the first time Geno could see that he mattered to the detective. "I'm serious, somebody either wants you dead or in prison. Tonight, Lyna Marchel was murdered in the same way your parents were murdered. In the same way Noemi and Caio Diliberto were murdered. In the same way Viola and Marcelle Marino were murdered. A similar weapon was used on the young woman murdered on the porch of Miranda's Miracles."

Beside him, Amaranthe placed her fork on her plate and turned her face up to his, shock in her eyes. "Lyna? Why would anyone kill Lyna?"

"They dipped her finger in blood and wrote your name, Geno, as if she named you as her killer," Patrick persisted. "It was your good luck that you went straight from the studio to your home, and every traffic light confirmed it, and then the security cameras in this building confirmed it. Your car was easy to track. The time of her death was easy to establish. At that time, you were going into the condo. You have enemies, Geno. I want to know who they are."

"Patrick, if I knew who killed my parents, don't you think I'd tell you? If I had a clue who was doing this, targeting people who matter to me." Geno gestured around the table to his cousins. "I was afraid to have my brothers here in New York with me. I asked them to stay away. I was afraid to have my cousins and their wives here. I don't like

Amaranthe going to work. She's supposed to perform and needs to go to rehearsal. It terrifies me to have her go because I'm afraid she's a target. Honestly, I even worry about you," Geno admitted. "That someone might find out you matter to me."

There was a short silence. "The lasagna smells good," Terence said hopefully, looking at Raffaele. "I'm practically family with that admission."

"Patrick's family. You're—I don't know what you are," Raffaele denied. "Fine, sit down. Food's great. Amara, I'm sorry about Ms. Marchel. You've been having a difficult time of it."

Terence hastily filled a plate with food and sank into a vacant chair. "We've been at this for hours. I'm starving."

Patrick sat, but he didn't take any food. He looked more distressed than ever. "Geno, your people must have files on threats made to you."

Francesca got up, moved around the table to the sideboard and immediately fixed a plate of food for the detective.

"I'm Stefano Ferraro," Stefano introduced himself, "Geno's cousin. My brother Taviano; his wife, Nicoletta; my wife, Francesca. We've looked at all those threats numerous times. We have teams of investigators looking at them. We have other cousins with teams of investigators looking at them. Like you, we feel the threat to Geno and his family is very real. We have no idea why, and we're searching for a reason."

"I buy and sell companies," Geno offered. "I try to save them, if possible, but there are times I can't. People lose their jobs. I have no way of knowing if someone lost their job years ago and is holding a grudge. Why would they kill my parents? Or relatives my mother was raised with, but I had little interaction with? It wasn't like my brothers and I spent holidays at their homes."

Patrick looked up at Francesca when she put the plate in front of him. "Thank you, ma'am. That was kind of you."

He picked up the fork she laid by the plate, looking for all the world as if he was on automatic pilot when it came to food.

"You need to eat if you want brain cells working," she replied.

I love you, Francesca, Geno said. *You're an amazing woman.*

Francesca flashed him a smile and took a seat beside her husband.

"My brain cells haven't been working for a while now," Patrick muttered. His eyes met Geno's. "This may have nothing to do with it, but it's been nagging at me. When things bother me and won't let go, I find I'm usually on the right track." He indicated Terence. "My partner and his wife like to go clubbing."

Terence grinned. "Met my wife at a dance club. We go out most weekends. Try to drag Patrick as often as possible." He took the salad bowl Salvatore offered him. "This is damn good. I was starving."

Patrick ignored the byplay. "I was at the bar, and a woman came up to me. She was really cute, had an accent and was flirting like crazy. That doesn't happen in my world. I'm not very outgoing. The club, by the way, was your club, The Fast Lane."

"She was all over him," Terence confirmed. "Little Australian woman. She danced the night away with him."

The moment Terence identified the woman as Australian, Geno went on alert. "How long ago was this, Patrick?"

"About seven months. We dated for approximately two months, although not steady. I was uncomfortable with her questions. When we were in the club, she asked if I knew the owners. I didn't answer her, but she was persistent and kept repeating the question. Eventually, I said I'd met you in passing, but we obviously didn't run in the same circles. I told her I was a cop, and you were a billionaire. I think I laughed, and she let it drop. At least that night she did."

Geno glanced at Stefano. Seven months earlier. Someone had been already setting them up. They did know about Patrick, so they'd done thorough research on Geno and his family. They knew about the connection between the Bowden and Ferraro families, which meant Patrick could be a target.

"Sometime after our third or fourth date, your name came up again. She asked casually if I'd been to your house. If you lived with your parents. If I had ever been to the house. She said the reason she asked is because she had been sightseeing and she saw the house your parents lived in, and it looked huge and quite cool. She claimed it looked like a mansion. Had she kept the conversation to the house, it wouldn't have raised a red flag, but she kept bringing you into it and asking personal questions about your parents."

"You dumped her," Lucca stated.

"At first, I was polite and just tried to fade away by being busy. I'd told her from the beginning that I worked quite a bit. But she continued to call me," Patrick admitted.

Geno had to smile. That was Patrick. He didn't like hurting people. He might be a brilliant detective, but he was still that kindhearted kid his mother had raised.

"I think that Australian woman was a scout for the people who murdered my parents. My father had lost his leg and was using a wheelchair the night he was murdered, but both he and my mother were excellent at self-defense," Geno said. "When I say *excellent*, I mean that in every sense of the word. My mother was facing my father. She wouldn't have been so frightened she suddenly froze in place. She would have reacted in the manner she had trained in for years. There had to be a reason she didn't. Patrick, we believe this killer isn't acting alone. We believe there are two of them."

Geno was watching the detective's eyes, and he realized Patrick had already come to that same conclusion. "We also think the second killer is using a drug to incapacitate the second victim so they can't move. We've asked our cousin to help us identify what might be used in such a scenario.

The drug would have to be very fast-acting but then disappear from the system so the medical examiner wouldn't find it."

Patrick finished chewing and then sighed. "I'm going to have to remove myself from this case. I didn't want to. I thought because we hadn't seen each other in years our connection wouldn't taint evidence for a conviction. I can't take that chance."

"You also can't take chances with your life. I think that woman contacting you means you're in danger," Geno said. "You're most likely on their hit list. We need to get you to a safer environment."

"I'm a police detective, Geno," Patrick reminded. "I can't turn tail and run. And I can't just disappear."

"Sure you can," Terence said cheerfully. "You have enough vacation time coming to you for fifty people. We can make it happen by tomorrow morning."

"My wife will be flying home in our personal jet. You can stay at the hotel and help keep watch over her and my family. I'd take that as a personal favor," Stefano said. "She's an excellent cook, which is the upside, but she never does what she's told. I'll warn you ahead of time, she smiles sweetly, and you think she isn't going to go visit that sick woman down the street, but she is. Take extra bodyguards and insist on going with her whether she says you don't need to or not."

Geno could have kissed his cousin. Stefano made it seem as if Patrick were doing him a huge favor by looking after Francesca, who just laughed without one ounce of remorse. Geno felt better now that he knew Patrick would be safe. He had no idea why Lyna was targeted, but at least Patrick would be alive and well when all this was over.

CHAPTER SEVENTEEN

Amaranthe didn't know how to seduce her fiancé. She wasn't good at that kind of thing. Moreover, she was very nervous. Things hadn't gone that well the first time around, but she knew he was a man who enjoyed sex and wanted it often.

They slept in the same bed, and she could feel—and see—his body reacting to hers, so she knew he wanted her. It wasn't that he didn't find her attractive. He was worried he'd hurt her. She had been sore after that first time. She couldn't deny that. She hadn't achieved an orgasm, and that had really bothered him. She tried not to feel like a failure, and she hated that he did.

Francesca had left New York as soon as Patrick Bowden had arranged with his boss to take personal time. He went with her, and Geno was noticeably relieved. She found herself falling more in love with him when she realized just how much the detective meant to him. Lyna Marchel had no family, and the Ferraro family claimed her body, making the necessary arrangements to take the body when it would be released. She knew the Ferraros made a habit of caring for the people in their territory, but seeing it in action emphasized that care.

Amaranthe wanted to be a part of Geno's family. Mostly she wanted to be a part of him. She looked out the thick glass that made up one wall of the room. She loved that the master bedroom was open and spacious. The platform bed sitting at the top of the spiral stairs gave them a great view of the river. There was a library and an enormous master bath with soaking tubs and a double shower. The walk-in closet could have been a small apartment. At the far end of the floor was a grand piano. She thought it had been there for show. Now she knew Geno could play.

Geno was a wonderful man. Kind and caring. Much more so than he believed he was. He had admitted, in front of his family, and in front of Patrick Bowden's partner, that the man mattered to him. Geno thought of himself as impassive, unemotional, with a heart of stone, but he wasn't. He had a marshmallow for a heart. He just protected it, and with good reason.

He'd been deserted by his parents and forced to grow up almost overnight. He'd been thrust into a position of immense responsibility, and he'd taken that very seriously. He was an adult for years before he'd become one biologically. He learned not to trust those closest to him. Like all children, he blamed himself for his parents' desertion. He thought something was wrong with him. He believed he wasn't lovable. He was certain he did things wrong. Now he believed he'd let Amaranthe down.

Amaranthe found herself drowning in love for him. She told herself it was too soon. She shouldn't fall so hard— so fast. It didn't matter. She saw him. Into him. Into the heart of him, and everything she was immediately fell in love. She was protective and loyal. She wanted to care for him. Make certain he had everything he ever wanted or needed. She wanted to be the one person in his life who he counted on, who he talked things over with and knew he could rely on. She wanted to be his home.

There was just this one hurdle she didn't quite know how to overcome yet, but she was determined that she would. Geno loved sex. She knew he did. It wasn't just up to him to see to it that they had a good sexual relationship. It was up to her as well. She wanted to be his partner in every way. Not just an adequate partner, or good—she wanted to be fantastic. One didn't become fantastic without experience, and she wasn't going to get that if they didn't have sex.

She did her research. That was the only way she knew how to proceed. Step one was study the subject, and she studied. She went online to every site that gave tips on how to best have sex when she was smaller and he was larger. She got lots of great advice, much of it the same. She was determined to put it all to use—if she could do so without being too shy. The advice called for her to be the seducer. She felt she wasn't going to be good at being the one directing the evening, but she was going to try because Geno was worth it, and she wanted to enjoy sex with him.

Foreplay was important. Very important. Lots and lots of foreplay. Toys, even. Orgasms would be excellent. Even for Geno prior to penetration. Lube was extremely important. Positions mattered so she could control entry and how deep he penetrated. She blushed thinking about what she intended to do, but she was no shrinking violet. This was important for both of them.

Amaranthe was determined to give Geno everything he could ever want if it was in her power to do so. She wanted him to feel loved. Deeply loved. She wanted him to know, the moment he laid eyes on her each day, that he had one person who built her life around him.

She put on her ballet slippers—not her pointe shoes, this wasn't a formal ballet, but one of her nicer pairs and took out the chain she had purchased to go around her hips. It wasn't diamonds, but when she looked at the price of a diamond chain, it was outrageous. No way could she afford it, not even if she wanted to spend the majority of her savings, which she didn't.

She laid out the toys and lube in plain sight so Geno couldn't fail to see them when he came out of his office. She put on music and wrapped the fine gold chain around her hips. The music immediately put her in the mood to dance. It always did. The moment she heard music, it would play through every muscle and cell in her body urging her to move to the rhythm. It had always been that way for as long as she could remember. She could lose herself in the beauty of the rhythm, her mind in complete harmony.

She shed the little robe and went to the open space where she'd chosen to dance. The room was purposely dim, with just a faint light shining on that section. It had taken her some time to figure the lighting out. She'd even set up her phone to record a couple of short dance moves to see how the lighting played over her body. She liked the way her hair moved, one moment covering her and the next revealing her slight curves. Geno had been right about the diamond chain. It would have glittered beautifully in the light.

"What is my sexy little *danzatrice ombra* up to?"

Geno's rasp was more of a growl than a rasp. The sound sent goose bumps erupting all over her body. She turned to him, suddenly feeling very seductive. Very provocative and surer of herself than she ever had. She hadn't even gotten started, and he was reacting exactly as she wanted him to.

She flashed him a smile. "I've got a surprise for you. You have to strip though. No clothes for you."

His gaze dropped to the toy and the lube she'd laid out and then to her naked body. "You're certain, Amaranthe? This could be dangerous."

"Dangerous for you. I have a plan. We followed yours, now we're going to follow mine. I wanted to give you something special. It's going to take a while, but I promise you, you're going to have a very good time."

"I did buy you a diamond chain, Amara, in the hopes

that you'd dance for me," he said. "My cousin Damian made it for you."

He shrugged out of his shirt, his back to her, and she couldn't help but admire the way his muscles rippled as he walked toward the raised platform. Pulling open a drawer, he took out a rectangular case.

"Come here, baby." Sinking onto the bed, he pulled off his loafers, letting them drop to the floor. "I want to put it on you." He picked up first the small toy that fit over her clit and then the dildo, which wasn't quite as large as he was. "Are you going to use these?" He raised his gaze to hers, and the desire creeping into all that dark blue sent a wave of weakness through her.

She moved between his thighs and unhooked the fine gold chain. "Yes. I'm going to dance for you first. Hopefully, you'll find my dancing sexy. I'll find it sexy if you're using that lube and getting yourself off while I'm getting myself off. We'll just be getting started." She wanted to reassure him that they would be doing more than watching each other.

Geno leaned forward and brushed kisses over her lips. Featherlight. As if he were painting them with an artist's brush. Her heart stuttered. Her sex clenched. His hands dropped to her hips, and he pulled her closer to the heat of his groin. He was so hot. Only the material of his trousers separated them. She was completely naked other than her ballet slippers. She pressed tight against the thick evidence of his desire. He was long and thick, so hard, his girth wide. She rubbed against him without conscious thought, trying to alleviate the building ache.

She'd been thinking about making love with Geno for days, looking up the best ways to make things work between them. She'd spent so much time thinking about him and working out the details, planning for this night, that she was already aroused.

Geno leaned closer, kissing his way over her chin and down her throat to the curve of her breasts as he reached around her to clip the thin chain of diamonds around her hips. His mouth closed over her right breast, and he sucked, his tongue fluttering against her nipple. Fire streaked from her nipple straight to her sex. She circled his neck with one arm and stroked the front of his trousers with her palm.

Anticipation was very necessary when it came to sex. She was so ready after thinking about Geno for so long and planning everything out for him. She loved those sensual lines carved so deep in his face. The way his eyes lit up for her. Not just lit up. It was far more than that. There was love there. So much she could drown in it. She couldn't remember having anyone love her. Not like this. Wholly focused. Intense. Overwhelming. Real.

Geno was a sexual man. Not just sexual, but everything he did was sensual. He might look different from his suave and sophisticated cousins, but his dark, dangerous appearance only added to his sensual attraction. She saw the way other women looked at him. There was a natural, primitive appeal. He would never want for sexual partners if he looked for them.

"You always look so beautiful, Amaranthe," Geno murmured.

His breath felt hot against her skin, adding to the desire coiling like a hot fist deep in her abdomen. The pressure built faster and stronger than she expected.

She was very certain Geno was the only one who thought she was beautiful, but she knew he genuinely believed her to be, and that knowledge made her feel beautiful. And sexy. She'd never considered herself sensual, but right at that moment, with Geno looking at her the way he was, she felt sensual. That feeling and the way he looked at her gave her the necessary courage to continue with her plan.

She stepped away from him reluctantly. "I think you really need to strip, Geno. Everything off." Desperately trying not to blush, she indicated the items she'd laid out on the tray. "I'm dancing for you and hopefully you'll enjoy yourself. *Really* enjoy yourself."

Geno flashed her a dark sensual smile, one that took her breath and sent heat spiraling down her spine. He had no inhibitions at all. He shed his clothes with an easy casualness, his fist circling his heavy cock as he stretched out, one hand lifting the toys on the tray.

"You did a good job shopping, Amara. I did some shopping as well."

More color swept up her skin. "You did? Were we reading the same articles?"

"We seem to be on the same page when we decide on things," he said. He put down the thick dildo and used the lube. "Nice that this is good-tasting."

Her blush deepened. "I'm all about thinking ahead."

Geno's body was already as hard as a rock. He couldn't take his eyes off his shadow dancer. He'd done everything wrong his first night with her, although he'd been determined to do things right. He'd been too rough, gone too deep, made her sore. He wasn't going to repeat his mistakes. He'd done research on the internet, but he'd also consulted with an expert on how someone his size could have the best sex possible with someone Amaranthe's size. It seemed as if Amaranthe had done the same. He loved her even more for caring enough to spend the time researching and then putting a plan into action.

Just seeing the toys and lube on the tray had Geno choking with emotion. She loved him enough to want to research the same way he had. She hadn't retreated from him the way many women might have, instead she'd looked for ways to make their sex life good. Instinctively, he knew she wanted that for him because he mattered to her. When he considered having a partner, he hadn't really envisioned her loving him or even caring enough to do little things for him, let alone finding ways to make their sexual relationship as amazing as possible.

Geno had always thought he would be the one to make

or break the relationship with his wife. He knew he would be faithful, and he would demand her fidelity, but in all honesty, he didn't expect her to remain loyal to him. He really didn't expect her to love him. Along came Amaranthe. His heart clenched hard in his chest as the fireplace sprang to life and the music started.

His dancer was so small, tiny really, in comparison with him. She glided across the floor looking ethereal in the dim light she'd created. He could imagine her in a forest of trees with fog surrounding her, a fairy princess dancing in and out of the veil of silvery light, believing no one could see her as she spun and swayed so gracefully.

Her hair fell in thick waves, covering her feminine form, and then the long waves would part to reveal the smooth line of her back or her small, perfect breasts. Sometimes as she spun or leapt or swayed, it was only the glitter of diamonds on her hips and the enticement of the vee between her legs he caught glimpses of.

Geno thought the dance was the most sensual performance he'd ever seen. He'd been to many clubs, and this wasn't a bump and grind. She wasn't consciously trying to be sexy for him. She'd given herself up to the music, become totally lost in it. The moment she did, her natural sensuality took over. She moved through the light and shadows, holding him spellbound.

His body reacted to the erotic vision, his cock pure steel. Without conscious thought, his fist tightened, moving faster to the beat of the music. Heat racing down his spine, radiating out from his groin so that intense pleasure burst over him. Then his cock was erupting like a volcano, jerking over and over while he shuddered with euphoric release and didn't want the feeling to end.

Through his climax, he hadn't taken his gaze from his shadow dancer. She was exquisite. Perfect. Sexy. Everything he could have dreamed of but hadn't had the imagination for. He'd never once conceived of having a woman like Amaranthe for himself. The music began to slow. To fade. She slowed her pace. He became aware of the sticky mess on his stomach, thighs and fist. In a warmer on the bedside table were a towel and a wet cloth. Amaranthe thought of everything. He cleaned himself, unable to keep his gaze from straying back to her.

"You are not only beautiful, Amaranthe, but you dance like a dream," he said. The rasp in his voice was more pronounced than ever. He sounded gruff. Primal.

She hadn't come up the stairs to him yet but stood in the middle of the floor with the dark cloud of hair falling around her. Her hair was wild, the waves and curls adding to her sexy appeal. She tilted her chin, her eyes bright, both hands moving over her body, following the path his would have taken if she were close to him. She traced the upper curves of her breasts.

"I always thought I was too small until I was with you. Suddenly, I not only feel beautiful, but sexy. You make me feel that way, Geno."

His breath caught in his lungs as her hands framed her breasts. His cock was coming back to life that fast. It was difficult enough to pull his gaze away from his fiancée when she was anywhere near him, but when her hands moved in a slow seduction over her body, it was impossible.

She glided up the stairs toward him, once more moving in and out of the dim light provided by the lamps in the room so that she appeared to be behind the silvery veil again. The light from the sliver of moon burst out from behind a dark cloud to spotlight her, turning the mass of dark hair into shiny, wild silk. The chain of diamonds glittered invitingly, drawing attention to the shape of her hips, her feminine belly and the dark curls hiding treasure at the junction of her legs.

His heart stuttered in his chest. It wasn't just her beauty—and he thought her the most beautiful woman in the world, it was the look in her eyes when her gaze settled on his. Desire was there. Lust even. But most of all love. Deep love. When she looked at him, her entire face softened. That look was priceless to him.

She climbed right up onto the end of the bed, her gaze dropping to his cock he'd once again fisted in his hand. He barely knew he was pumping slowly; he was so mesmerized by her. The tip of her tongue touched her bottom lip and then she began to crawl up the bed, looking as if she were stalking him. His heart accelerated as she crawled right over his legs, licking and nipping his thighs, so he shifted to give her better access.

Geno brushed back the silken strands of her hair to better see her face, although the sensation of the hair moving against his bare skin combined with the sight of her was nearly his undoing. He couldn't allow himself to lose control again.

"Danzatrice Ombra, you gave me such a gift, it's my turn to give you one." Easily, he caught her under her shoulders and pulled her up beside him, rolling her over onto her back, almost all in one motion.

She gasped as she sprawled out beside him, her gaze jumping to his face, eyes moving over him with that loving adoration he knew he'd never get used to but would always crave. Her skin was flushed a beautiful rose, her breathing ragged. Never once did she take her gaze from his. There was trust mixed in the dark beauty of desire raging in her eyes.

He bent his head to hers, finding her mouth, those soft lips that drew him like a magnet. Kissing her transported him to another world. The truth was, he didn't remember kissing any other woman before Amaranthe. No one tasted the way she did. No one poured fire into his veins or love into his heart the way she did. No one was memorable, or maybe it was just that she was so extraordinary she drove everyone else from his mind.

He kissed his way down her throat, lingering for a moment on her pulse, tasting her heart beating wildly, matching the primal beat of his. He found the curve of her breasts. Her tight nipples, responsive to the gentle rake of his teeth and tugging and pinching of his fingers along with the intense heat of his mouth. She arched her back, offering herself to him with those little soft moans that played like music in his head.

He moved his palm down her belly, taking in all that soft, satin skin. His. She gave that to him. Shared with him. She was such a miracle. Her tiny curls were damp with need, her entrance slick, already hot and inviting. Just what they wanted and needed. He kissed his way down her belly and inhaled her feminine fragrance, unique to her, triggering the addiction for her taste she'd already set up in him.

He settled between her legs, using his wide shoulders to hold her legs open for him. He wanted to take his time. Do this right. Give his woman as much pleasure as possible. Not just one orgasm, but multiple. She needed to be very slick to take his cock. This time he was determined she would feel nothing but absolute pleasure.

Geno used his vast skills, mouth, tongue and fingers to bring her to orgasm several times. He took her up slow, letting the burn smolder and then burst into flames so that the orgasm took her by surprise. As she was coming down, he took her back up again, using his tongue and the flick of his fingers on her clit, so that one orgasm rolled right into another.

By her third orgasm, Amaranthe's head thrashed on the pillow, and she dug her heels into the duvet as if she might escape. He wiped his glistening jaw on the inside of her thigh and reached for the toy on the tray on the end table.

"What are you doing?" She sounded breathless.

"Making certain you're ready for me." The rasp in his voice was more pronounced than ever. She might not be ready, but he was. His cock was pure steel. Painful even.

"I'm sure I'm more than ready, Geno," she assured.

"We're going to make sure," he decreed. "Not to mention, this helps prepare your body for my size."

The smallest smile flashed across her face. "You like this."

"I do," he admitted. "Sexy as sin."

It was. He was easy about it, sliding the toy into her as gently as possible. Pleasure washed over him watching her body take the toy, watching her hips jolt, hear the moan, the gasp as her body fought to accommodate the girth of the dildo. He set the toy on the lowest setting as he slowly watched her body swallow it. The sight was sexy as hell. He couldn't help fisting his cock, wishing the lube were closer.

"Do you want to take over?" He didn't want her to, but he didn't want to go too deep.

She shook her head. "It isn't burning. I'll say stop if you need to. I'm already close. So close."

He could hear it in her voice. He turned the toy up another notch and let the dildo go another half inch deeper. She exploded, crying out, a soft little musical hitch. He pulled the toy out and put it on the tray, caught up the lube as he rolled to his back and beckoned to her.

"All right, *la mia danzatrice ombra*. You're going to control how deep you go. Straddle me. Just lower yourself over the top of me. Like a cowgirl."

Amaranthe didn't hesitate. She was still feeling the aftershocks of the orgasm, and the expression on her face was beautiful. Her eyes met his in a startled, shocked, nearly dazed wonder. Geno had to help her, his hands on her waist, lifting her, so that she sat on his hips, legs on either side of his.

"That's it, baby. Go slow," he encouraged. He once more fisted his cock at the base, making certain she wouldn't go so deep, and there wouldn't be pain or damage. He had listened carefully to everything the expert had said to him, and he was determined to ensure Amaranthe had the best possible experience. He was not going to get so caught up in the pleasure that he lost control of the situation. Still, it was the biggest challenge of his life.

Amaranthe's heat hit the sensitive head of his cock and

then slowly swallowed him. The fit was exquisitely tight despite all their preparation. She was slick and hot, very ready for him, but his girth still strained her capacity to take him. She took her time, allowing her body to adjust, using a little twist that sent flames spiraling through his veins. His fingers dug into her hip, but he didn't take control, allowing her to go at her own pace.

She was incredibly sexy sitting astride him, undulating with little twisting hip motions to take his cock deeper, and then stopping to allow her body to adjust. Each time she stopped, he felt the grip of her sheath, that strangling silken heat surrounding his shaft, gripping like a thousand fists.

Her lashes fluttered, her breathing turned ragged, and the musical notes rose to a crescendo as she began to rise and fall in a rhythm, taking him deeper and deeper. At first, almost in slow motion, her body seemed to ripple to a beat that began to climb in pace—like a sensually moving dancer. It was impossible to take his gaze from her as she rode him.

He felt her heartbeat with every inch she took of his cock as she swallowed his girth and that silken tunnel surrounded him. Then she was moving faster and faster, throwing her head back and singing her little moan. Tentatively, he loosened his grip on his cock to allow her to sink deeper. It also allowed him to turn the overhead lamp on—to cast a shadow so he could see what she felt.

Hot pleasure rose like a tidal wave, swamping both as she rode him. Each jolt sent streaks of lightning rushing through their veins. Flames danced through them, arced over them. Rose higher and higher as the tension coiled tighter. Geno murmured softly to her, telling her he loved her, stroking caresses over her breasts, tugging at her nipples.

"Geno," she whispered.

"Let go, Danzatrice Ombra, fly with me." He flicked her clit as he whispered the invitation.

Her silken sheath clamped down on his cock, a hungry

mouth milking him, pulling at him, determined to milk every last drop from him. Flames threatened to destroy them both, burn them to ashes. Colors flashed behind their eyes. Stars surrounded them. They floated together, bodies joined through their sensual experience and minds joined by the shadows.

Eventually, Amaranthe collapsed over the top of him, her head colliding with his shoulder, the movement of her body tightening her sheath even more around his shaft, sending aftershocks rippling through them both. Her breath was warm against his skin. Geno slid his fingers into her hair and held her to him, listening to the combined wild beating of their hearts.

"You all right, *bella*?" Geno murmured. He kept his eyes closed, savoring the feeling of the two of them joined together. Skin to skin. Sharing the same body. Sharing her mind. Feeling every beat of her heart. Already her body was relaxing around his.

"Perfect. Absolutely perfect." Her voice was a mere thread of sound.

"Don't go to sleep yet. Doc said you had to bathe with these special healing salts." He massaged her scalp and then her nape, amusement creeping into his voice.

"I'm going to sleep. You can take a bath with the salts. I'm sleeping right here."

He wouldn't mind if she fell asleep on him. She didn't weigh anything, but his body wouldn't relax as he was surrounded by her heat.

Suddenly, she lifted her head, eyes glittering at him. "What do you mean, *doc*? You consulted a *doctor*? I did research on the internet. I thought you did as well."

He did his best to keep from laughing. That little disapproving frown of hers was adorable, but clearly it was best not to say so. "I did research on the internet," he admitted. "But I wanted to know I was doing my best for you."

Very slowly, she rolled off him to curl beside him on the

bed. The friction her tight sheath created sent a shudder of pleasure through his body.

"Geno, you're so sweet. Thank you for caring so much."

He turned to wrap his arm around her and drag her even closer. "You amaze me, Amaranthe. You did all this for me. Arranging the entire evening. Do you have any idea how it makes me feel to know you did this for me?"

"I hope it makes you feel very loved, because you are."

He took a deep breath. "It does make me feel loved, baby. I need us to be together like this all the time. I don't want you to feel as if I'm pushing you too hard into marrying me right away, Amaranthe," Geno ventured carefully. "But the truth is, I am. As soon as this is over, I want us to get married. Immediately."

Her gaze jumped to his. "We talked about this briefly, but we did talk about it. We have the license. I said yes. Are you worried I'm going to back out—because I'm not. I'm absolutely certain I want to be your wife, Geno."

"There's uncertainty, Amaranthe, I feel it when our shadows are connected and when we're speaking mind to mind."

The pads of her fingers slid along his jaw as if she could smooth the shadow of bristles there. "If you feel any hesitation on my part, it isn't about being your wife. I think it's more the wedding. I don't have family. You have so many. It's awkward enough knowing the headlines are going to be all about speculating that I'm a gold digger, but if we have a wedding and the entire side of a church is filled with your family, and no one is on my side, and no one is walking me down the aisle, I'd just feel . . ." She trailed off.

Geno would always feel as if his parents abandoned him and his brothers, but he had a huge family. Stefano and his siblings in Chicago. Severino and his siblings in LA. Lorenzo and his siblings in San Francisco. The cousins were all very close and they backed one another without question. He had family. Amaranthe had no one. He couldn't imagine what it would feel like to be completely alone. The last thing he wanted was for her to feel isolated at her own wedding.

She didn't have friends to be bridesmaids or a maid of honor. His female cousins hadn't had the time with her to make her feel part of the family yet, so she wouldn't feel comfortable asking any of them. He understood.

"Amara, I want to marry you as soon as possible. Planning a wedding in our family takes months. As soon as this is over, we'll not tell anyone, other than a judge I know. He'll make us legal. Unless you want to go to Vegas."

Amaranthe smiled up at him, settling her head against the pillow. Her dark hair spilled around her, giving her that otherworldly look. "I think getting married right here in New York will be perfect. Should we ask your brothers to come? I don't want them to be hurt."

"The two of them seem like they're trustworthy, don't they?" Geno said. "But don't let their charm fool you. Those smiles are deceitful."

Amaranthe turned her face into the pillow to muffle her giggle. "Geno. They're sweet boys, although never tell them I called them boys."

"They're older than you are, but half the time they act like sneaky teens defying me." He tried his best to sound annoyed, just to get another musical laugh out of her. He *loved* when she laughed. She didn't let him down. Again, her soft little giggle floated up to him from where she had turned her head into the pillow.

"You make them sound like they're ten."

He swallowed the sudden lump in his throat as a million memories washed over him. Was this the way parents felt at times? He'd been a parent as well as a brother to Salvatore and Lucca. He'd never once resented them. He'd been angry with his parents for the hurt they caused the two boys. He'd gotten upset at his brothers for their behavior occasionally, but never once had he resented having to take care of them.

Geno knew he would forever feel as if at any moment he could be abandoned, that he wasn't lovable. His parents had done that to him after being amazing parents for thirteen years. They'd done the same to his brothers. Salvatore was very sensitive and compassionate. In his younger years, he'd been very close to his mother. When she'd turned cold and turned away from him, he'd been devastated. Something inside Geno had become so protective of his youngest brother that he felt almost murderous. That was when the rage had begun to form in his gut, and it never quite went away when it came to anything hurting either of his brothers.

He was proud of them. He wanted the best for them. He worried about them every day just as a parent would.

Her fingers were back tracing the line of his jaw, featherlight then moving over his bottom lip. It felt like caring. Like love. His gut tightened into hard knots. At the same time there was a curious melting sensation in the region of his heart. She didn't make grand gestures, but he didn't want or need them.

There was the look in her eyes. The touch of her fingers. The way she seemed to know whether he was happy or sad.

"Geno, I don't mind your brothers being with us. We don't want them hurt. We can tell them at the very last minute. I know you want them there. I do as well. I like the idea of having brothers, even though they are terrible teases."

He took her hand, turned it over and pressed a kiss into the center of her palm, love for her overwhelming him, the way he found it did more and more. She understood him. He didn't need to tell her that he wanted his brothers to be with him when he married the woman he was in love with. He had to swallow the lump in his throat before he could respond. As it was, his normal rasp was deeper than ever.

"Fortunately, you have a good sense of humor. You'll need it with those two."

"I think they like the idea of having a sister," Amaranthe said. "Lucca, in particular, loves to give me the worst nicknames."

Geno couldn't help laughing. "The sad truth is, Lucca doesn't even need time to think up the crap he comes up with. He's quick-witted. Staying in front of that one can be a full-time occupation."

"I'm up for the challenge," Amaranthe assured. "In fact, I welcome it." She covered a yawn and sank deeper into the pillows. "I'm sorry, honey, I can't seem to keep my eyes open."

He brushed a kiss along her temple. "You go to sleep, while I run your bath. I'll come back and get you when it's ready."

Her laughter was smothered by the pillow. "You do follow rules when the rules are for someone else, don't you?"

Geno looked down at the woman who had changed his life completely. He'd do anything to keep her healthy and safe, and that included following rules even if he had never really followed them in his life.

CHAPTER EIGHTEEN

"Did you break into my house?" Geno demanded. "Even shadow riders can't break in."

Dario waved the question away and pushed aside Fiero's weapon. "Don't point that at me. It just pisses me off. You need to see this report Brielle turned in." He turned his head to look over his shoulder. "Where the hell are Elie and Val?"

"They probably have a sense of decorum," Geno muttered, but he took the papers out of Dario's hand.

"Not decorum," Elie denied, sticking his head a lot more cautiously above the stairwell. "A very healthy dose of self-preservation."

"Fucking pussy," Dario muttered. "Ever since you and Val married, you've turned into a couple of babies afraid to stick your necks out. Geno could have been dead by now. He needed this information as soon as possible. It's not like we could send it over a computer."

He looked past Geno to Amaranthe, who sat up cautiously,

pulling the covers over obviously bare skin. "Good morning, Amara."

"I'm not certain it is morning, Dario, but hello to you, too. Thank you for risking your life to bring Geno whatever news you have. That was terribly courageous of you."

"Don't encourage him, Amaranthe, or you'll regret it for life," Geno said. "If you don't mind vacating our bedroom, Dario, we'll meet you downstairs. Light the fire so the room warms up faster. I'd text Stefano rather than go into his bedroom. Francesca is home, but that doesn't mean he isn't sleeping with a gun."

"You should be sleeping with a gun," Dario said. "You have your woman to protect. You shouldn't rely so heavily on your bodyguards or your security."

Geno drew back the covers and showed Dario the firearm that had been aimed directly at him. Amaranthe did the same.

"You would have been a dead man if I hadn't recognized you immediately, or if you'd made one wrong move toward my woman," Geno said.

Dario raised an eyebrow. "Good to know. I'll meet you downstairs."

Amaranthe waited until Dario and the others had gone downstairs before she turned to Geno. "That was certainly risky on Dario's part, and he didn't have to do it. Why do you suppose he did? He doesn't seem like the type of man to show off his skills. If anything, he seems like he prefers to fade into the background."

Geno noted the worry in her voice. It echoed the uneasiness he'd been feeling for a long time when he was in Dario's presence. Amaranthe had good instincts. She seemed to be confirming what had been lurking at the back of his mind for some time.

"I haven't discussed my concern for him with anyone yet. I think Valentino and Emmanuelle should be able to see the self-destructive behavior. Certainly, his personal protectors see it in him, and they can't be happy. He has no concern for his safety. I think he wants to die."

"Why, Geno?"

"I don't know anything about his past. I know Stefano had his investigators look into him, but they couldn't find much. He's shrouded in mystery. He's pretty fucked up. And I mean that. He knows it, too. He talks as if he could never have a woman of his own, and honestly, I think if he ever falls for someone, he'll deliberately sabotage the relationship. Not in a small way, but so bad it will never recover. I think he knows that, too."

Amaranthe frowned. "Why would he do that when he can see how happy Val is with Emme? Dario obviously loves Emme."

"It makes him vulnerable. He can't be vulnerable. He just can't. Worse, the things he needs sexually are beyond my comprehension. He owns a club, and the things that go on there are more than kink. To me, it's disturbing. I try not to judge because everything is consensual, but it isn't exactly play with him. His lifestyle would be difficult for a woman. His personality would be difficult for a woman. On top of that, his constant need for her to prove that she'd stick with him when he deliberately sabotages the relationship would only lead to the inevitable breakup. He's extremely intelligent, Amara. He knows the match would be doomed."

"Do you think that's why he's taking so many risks? He doesn't think he has a chance at having a permanent partner? Does he really care so much? He can't hurt for women. He probably draws them like flies." Amaranthe was up, peering into the closet.

Geno came up behind her, towering over her. He reached for her favorite sweater and pair of leggings and handed them to her.

"Dario is very popular, and from what I understand, he has a strong sex drive. He doesn't go without—at least according to Elie, women are all over him. But he's not happy, and it's been getting worse, from what I've been observing. He covers it, but I can feel it. His behavior has been getting extreme."

Geno couldn't help watching Amaranthe dress. She was so beautiful to him. Every movement was graceful and flowing, but it was so much more than that. He knew what she was like on the inside. She didn't know Dario the way he did. On the surface Dario was the worst kind of criminal. He had a reputation that was deserved, and yet he wasn't that man. Geno knew that he loved Valentino fiercely and protectively. That love eventually extended to Emmanuelle. Brielle and Elie had been added to the circle he included as family. Stefano and Francesca had slowly, over time, changed him. To begin with, Geno had thought it a good thing. Now, he wasn't so certain.

He understood Dario on many levels others might not be able to. Geno loved Amaranthe deeply. Fiercely. Protectively. He also didn't feel worthy of Amaranthe, although he wasn't about to sabotage their relationship, not intentionally. He wanted her to know he loved her and would put her first. Dario feared making himself vulnerable, not only to the outside world, but to his woman. Geno had no idea what the man had been through to make him the way he was, and he had no idea how to make things different for him. Dario was resistant to help.

Geno pulled on his clothes, texting Stefano as he did so. Stefano assured him he was already up and would be meeting Dario and the others in the great room.

The sound of Emmanuelle speaking in a low, furious tone reached him as Geno and Amaranthe stepped off the stairs. She was rarely angry. Emmanuelle had attitude, and because she was outnumbered by the men around her all the time, she'd learned to give as good as she got in the teasing department, but she wasn't a woman to lose her temper that often. When she did, most times they all just stepped back and stayed quiet.

"If you two can't stop Dario when he decides to put himself in danger, then you're not going to be his primary personal protectors. I get that you're his friends and you go way back, but that isn't going to save his life if you can't stand up to him."

"Emme," Dario broke in softly. "Stand down. It isn't on Marcu or Vicenzu. You know me. When I decide to do something, no one is going to stop me."

She spun around to face him. She was much shorter than he was, her figure curvy. Her dark blue eyes shot sparks at him. Her dark hair seemed to crackle with fury. "I'd stop you, and you damn well know it."

That was another thing, Emmanuelle didn't swear. She was really pissed. Or scared. Geno tucked Amaranthe's hand into the crook of his arm as they entered the room. Valentino and Elie stood to one side of the fireplace, neither interfering in the drama being played out across the room from them.

The two men she was dressing down towered over her. Both looked stoic, their faces masks, their eyes cold. Neither flinched under her declaration, but it was obvious she meant what she said. Ignoring Dario, she turned back to them.

"You may think Dario is the boss, but he isn't when it comes to his security. *I* am. What I say goes. You can be his friends. You can hang out with him as much as you want at that kink club of his and share women with him. Whatever floats your boat. What you *can't* do is let him get away from you. You don't get to neglect his security. Just because he wants to kill himself doesn't mean he gets to do it. You hear what I'm saying?"

Both men nodded. That surprised Geno. Neither spoke much. They clearly were still uneasy around the Ferraro family. Like Dario, they were used to ordering women around and having the women do whatever they were told. As a rule, Emmanuelle played things low-key. She didn't throw her weight around as Valentino's wife, or as head of security.

Dario would never talk about shadow riding to anyone, Geno was absolutely certain, not even to the two men he trusted with his life. Dario was many things, but he was loyal to a fault—and he was loyal to the Ferraro family.

"Babe, you're head of Valentino's security, not mine," Dario said.

"Don't you 'babe' me, Dario," Emmanuelle hissed, the sound deadly. She pushed past the two towering bodyguards as if they weren't there and got right into Dario's personal space.

"Don't you *ever* patronize me like that. I *am* head of your security whether you like it, or they like it. I don't give a damn whether you want a woman calling the shots. I'm the best at keeping you alive, and you're getting the best. When it comes to your safety, you are going to follow my orders, and if your men don't follow my orders, they're gone. As in *permanently*. If you think I'm kidding, you fucking try me."

She whirled around and stormed out of the room. There was complete silence following Emmanuelle's threat. The two bodyguards, Marcu and Vicenzu, clearly thought she meant she'd fire them. Geno knew she just told Dario she was willing to assassinate them if that was the only way to get rid of them. A declaration like that from Emmanuelle was unheard-of.

It was obvious to Geno that Emmanuelle knew Dario was pushing closer to the edge, and she was moving to counter him. Emmanuelle loved Dario like a sibling. She wasn't about to lose him, and she'd just told him so.

Valentino made a move simultaneously with Stefano to go after her.

Dario shook his head. "I'll go."

"You know Emme," Valentino said. "She needs time when she's really upset."

"I know Emme," Dario assured. "She'll be in good hands, Val." He walked out without looking back.

There was another silence. It was Marcu who broke it.

"We're going to have to learn the dynamic here, Valentino. Clearly, your wife *is* head of security for Dario."

"Yes, she is," Valentino said. "Dario should have made that clear to you. She means what she says. Dario's safety must come first before friendship."

"She's risking her life talking to him that way."

"Don't ever make the mistake of underestimating her," Valentino said. His voice was still very low, but it had gone hard. "She's lethal as hell. And never make the mistake of thinking she's not protected. Anyone touches her and not only would I retaliate, but Dario would also. And then there's her family. Emmanuelle on her own is enough to contend with, but she isn't alone, never forget that."

Geno walked with Amaranthe across the room to the small bar where the espresso machine was located. "Whatever is in the report Dario brought must be good or he wouldn't have been so eager for all of us to read it."

"My wife is thorough," Elie assured. "She has trouble stopping once she's onto something. She starts out in one direction with some faint clue, and the next thing I know she'll be at the keyboard for days without eating or sleeping, following a trail that no one else can see. It's a thing of beauty."

Stefano sighed. "Damn Dario and Valentino for stealing her right out from under us. Brielle's brilliant at what she does. Clearly, she has a gift. I've asked Renato and Romano, two of my investigators, to send me their report encoded."

"Beniamino, one of our investigators, is on his way with our report. He should be here any minute," Lucca said, glancing at his watch.

"Marcu, Vicenzu, I expect the two of you are tired. Has anyone shown you where you can sleep?" Geno asked. He wasn't really asking so much as telling them that they were to retire to the guest suites. The meeting was private. The bodyguards were fairly new to the family and not quite trusted fully. "Dario is safe enough with all of us."

"I'll take you to the guest suites and show you where Dario always stays when he's here," Lucca volunteered.

"Might not be the best idea after Emmanuelle just read us the riot act for not staying on top of Dario," Vicenzu ventured.

"Text her," Geno ordered. He tried not to sound like it was an order, but he knew it came out like one. These men were guarding Dario Bosco, the man running a huge territory, a well-respected crime boss. They weren't used to taking orders from anyone. People were mostly afraid of them. Terrified, in fact. They didn't understand the relationship with the Ferraro family or the deference given to them.

Marcu took out his phone and texted not only Emmanuelle, but also Dario. Geno could see he made certain to include both.

The answer came immediately. Marcu turned to Lucca with a nod. "We'll take you up on the beds. Haven't had much sleep in days."

That alarmed Geno. Was Dario spiraling out of control? He glanced at Valentino but refrained from asking until the two men were in the elevator and heading down to the floor below them with Lucca.

"Just how bad has this thing with Dario gotten?" Geno asked Stefano as he made Amaranthe a café au lait. He handed it to her and then made himself a latte.

"Emmanuelle says he isn't sleeping at night. At first, he'd go running on his property and afterward work out on the heavy bags or with Marcu and Vicenzu. She said it was fairly vicious, but they'd go inside and he'd make them breakfast. After weeks of that, he began going to his club. In the beginning, she didn't follow, but she began to worry when his behavior during the day became more and more erratic. He didn't seem to give a damn whether he was confrontational when his life was clearly in danger. He'd step away from his personal protectors and put his life at risk.

"Emmanuelle followed him to the club in the middle of the night and was horrified at the nonstop sexual behavior, which never seemed to satisfy Dario. It didn't seem to matter how many women he was with, what he did or who he shared them with, he sought out others. He clearly cared nothing for them. The woman fell all over him, followed him around, begged and pleaded for the honor of having him abuse them—at least she considered his brand of sex abusive.

"He left without looking back. She was certain he didn't know the names of the women he used. The next night they were waiting, eager for his attention. She told Valentino, who hated that Dario became colder and even more disconnected from the women he was with. There was no love lost between them. There wasn't friendship. There was no emotion whatsoever unless it was contempt."

"He's looking at the difference between the women he sees and loves, Emme, Francesca, the others in the family," Stefano continued, "and the ones he carries out these acts with he seems to need." He glanced at Elie but refrained from continuing.

Elie shrugged. "I like to play in the bedroom, but I don't do the kinds of things Dario does, nor would I ever share my woman with other men. Dario is driven to be very sadistic. I think he's tried to stop but has never succeeded. Seeing Val and all of us happy has just proved to him it's impossible for him to ever have a decent life."

Geno swore under his breath. "These men from his childhood, Marcu and Vicenzu, are they the same way? Are they reinforcing those needs in him?"

There was silence again. Valentino wandered over to the chair beside the fireplace. "I fucking hate watching him spiral. His life has been shit from the moment he was born. He's saved my life so many times. And he's the most loyal man I know. If anyone deserves better, it's Dario, and I've never been able to think of a way to give him better."

"You gave him Emme," Amaranthe said unexpectedly. "She's that beacon of hope for him. You think she isn't, that she represents the beginning of the end—all of you do, but it's really the opposite. He can choose not to grow as a person . . ."

"Honey," Valentino interrupted. "He's a sadist. There's no growing out of that."

"That doesn't mean he can't grow as a person. He can find ways to be a better person, so that if he finds a woman, he can balance his needs with being a good man," Amaranthe said. "Everyone should continue to grow. Aren't we all trying to be better people?"

"That's the hope," Valentino said.

Amaranthe curled up in the love seat, giving Geno plenty of room to sit beside her. He set their drinks on the little table close to their chair. "The sun is coming up. I guess it wasn't as early as it seemed."

We didn't get much sleep last night, did we? He couldn't help giving her a faint grin, remembering the long night of making love to her. Or Amaranthe making love to him.

When her eyes met his, there was a curious melting sensation in the region of his heart. It was pathetic, and he wasn't about to admit that to anyone—unless it was her. One shouldn't have such physical reactions just by looking at a woman and seeing love in her eyes—but he did.

We didn't need to sleep.

Amaranthe smiled at him, and his breath caught in his lungs. She was right. He would give up sleeping every night to spend the time just watching her dance for him, let alone making love to her. Or even just lying next to her watching her sleep.

Emmanuelle and Dario entered the room side by side. It was impossible to see beyond Dario's mask, but Emmanuelle looked tired. She went straight to her husband and buried her face against his chest. He wrapped his arm around her, his eyes meeting Dario's over her head.

"We're good," Dario confirmed.

"I don't know why Geno didn't shoot him." Emmanuelle's voice was muffled by Valentino's shirt. She didn't lift her head. "Geno usually shoots first and asks questions later."

"I smelled lavender," Geno said with a straight face.

Dario gave him the finger when the others burst into laughter.

What does that mean? Amaranthe asked.

Dario bought a beautiful piece of property on the lake in Chicago, a working lavender farm. He didn't shut it down. He's kept it running. When he had to give Brielle CPR, she said she remembered smelling lavender. It's been a running joke ever since.

From across the room, the elevator doors slid open and Beniamino Latini, Geno's cousin and one of his top investigators, handed Salvatore a folder and stepped back into the elevator without speaking to any of the rest of them.

"I think all the reports are available now," Geno announced. He wanted to read the one Dario had brought.

Dario was included, along with Valentino as the various reports were distributed. Amaranthe and Geno pored over Brielle's very detailed dispatch.

Geno found himself looking to Stefano, his gut churning. If what Brielle found was confirmed by even one other report, the implications were damning. He didn't want to look at Amaranthe. She was an elite rider sent by the International Council to ferret out the reasons behind the murders as well as to find the murderers. Amaranthe was extremely intelligent. If he thought there was a direct correlation between Brielle's findings eighteen years earlier and the murders now, so would she.

"Geno?" Salvatore asked. "Brielle's report is very thorough. She doesn't make mistakes. It looks as if she's the only one of the investigators who caught that there were two branches of the Boutler family working in Queensland at one time."

"It was well over a hundred years ago when the two families began working in Queensland," Stefano murmured, resignation in his voice. "That woman is amazing. She doesn't miss anything. One branch lived on the coast and one in the interior, but from what Brielle could tell, they were close. Apparently, it took some digging, but she found documentation of the families getting together often when the first shadow riders were assigned there. Theo and Meghan Boutler resided on the coast, and Theo's brother Hamish with his wife, Felicia, took up residence hundreds of miles away in the interior, but they visited as often as possible. There's a reason the other investigators didn't go that far back."

"Why would they?" Taviano murmured. "They were thinking in terms of eighteen years ago, not a hundred. Brielle is amazing. We're all very sad we lost her to those underhanded sneaks Val and Dario."

His comment provided some much-needed levity. Even Emmanuelle smiled.

"We were just faster at seeing how brilliant she is," Valentino pointed out. "For once, Stefano, you didn't win."

"Don't remind me," he groused, staring down at the report Brielle had prepared for them.

"Theo and Meghan had five sons and a daughter," Elie continued with the information aloud. "They trained all their children to be shadow riders. Of the six children, only the oldest, Erik, and the daughter, Rachel, married and had children. Erik had three sets of twins and a daughter. Rachel had two boys and a girl. Interestingly, Rachel left home early. Once she left, she never returned. She ceased shadow riding altogether, married and lived in Italy. Her husband, according to Brielle's report, knew nothing of shadow riding and had no connection with it whatsoever, nor did any member of his family."

It was Emmanuelle who continued with the reading of the extremely thorough report. "Hamish and Felicia Boutler had three sons. Lewis, Nate and Rogan. All three married and had children. They were trained as shadow riders and the women they married were shadow riders. They appeared quite close to the coastal Boutlers. Despite the distance, they were able to get together often presumably using shadows to travel back and forth. Brielle even uncovered several old photographs of family celebrations."

Geno studied the faces. The pictures were grainy and in black and white. Not really black and white, more like faded brown.

"Despite the condition of the photographs, the resemblance of Hamish and Theo to the assassin who murdered the younger Australian woman on Miranda's back porch is uncanny," Geno told the others. "He was in his late fifties or early sixties, and very experienced at riding the shadows."

Geno frowned down at the report. He almost wanted to snatch it away from Amaranthe as she studied it. The conclusions he was drawing, he knew she would come up with as well. How could she not? She was looking at it the same as Elie Archambault was. Geno figured he may as well just put it out there as calmly and matter-of-factly as if his parents weren't part of some huge criminal conspiracy that had unimaginable repercussions eighteen years later.

"The same night Papa's leg was amputated, there were twelve members of the Boutler family killed in accidents or assassinations. They were scattered all over Europe, which was why no one caught it. Some weren't riders. Some were former riders. But all were members of the Boutler family formerly from Queensland."

"Erik Boutler was the oldest of the five coastal brothers. He'd just turned seventy and resided in Vietnam. As a highly sought-after engineering professor, he taught at one of the universities in Vietnam. He took a fall from a third-story balcony. There wasn't a hint of drugs or alcohol in his system. Erik was the only brother that married. He had seven sons and a daughter. Three sets of male twins and the girl. His wife died in a climbing accident, and it was right after that when his daughter, Rowina, left."

"A climbing accident?" Stefano echoed. He tapped the

table. "That doesn't seem likely for a rider. "I'm not certain I buy that. Was her death investigated?"

"They lived in Queensland, far away from everyone else. No one raised questions about her death that I can see," Elie said. "Brielle noted she was a little suspicious, but there was no way to investigate further."

"Jerico Boutler had a small farm in Costa Rica. He was in his sixties. He'd never married, and he'd been a rider for years in Queensland," Stefano said. He frowned down at the report in front of him. "He died in his field when he was off his tractor, and it somehow continued moving and ran right over him. It was ruled a freak accident as no one was around."

"Shawn Boutler lived alone in Indonesia," Lucca added. "He was very wealthy, owned a thriving farm and employed quite a few locals. He was also in his sixties and one of Theo and Meghan's sons. He died in his shower. The door was locked, and he was alone. It appeared that he slipped and fell on the wet tiles. His neck was broken."

Valentino looked up. "Percy Boutler, in his sixties, also one of the brothers, lived alone in India. He ran a brothel there. He was found in the street just outside his home. It appeared as if he had been in a very vicious fight. There was a knife in his hand, but no blood on the blade. He had been beaten and he had several broken bones. He died of a blow to the chest hard enough that it literally stopped his heart. Whoever killed him was immensely strong."

Geno glanced at Amaranthe. "These are classic kills."

She shook her head. "Not classic, but the deaths seem to be planned and carried out all on the same timeline. The same night."

"Then there was Arlo, the youngest of the five Boutler brothers," Geno continued. "He lived in Thailand. Like his brother in India, he ran a brothel, but this one included underage children. It seems the Boutler brothers weren't very socially conscious. Arlo was killed inside the brothel in the common bath. Arlo was drowned. That's all five boys Theo and Meghan gave birth to. They all died on the same night no matter where they were living."

"The only inland Boulter from that generation who died that night was Nate Boutler," Dario said. "He was sixty-five, living in Pakistan. His wife left him when their sons, Mitchel and Monti, were teens. He was unable to ride the shadows, and she had nothing to do with the family, unable to remember them obviously. She died several months later in a horse-riding accident. The boys lived in Pakistan with Nate until they went off to college, still training as riders, but they never returned to Queensland. Nate died hard, of several stab wounds, mostly in the genital area. It looked as if it was a very personal attack. No witnesses and the murder occurred in his home."

"That's six of the twelve members of the Boutler family killed. The five male members of the coastal family and only one of the inland family, at least of that generation," Geno mused.

"That brings us to the next generation, Erik's children," Stefano said. "Jaspar and Beau were the bastards Taviano talked about. They were living in Queensland on the coast. I believed Eloisa killed them. Why I thought she might be outraged enough to risk her career or at least report the abuse to the Archambaults when she never gave a damn about her children, I don't know, but when I heard they were dead, I believed, and so did Taviano, that she killed them. I asked my investigators to check if it was possible. They said no. She never left Chicago. As far as reporting to the Archambaults, no investigation was launched into Jaspar and Beau Boutler."

"How could Brielle possibly know that?" Amara asked. "She didn't ask them, did she? We wouldn't want them connecting the dots on this until we know what we're looking at and how to handle it."

"Brielle is very discreet. She would never ask questions of the Archambaults, Amara," Elie assured, keeping his head down as if reading over the report. "We know for certain the Archambaults did not bring justice to Jaspar and Beau Boutler, but they were killed by shadow riders. At least both had broken necks and appeared to have been killed by an assassin sent out to serve justice to them. The two men were in their forties."

"Edwin Boutler and his twin, Gef, lived in Laos," Dario continued. "Like Jaspar and Beau, neither married and they were in their early forties. They had a large farm where they bought unwanted children, paying top dollar for them, which was a real incentive for poor families. The farm produced crops they sold in the marketplace. The Boutler brothers were stabbed and beaten in their home. They were both in the same room. Big men, lots of muscle and well trained in self-defense, yet they were both killed."

"Rowina, the daughter, left home for training in Greece," Emmanuelle said. "She ended up marrying into that family of riders. They seemed to have a happy marriage. When her children were eight and five, the boy eight, the girl five, her brothers Edwin and Gef showed up for a visit. About two weeks after they left to go back to Pakistan, Rowina died by her own hand. If her husband knew why, he never said."

There was a long silence. Amaranthe pushed her forehead into the heel of her hand. Stefano swore softly. "This is one fucked-up family. They got away with abuse for years because in the old days there was little communication."

"And no one talked about it," Geno said. "Especially if it happened to boys."

"Generations in the same family?" Valentino asked. "Is that what we're looking at? These men sexually assaulted children and eventually someone retaliated?"

"Several someones," Amaranthe corrected. "We accounted for ten of the twelve deaths eighteen years ago. "Who else died that night?"

Geno scanned the report. A couple of the men had put up a fight, but it didn't seem as if his father's severe injury could have been gotten in either of those instances, and both were too far away for Eugene Ferraro to have survived.

"This is it," he murmured aloud. "Salvatore. Lucca." He wanted them to see the significance. "Nate Boutler lived with his two sons, Mitchel and Monti, in Pakistan. They were reputed to be good shadow riders from all the reports by the trainers, yet when they were old enough to be given a territory, they refused to return to Queensland or Pakistan. They migrated to Canada. Given where they grew up, it isn't surprising they preferred wilderness and ended up in New York, establishing businesses guiding wealthy clients into the West Canada Lakes Wilderness area. They also took troubled teens into leadership and survival programs. Most of the time, they worked separately from different areas around that region."

"Were they working that night?" Lucca asked. He turned the papers over as if that would answer the question. "Why were they both there?"

"Mitchel had finished a week's work with a company, so he had a bigger group than usual," Dario said. His voice had turned grim. "His usual routine was to take a couple of days alone time, but his brother had come to camp out with him. When they found the bodies of Mitchel and Monti, they also found the body of a young boy who had been buried in a shallow grave. He was covered in bruises and had been sexually assaulted."

Amaranthe slipped her hand into Geno's. He slid his thumb along the back of her hand, needing the contact.

"Hikers found the bodies," Geno said. "It looked as if the two men had been in a vicious battle with bears, because they seemed to be torn apart. Around them the ground was saturated with blood. Wild animals and insects had gotten to the bodies. An investigation was launched, and the conclusion was the two men had sexually assaulted the boy, strangled and buried him and then were attacked by an unknown man or men. The axe the brothers used to chop firewood was missing. Not only did both men have cuts from an axe, but the cuts also matched the slices on the firewood. The police concluded whoever had attacked them had used the brothers' own axe against them."

Geno looked at his brothers. "Papa must have had his leg chopped open by the axe. That's how he got that hideous injury. I don't know how they didn't get his DNA. His blood had to be all over the ground along with Mitchel's and Monti's."

"They did get his blood," Stefano confirmed. "Keep reading. Somehow it disappeared from the evidence room before it could even be logged."

"That's the twelve members of the Boutler family who died all on the same night eighteen years ago," Lucca said. "And now we know what really happened to Papa's leg."

"They were part of a conspiracy to take the law into their own hands," Stefano said. "The shadow riders taking part in the killings must have known these men were pedophiles. The only way they could have known was when they went for training. The riders had to have been assaulted when they were sent out for training."

CHAPTER NINETEEN

Brielle searched to see if other shadow riders stepped down that same night or right after the way Geno's parents did," Emmanuelle said. "There were twelve couples that ended their shadow-riding careers. Eugene and Margo Ferraro lived the longest of all of them. They're the only couple from here in the States. The eleven other couples were scattered over other countries. Finland, Switzerland, Germany, Spain, Russia, China, Argentina, United Kingdom, Croatia, India, Venezuela. Every one of those countries had their top shadow riders stand down and turn their leadership over to another family member or someone else. They became greeters."

"Even eighteen years ago, shouldn't that have raised an alarm?" Valentino asked. "That should have been considered unusual behavior."

"It would have been," Stefano admitted, "but there appears to have been a good explanation in every case. Brielle took the time to check everyone. Health reasons, accidents, failing eyesight: these were all legitimate excuses the International Council would believe. In most cases, leadership was turned over to an adult, so no one had to be sent to the families to be trained. The council wasn't informed that the leaders stepping down no longer participated in any decision-making."

Geno pressed his fingers to the hard knots gathering in his neck. Those riders had broken the sacred laws of shadow riders. Breaking those laws was done when there was no time to send for the Archambaults and you had to administer justice, but you informed the council immediately and turned over the evidence you had gathered against those committing the crime. Geno knew Stefano's family had done so on more than one occasion. He'd even participated. As a rule, they informed the Archambaults after the fact and explained why it had been necessary not to wait.

"Stefano, you said the other couples are all dead. Were they murdered? As far as Brielle or any of the other investigators could tell, did the Archambaults serve justice on them?" Geno didn't want to look at the report anymore. There was too much there. If his father had been sent to one or more of the Boutlers to be trained as a rider and was assaulted and years later decided to be part of a revenge conspiracy, that meant not only his father but his mother was willing to give up shadow riding, the leadership of the riders and their family to carry out their plot. They'd done all three. His parents had participated in a global conspiracy against a single family, a crime punishable by death.

"There was no investigation or evidence that the Archambaults were involved in the deaths of any of the shadow riders who abdicated their positions," Stefano said. "The first person to die was in Finland, the woman. She drowned although she was considered a good swimmer. There was no evidence that anyone else was around her. Her husband died two months later. He'd been fishing. There were no signs of a struggle. It appeared as if he'd had a heart attack."

"They were testing the poison," Amaranthe guessed.

Geno thought it was a good deduction.

"They would go after the woman first when she was alone," Amaranthe continued. "They needed to see if it would paralyze her and leave her system so no trace would be discovered. They did the same thing to her husband later. That was the first pair they killed, testing their drug."

"They must have done the same thing to the next three couples. Each died in a similar fashion, always the woman first and in some accidental way," Stefano said. "These people were patient. They wanted everything in place before they began to exact their revenge."

Emmanuelle tapped her fingers on the end table. "Brielle thinks that's when they started experimenting with drawing in locals, using various means. It changed from region to region, but there were reports of unrest in the shadow rider territories before the greeters died. All of them died by accident until those in Croatia."

"I was sent to Croatia to investigate," Amaranthe admitted. "I had a bad feeling the murderers weren't finished. I believed eventually they planned to go back and kill the rest of the family. I wasn't certain why they left, but I'm positive they plan to go back."

"You believe, like Brielle, that their intention is to wipe out the shadow riders. *All* shadow riders," Elie said. "Her conclusion isn't in the report, but privately she conveyed that worry to me."

Amaranthe nodded. "They planned this out very carefully, from developing weapons that can be carried into the shadows to a compound that paralyzes their victim so they can't move but keeps them awake so they know what is happening to them. They want them to see their partner killed before they're murdered. Every single step was planned with patience and cunning."

"Why wait eighteen years? Why now?" Stefano asked.

There was a long silence. Beside Geno, Amaranthe moved restlessly, very unlike her. Geno glanced down at her. Her fingernails dug into his palm.

"You may as well tell us what you think, Danzatrice Ombra," he said. "We know it's speculation."

"I honestly believe they want to come after all the shadow riders eventually. Whoever is running the show has a taste for power and even for killing now. The hatred toward the Ferraro family really stands out." Amaranthe hesitated briefly and then stated her opinion. "I think Francesca was the catalyst."

Stefano's head went up alertly. "You're just now telling me that?" He demanded. His eyes slashed at her, furious. "That would make her a target for these maniacs."

"It just now occurred to me when I was putting everything together," Amara returned calmly. "In the shadow tube, when the Australian was confronting me, he seemed as if he wanted to allow me to go, almost as if he thought I was being taken in by all of you. But I made the mistake of saying something about having Geno's baby. The moment I did, he turned on me and there was no going back. He wanted me dead."

"This all is beginning to make sense," Salvatore said. "Shadow riders couldn't find one another and were slowly dying out naturally. Not just here but everywhere. We couldn't find our partners. But Stefano found Francesca, a natural love match. They were happy, more than happy, and they had Crispino. Then little Luciana. That wasn't to be tolerated. A Ferraro, happy? After Stefano found Francesca, every one of his brothers found a love match. Elie did. Now Geno."

"That had to have been a blow to them if they wanted the riders to die out," Lucca said.

"I think the worst blow was that Stefano and Francesca were happy and had children," Amaranthe said. "I'm just judging by how quickly the Australian changed his entire demeanor when I said the word *children*."

"I've texted my brothers. They'll put extra guards on the women," Stefano said. "And take precautions as well."

"The next step is to find out who is still alive from the Boutler coastal and inland families," Lucca said.

"Brielle has that information listed," Dario said. "From the coast, a set of twins is still alive, Cooper and Calen. They are in their midforties. Their sister, Rowina, married a man in Greece, but after a visit from her brothers, she died by her own hand." There was speculation in his voice. "Until then, she seemed to have had a happy marriage."

"There's no way to tell, but my guess would be they assaulted her son. The preference seems to run to boys," Valentino said. "She knew it when she left home, and she thought she was done with her family."

Unfortunately, Geno's gut was telling him they weren't wrong. He rubbed the back of his neck in an effort to ease some of the tension.

Salvatore took up the findings in the report. "The inland Boutlers faired better. Mostly because they left the area and were under the radar, I think. Lewis and Rogan would both be in their sixties. Nate was their brother. Lewis has one son, Lincoln, and he's still alive. According to this, he's forty-two and has never been married."

"Rogan has three sons," Lucca continued. "Neil is thirty-nine, the oldest, Owen is thirty-six and Parker is thirty-four. The sons never married."

Geno sighed and shoved his forehead into the heel of his hand. "If what we suspect is true, communication would have prevented so much damage, both to the Boutler family and to so many children. There seems to be a code of silence surrounding sexual assault."

Stefano nodded his agreement. "Not that I think much can be done to save these men when it's been so ingrained in them, handed down for generations."

"We'll need up-to-the-minute tracking on each of the Boutler family members left alive," Geno said. "Ask the investigators to track any additional cousins no matter how distant they might be. Look into Rowina's family just in case. Also, tell them not to overlook Rachel Boutler. She went to Italy, married and had children. That doesn't mean she wasn't loyal to her family when they all started dying. Her children might be capable of shadow riding. We'll need to find out if they are."

Stefano nodded his agreement. "We'll need the answers fast, so tell your investigators to put a rush on it but to be thorough."

"I have a performance coming up," Amaranthe announced. "Two full rehearsals including a dress rehearsal. They'll either strike during one of the rehearsals or the performance itself if they think a large number of riders will be present."

"Cancel," Salvatore ordered. "Say you're sick."

"That's one way to handle it," Amaranthe agreed quietly. "Or we can use this opportunity to get out ahead of them and for once be in a position to stop them."

Geno forced himself to breathe through his every protest. Amaranthe was trained for this very thing. She was his *partner*. His every instinct roared at him to lock her up somewhere safe, but she needed to know he saw her as an elite rider. Being a rider was a good part of who she was.

Although he knew everyone was waiting on his decision, he didn't make the mistake of speaking too soon. He waited for his mind to stop spinning out of control and work the way he was taught. He was leader of the New York shadow riders. He'd been taught for years by the Archambaults. He had the intellect to work the problem and get it right if he just allowed himself to think like the head of the family.

"We'll need volunteer riders, Stefano. If not from Chicago, we can call them in from San Francisco or LA. We might need both. We'll have to find a way to bring them in without anyone knowing. Dario and Valentino are already here. They arrived in a private jet. It makes sense that they would attend Amaranthe's performance. It also makes sense that they have bodyguards with them. We have box seats allowing us to keep other audience members safe."

"I see where you're going with this," Lucca said. "If it's leaked that Stefano will be in the audience and the three of us will be there, along with Valentino, Emme's husband, you believe they'll wait to make their strike."

Geno nodded. "Why go after just Amaranthe when they can get several of us in one big swoop? It would be natural for my cousins to come in to see my fiancée's performance. We make a big deal of it."

He felt Amaranthe's body relax into his and knew he'd played it smart. The more he laid the plan out, the more it felt right. "We can set the theater up in advance. We'll have tracking on the known survivors of the Boutler family and any of their associates."

"It's still a risk," Lucca pointed out.

"There's always a risk," Geno agreed, "every time one of us walks out the door. We're riders, Lucca. We're sworn to protect others. We're not going to hide from these bastards. They're coming after us and everyone we care about."

"They declared war," Valentino said. "Just the way my dear uncle Miceli did when he got so greedy; he wanted to sell human beings to make more money. He killed his own brother and then went after another brother just for power."

"We're going to have to send a report to the International Council and also the Archambaults," Amaranthe said. "Although I don't believe any of these people are official riders. It's possible they will ask us to delay, but they'll know it's impossible to do so. Jean-Claude will give the go-ahead, as will the rest of the council. Jean-Claude is leader of the Archambault riders, so I very much doubt that he'll tell us to delay until the French riders can get here."

"They can get here overnight," Stefano pointed out. "Do we delay sending in our report?"

"We need to protect Brielle," Dario said, pointing to the

papers, snapping his fingers, all business, indicating he wanted every copy. "I'm burning these. That's why I didn't bring a digital copy." There was an edge to Dario's voice. Even a mild threat if one wanted to read it that way. That was interesting to Geno. That meant Brielle had joined Dario's inner circle whether Dario was aware of it or not.

Geno could have told him he had that report imprinted on his brain nearly verbatim. He didn't need the written one, and he was sure Amaranthe didn't, either. He handed the papers over immediately.

"The Archambaults and the council are going to want to know where we acquired all the information," Stefano said.

"That's not my problem," Dario stated. "We asked her to do this for us and get as much data going as far back as she could and to be thorough. When you demand that of Brielle, you can't ask her where she gets her information."

Valentino looked every bit as protective. "Brielle is very driven as a researcher. She's instinctive on a keyboard. I don't think she knows where she's going half the time, she just follows the trail no matter how faint it is. Nothing gets in her way."

Geno felt very fortunate that he had practiced for years keeping his face a stone mask, otherwise he'd be smiling. Neither man was going to come out and state Brielle Archambault could hack her way through anything, but everyone in that room knew the implication was there.

Elie covered the lower half of his face with his palm, but his eyes were bright with pride. "My woman is hell on wheels with a keyboard."

Stefano made a growling sound and glared at Dario and Valentino. "If you two weren't family, I'd stick you back on the top of the hit list for stealing that woman out from under me. I needed her as an investigator for the family."

Dario's eyebrow shot up. "Technically, since we are family and she works for us, she is working for the family." He sounded like he was speaking to a child, enunciating every word deliberately as if Stefano might not get the concept.

Stefano gave him the finger.

Geno couldn't help the slow grin that he exchanged with his brothers and Amaranthe.

Dario didn't look in the least bit intimidated or offended at the rude gesture. "We can't help it if your work was just too boring for her, Stefano. You Ferraros sit around eating pasta all the time, and that makes you sleepy. Your women spoil you and that slows you down."

Dario was back to looking down at the screen on his phone as he made the observations. He texted one-handed, lightning fast, giving Brielle instructions.

"Are you including Val and Elie in your candid opinion?" Stefano asked.

"Like you, they're totally pussy-whipped. I tell them all the time. Emme knows I tell Val he needs to beat her once in a while just to get the upper hand."

"How does that go over?" Stefano asked.

"Emme just laughs because she knows he would never do it even if he threatened her." Dario poured disgust in his voice.

"Emmanuelle just laughs," Emme corrected, "because she knows if Val ever hit me, Dario would cut off his balls and that's the truth."

"Is that the truth, Dario?" Geno asked.

Dario shrugged his very muscular shoulders, not looking up from his phone. "Well. Yeah. No one lays a hand on Emme. Not like that." He sounded bored.

Geno exchanged a look with Amaranthe.

I see why you like him, Geno. It's very hard not to. He's very different on the inside than he is on the outside.

Geno didn't want her to have the wrong impression. *He is a sadist through and through. He has no problem torturing someone. He doesn't feel sick or disturbed by it. In fact, he gets off on causing pain to others, men or women. That's what he fears the most in his relationship with any woman he ends up loving.*

Evidently, not Emmanuelle, Amaranthe pointed out.

Geno turned that over in his mind. Dario certainly would kill someone who dared to hurt Emme. He was certain if anyone touched Brielle they'd suffer long and hard before they died at Dario's hands. What did that mean exactly? If they were really going to save Dario from himself, that was the question they would have to answer.

"Let's get a plan in place," Geno directed aloud. "Emmanuelle, you're good at writing up whatever we need to put in the papers. Make it good. We want everyone to see that the family is coming together to support Amaranthe in her first performance in New York City. We have reserved boxes, the best in the theater, and for the first time, they will be filled with Ferraro family members."

"Way to put the pressure on," Amaranthe said. "I'll probably make a fool of myself."

"That would be impossible," Geno stated.

Two hours after the news broke that the Ferraro family intended to support Amaranthe's first performance, they received a report from Deangelo Rossi, one of Geno's investigators. He'd been keeping a close eye on Jenny Porthman's devices. Lucca had provided the necessary way in, and once Rossi had that, he was able to see whatever Jenny was doing and who she talked to.

"Jenny Porthman received a message from an unknown person. He instructed her to have her mother ensure Jenny and three others are hired as ushers in the theater for all performances. It's common practice to hire extra staff during performance week. Jenny's mother is on the board of directors, and she has a lot of pull. She can easily get Jenny and the others hired," Rossi informed Geno.

"Were you able to trace where the text originated from?" Salvatore asked.

"It bounced all over the world," the investigator said, "but in the end, the message came from a café here in New York. The café is one known to us. A lot of hackers use it."

They talked it over, deciding whether it would jeopardize their plans if they prevented the four girls from being hired as ushers. Priscilla Clake was known to them. She was seventeen and had been taking dance lessons in the studio for several years. She had been a friend of Jenny's until recently. Amaranthe noticed there appeared to be a rift between the two teens, yet she was one of the girls the unknown person had instructed Jenny to have hired as an usher.

Deana Miller took lessons at the studio in Little Italy. Amaranthe had never instructed her, but she had been a student there for going on fourteen years. Two months earlier she suddenly stopped coming to dance. She had a good reputation as a hardworking student and the other instructors had told Amaranthe it was a pity she stopped coming because she was an excellent dancer and had such potential. She was seventeen years old. Amaranthe had made a note to visit her and determine whether she needed a scholarship to continue the program. Reading over her file, Amaranthe could see her family had struggled to pay the fees. Deana always had a part-time job to help. She seemed an unlikely candidate for the Boutlers to get their hooks into, but then so was Priscilla.

Leslie Van Ray was the final girl on the list that the Boutlers wanted as an usher. She was sixteen and also trained at the academy in Little Italy. There didn't seem to be a connection between Jenny Porthman and either girl from Little Italy. Certainly the two girls didn't move in the same circles as Jenny. Rossi had looked for a connection between the Leslie Van Ray, Deana Miller and Priscilla Clake and hadn't found one there, either. It appeared as if the girls were chosen at random.

Geno didn't believe the four girls were chosen randomly by the Boutler family to assist them. Jenny's family had money, and she had access to that money. She was good at manipulating her mother into giving her whatever she wanted, but the other three girls didn't have nearly her wealth. Priscilla came the closest to Jenny's family financially, but the other two weren't even close.

He considered what Amaranthe had told them about sextortion. Had the Boutler family managed to con the girls into sending nude pictures of themselves? Or videos? Had they been compromised and now were they being threatened with sextortion if they didn't do what they were told? Geno was certain that was the most likely possibility.

Since the girls were minors, Geno would have preferred they be far away from the theater when the Boutlers made their move, but he didn't want to chance tipping the family off that they were walking into a trap.

The days of rehearsals went without incident. Amaranthe had her own personal protectors in the form of riders hidden in the shadows in her dressing room, in the wings of the stage and everywhere else she went. She was never alone. Geno and his brothers listened to her every argument, but they ignored her protests. In the end, he was grateful she found humor in the situation, rather than get angry over it. She could have. He even accompanied her into the bathroom. He was that paranoid.

Geno despised the fact that he'd agreed to allow Amaranthe out in public. He didn't care that she was an elite rider. He only cared that she was his world, and if anything happened to her, it was on him because he hadn't protected her adequately.

The night before the opening of her performance, he couldn't sleep. He couldn't even stay still. He'd made love to her slowly and gently, but once she had drifted off, he had to pace the length of the room, back and forth like a caged animal, furious with himself for giving in because she had those eyes, and he couldn't bear to see her unhappy.

"Geno." Amaranthe sat up, pulling the covers over her breasts. "What is it?"

He tried not to snarl like a wild animal, but he felt like one. Feral. With the way he'd been shoving his hand through his hair, he was certain he looked a little wild. "I was crazy to agree to this. To risk your life."

Her dark eyes drifted over his face with that look that should have made things better, but only made them worse because he could lose her. He could lose seeing that expression he knew was love.

"I wouldn't survive, Danzatrice Ombra." He shoved both hands through his hair again and faced her. "I know that makes me sound pathetic and weak. I don't really give a damn if I sound that way. It's the truth. I've never had what you give me. Not from anyone. Is giving you what you want really worth risking your life? Is it, Amaranthe? Because I don't think it is."

She thought for a long time before she spoke. "Honey, it wouldn't be worth the risk if this was just something I wanted to do. But it's something I *need* to do. I've trained to bring justice to people like this since I was a toddler. I don't know any other way of life. Essentially, it's who I am. In my deepest core, it's who I am. I know it's hard on you to stand aside, and I love you all the more for it."

He turned away from her abruptly so she couldn't see his face. "It won't matter how much you love me if you're dead."

Again, there was a long silence. He detested hurting her. He forced himself to go the staircase railing and stand in front of the bed. "It isn't that I don't believe in your skills. I know you're good, maybe one of the best riders in the world, but you're *mine*. My heart and soul, Amaranthe. My everything. I didn't have a reason for living. I know I'm supposed to live to serve the people in my territory and the other riders. I know my duty should keep me going, but I'd run out of reasons to stay alive. I understand Dario because I felt the way he does. Until you."

Her dark gaze moved over his face. She never just touched him on the surface. She seemed to find her way inside of him and connected deeply. He rubbed his chest over his aching heart. He hadn't known he was capable of loving someone the way he loved her.

"My entire life centers around protecting people, Amaranthe, and I'm damn good at it. The one person who matters the most to me is the one who doesn't want my protection. You make me feel . . . helpless. Useless. As if my world is spinning out of control."

He dug his fingers hard into the back of his neck, into the knots that were so tight they felt like concrete. "I want to lock you up somewhere safe until this is over."

She nodded slowly and the mass of silky hair shifted and moved enticingly. "I understand completely, Geno." Her long lashes lifted calling his attention to the length and thickness of the dark frame surrounding her eyes. Her gaze met his steadily. "I've never had a family or anyone to accept or love me, at least not that I remember. Only you. You're my world. I was raised to give my life protecting others. While I'm onstage dancing, you're going to be a target and I won't be able to do anything about it. I'll have to rely on others—people I don't know—to keep you safe. To keep your brothers safe."

For the first time he heard her voice tremble. She pressed her fingers to her lips as if she was trying to contain all emotion.

"I know what I can do, Geno. I know I'm capable of keeping you alive, but you insist on putting yourself in harm's way. I don't love you any less than you love me. As afraid for me as you are, I'm terrified I'm going to lose you, too. I'm small, and to make up for that, I've had to learn to use speed and other ways to best my opponent. You go straight for them, Geno. You're very strong. You just go for it because you're used to always being the best. I've already watched you go down twice. *Twice.* Right in front of me."

Her voice broke and she looked down at her hands. "You aren't the only one in this relationship that's worried, Geno. Every instinct I have demands I keep you safe. I'm petrified with fear because I know when these people come after me, you'll stand in front of me. I won't be able to stop you."

Geno studied her face for a long time in silence. The tight knots in his neck and gut slowly began to unravel. His little dancer. She didn't know it, but she had a way of making sense out of everything. He hadn't considered that he was being selfish, but in fact, that was exactly what he was being. He had promised himself he wouldn't be that man. He would look after her, put her first, but in the end, he wasn't thinking of how she was feeling, although they were in the same situation.

"I didn't think about what it must be like for you, Amaranthe. I was only thinking about myself. I apologize." He was sincere when he told her he was sorry. "I want to be a good husband to you. I know you're an elite rider. I try to believe that you love me. You show me you do, but to be honest, I've never gotten to a place where I believe anyone can love the real me. I'm always afraid I'm holding you too tight, or not tight enough. I'm so afraid of losing you it's entirely possible I'm pushing you away before you can walk away first."

He ran his hand through his hair again. "That does make me somewhat of a coward."

Amaranthe caught up the short, nearly transparent robe and slipped from the bed. "It makes you human. It means you have repercussions from your very strange childhood, just as I have them and your brothers have them."

She came down the steps with her usual grace, straight to him, and took his hand. "I want to hear you play the piano. Neither one of us is going to get any sleep tonight. Play for me."

"Wear the diamond chain around your hips. I'll play something you might feel like dancing to."

Amaranthe didn't hesitate, but then she never did. She moved back up the stairs, her hips swaying under the gossamer fabric. She looked so beautiful. Ethereal. Just as she did onstage. A woman from another dimension. Her long hair flowed down her back in waves and curls, nearly reaching her small tucked-in waist. Her bottom, like the rest of her, was small but perfectly shaped. He enjoyed watching the movements of her body beneath the transparent robe as she opened the rectangular box sitting on the shelf above the headboard.

"I'm never going to like that you put your life on the line, Amara," he admitted. "There's always going to be that part of me that insists on protecting you. And I will. I refuse to lose you. But I'll do my best to understand that you feel the same way about me and my safety."

He narrowed his eyes as she turned toward him. The edges of her robe were separated so she could reach around and link the diamond chain at her left hip. His breath caught in his lungs, staying there until he was burning for air.

"You're so fucking beautiful, Amaranthe. Why did you even give me a second look?"

She had been looking down at the chain, but her head came up, that adorable little frown on her face, her eyes blazing with a warrior's light. "Geno Ferraro, there is no man to compare with you. I can't see anyone else. I never will be able to." A mischievous smile lit her face. "And now that I know you play the piano, there is no way to resist you."

Amaranthe came down the stairs straight to him, the edges of her short robe still open. She was comfortable with him now. That was a victory he was happy he'd scored with her, making her feel comfortable as a woman with him. She reached up to run the pads of her fingers along his heavily shadowed jaw in a caress.

"I love you, Geno. Every part of you. Even the overprotective, bossy part. I love that side of you very much. *All* of you. I don't mind telling you. Or showing you. Play the piano for me. I'll dance for you, but I do have other things in mind. It's time for me to practice the art of making you very happy."

His cock jerked. "Baby," he countered cautiously. She couldn't possibly mean what he thought she did.

She took his hand and tugged, starting toward the piano at the far end of the floor. "It's going to take a lot of work on my part to learn to be good at pleasing you. I think distracting us both with your significant skills on that instrument while I practice on your beautiful instrument will work quite nicely."

CHAPTER TWENTY

The atmosphere in the theater was electric. As most people watching the performance would know nothing about the assassins that had gathered to kill some of the patrons, Geno knew, like him, it was the amazing dancers telling the story of Romeo and Juliet that would capture their attention.

Granted, it would be his first live performance with the lighting, the music and all the dancers, men and women in their costumes, but he expected after watching rehearsals for it to be powerful and mesmerizing. During the dress rehearsal he hadn't been able to take his eyes off Amaranthe dancing, every movement so expressive and emotional it was impossible not to understand the story. The spotlight didn't need to follow her. Amaranthe was spellbinding.

Amaranthe had explained that the ballet, *Romeo and Juliet*, was difficult to perform for several reasons. The music was powerful, and a superb orchestra could overshadow mediocre dancers easily. Aside from the fact that the choreography was technically challenging, this particular adaptation they were performing required athleticism, skill and a partnership of matching body types. As the principal dancer, Amaranthe was far too short to have a male dancer match her height. In order for her to be able to match the steps perfectly with her partner, they had to practice hours and hours for months together.

Jason Donagon, originally from New York City, according to Amaranthe, was a flawless classical dancer. He had beautiful, effortless leaps, taking to the air with amazing heights, and yet never once complained that he had to shorten his strides to dance the choreography with her. It took considerable skill to shorten his steps and still look as if he were at full extension. Jason was a powerful, explosive dancer, and at five-seven he was shorter than most of the other principal male dancers, but he could gain more air and do more turns. He looked out for his partner.

Geno hadn't met the man, but he'd read his very impressive résumé. If Amaranthe admired him, he was certain Jason was even better than everything he'd read about him. Geno was very aware that there were several people there looking specifically at him. Two representatives of the American Ballet Theatre were in the audience by special invitation. National Ballet of Canada also had two people representing them watching the performance. The Royal Ballet had also sent a small group to watch the opening-night presentation.

Geno was nervous for all the performers. Those companies were three of the most prestigious in the world for a reason. The demands for a dancer to be the best were always there. He knew Amaranthe had not applied at any of the companies, but Jason had. Geno had issued a special invitation to the two women representing the American Ballet Theatre because he had done a favor for one of them. He'd never mentioned it, of course, nor had his family taken money. There were no ties back to the Ferraro family.

He had carefully worded the invitation making it clear there were no expectations of them hiring anyone. He simply sent her tickets to the event if she was free to attend. If Jason was good enough to qualify for an actual audition, that was up to him. Amaranthe had told Geno sending Jason's résumé to the companies might not get him looked at when he barely met the height requirement of five foot seven.

Geno wanted to be the one in the shadows guarding Amaranthe when she wasn't onstage performing, but he had to be in the box making himself a target. The Ferraro family had taken up six luxury boxes, all in one row. His two brothers were in the box with him. Stefano was in the box on his right with Vittorio and Giovanni. Taviano, Nicoletta, Ricco and Mariko were in the box to Geno's left. On the other side of Stefano's box, Valentino, Emmanuelle, Elie and Dario were seated in one of the luxury boxes.

Geno made it clear he didn't want their bodyguards to be in the boxes or even outside of them. Any shadow rider could easily slip up behind them and kill them. He had a feeling the Boutler family was feeling murderously vengeful. The bodyguards didn't like it, but they understood unusual circumstances were happening and didn't want to be in the way of the plan—and there was a plan.

To entice the Boutlers further, the LA cousins had arrived to support Amaranthe in her performance as Juliet. Afterward, they were going to Luna D'Argento to celebrate. There were plenty of photographs of Geno's cousins deplaning from their private jet, being met by a limousine and being driven straight to the theater. What no one saw, as the cameras went off, were the San Francisco cousins, also aboard that same jet, sliding into the shadows and making their way to the theater.

Lorenzo was the oldest, head of the San Francisco family and leader of the shadow riders in the Northern California and Oregon regions. His brothers Franco and Brio were twins, followed by triplets, Santo, Matteo and Lucio. The last twins born were female, Zenita and Zeta. Lorenzo had his hands full with his younger siblings, all reputed to be fast in the shadows as well as quick, independent thinkers.

The latter was a trait one wanted in a shadow rider but maybe not so much in a sibling one was responsible for.

The outside luxury box next to Taviano, Nicoletta, Ricco and Mariko held their LA cousins Severino, Veila and Remigio. Santo, from San Francisco, was in the shadows watching over them. Matteo remained unseen in the shadows guarding Taviano and the others in their box. Lorenzo guarded Geno and his brothers. It was up to Franco to ensure no one got into Stefano's box. Lucio watched over Val and Emme's box. And in the last luxury box holding Max, Tore, Vico and Marzio from LA, their cousin Brio, from San Francisco, remained in the shadows, guarding them.

Geno knew Zenita and Zeta were excellent, skilled riders. He was certain they could protect anyone—just not *his* Amaranthe. He couldn't shake the idea that he was failing her by not being with her every moment. It made sense that the two women would shadow her. They could be in her dressing room and would be able to stay close. He was uneasy, and it took discipline to stay in his seat rather than pace up and down in the hallway as he would like.

Brielle had checked on the survivors in the Boutler family and any known associates. She had sent her findings to the family and continued to track them, sending updates if anything changed, such as she could tell they were on the move.

Rogan Boutler was the man who had murdered the Australian girl. He was sixty-six years old and had been a shadow rider in inland Queensland for a number of years. He'd been married and had three sons, Parker, Owen and Neil. His wife, Irene, died in a hunting accident. She had fallen from a cliff into a ravine. Rogan left Queensland with his three boys within weeks after her death. The boys had been in their early teens.

It seemed to Geno that the wives of the Boutler men ended up dying in tragic accidents that no one could quite believe of a shadow rider. Brielle questioned the accidents as well. In any case, Rogan was dead. Vivian Brown, the

Australian woman Rogan had murdered, was twenty-six years old and distantly related. Rogan had started up a family genealogy site online, and she was one of the interested parties who had joined. She'd begun corresponding with him and asking all kinds of questions about the family.

Brielle said both Rogan and his brother, Lewis, seemed to be very charismatic and would post videos talking to their followers. Those videos were viewed over and over, hundreds of times, by the same younger relatives as if they were mesmerized. Geno believed in psychic gifts. Rogan and Lewis seemed to possess the ability to bind followers to them. Not all joining the genealogy site became fanatical followers; in fact, many seemed to be refusing to have anything to do with the two men once they left the site.

Brielle had added a few names she was keeping track of—men and women she believed might aid Rogan and Lewis in their plan for revenge against the shadow riders, but Rogan's sons, Neil, Owen and Parker, were in New York. Not only were they in New York, but they were close to the theater. Not in it, but close. It wouldn't take much for them to catch a shadow, slip inside and murder their assigned targets and leave.

Lincoln, Lewis's son, was also in New York. He'd lived there for seventeen years. Like his cousins, he wasn't married. He was part owner of a thriving art gallery and illustrated graphic novels. From what Brielle could tell, he lived quietly, dated Fiona Alley, an artist whose work sold very well. They kept their relationship out of the spotlight and attended few public events together. At her showings, they were never seen together.

Geno considered why Lincoln would put an ocean between his father and himself. Why he would live so quietly, almost as if he were living in the shadows. He had dated the same woman for years but didn't live with her and didn't appear in public with her, as if hiding that relationship. Late at night, Geno had discussed his conclusions with Amaranthe, and she agreed with him. Lincoln wanted his family to forget all about him, just as Rowina Boutler had hoped would happen when she married in Greece. Still, Brielle kept a close watch on Lincoln and Fiona.

Cooper and Calen Boutler, sons of Eric, had arrived in New York a good six months earlier. They frequented one of the internet cafés the hackers used. Now that Amaranthe was able to see photographs of them, she realized she had seen each of them separately on more than one occasion in the business district near a coffee shop she sometimes stopped at before going to work.

It was a sign that the Boutlers were entrenched in the Ferraro territory as well as in Little Italy. The times she saw the two men, they had teenagers with them, and the boys or girls were following their every word with rapt attention. It seemed one of the gifts some of the Boutler members inherited was charisma.

Finding a way to track Cooper and Calen hadn't been easy. Amaranthe and Salvatore had slipped into the shadows and waited for them to go to the internet café, knowing they were using it to direct the others in the conspiracy and to get their orders from Lewis Boutler.

Several years earlier, Giovanni and Taviano had made a tiny tracker that could be inserted under the skin of a rider. They'd turned it over to their cousin Damian to find the right element so the device could be in a rider and could also travel through the shadows. At the time, they thought to put it in the young trainees so they wouldn't lose any of them. Now, they were able to use it on Cooper and Calen, inserting the tiny device into their skin as they brushed past them entering the shadows. Both men had to feel the slight sting as if an insect had bitten them. The needles were thin enough that no evidence was left by the time the two men were once again out of the shadows.

Clearly, Lewis was the leader of the conspiracy against the shadow riders. Now that Rogan was dead, more than ever, Geno believed he would be determined to kill every shadow rider he could. By bringing his cousins together in a crowded theater, he made them appear to be easy targets. The Boutlers would believe that the Ferraros would be enthralled with the performance of Geno's fiancée, arrogant and secure in the knowledge that they were shadow riders, and no one could get to them. Brielle was still trying to unravel Lewis's actual location. He was communicating with his nephews but in short bursts, difficult to pinpoint when the transmission was being bounced all over Europe, the United States and Canada. She and Bernado, Val and Dario's other investigator, were working on ferreting out his location together.

Amaranthe had easily solved the problems they had with the Archambaults. Geno, Stefano and even Elie had been agonizing over when to give them the report on what was transpiring, but Amaranthe simply raised an eyebrow and said she was sending in her report immediately and Geno and Stefano should do the same.

She pointed out that not a single Boutler was an active shadow rider taking rotations. They had trained when they were younger, but they were no longer working. In fact, they had faded from most people's memories. This was an attack by nonriders on multiple shadow-riding families. It didn't matter why. The present generation had no knowledge of crimes committed by their parents or grandparents and wasn't responsible for what other family members had done in the past.

There was a brief rustling at the heavy velvet curtain behind them. Instantly, Geno was out of his seat and in front of his brothers, gesturing for them to give him room. They did, standing, spreading out to allow themselves fighting room as well. They had ensured no shadow could find its way into the boxes other than the one Lorenzo stood guard in.

Priscilla Clake, wearing the uniform of an usher, came hesitantly into the box looking strained. She stopped the moment she saw Geno looming in front of her. Nervously, she glanced first at Salvatore and then Lucca before her gaze tracked back to Geno. Clearly, she was terrified.

"I have to talk to you, Mr. Ferraro," she whispered. "You're going to think I've lost my mind, but please listen to me. I would have gone to Miss Aubert, but I couldn't get near her, not before her performance. I don't have much time. Someone is going to try to hurt her. Or you. I know something bad is going to happen tonight. These horrible people have been blackmailing me and a couple of the other girls."

There was a little sob in her voice. She pressed her hand over her mouth and made a visible effort to pull herself together. "They insisted I usher tonight. That means they'll tell me I have to do something I'm not going to like. If I don't do what they tell me to do, they're going to put a video they have of me all over the internet. I'm not willing to let them hurt your family or Miss Aubert. I just don't know how to stop them. When I heard Ms. Marchel had been murdered and Jenny implied you had killed her, I knew it was them. And I knew they told Jenny to get everyone to believe it was you. That's what they wanted us to do, get everyone to believe you were stealing from them."

Geno nodded his head. "Thank you, Priscilla. It had to have taken a great deal of courage for you to come up here and tell me all this. I'm glad you didn't try to stop these people on your own. Have you met any of these people face-to-face?"

She shook her head. "Jenny has. Several times. She's bragged about it. I didn't want to. I knew as soon as I sent the video that I'd made a big mistake."

Geno deliberately dropped his voice another octave and used a much more compelling tone. "Everyone makes mistakes, Priscilla. When you're young and someone does their best to persuade you there's only one way out, you believe them, but it isn't true. When this is over, we'll help you resolve the situation."

"I'm sorry I couldn't find a way to stop them."

"If you're right and they're that ruthless, they would have no problem harming you. It's best you just do your work, enjoy the show, and if they contact you again to do something you find uncomfortable, come up to the box immediately and stay with us. Don't talk to them or say anything to any of the other ushers. Just come straight to this box."

Priscilla nodded. "I have to go. I know they're watching me. They'll send Jenny to ask why I came up here."

"Did you bring your cell phone?"

"Yes. We're supposed to have them off, but the watchers said we need to have them on but on vibrate so they can send messages to us."

Geno held out his hand. He put a number he used occasionally into her phone and sent her a text asking her to come upstairs, that he wanted her to take a gift to Amaranthe's dressing room. He handed her a small box. "They won't allow you to take it to her, but a guard will take it from you and give it to her. I was going to give it to her after. Tell Jenny I spotted you in the crowd."

For the first time, Priscilla looked as if she wasn't going to implode or burst into tears at any moment. "Thank you, Mr. Ferraro."

Geno inclined his head and started to follow her out of the box to ensure her safety. Lorenzo's voice stopped him. *Stay inside the box where we control the shadows, Geno. You don't know whether she was sent to draw you out of the safety zone.*

Geno swore under his breath. He knew. His gut told him Priscilla was terrified and it had taken every ounce of courage she possessed to warn him. Lorenzo could hear lies just as well as he could.

She's a kid, Lorenzo.

You come out of the safety zone; you leave me no choice. I guard you or your brothers, and you're the main target, so I'm sticking with you. We're stretched thin, Geno.

Geno understood how frustrating it was for men like Val

and Dario to be surrounded by personal protectors who re-fused to give them space—especially when one of them was a shadow rider like Emmanuelle. She could follow them anywhere. Geno had bodyguards, but he could escape them using a shadow anytime he wanted—unless—like now—his protector was a shadow rider. His cousin from San Francisco wasn't going to be shaken off easily.

Fuck you, Lorenzo.

Lorenzo's amusement slipped into his mind, reminding Geno of Stefano. All of them were so alike. He might have found the situation a little comical had it been one of his cousins.

Check to see if the kid made it safely onto the main floor. I don't have the best visual.

Geno bared his teeth toward his cousin and growled low as if he were a feral animal. Salvatore and Lucca lifted an eyebrow simultaneously. He used to intimidate his broth-ers, but ever since he'd been with Amaranthe, he seemed to have lost his edge. Sighing, he ignored them and went to the railing to look down. Immediately, he spotted Priscilla.

Jenny cut Priscilla off from the hallway leading to the back dressing rooms. The two girls appeared to have a heated exchange, with Jenny holding out her hand for the rectangular jewelry box Priscilla had for Amaranthe. Pris-cilla stepped back, shaking her head. Jenny looked furious.

Geno willed Priscilla not to get overconfident. Fortu-nately, the head usher came up behind Jenny and directed her to the other side of the theater before speaking with Pris-cilla. She listened and then glanced up toward Geno's box. He nodded to indicate Priscilla was telling her the truth. The head usher took the jewelry box from Priscilla, giving her a smile and clearly telling her where she should be working.

Geno took a deep breath and turned back to his brothers. "I detest not being able to communicate with Amara. She'd answer me if I reached out, but it wouldn't be fair when she needs to concentrate on dancing."

"She must be just as worried about you," Salvatore said.

Lucca agreed. "You know how she is about you, Geno."

"About all of us," Geno corrected. "She'll reach out if she needs to." This was her time to be a dancer, not a shadow rider. Not his fiancée. She was wholly Amaranthe, a trained classical dancer.

Geno knew Amaranthe loved what she did, and she deserved her time on the stage. If she truly wanted to dance with the American Ballet Theatre, she could apply, and he would support her decision, but he would travel with her. He considered that he might prefer her dancing to her shadow riding.

The International Council couldn't send her out on elite investigations once she was married to him, not unless he agreed to go with her. Six months was a very long time for him to be away from his territory. He doubted he would ever agree to such a lengthy time, but he didn't rule out anything when it came to Amaranthe. Right now, he needed to remain focused on her safety—and that of his brothers and cousins. They were all bait to draw out the murderers.

Bells dinged and the lights dimmed three times before they went off and the theater darkened. A hush of anticipation fell over the audience. Geno found himself sitting again, his breath catching in his throat. He'd seen Amaranthe dance in the privacy of their bedroom, and he'd been utterly mesmerized by her. He couldn't imagine what it would be like to see her perform on the stage in a full-scale production.

The marketplace scene was a whirlwind of activity where the fair Rosaline turned down a proposal and the Montagues and Capulets showed a fierce rivalry. Tempers flared, but before a fight started the Duke of Verona appeared and threatened them with death if they didn't stop the feud.

Geno leaned forward when Amaranthe appeared in the next scene in the garden receiving her ball gown. Her parents had accepted a marriage proposal on her behalf from noble Paris.

Amaranthe was stunning onstage. Her jumps were beautiful, elegant and astounding in the height she could reach. Her kicks were effortless and so high she appeared to have legs that went on forever.

Guests arrived at the ball. Romeo and his friends, wearing masks, followed Rosaline and gained entry to the Capulets' home. In the ballroom, Romeo and Juliet saw one another across the room filled with people. Geno thought it was a highly emotional moment. He wasn't the only one. He heard the swift intake of breath from the audience. The hush shared throughout the theater as the onstage chemistry became apparent. The chemistry was so believable between the principal dancers, it was easy to see the two had fallen in love at first sight.

Jason had strong, clean technique. The lines of his body were superb. Although he was significantly taller than Amaranthe, the height difference was never a problem due to her outstanding ability to leap into the air effortlessly as well as the way Jason matched her stride while appearing to be at full extension every time. Geno had no idea how the man could accomplish such a feat, but he certainly was generous to his partner, always spotlighting her.

Geno was suitably impressed with him and held spellbound by Amaranthe—by the two of them. Their onstage chemistry made for a magical partnership, creating the illusion of two young people from rival families falling deeply in love. The audience couldn't help but feel every emotion as the dancers portrayed the depths of their feelings for one another through dance.

Geno did his best to scan the audience for any movement, not that he expected to see any of the Boutlers, but even the best of the best made mistakes. A rider could make a transfer from one shadow to the next but step out into the open for the briefest of seconds to make the exchange.

Intermission gave him a reprieve and what he hoped would be the ability to be stronger. Time was against them now. If the Boutlers were going to attack, they would do so in the next hour. Geno stood up to stretch, to keep his body loose and ready for action. Salvatore and Lucca did the same.

Brielle sent word to Elie, Emmanuelle reported telepathically to her family. *Our little theater is suddenly crowded with the enemy. They came in while the audience was getting drinks and food.*

Is anyone going near Amaranthe? Geno asked, doing his best not to sound like he was snapping her head off.

It appears they're all coming up here just as we expected them to do, Emmanuelle said.

Geno wished he didn't have the gut instinct that told him things weren't going to go as well as they all were expecting. They were missing a key component. He kept his hands on the railing, not joining his brothers near the shadows, where they could help Lorenzo if they were attacked. He needed to be able to think clearly.

Geno, are you certain you're on alert? Amaranthe poured into his mind, filling him with her essence—the beauty of her. The promise of a life of companionship, laughter, loyalty and most of all love. In that moment, he realized she would leave the stage, blow her reputation as a dancer and come to him if she believed he needed her for any reason. She wouldn't hesitate. He felt that as surely as he drew air into his lungs. He didn't know why he'd gotten so lucky, but he recognized that he had, and he knew what he had in Amaranthe—a miracle. A treasure.

I'm covered, Amara. Lorenzo is controlling and getting joy out of telling me what to do. No one is going to slip past him. He poured reassurance into her mind.

We're missing something. I know we are. I can feel it.

That really put him on alert. All along his radar was blaring a warning. *We're on the same page, baby. I'll make certain the others know that both of us feel something else is in the works. They'll pay attention.*

They'll strike when the play is at its most intense, she warned.

He agreed. *It's difficult to keep from being mesmerized by your performance*, he told her. *I'll admit, even knowing we're being stalked, when you're dancing, I just want to watch you.*

Well, don't. I really have this bad feeling, Geno. I'd rather be in the shadows protecting you than up on the stage.

Funny thing, la mia danzatrice ombra, *I feel the same way. I want to be right there with you.* He poured love into her mind. He didn't have his protection to give her—he was trapped in the luxury box, bait for killers—but he could give her everything he felt for her. Let her know she was his world. He might not have the words, but he had the ability to share her mind and give her the absolute honesty of his true emotions.

Geno despised allowing her to slip away from him, but the lights dimmed, signaling the audience to return to their seats. The bells chimed softly, alerting everyone the dancers were in place and act two was about to start.

The second half of the performance was even more emotional than the first half. Geno realized it would be so easy to forget his family was being stalked. He couldn't take his eyes off Amaranthe and Jason as the tragic love story played out. Geno realized the story wasn't just about the tale of two innocent hearts being destroyed, it was about power, greed, ego and pride. Those particular values played out in families across the globe in modern times. Often, the young lives being destroyed, the hearts broken, didn't seem to matter as long as those in power got their way.

Some parents wanted control and insisted their children follow their dictates no matter how soul-destroying those demands were. The consequences were often the loss of the child, but those in power would rather sustain that loss than entertain a different way of thinking. Geno could see the parallel so easily between the tragic play written long ago and what was happening in the modern world.

It was difficult not to fall in love with the dancers, not just the roles they were playing. While it was true that Geno didn't know that much about classical ballet, both principal dancers seemed world-class to him. He'd taken a lot of time to study the dancers considered best in the world, and Jason and Amaranthe were up there with them in the performance they were giving.

The audience was enthralled. Spellbound. They believed the two young lovers as they declared their ardent feelings for each other and then later met at Friar Lawrence's garden to be secretly married. The passionate scenes were riveting, the dancing taking each act to new heights.

After killing Tybalt in the marketplace, Romeo spent the night with Juliet but had to leave at sunrise under sentence of exile. There was so much emotion between the two principals, it brought many in the audience to tears.

Geno's warning system began to blare at him as Juliet went to the friar and he gave her a sleeping draft that would make her appear as if she'd died. The Ferraro enemies were closing in just as the Montagues and Capulets were coming to a crucial point.

Geno reached out to his brothers and cousins. *The Boutlers are moving into position. Be alert.*

He leaned closer to the rail, his gaze fixed on the stage and his woman dancing there. The spotlight created all kinds of shadows on the set, where she took the sleeping potion and her parents discovered her, believing her dead. The shadows made him nervous. There seemed to be more than usual.

The final scene was the most dramatic. Juliet lay as if dead in the tomb. Romeo rushed in and discovered Paris mourning her. A fight ensued. The timing was perfect for the Boutlers to attack.

Simultaneously, all six boxes were hit. Cooper and another older man slid out of the shadows into Geno's box.

Each held a knife in his hand as they went straight at Geno, who had turned to face them. Salvatore and Lucca closed in on them from either side, controlling the wrist holding the knife while Lorenzo glided silently up behind first Cooper and then the older man, snapping their necks and murmuring the traditional "Justice is served."

Lorenzo dragged Cooper into the shadows and Lucca followed with the older man. The entire incident took seconds. Geno returned to the balcony railing, his gut still knotted. Salvatore kept his gaze fixed on the other boxes just in case his cousins might need help.

Neil and another younger man entered Stefano's box, riding the shadow directly to Stefano. Neil's knife was held low, stabbing upward toward Stefano's abdomen. Giovanni slapped the knife away, hitting Neil's arm so hard there was an audible crack. At the same time, Vittorio caught the younger man's wrist, yanked him forward and turned hard, snapping his wrist and putting pressure on him until the knife fell. Franco came up behind him and snapped his neck as Stefano easily spun Neil around and broke his neck. Franco dragged the younger man into the shadows and Vittorio followed suit with Neil.

Calen rode a fast shadow with his partner, a young man of around the same age straight into the box where Taviano, Nicoletta, Ricco and Mariko waited. The four Ferraros closed in on them while Matteo Ferraro followed them into the box. Calen and his companion went from sheer confidence to shock and horror, realizing too late that their victims were waiting for them.

Ricco took control of the knife, turning it on Calen while Matteo snapped his neck. It was Taviano who blocked the weapon the stranger wielded, and Mariko administered justice. The two assassins were dead within seconds of entering the box. Matteo and Ricco took the bodies into the shadows to dispose of them a great distance from the theater.

Owen Boutler and Martin, a distant cousin discovered

through genealogy research on the internet, rushed through the shadows into the box where Dario, Val, Emme and Elie sat watching the performance of *Romeo and Juliet*. Val and Dario looked up at the two men as they entered, Val raising an eyebrow, Dario smirking.

Owen tried to stop his forward momentum, ducking behind Martin, nearly skimming the poisoned blade of his knife across his cousin's back as he half turned to face the man emerging from the darker side of the box. Elie Archambault had a well-earned reputation for being very fast. He moved with blurring speed, kicking the knife from Owen's hand and catching his head in his hands, snapping the neck almost in one move.

Elie turned to help Emmanuelle with Martin, but Lucio was already there, not that Emme needed any help. She'd already disarmed Martin, and Lucio was behind the assassin, meting out justice and dragging the body into the shadows. Emmanuelle calmly returned to her seat as Elie removed Owen's body.

Parker Boulter rode the shadows into the box nearest the stairway. The box contained cousins who had come from Los Angeles to watch Geno's fiancée perform. Severino, Veila and Remigio should have been watching the last act with rapt attention, but only Veila faced the entrance to the box and Parker. She smiled sweetly at him, ignoring the knife in his hand as if she didn't even see it. Warily, Parker looked around the box seats before he took a step toward Veila.

The moment he took that step, he knew it was a mistake. Her brothers emerged on either side of him, gripping him with tremendous strength so he was unable to wield the knife. Behind him, Santo Ferraro from San Francisco caught his head in his hands and wrenched, breaking his neck. Santo calmly pulled him into the shadows while his cousins seated themselves to watch the fight play out between Paris and Romeo in the tomb.

At the last box on the far left, Max and Tore sat in the

seats, swinging around to face two strangers as they emerged from the shadows. Both stood slowly, waiting in place as the two Boutler assassins came closer. Vico and Marzio closed in on either side of the two men. Instantly, Max and Tore moved with blurring speed, both going for the wrists holding the poisoned knives while behind them, Brio, their cousin from San Francisco, caught first one neck, then the other, administering justice.

Romeo had killed Paris by the time Tore and Brio dragged the two bodies into the shadows to take them away from the theater.

I believe all the Boutlers have been disposed of, Stefano said as the cousins checked in with one another. *With the exception of Lincoln, and we haven't identified him as an enemy.*

That wasn't so. The leader, Lewis, was still unaccounted for. They didn't have his location, and worse, that radar telling Geno something was very wrong was stronger than ever.

Come on, Brielle, he murmured softly to himself. *I need to know where he is.* He knew the investigator would never give up. She would take it down to the wire—the very last minute.

Geno placed both hands on the balcony railing intent on the scene taking place onstage. Romeo embraced Juliet and then plunged a dagger into his heart, taking his life. The note the friar had sent explaining the plan never made it to him, and he believed his love was truly dead.

Lewis Boutler is Lewis Mainlander. Mainlander was his mother's name, Elie related. *He has worked for years in the corporate office of the Australian Ballet. He's here in New York and is attending the ballet.*

By now, Boutler would know his plan had failed. He would choose his time during the scene in the shadowy tomb, and all eyes were on Juliet as she awakened and realized her beloved was truly dead. That's when he would strike.

Geno knew timing was everything. A dozen shadows played over the stage. He kept his gaze fixed on the front of the stage. Lewis was seated in front, Geno was certain of it. The man was waiting for that moment when Juliet would plunge the dagger into her breast and take her life. That was the perfect moment to kill Amaranthe. Lewis would need to pick the perfect shadow to get onstage, get behind Amara, use his poisoned knife and get back to his seat before anyone knew what had happened. Lewis was bound to find deep satisfaction in killing Geno's fiancée in front of an entire theater and all the Ferraros.

The dance portrayed Juliet's deep sorrow, allowing the audience to share the emotion with her. She sank gracefully to the floor beside her beloved Romeo, clasping the dagger in her hands. Geno had planned out every move a hundred times in his head. He pushed off the railing with both hands, leaping into the smallest of the shadows, a feeder tube, the fastest one that would take him directly onto the stage.

The tube was so fast it nearly tore him apart, ripping at his skin, tearing at his eyes and scalp, turning him inside out as he streaked across the theater and nearly spilled right out on top of Lewis as the assassin emerged from a long shadow to step into a smaller one that would take him behind Amaranthe as she portrayed a dying Juliet.

Geno wrapped Lewis up tight in his arms and continued his forward momentum, carrying the assassin into the feeder tube so the two of them streaked across the stage toward the curtains. He had to time his step exactly so there was no exposure to the audience as he took the struggling man into the larger shadow, which would take them backstage, where he hopefully could find another shadow that led outside.

All the while, he pinned Lewis's wrist tight against the man's thigh to keep him from turning the poisoned blade on him. As they shot backstage, Geno rolled Lewis over, coming to a halt to find another shadow. He kept his grip on his wrist. Unexpectedly, Zeta, his cousin from San Francisco, joined him. Placing her knee on Lewis's back, she gripped his head in her hands and ended his life in the classic way of a rider.

They could hear the thunder of the audience as they gave the cast members a standing ovation.

"I'll take him out," she whispered. "You get back to your seat."

CHAPTER TWENTY-ONE

Lincoln Boutler contacted the Archambaults to warn them that his father was in New York to try to kill members of the Ferraro family," Elie stated as he helped himself to the eggs Benedict. "He told them his father was a pedophile and that many of his cousins were, and that he left home years ago to get away from them."

Geno leaned back in the high-backed chair, his legs sprawled out in front of him, regarding his cousins as they gathered around the food warmers. The morning sun spilled into the room, reflecting off the water, casting diamond-like patterns across the far wall. He was absolutely, utterly relaxed. And happy. He hadn't known that emotion for a long time, but now each morning he woke with the knowledge Amaranthe was in his life. Not only was he happy, he felt content, at peace, something he hadn't thought possible.

He was acutely aware of Amaranthe standing beside Salvatore at the coffee station. He knew exactly where she was at any given moment, his radar tuned specifically to her. She spoke in a soft voice to his brother, and his reply made her laugh. Geno loved the sound of her laughter, the way it seemed to brighten up the room. She had already made a difference, not only in his life but in his brothers' lives.

"Are you paying attention, Geno?" Elie demanded as he seated himself at the table.

"I'm trying not to think about the Boutler family," Geno admitted.

"He was thinking about his woman," Dario murmured. He was staring down at the screen of his phone. "He's got that vacant look you all get on your faces right before you make total asses out of yourselves."

"You're just jealous," Emmanuelle said.

Dario's eyebrow shot up, but he didn't take his gaze from the screen. "You think I want to look like a jackass? I don't think so, babe."

Emmanuelle threw her napkin at him. "You call me *babe* again, I'm going to shave your hair off and you won't look all rakish for your ladies."

Dario picked the napkin out of the air with one hand, ignoring her threat. "Brielle also said Lincoln suspected his uncle murdered his wife. He believed it possible that his father had done the same. He warned the Archambaults several times that they shouldn't be allowed to accept trainees. She sent a screenshot of the reports asking for investigations multiple times."

Amaranthe set a cup of coffee on the table beside Geno's hand. "Was there an investigation? Is that why the inland Boutlers moved out of Australia?"

"According to the documents Brielle discovered, it wasn't the first time the Archambaults had been asked to investigate that particular family," Dario continued. "Years earlier there was a handwritten report."

Stefano brought a plate back to the table and placed it in front of his chair. "No doubt the Archambaults are going to want to know why the Boutlers decided to attack us now."

"Fortunately, we don't know why for certain," Lucca pointed out. "We can only speculate like everyone else."

"The Archambaults should consider themselves somewhat complicit in that they didn't investigate when they were asked numerous times," Amaranthe said, a frown on her face.

Geno couldn't help himself. He leaned into her and rubbed at her lower lip with the pad of his thumb. "I honestly don't give a damn about the Archambaults, other than Elie and Brielle. And I could not care less about the Boutlers. I'm just very thankful I have my family and friends alive and here with me."

Taviano waved at him, the scent of cinnamon and apple following the motion of his hand. "You just like me here because I cook for you."

"That could be true," Geno admitted.

"It's the only reason I tolerate him," Stefano said. "Otherwise, he's a pain in the ass." He stretched and sent a quick grin to Lucca and Salvatore. "We do have another important matter to discuss. I had no choice, Geno. When I leave the women behind and they know we're in danger, it's important to give them something to occupy their minds to keep them from worrying."

Geno reached for Amaranthe's hand. *Brace yourself, Danzatrice Ombra. He's up to something, and my knuckleheaded brothers are in on it.*

He glanced around the table. His brothers weren't the only ones. Even Dario was smirking. "Spit it out, Stefano."

"Apparently, the two of you got your marriage license."

Geno sat up straight. "Do you have spies in that office?" He glared at his brothers. "Are you shadowing us?"

Lucca looked unrepentant. "Someone needs to keep you safe. You have enemies, Geno."

"Welcome to the club," Dario said. "Now you'll never have a minute to yourself."

Geno tightened his hand around Amaranthe's. "What did you do, Stefano?" He knew he sounded wary. When his cousins looked as they did right at that moment, with their shit-eating grins, he knew he was in trouble.

"Grace is an event planner." Stefano stated it as if that answered all questions.

There was a sudden silence as around the table his cousins began to eat with great enthusiasm.   .

"What does that mean?" Amaranthe asked, looking up at Geno. "What event would Grace be planning?"

"Our wedding," Geno said tightly. "We're eloping," he added.

Amaranthe nodded vigorously. "We're eloping," she echoed.

"That's what the women are planning," Stefano said. "The family will be here . . ." He glanced at his watch. "In under an hour. They planned your elopement."

"But . . ." Amaranthe pushed her coffee cup along the table beside his. "Elopements aren't planned, Stefano. They're spontaneous. We run off alone, together."

Stefano sent her a look of pure amusement. "Did Geno deceive you into thinking you could really get away with running off alone to get married? You're engaged to a Ferraro, Amara."

"Eloping," Geno cut in. "What part of that word don't all of you understand?" He glared at his grinning cousins and then brought Amaranthe's hand up to his mouth to press kisses over her fingertips. He knew, from experience, this wasn't going to end well for them—at least not have the outcome they desired.

"Eloping doesn't mean getting married without guests, Geno," Emmanuelle said. She sipped at her coffee and then began to eat again, looking every bit as smug as Stefano.

"Eloping means running off to *secretly* be married," Geno corrected.

Amaranthe pulled out her phone. "I don't think one has guests at an elopement."

"Don't bother," Dario said. "You can bet this has been researched heavily."

Val nodded. "Twenty guests, and it's still considered an elopement, especially if no parents are present. Up to fifty guests is a micro-wedding."

Geno's growl rumbled in his chest. His cousins just grinned at him. Amaranthe looked more confused than ever.

"Stefano, did the cousins go home?" Geno asked. It was impossible to keep the suspicion out of his voice. "Lorenzo and his family? Severino and his family?"

"I believe they were tired after all the excitement yesterday at the ballet. They opted to spend the night," Stefano said.

"Who is coming in on this plane you have in the air?"

Amaranthe gripped his thigh, her nails digging into his leg.

Stefano shrugged casually. "Just the *famiglia*."

"That would easily make it over thirty people attending, which puts it over the required number for an elopement," Geno pointed out.

Valentino laughed. He didn't bother to cover it, he just laughed aloud. "Do you have anyone in mind you want to throw out?"

"All of you," Geno said.

"I don't even have a dress." Amaranthe's voice held a hint of a wail. "Geno, they're joking with you, right? This is all a joke."

Geno wrapped his arm around her shoulders and leaned closer to give her some protection against his insane family. "Unfortunately, I doubt it."

"No worries on the dress, Amara," Nicoletta assured. "Grace contacted Andrea at Ferraro Designs and she has everything ready for you."

Amaranthe pressed her forehead against Geno's side. "Is there no way to make them all just go away?"

"I could shoot them." He kissed the top of her head. "I'd do it for you, Danzatrice Ombra."

"I'd help him," Dario volunteered.

Emmanuelle wadded up Val's linen napkin and flung it at him. "You will *not*. You're part of the family whether you like it or not, you cretin. That means Geno shoots you, too."

"Francesca wouldn't like it if Geno shot me, Amara." Stefano sounded complacent, as if the mere mention of Francesca's name solved the issue.

"Well, Francesca isn't the one being railroaded into a wedding." Amaranthe sat up straight, narrowing her eyes at Stefano. "We were eloping for a reason. A big wedding freaks me out." She looked away from him. "It's not like I have any family on my side."

Geno's temper rose when he felt the sudden surge of sadness in her. Before he could say anything, Dario stood up and walked around the table to stand in front of Amaranthe.

"I know Stefano is the head of the Ferraro family, and he's going to tell you he'll walk you down the aisle, but I'd consider it an honor if you'd allow me to do it. I'll hand you off to Geno safe and sound. Just so you know, I clean up in a tux. And I know what it's like not to have family. Until these dumb fucks took me in, I had the dubious honor of calling Val my only family."

Geno was shocked. Looking at his cousins, he could see they were as well. There was absolute silence in the room.

Amaranthe stroked her fingers along her throat. "Thank you for such a beautiful and kind offer, Dario. I hope you mean it, because if they're really going to railroad us, I'll accept."

Dario grinned at her, nodded abruptly and walked back to his chair.

"You bastard," Stefano sniped. "You knew I was going to walk her down the aisle."

"You're getting slow," Dario said. "Old age, Stefano."

Geno knew Stefano had taken the spotlight from Amaranthe, but it was more important to him to figure out why

Dario had volunteered to walk Amaranthe down the aisle. Geno could hear truth, and Dario meant what he said about knowing what it was like having no family. At the same time, it was more than that.

Dario was a master manipulator. He was charming when he wanted to be. He was also ruthless and deadly. Clearly, his offer to escort Amaranthe down the aisle cemented Dario's position in the Ferraro family more than ever. Geno glanced at Stefano. They had discussed more than once what a shame it would be if they had to kill the man. They wanted to believe everything he said and did was genuine, but they were responsible for their family members, and Dario was just too dangerous to take every action at face value.

His offer was sincere, Stefano said.

Geno nodded, indicating he was aware it had been. At the same time, Dario knew Amaranthe was an elite rider, and she questioned why the Ferraro family kept him so close to their inner circle. By declaring he was aware of how isolated she felt, by showing her that vulnerability, he had aligned himself with her. She couldn't help but identify with him. It was a strategic move on his part. A brilliant one. Perhaps Dario had been one hundred percent genuine, but then again, because he was a brilliant strategist, and he took advantage of an opportunity when it presented itself, Dario more than likely had multiple reasons for his offer.

We can't fault him when we think just like him, Stefano pointed out.

Once again, Geno inclined his head. He did think that way. He had to.

"The family is here," Stefano announced. "Coming up now. All of them."

Geno's phone went off continuously. "Andrea is here with a trunkful of clothes. Penelope says the restaurant is being transformed." He brushed another kiss on top of Amaranthe's head. "Welcome to the Ferraro family, Danzatrice Ombra. It's a damn good thing you love me. Anytime the family is together, chaos ensues."

"I do love you," Amaranthe assured. "Although your family is crazy."

He couldn't help smirking. "You're about to become part of the crazy."

Keep reading for an excerpt from
the next thrilling novel in the Carpathian series
by Christine Feehan

DARK MEMORY

The breeze coming off the Mediterranean Sea brought a hint of the coming storm with it. Safia Meziane stood at the very top of the hillside overlooking the turquoise water, which was now beginning to grow choppy as little fingers of wind touched the glassy surface. The knots in her stomach tightened as she watched the water begin to churn. Ordinarily, she loved storms, but she was uneasy, certain the weather heralded something much more sinister than lightning and thunder.

"I will never tire of this view," Amastan Meziane said, his gaze on the sea. "As a young man, I would stand in this exact spot with my father and feel fortunate to live in this place."

"Just as I do," Safia admitted, looking up at her grandfather.

Safia's family was Imazighen. Outsiders sometimes referred to them as Berbers. Their family owned a very prosperous farm located up in the hills outside the town of Dellys. They had extraordinary views of the sea and harbor.

The farm kept a variety of animals, mainly sheep and goats. Safia's family harvested the wool, spinning and dyeing it for clothes and rugs they sold at the local market or sent with Safia's oldest sister's family across the Sahara to markets. Some of the members made jewelry and others pottery. All contributed to the success of the family.

Her grandfather was the acknowledged head of her tribe. Like her grandfather, Safia had always felt very lucky to have been born into her family. To live where she lived. To be raised on her family farm. She had two older sisters who doted on her and three older brothers who always treated her as if she were a treasure, just as her parents and grandparents did. They all worked hard on the farm. When her oldest sister, Illi, married and left with her husband, Kab, no one resented the extra work. They were happy for her, although Safia missed her terribly and looked forward to the times when she returned from her travels.

Beside her, Amastan sighed. "Our family has had centuries of good years, Safia, and we can't complain. We've always known this time would come."

He felt it too. It wasn't her imagination. Evil rode in the wind of that storm. It had quietly invaded their farm. She had known all along but had done her best to tell herself it was her wild imagination. The number of invasive insects had suddenly increased. Three weeks earlier, she had begun to note the tracks of an unfamiliar predator. One week ago, several predators had eviscerated a goat near the cliffs. Whatever it was seemed to disappear into the ground when she'd tried to follow it. There had been more than one, but she couldn't determine the number or exactly what it was.

"I love the way Dellys looks, *Jeddi*, day or night. The blend of beautiful modern built so close to the ancient ruins, and the way the ruins are on the hillside facing the sea. I love the sunrises and sunsets, and the sea with its colors and ever-changing mood, the markets and the people. Dellys is so modern, and yet our history, our culture, is right there for everyone to see. And on the hillside, evidence of our history remains. We're like that. Our family. Like Dellys. So modern on the outside. Anyone looking at us would believe we're so progressive." She loved her life. Mostly, she loved the huge tribe she called family.

Safia didn't look at her grandfather; she kept her gaze fixed on the beauty of the sea. The women in her family were well educated, unlike many females in other tribes. They spoke Tamazight and Arabic, but along with that, they had learned French and English. Safia had been required to learn an ancient language that none of the others had to master. Her grandmother and mother were able to speak it, and she had one friend, Aura, who knew the language, so she was fortunate to be able to practice with her. Safia never questioned why she had to learn such an ancient language that no one spoke in modern times. When her grandfather or grandmother decreed anything, it was done, usually without question.

Her grandfather not only believed they should expand their thinking, he insisted his daughters and granddaughters learn to use weapons and how to fight hand-to-hand combat just as well as the males in the family. The women took care of the house, but they also worked on the farm. They learned to do everything needed and were always treated as valued members of the tribe. Their voices were heard when it came to solving problems. It was all very progressive and different from tradition.

Her grandfather arranged marriages in the traditional way. His word was law. He held the men they married to a very high standard. She couldn't imagine what would happen should he ever find out his daughters or granddaughters were mistreated. Amastan appeared stern to outsiders, but he was always soft-spoken and fair. No one ever wanted to get him upset. It was a rare event, but when it happened, he had the backing of the entire tribe, not that he needed it. He was a force to be reckoned with.

"We must go inside, Safia. I told your father to call a family meeting. We can't continue to put this off. You will read the cards, and I'll consult with the ancestors tonight. We need to know exactly what we are facing and how much time we will have to prepare." He placed his hand on her shoulder as if he knew she needed encouragement.

Her heart sank. All along, she had told herself the tales she'd been raised with were simply fictional stories handed down for hundreds of years. They weren't real. Demons and vampires didn't belong in a modern world any more than the myths and legends that had sprung from the area where they lived.

"I tried not to believe it, *Jeddi*," she confessed. "I've trained from the time I was a baby to fight these things, but I still didn't believe. I read the cards daily, but I still didn't believe."

"You believed, Safia, or you wouldn't have trained so hard. You're very disciplined, even more so than your mother and grandmother ever were. You work on the farm and at home with your mother, but you never once shirked your training. You believed; you just hoped, as we all did, that the evil wouldn't rise in our lifetime."

She turned her head to look at her beloved grandfather. For the first time, she really saw the worry lines carved in his face. There was unease in the faded blue of his eyes. That alone was enough to make all the times her radar had gone off and the knots in her belly very real.

"When you were born," he continued, "we knew. Your grandmother, your mother and father. I knew. I consulted the ancestors just to be certain. None of us wanted it to be true, but the moment you came into this world, all of us could see you were different. You were born with gifts." There was sorrow in his voice. "You were born with green eyes."

She was the only one in her family with green eyes, it was true, but why would that make a difference? Still, she didn't question him. "I did prepare," she whispered. "But it feels as if it can't be real, even now, when I feel evil on the wind. When I know the accidents on the farm were actual attacks on our family. I *know* these things, yet my mind doesn't want to process the reality."

She turned back to look at the town of Dellys, spread out in the distance. "All those unknowing, innocent people living there. The restaurants. The shops. The market. I love the market. Everyone is so unaware of the danger coming. It isn't as if soldiers are attacking them and they can see the enemy coming. No one would believe us if we warned them. I wouldn't even know what to tell them."

"You don't know what you're facing yet," Amastan pointed out, his voice gentle. "I've told you many times, Safia, prepare, but do not worry about something you have no control over—something that may or may not happen. That does you no good. If you have no idea who or what your enemy is and you dwell on it, you will make him much more powerful than he is."

She knew her grandfather was right. She trusted him. Throughout the years growing up, she hadn't known him to be wrong when he gave his advice. He was always thoughtful before he spoke, and she'd learned to take what he said to heart.

Once more, she looked at the harbor. The port of Dellys was small, located near the mouth of the river Sebaou and east of Algiers. Many of the men permanently living in Dellys were fishermen, sailors or navigators. The fishermen provided fresh fish daily to the local restaurants. The harbor was beautiful with the boats and lights, so modern looking. Everything looked modern—so this century. Just by looking at the beauty of the harbor and the town, one wouldn't imagine it had been around since prehistoric times.

"We must go in," Amastan reiterated. "The others will be waiting. Hopefully, Amara will have fixed dinner for us, and it will be edible."

Amara was married to her oldest brother, Izem. Safia really liked Amara; who could not? She didn't understand how the match worked; yet it did, perfectly. Amara was a tornado moving through the house and farm, one disaster after another. Through it all, her laughter was contagious. She was bright and cheerful, always willing to pitch in and help, eager to learn every aspect of farming. Clearly, she wanted to be a good wife to Izem, but her youth and exuberance coupled with her total inexperience and clumsy energy were sometimes recipes for disasters.

At the same time, she was an amazing jeweler. One would think when she was so clumsy around the farm, tripping over her own small feet, she wouldn't be able to make the fine necklaces and earrings she did. Her artwork was exquisite and much sought-after. She was an asset to their family for that alone, but most importantly, because she made Izem happy.

Despite the two appearing to be total opposites, Izem was very happy with Amara. Izem was very serious. He took after Amastan in both appearance and personality. His name, meaning lion, epitomized who he was and what he stood for. He was always going to be the head of his family. He was a man to be counted on, and maybe that was exactly why the match worked so well. Amara needed the security of Izem, and he needed the fun and brightness she brought him.

Safia loved watching her oldest brother and his wife together because she was a little terrified of her grandfather choosing a husband for her. She knew several offers had been made for her and he'd turned them down, stating she was already promised to another. He'd never explained to her what he meant. She'd never met a man she'd been promised to in marriage. Her father seemed to accept her grandfather's decree, as did her brothers. No one ever questioned her grandfather, and for some reason, even on such an important subject, she couldn't bring herself to either. Seeing Izem and Amara so happy made her feel as if there were a chance she could find happiness with a man, a stranger, her grandfather believed would be the right choice for her.

They walked together, side by side, through the field and

toward the house. "Your leg is hurting," Amastan observed. "You were injured today."

She wasn't limping. She'd been careful not to show any signs of pain. Instantly, she felt shame. How could she possibly be ready to protect her family if Amastan could so easily read her discomfort? Her enemies would be able to do so just as easily and take advantage during a battle. All those years of training and she couldn't cover a simple injury?

"I'm not ready, *Jeddi*," she whispered. "How can I defend the farm? Our family? How can I defend the people in the town if I can't hide a small injury from you?"

He spoke in his gentlest voice. "*Yelli*, I observed the tear in your trousers, along with the dirt and bloodstains. You have not given anything away by your actions or expression. It is the condition of your clothes that tells me something happened."

"I did have a little accident today when I was herding the sheep in from the back pasture. They were far too close to the cliff and very uneasy." It had been in the same area where those strange tracks had been. She had been searching for them.

She didn't look up at him, but she felt her grandfather's piercing eyes on her, drilling into her, seeing right past her casual tone to the truth.

"Safia?" He stopped abruptly right in front of the house.

More than a question, it was an order. Reluctantly, she halted as well and forced herself to look up at him, holding her gloves in front of her as if the thin leather could protect her from his close scrutiny. His gaze moved over her, examining her inch by inch.

"It was no accident, any more than what happened to me or any of the others, Safia. We can't pretend this away any longer. How badly were you injured?"

She pressed her lips together, reliving the terrifying moment when the dirt gave way on the cliff and she went over.

She had clawed at the dirt, rock and scraggly tree roots as she slid over the side. It seemed to take forever before her fingers dug into the mud and roots, and she gingerly found a grip with her fingertips. She clung there, legs dangling, heart pounding, head resting against a tough rope of knotted wood.

Insects began to emerge from the mud, crawling toward her from every direction. Stinging bugs flew around her hands and face. A hawk screamed and rushed out of the sky straight at her. In that moment, she knew exactly what she faced, and calm descended. She forced air through her lungs, calling on her training to keep from panicking.

Evil had come to her family's farm. She couldn't deny it any longer, as much as she wanted to. She had known for the last three weeks the small "accidents" happening on their farm were attacks against their family. She felt guilty that she hadn't been able to protect the animals or her family members from the escalating violence. It was just that she had no idea how to stop it, because she wasn't certain how to fight what she couldn't see. Right at that moment, evil was striking at her as if it knew she was the primary defender.

"I was more frightened than anything else. A few scrapes and bruises." She had dug her toes into the rocks for purchase and reached with her mind for the hawk. She had gifts—incredible gifts she'd been born with. Before that moment, she had thought it was just plain cool that she had an ability to connect with animals, but the hawk turned away from her at the last moment, pulling up sharply at her command.

"Lacerations," her grandfather corrected.

She nodded. "When I was climbing back up the cliff, there were a few jagged rocks poking out. It really was more the scare of feeling the dirt give way under me, and then having to admit to myself that all these little accidents haven't really been accidents at all."

Her grandfather continued to look at her.

She sighed. "I'm sore, shaken up, but really, nothing broken or sprained, so I got off easy."

Her grandfather remained silent far too long, thinking over her revelation. There had been too many small accidents lately. Both had become aware over the last few weeks that something was very wrong. Her father, too, had become suspicious. Even her brothers had grown quiet and exchanged worried looks between themselves.

"You're certain all the animals are in for the night?" Amastan asked.

Safia nodded. "Usem and Farah brought in the sheep."

Her brother Usem and his wife, Farah, were fast at moving the sheep. She was certain Usem had his own gift with animals. They always seemed to respond to him, especially the sheep. Usem was the third oldest and, like Izem, was steady and a hard worker, but much more inclined to laugh and take time to play pranks on his siblings. Farah was quiet and sweet, her gaze following Usem lovingly. She was a very good cook and did her best to help Amara learn. She treated Amara like a younger sister, welcoming her with open arms.

"Badis and Layla took care to round up the goats and get them into the shelters," she continued, turning to survey what she could see of their land.

Layla was nearly as tall as Safia's brother Badis. Layla was confident and beautiful. There was very little she couldn't do. She excelled in combat just as she did in keeping house and making rugs. She was also kind and showed endless patience toward Amara. Badis and Layla were a wonderful match and were never far from each other, especially now that Layla was pregnant.

Her grandfather laughed unexpectedly. "That left your sister, Lunja and Zdan to round up the chickens with their children."

Despite the gravity of the situation, Safia couldn't help smiling too. Her two nephews and her niece loved the chickens. They spent quite a lot of their day chasing after them, collecting eggs, naming the chickens, finding new nests, whatever they could interacting with them. The chickens were given free range over the farm for the most part, only being brought in at night when predators would attack and eat them. The children were very enthusiastic about their jobs.

Zdan, Lunja's husband, was a great bear of a man, the largest in their family. He certainly looked intimidating, or he would to an outsider. It was difficult to think of him as scary when his children clung to his arms and legs, winding around him and riding on his shoulders every chance they got. Lunja looked at him as if the sun rose with him every morning, and for her, it most likely did.

"I love my family so much, *Jeddi*," she whispered, more to herself than to her grandfather. "I'm so afraid I can't protect them. My brain refuses to really acknowledge what's happening because I worry I'm not up to the task. If something happens to any of you because I failed to train hard enough . . ." She trailed off.

Throughout the years, she had considered her training fun. It was extremely difficult and demanding, but she had fast reflexes that only sharpened as she got older. Every muscle and cell in her body sang when she ran or climbed or when she picked up weapons or fought hand-to-hand.

"You are ready, Safia," Amastan confirmed. "You must have faith in yourself and in your training. You were chosen. You have two older sisters, but the gift was not given to either of them. It was given to you. You were born with the talents you have, Safia. You must know, when you train with your brothers and father, when you did with your mother and grandmother or with Aura, no one is faster or more intuitive than you are."

She took a deep breath and let it out before she nodded. "I just never believed it would come to this."

"None of us wanted it to come to this, not in our lifetime, but it has, and we'll do whatever is necessary to defeat our enemies, just as our people have done for over a thousand years." He opened the door and waved her inside.

At once, Safia's stomach reacted to the delicious aroma filling the house. Amara had been busy in the kitchen, and her efforts filled the house with the inviting scent of one of the staples the family often relied on. Tajine was a delicious stew Safia particularly enjoyed after a long day working in the field. She was suddenly very, very hungry. She knew Amara had been trying hard to get the tajine just right.

Tajine was slow cooked with lamb or poultry as a rule. Vegetables, nuts and sometimes even dried fruits could be included. Spices such a ginger, cinnamon and turmeric, along with a host of others, were used depending on whether it was a vegetable, poultry or lamb tajine. Amara had trouble with the spices, sometimes dumping all kinds into the stew, or trying to make it first sweet and then savory, but she hadn't given up, determined to master the craft of cooking.

Amara had made loaves of bread to go with the tajine, and the one thing she was very good at was baking bread. Couscous was the dessert—her grandfather's favorite. Amara often struggled with couscous as well. Safia knew it was important to her that she get that right. Amastan never said anything when the dessert was doughy or overly sweet. Although Amara laughed at herself, it was obvious to Safia she was disappointed if the meal wasn't good. Safia hoped this would be the one to turn things around for Amara.

One by one, family members washed and gathered to eat together. After prayers, there was much laughter as the hot stew was served up in bowls of clay their ancestors had made. This was one of Safia's favorite times of day. She knew it wasn't the same for all other families, but in hers they were encouraged to talk to one another, to laugh and share their day.

She recognized Amastan's wisdom in encouraging family members to give input on the farm, the gardens, livestock and even the children. Her brothers had secured land around the original farmland handed down through generations, adding to the flourishing tribal business. The livestock was healthy, the soil was rich, and every member of the family meticulously worked to produce beautiful rugs, carpets and clothing for sale. Many of their items were sent with her eldest sister, Illi, and her husband, Kab, across the Sahara to the markets in the Middle East. Kab's family was one of the few very familiar with the Sahara Desert and the places one could find water.

Kab's family were also artisans. Illi had been welcomed into their family not just because she had caught Kab's eye but because she knew the old ways of making pottery and her work was sought-after. Their grandmother had handed down the history and designs that went back centuries. Illi not only had the skills but could pass those skills and her knowledge on to new generations.

Safia realized just how difficult her grandfather's job as head of the tribe and head of the family really was. Choosing others to bring in when they had so many secrets had to be extremely challenging. She looked around the table and realized just how carefully Amastan had chosen those he had allowed into their inner circle.

They had to be loyal and willing to keep secrets. They had to train every day to fight as both modern and ancient warriors. Anyone coming into their family would have to fit their personality into a unit that was already tight-knit and learn to accept their very different ways. It wasn't an easy ask. Every one of the chosen brides had done so, as had Zdan, Lunja's husband.

It was unusual for the man to choose to come to his wife's family rather than for her to go to his. Zdan's family had become very small. His two sisters had married and left home. His parents were dead. One aunt remained and he offered to bring her with him, but she had refused. He checked on her daily. She was very set in her ways. Safia knew Zdan's aunt would never have accepted Amastan as head of the family. He wasn't traditional enough.

Safia couldn't help noticing how anxious Amara looked as everyone began eating the tajine. Twice Amara's gaze went to Izem's, and he shifted slightly toward her, giving her a reassuring smile. Deliberately, Safia took a spoonful of the stew, expecting it to be a little better than the last time Amara had made it, but this time, it was far, far better. The blend of spices was nearly perfect.

Safia looked across the table at Amara, unable to keep the huge smile from her face. She didn't want to make a big deal about the fact that the tajine was so good because that might embarrass Amara and point out all the times she had failed.

"Charif," Amastan said with a false frown. "Are you already finished with your first serving? Leave some for your elders."

Charif looked up at his father, puzzled, with a spoon halfway to his mouth. Zdan ruffled his hair and leaned down to whisper in an overly loud voice. "I have a much longer arm, Charif. I'll get you extra helpings."

Mock fighting over the stew was the perfect way to convey to Amara that she had gotten it right and everyone was devouring her efforts gratefully. Safia once again noted the exchange between Amara and Izem. This time there were tears in Amara's eyes, which she hastily blinked away, and pride on Izem's face. He smiled at her lovingly. The look her eldest brother gave his young wife was enough to make Safia wish, just for that moment, that she wasn't so alone, especially now, when she faced something evil and her family depended on her to lead the defense against it.

She felt her father's gaze on her, and she sent him a small smile that she hoped was reassuring. When her mother was alive, Gwafa Meziane had laugh lines around his startling blue eyes and a ready smile for his six children. He teased his mother and wife continually, but was his father's constant companion and adviser. He worked harder than any other on the farm. He was loving toward his children, but when it came to teaching them to wield weapons and defend themselves, he was every bit as fierce and demanding as Amastan, her grandmother and mother and even her friend, Aura.

Since the death of her mother, Gwafa's laugh lines and smile had faded. Several of the "accidents" on the farm seemed to have been directed at him and Amastan, but the majority were definitely aimed at Safia. He'd grown even quieter, and he and Amastan had taken to staying up and talking for long hours into the night. She lay in her bed and stared up at the ceiling or paced back and forth in her room, wondering if she should reach out to her closest friend, Aura, while her father and grandfather were whispering in the other room.

She couldn't talk about her fears to her family, not when they would have to depend on and look to her for guidance. It didn't matter that she was the youngest of the six siblings. She had been born with the "gift." Amastan had decreed it was so. Her grandmother and parents concurred.

"We have many things to talk about before night falls," Amastan announced once the dishes were cleared. "Everyone needs to gather close."

Dread filled Safia as they adjourned to the wide-open room they preferred, where they could sit in front of the open fire on the carpets woven by their ancestors. There was a connection always felt from past to present. Safia found it comforting to be in the room with her family, sitting on the carpets surrounded by other keepsakes from those who had gone before her. She felt their presence stronger than ever, as if they were there to give her courage.

Amastan waited until everyone had settled comfortably and looked up at him expectantly. So many nights this had been storytelling time. This had been a favorite time for everyone as they gathered together to hear stories that had been handed down for generations. Children sat on laps and listened with wide eyes. Safia remembered sitting on her mother's lap and snuggling close to her father's side when

Amastan regaled them with tales of brave men and women defending their lands from invaders.

They were Imazighen, free people and very peaceful, but they would defend themselves fiercely when needed. They were proud of who they were, and with their last breath would always declare to the world they were Imazighen.

"All of you studied the history of our country and are aware that many wars have taken place here. One of the most significant for our family was one that started with the continual political wars as one faction after another invaded Algeria. In 17 to 24 AD, the Romans invaded. They cut a road right across the migration route. Where there was once wild grass to feed livestock, now there were fences to keep out the nomads' flocks from wheat the Romans needed.

"An entire way of life was disrupted. The Romans sought to take the tribal lands and divide them up for settlers," Amastan continued. "The free people rebelled. The fighting became quite fierce, and those living here refused to bow down to outsiders. As Imazighen, we do not accept the dictates of any other."

Amastan paused for a moment and looked around the room at his family. "Had the tribes been fighting only men, the battle would have been won very quickly, but that was not the case. It was not mere mortals our ancestors fought. The underworld chose that time to enter our world and turned neighbor against neighbor, sending an army of vampires and demons mixing with the invaders from Rome."

An icy shiver crept down Safia's spine. She glanced out the window. The sun was beginning to sink, and small fingers of fog began to drift in from the sea.

"Our male ancestors have gifted us with their presence and wisdom. They share, through the elders, advice and knowledge. Through the female side, handed down for centuries, we have been given the wisdom and direction of the cards. The gift of reading is given to only one female in the family. She not only holds the power and responsibility of the cards, but should the demons rise to attack again, she must lead us to slay them. Without her, this will be impossible."

All eyes turned to Safia. She heard Amara gasp and then hastily cut off the sound. Glancing up, she could see that Amara had her hand over her mouth and was leaning into Izem.

Amastan's sharp gaze was on her as well. "Amara." His voice was gentle. "You have known of this from the day you married Izem."

She nodded. "That is true, *Jeddi*, but it wasn't real to me. Lately, I've felt the presence of evil, but even with that, I've done my best to ignore it. I often spoke to Izem, urging him to speak with you and *Eemmi* about finding Safia a husband. It didn't seem right that we were happy and she had no one. She loves children and she works harder than any of us. Because fighting something we can't see and that the family would send her out to fight unknown evil entities didn't seem real to me, I just wanted someone very special for her. Now, it feels like we're all abandoning her. Forgive me, *Jeddi*, but I don't understand."

Amastan's expression remained gentle. Safia loved him all the more for the way he had always allowed every family member to ask questions and share opinions. That had been a difficult concept for Amara, and Safia knew it had to have been very hard for her to express her concerns, especially in front of the entire family and Safia.

"It's natural for you not to understand completely, Amara. You weren't raised from childhood with the knowledge those born into this family have. Perhaps it was already imprinted on us for our family to accept these ideas so easily. I have never asked the ancestors this, but it is a good question. I admire you for caring so deeply about Safia, but I assure you, she is spoken for."

It was Safia's sister Lunja who questioned their grandfather next. "*Jeddi*, I have heard this on more than one occasion, that she is promised, and you would never say this unless it is true, but we are now in a dire situation, and she will need all the help she can get. If that is so, where is he?"

"He will come, Lunja. You must have faith. He is a great warrior."

It was Izem, her oldest brother, who brought up what Safia worried about the most. "Is this wise, *Jeddi*? Bringing an unknown into a complicated battle and having Safia get used to a relationship that will need time to develop? She is used to coping on her own with just us. If this man decides to take over and has his own strategy, it may well throw her off balance."

Ordinarily, Safia would have had several questions of her own, but it was nice to have family members addressing the concerns for her. Her heartbeat stayed steady, under control, a win for her. She'd trained hard to keep her heart and lungs functioning under every circumstance. The accident in the afternoon that had sent her plunging over the cliff had shaken her confidence in her abilities for a brief period of time. She'd lost that control, sending her brain into chaos. She had to be able to think at all times, no matter what was going on around her.

"You raise a legitimate concern, Izem. Gwafa and I have worried about the same thing many times. We prepared Safia as best we could. She knows many of the customs of his people and she speaks his language."

The breath caught in Safia's lungs. A stunned silence filled the room. She pressed a hand to her throat in an effort to stay grounded. For a moment, she couldn't feel her own flesh.

"He doesn't speak our language? He has different customs?" Izem echoed. "Are you saying this man you have chosen for our sister is not a member of our tribe? He is not Imazighen?" He looked to his father and then back at his grandfather. "You would have Safia leave our family? Our tribe?" He was shaking his head even as he spoke, rejecting what his grandfather implied.

He wasn't the only one. Her brothers and sister were also indicating a strong disapproval of the choice selected for their sister. It was extremely rare for anyone to disagree to such an extent with Amastan, and never over an arranged marriage.

Safia had never considered that she would be sent away from her family, especially since she had been trained to protect them. She had the family cards. She had spent her entire childhood, her teens, her early adulthood training to fight, to hone her skills. She'd been devoted to her family. She couldn't believe her grandfather would arrange a marriage to an outsider. It felt like a betrayal.

"Jeddi." It came out a choked whisper. She turned to her father, knowing she wasn't successful at hiding the shocked horror on her face. She did feel as if her father and grandfather had deceived her all these years. They had known they were going to send her away and yet they had demanded the long, grueling hours of training from her. They had forced her to accept her fate as the defender of her family and she had done so willingly.

This felt like sheer treachery. Disloyalty. It didn't just feel that way; it *was* betrayal. Her parents and grandparents had treated her as if she were special to them, and yet they would send her away with a perfect stranger, someone not even of their tribe, not of their people. Worse, they would do so after she risked her life to save them.

Even Illi's marriage was closely monitored to ensure she was treated with kindness, acceptance and love. Her husband was Imazighen. Once Safia was married to this stranger, her family would have no say in how he treated her. If he took her away from them, they would never know if he beat or even murdered her.

Still, with all that, she had the years of love and kindness her father and grandfather had shown to her. Could they really have betrayed her in such a terrible way? Amastan stated plainly that she was to marry outside their people.

She had to get away from everyone, go somewhere to think. She couldn't breathe properly. She had to leave. Pushing up with one hand, she managed to get to her feet. All the years of training made her look good, calm, steady. "I can't stay here right now. I must leave."